Look The Other Way
Galveston Crime Scene Book One

Leigh Jones

Galveston Crime Scene Press

Galveston Crime Scene Press
3209 Autumn Court
Pearland, TX 77584
www.galvestoncrimescene.com

Publisher's Note: This is a work of fiction. Names, characters, places, and incidents are a product of the author's imagination. Locales and public names are sometimes used for atmospheric purposes. Any resemblance to actual people, living or dead, or to businesses, companies, events, institutions, or locales is completely coincidental.

Book Layout © 2017 BookDesignTemplates.com

Cover art by Elizabeth Mackey

Look The Other Way/ Leigh Jones -- 1st ed.
ISBN 978-1-7334900-4-7

For Galveston, with love.

Prologue

Her heart beat a staccato rhythm against her ribs, pulsing terror through her chest and down her arms and legs until her whole body trembled. Every instinct told her to run. But a small voice in her head screamed, "Wait!" She had come so far. Freedom beckoned.

Her body ached with the effort to lie still. Her captors thought she'd taken the pills. They told the girls they were for the motion sickness that roiled their stomachs and spun their heads in dizzying circles. But suspicion prompted her to tuck the small white capsules under her tongue and only pretend to swallow. Her two companions slipped into a heavy slumber about 30 minutes later. When the men stepped out of the room, she spit the pills into her hand and tossed them under the bed.

As the hours ticked by, she almost wished she'd swallowed them. Fear about what was coming next crept across the floor of the tiny, cramped room, snaked up the side of the bed and wrapped itself around her throat. With every thought about the end of the journey, it tightened its grip. She tried to shake it off by picturing herself walking into a new life, a limitless life. But once fear had taken hold, it refused to let go.

She wrestled with it until exhaustion won out and she slept. When she woke, the gentle rolling propelling her forward had stopped, and the grinding engine had quieted to a menacing rumble. Her captors' muffled voices undulated outside the room, whipping her fear into a frenzy again.

The door opened and two men strode in, pushing a luggage cart. Through barely cracked lids, she watched as they put her two sleeping companions into the cart first. She willed her arms and legs to hang limp as the men hooked their hands under her shoulders and knees and lifted her in next to them. With the curtains on either side of the cart pulled closed, the girls were completely hidden from view. Her pulse surged, roaring in her ears. An involuntary whimper pried its way past her tightly clenched teeth.

"What was that?" one of the men barked.

"I don't know. They may be waking up. Let's get them out of here. Then they'll be someone else's problem."

Her breath came in short gasps as the cart started to roll. To keep herself calm, she began counting backwards from 100. It took all her concentration. She made it all the way to one and was about to start again when the cart stopped.

"Hurry up! We're running late. They're going to wonder what's going on."

The other man grunted. A metal door scraped open and a wave of warm, wet air washed over her. Through a gap in the vinyl curtain hiding them from view, she could see lights puncturing the darkness. Her heart skittered, sending a dizzying surge of blood to her head. Freedom was one lunge away. Did she dare risk it?

"Hold up a minute," the first man said. "I don't see them."

The cart stopped rolling. She heard seagulls crying and the chugging of big machinery in the distance. She took a deep breath and a salty tang filled her nose.

"Where are they? We can't just stand out here forever. Someone's going to wonder what we're doing and start asking questions."

"Relax. They'll be here any minute. Just roll the cart over there, out of the way. Let's have a smoke. If anyone sees us, they'll just think we're taking a quick break."

Disbelief tingled up her spine and ignited determination in her heart. Through one curtain, she could see her captors about 10 yards away. On the other side of the cart, a dumpster offered the perfect hiding place. She pushed the curtain open just enough to slip through and scampered around to the other side.

One. Two. Three.

She held her breath and counted to ten. The men hadn't noticed she was gone. The dock stretched out in front of her. A darkened building beckoned on the other side. She said a quick prayer and dashed across the open space, flattening herself against the wall, set deep in shadow. Her heart hammered so hard her pulse pounded in her fingertips. She glanced over her shoulder and caught sight of the orange glow of her captors' cigarettes. They still hadn't noticed anything was wrong. But she didn't have long.

"Here they come," she heard one of the men say. "Let's get the cart over to the curb."

Adrenaline coursed through her chest. She didn't bother looking back as she pushed herself off the wall and sprinted down the sidewalk. They would know something was wrong as soon as they got back to the cart. She willed her legs to pump faster.

To her left, the outline of cranes tattooed the sky. In front of her, rows and rows of shiny new cars, their hoods and tops covered with white plastic, stretched into the distance in the other direction. She ran toward the cars, weaving between the rows, hoping they would hide her from view.

In the distance, several buildings towered over a few sparse palm trees. At the first sight of anyone who might help her, she would scream. Her breath came in ragged gasps, cutting the back of her throat with a fiery stab each time she inhaled. Her side ached.

It was dark when she snuck out of the cart. But now the horizon glowed a soft grey. Ahead, a chain-link fence forced her to veer, skirting around an open parking lot dotted with semi trucks. When she reached the corner, she saw water ahead and boats rocking gently back and forth in their moorings. But no people. She turned right and continued along the fence line. Ahead, trees and beneath them, houses. She would bang on the first door she came to and beg for help. She couldn't keep running much longer.

The dull roar of an engine sent terror crashing over her. She glanced back. A van was bearing down fast. She veered to the right, cutting across another parking lot. Tires screeched and she heard the van door slide open. If she could only get to the houses, she would scream and someone might hear. Surely her pursuers wouldn't drag her into the van where someone might see.

She tried to sprint ahead, but she had used up any burst of speed blocks ago. She heard footsteps behind her now, gaining quickly. With each ragged exhale, a keening whine escaped her lips. The first house was just across the street. To her right, the sunrise spread across the sky. Streaks of wispy pink clouds stretched along a pale blue horizon.

A small light glowed from a window in the house dead ahead. Someone was awake! But just as she filled her lungs to scream, a thump in the middle of her back knocked her off balance. She fell forward, hands outstretched, onto the thick lawn. She tried to scramble back up. But he was on top of her, one arm around her waist. He clamped his other hand over her mouth.

Strong arms lifted her up as she kicked and flailed. When he spun around, she saw the van driving fast toward them. She only had seconds to escape. Wrenching her body around, she jammed her knee up between his legs. It was a glancing blow but hard enough to make him loosen his grip. She broke free and stumbled backwards. He grabbed at her arm. In his other hand, he held a dull black gun. He had a firm grip on her left wrist, but she struck out with the other hand. She wanted to scream. But all she could think about was the gun and the frantic need to get away. While she tried to pull her left hand free, she swung at his face with the other.

Then he waved the gun, his mouth twisted in an angry snarl. He tried to block her blows. When the gun went off, she saw the flash of flame and heard the exploding pop before she understood what had happened. His snarl vanished. His eyes opened wide in surprise as she stumbled back and fell. She bounced on the spongy grass just slightly before a searing pain in her stomach stole her breath. A second man came running up and started pulling the shooter toward the van.

She sensed another light come on in the house just a few feet away. She told herself to get up, but she no longer had control over her arms and legs. She struggled to breathe. The sensation of falling overwhelmed her, the weight of the last few nightmarish days pushing her into a deep, dark hole. She remembered how it all started, how she never imagined it would end like this—her mama's hard, clasping hug goodbye. She hadn't liked the plan. Didn't want her to go. Would her family ever know what had happened? Would they have a chance to mourn?

She sensed someone on the ground beside her, looking into her face and touching her arm. But all she could see was her mama's face.

"Mama, lo siento," she whispered.

Chapter 1

Detective Peter Johnson exhaled a long, slow breath as he scanned the scene in front of him. A middle-aged man in a bathrobe, hairy white legs protruding below the hem, stood by his front door. Four uniformed officers dotted the lawn. One talked into the radio handset pinned to his shoulder. Another scribbled into a small, spiral notebook. Yellow caution tape wound around the mailbox and two conveniently spaced oak trees, cordoning off the lush lawn from the small crowd of curious onlookers that had already started to gather. The first gentle rays of dawn had given way to persistent beams of sun punching steamy holes through the thick morning air. It promised to be another scorching June day.

In the middle of the yard, a white sheet barely concealed the body.

Johnson arrived at the scene with foreboding and anticipation. He looked forward to the end of every investigation, when justice would be served. But he hated the way they began. Unlike some of his colleagues, he never learned to think of the victim as just another piece of the puzzle. Each body meant someone had a loss to mourn. Every grieving spouse, parent, sibling, friend tore at his heart. It always took several days before the tightness in his chest started to ease.

When Johnson ducked under the crime scene tape and stepped into the yard, the note-taking officer ambled over. His smug smile radiated barely restrained satisfaction. Most young officers relished being the first on scene, especially a murder scene.

"Nothing like a gunshot victim to start the week off right, huh boss?" Officer Dylan Conner said.

Johnson reminded himself Conner was only 23, and as one of the department's youngest officers, he hadn't had a chance to build up cynicism or sensitivity. Even so, his cavalier attitude grated.

"What do we know?" he asked, nodding toward the sheet.

"It's a young woman, with what looks like a single gunshot to the stomach. No purse or anything, unless she fell on top of it. The homeowner was making coffee when he heard the shot. He looked out his kitchen window but didn't see anything because it's on the side of the house, facing toward the marina. When he opened the front door, he saw the girl laying there." Conner pointed toward the sheet.

Bracing himself for the inevitable unveiling, Johnson headed toward the body as Conner flipped a page in his notebook.

"She was still moving, so he went over to see how badly she was hurt. He said she was gasping for air and trying to speak. Right before she died, she said, 'Lo siento.' Then he came in and called 911."

Johnson's eyebrows shot up in surprise. Conner flashed another grin.

"I asked Gutierrez what it meant, he said—"

"I'm sorry," Johnson finished, not needing the translation. He didn't speak Spanish fluently, but he'd been on enough domestic violence calls to know that one. Someone was always saying sorry by the time the police arrived.

"Yeah," Conner said, his grin flattened as Johnson stole the crowning glory of his report. "Why would the victim be the one apologizing?"

Johnson lifted his shoulders in a light shrug. Knowing he couldn't justify putting it off any longer, he motioned for Conner to lift up the sheet.

The girl couldn't have been more than 18. Her jeans, white polo shirt and well-worn tennis shoes looked like they'd been new several years ago. Her dark caramel skin and wide flat face made Johnson think of the indigenous people of central Mexico. Wavy black hair reached past her shoulders. She didn't appear to be wearing any makeup and looked rumpled, like she had slept in her clothes, maybe for a few days. Blood soaked the front of her shirt and saturated the thick St. Augustine lawn where she lay, turning the normally vibrant green carpet a rusty brown. The strong metallic smell mixed with the fishy brine wafting from the nearby marina created a nauseating bouquet of decay. Johnson wrinkled his nose and winced as he thought about how long that dark stain would mark the spot where the girl died. It would testify to her pain long after neighborhood residents had stopped talking about the shooting.

Johnson finished his inspection with the girl's eyes—deep brown and staring straight up into the trees. He swallowed convulsively to keep bile from filling his mouth. His stomach ached to empty its contents. No matter how many times he saw that vacant death look, he never got used to it.

Coughing several times to cover his discomfort, Johnson stood up and took a deep breath. He couldn't move the body until the coroner arrived, but he could at least check her front pockets for anything that might tell them who she was. He pulled a pair of latex gloves from his shirt pocket and snapped them on. He gently patted the outside of each front pocket. He couldn't feel anything, but just to make sure, he carefully slid his fingers into each one. They were both empty. The back pockets would have to wait. It didn't look like she had fallen on anything like a purse, as Conner had suggested. If he was right, and she didn't have an ID tucked into her back pocket, Johnson would probably spend the rest of the morning combing through missing persons reports.

As Johnson stood up, he heard another car pull up behind the police cruisers. Every cop in town knew *Galveston Gazette* photographer Doug Cowel's 1985 Volvo. It had to be the only one in the city, and it eventually made an appearance at just about every crime scene. Judging by the smokey black trail in its wake, it had another oil leak. Johnson didn't mind Cowel. He was a professional, and he knew how to do his job without getting in the way. But Cowel hadn't come on this call alone, and Johnson groaned when he saw the passenger climb out of the car.

Kate Bennett looked like she'd just gotten out of the shower. Her light brown hair hung in damp clumps. Clutching her reporter's notebook in her teeth, she hopped a few times as she tugged a shoe onto a sockless foot. While Cowel collected his camera from the trunk, Kate swept her hair back into a knot and secured it with a band pulled off her wrist. Despite her half-closed eyes and grumpy frown—sure signs she hadn't been awake when the call went out over the police scanner—Johnson knew from experience she had already absorbed much of the details around her.

Kate Bennett rarely missed anything. In the six months she'd been at the *Galveston Gazette*, she'd built a reputation for pinpoint accuracy with a flare for dramatic details. She knew how to tell a story and make a point, and Johnson could think of more than a few city officials who pined for her predecessor. The former city reporter never asked for detailed budget documents or noticed the sideways glances between city council members that gave away alliances and foretold voting patterns. Kate Bennett had an uncanny ability to sniff out hidden motives and see through pretense. And she was good at getting people to talk. Johnson didn't dislike Kate, he just knew he had to weigh every word when she was listening. She could tease the smallest details out of a mere hello.

~ ~ ~ ~ ~

Kate glanced back at Cowel to see if he had gathered his equipment. When she turned back toward the crime scene, she caught Johnson watching her and headed straight for him. By the time she reached the yellow crime tape barrier, she'd managed to force what she hoped would be a disarming smile, even though Johnson didn't look particularly happy to see her.

"This is an odd place to dump a body," she said, pulling a pen out of the rings of her notebook. "I guess they weren't concerned about getting caught."

"No comment," Johnson said, shrugging.

"Don't mess with me Johnson, I haven't had any coffee yet this morning," Kate grumbled.

"I thought you looked especially grouchy."

"Seriously, I'm about to start making up quotes." Kate raised one eyebrow and rested her pen on the paper.

"Okay, okay," Johnson said, holding up his hands in mock surrender. "But I'm not giving you anything more than the basics."

Kate rolled her eyes and regretted it when Johnson's lips compressed into a hard line. She never seemed to hit the right note with him. Some cops could be cajoled into talking if she pandered to their egos. Others opened up when she tried to act like she was just one of the guys.

Older officers responded to the helpless female routine. Kate had learned to tailor her approach based on what would get her the most information.

She still hadn't figured Johnson out.

"Look, I'm just trying to do my job," she said. "Think of me as chronicling the beginning of what is sure to be a brilliant investigation in which you single-handedly track down the bad guy and make sure he gets what's coming to him."

Johnson narrowed his eyes and shook his head. "I'm not doing anything single-handedly. Murder investigations are about teamwork."

"I'm on your team," she said, shifting her weight from foot to foot in impatience. "I want you to catch whoever did this just as much as you do."

"I doubt that."

"Seriously! Every unpunished crime is a blot on the universe."

His arched eyebrow suggested he didn't ascribe to her theory that injustice threw the world out of balance. Kate stifled a sigh. "I'm just saying, I don't have any interest in derailing your investigation. You don't have to treat me like the enemy."

Johnson's stern gaze softened slightly. "Fair enough. But I'm still only giving you the basics until I talk to the chief."

Kate clenched her teeth but wrote down what he told her without complaint. When follow-up questions earned her nothing more than a few more "no comments," she opted for retreat and regroup.

"I guess that's it then. Thanks, detective. I'll call you later to follow up."

Johnson just nodded. After six months, Kate had yet to persuade him to give her anything off the record or tell her anything beyond what he strictly had to. The other cops didn't call him "Detective By the Book" for nothing. But Kate refused to give up. She sensed more than a self-serving desire to get ahead behind his devotion to the rules. Something else compelled him to stick to the rigid structure of his department's command structure. She'd figure it out eventually, and in the process she hoped she'd discover the source of Johnson's other anomaly: compassion.

Pushing Johnson to the back of her mind, Kate focused on the homeowner. The man definitely looked like he wanted someone to talk to. Kate walked along the crime scene tape until she was almost parallel with the house and about as far away from the crowd of onlookers as she could get.

"Excuse me, sir?" she called softly. When the man looked over at her, she smiled reassuringly. He hesitated for about five seconds before he stepped off the porch and walked toward her. When he reached the yellow barrier, he suddenly seemed to realize it might be inappropriate to appear eager to talk to someone who was obviously a reporter. He glanced at Johnson.

"I'm not sure I'm supposed to say anything," he said.

"I understand," Kate said soothingly. "The detective gave me all the details. I'm Kate Bennett, by the way. With the *Gazette*. I was just hoping you could tell me a little bit about the neighborhood."

"I know you," he said, his eyes lighting up with recognition. "I've been a subscriber ever since I moved to the island in 1987. You do good work."

Kate beamed with her most docile and reassuring smile.

"Well, I suppose I can't get in trouble for telling you about the neighborhood," he said, stuffing his hands deep in his robe's front pockets as he glanced sideways at the investigative bustle marring his front yard.

He spent the next five minutes recounting his move to the island and his search for the perfect house in excruciating detail. The neighborhood was quiet, with lots of families and professionals, he assured her. People just didn't wake up to find bodies in their front yards.

"That must have been quite a shock," Kate murmured sympathetically.

He didn't need any more encouragement. Abandoning his previous reticence, he told her everything, from waking up a little later than normal to his horror at watching a woman take her last breath. Kate scribbled furiously to keep up. Her notes looked more like a timeline than a word-for-word account, but she didn't worry about remembering the details. Those would remain burned in her memory for weeks.

When he finished, Kate deftly tucked her notebook and pen in her back pocket as she continued to murmur sympathetic platitudes. He was just saying he probably wouldn't be any use at the office for the rest of the day when the coroner's van pulled up. The crowd, which had started to lose interest, perked back up again and the man's neighbors strained against the tape in an effort to catch every detail of the body's removal. After thanking him for his help, Kate headed for the crowd, walking around the vans and the police cars to stay out of Cowel's shots of the suddenly bustling scene.

Kate didn't have any trouble persuading the lookie-loos to talk. A few of them said they thought they heard the shot. One, a man who lived on the other end of the street, said he thought he heard a car speeding away. But no one saw anything. As Kate wrote down names and phone numbers, the coroner started to roll his gurney toward the back of the waiting van. With the help of a well-placed sheet held up by the police officers, he'd managed to scoop up the body before anyone saw anything. Now it was all over. The crowd began to drift away.

Kate caught Cowel's eye and they headed back to the car.

"Did Johnson give you anything good this time?" the photographer asked as he drove past the port, where two cruise ships had started to disgorge their passengers.

"Humph," Kate grunted as she watched the white-shirted attendants scurrying around the open decks, readying the vessel for the next round of passengers.

Cowel laughed. "I'm telling you, you're wasting your time with him. I can think of half a dozen other cops who would happily be your best police department source."

"Ha! Where's the fun in that? I like a challenge."

"Oh, I know. Anyone who would take on the state's mental health system while still in college definitely likes a challenge. Remind me again… how many awards did you win for those stories?"

Kate felt the blood rush to her cheeks along with the same mix of pride and embarrassment she always juggled when someone mentioned the investigative series that brought her to the attention of every newspaper editor in Texas. People couldn't believe a college student managed to stumble onto one of the state's biggest scandals in the last decade. She knew most chalked it up to luck. They had no idea she had an inside scoop and a vested interest in finding out why so many patients never recovered from their stay at Templeton Mental Hospital. Some never even came home.

"Shut up," she muttered.

"Aww, come on kid," Cowel said. "I'm just teasing. You're a reporting rockstar. Own it."

Kate mustered a weak smile. She had no interest in being a star. Her only motivation had been justice for the patients and their families. She found it, and now she had an addiction. Her need to right wrongs smoldered in her chest, pumping purpose through every fiber of her being.

"Have you heard anything more about the layoffs?" she asked Cowel as they neared the newspaper office.

"Nah. Just that Mattingly and the publisher are locked in a battle to the death over every penny in the budget."

Kate snorted. "My money's on Mattingly. But I still can't believe the publisher thinks he can run this newspaper with fewer reporters."

"Welcome to journalism in the 21st century. It's not as glamorous as it looked when you were in college, huh?"

Kate rolled her eyes at him as they climbed out of the car.

"What are you worried about anyway?" Cowel asked as he slung a camera over each shoulder. "Your job is probably the last one on the chopping block."

"It's not about my job. It's about the newspaper's ability to do its job. Exposing the truth and holding the powerful accountable, remember?"

Cowel guffawed and patted her on the top of the head. "We have an office pool on how long your breathless idealism will last. I'm going to extend my bet."

Chapter 2

At 8:30 a.m. on a Monday, the *Gazette's* offices echoed with an emptiness that spoke volumes about staff morale. Kate shivered as they stepped into the fluorescent-lit hallway that led from the back entrance to the newsroom. Although the publisher claimed he couldn't afford to make payroll, he didn't hesitate to keep the office ice cold during the oppressive summer months. How much of the budget went to energy bills? Staff members were expendable. Air conditioning was not.

Like everything else on the island, the newspaper had suffered through an inching decline since the turn of the 20th century. Circulation dropped along with the city's population. During the last 10 years, the *Gazette's* publisher had pared down staff through attrition, for the most part. He'd instituted the last round of layoffs two years ago, but another one appeared imminent.

Managing Editor Kenton Mattingly and the heads of the advertising and circulation departments had spent part of almost every day during the last three weeks haggling over the budget with Publisher Haviland Bells. Mattingly refused to say anything about the negotiations, but he'd chugged down two bottles of Maalox in the last week. That couldn't be a good sign. He normally kept it to one.

No one came in before 9 a.m. these days.

Kate could hear the ladies in the Classifieds department chattering into their headsets, taking orders for next weekend's garage sale ads, as she walked toward the break room. The warm, slightly burnt smell of caffeine drew her on, but the coffee in the pot was the color of strong tea, the most obvious sign no one in the newsroom had arrived yet. Sighing with frustration, Kate yanked out the filter basket, tore open two packets of Folger's and poured out the weak brew. She had just hit the start button for a new pot when assistant editor Hunter Lewis walked around the corner.

"I hear you beat Ben to a body this morning," he said, flashing her a grin.

Kate shrugged defensively.

"I was closer," she said. "Cowel swung by and picked me up."

Kate shared the cops beat with Ben Denison, the *Gazette*'s longtime crime reporter. Although her primary responsibility was to cover city hall, the editors wanted her to write about any crimes Ben couldn't—or didn't— want to cover. When she arrived in Galveston six months earlier, Ben said he was glad to have someone to share the load. The publisher had decided the paper needed more trial coverage, and Ben was running ragged trying to keep up with the daily grind of robberies and drug busts while he was holed up in the courtroom. Kate learned later he had boasted to his sources he would give her the grunt work and keep the best stories for himself. But Kate had no intention of being someone else's lackey.

She routinely beat him to crime scenes, which left Lewis to referee more than a few turf battles. She considered Ben more competition than colleague until one day she overheard him acknowledging to Lewis that she had talent. He gradually stopped protesting when she stepped on his toes, treating her like a protege and critiquing her work instead. Kate ignored him, for the most part.

While coffee slowly filled the empty pot, Kate gave Lewis the details of the murder.

"Get me a story for the web in forty-five minutes," he said, replacing the coffee pot with his mug in one fluid movement. While the machine chugged into his cup, he filled Kate's mug from the pot. "And stay on Johnson until he has an ID. This is going to be a great story."

Cradling her coffee cup in both hands, Kate hustled back to her desk to start typing. She'd worked out the first few graphs of the story in her mind on the way back to the office, so she beat Lewis' deadline by five minutes. Ben walked into the newsroom as Kate walked out of Lewis' office.

"How do you manage to get to crime scenes so fast?" he grumbled. "You've got to be sleeping with one of the cops."

"Yeah, you should try it," she snapped. "It just might save your career."

He was about to respond when Delilah Peters strode in behind him.

"So, we've got a body in Fish Village, huh? That hasn't happened in years," Delilah said. "Ben hasn't been whining about missing the story, has he?"

"Humph," Kate muttered noncommittally. "I figured I was doing him a favor. He's got that trial starting this week, and this story's going to take a lot of time."

"Yeah, right," Delilah said with a grin. "Don't whine, Ben. She beat you fair and square. I'm pretty sure you were busy this morning about that time anyway."

Ben just grunted. Kate raised her coffee cup to her lips to hide a grimace. Although Ben and Delilah lived together and everyone knew it, they usually kept up a facade of professional separation at work, notwithstanding occasional references to their domestic bliss.

"So, give us the details. What did you find this morning?" Delilah asked Kate as she dumped her laptop bag on her desk.

"Unidentified body in the middle of a well-manicured front lawn. No ID. No idea how she got there."

"Well, readers love mysteries. That should sell a few papers, at least for a week or two. Let's hope it takes them a while to figure out who she is."

At a few minutes before 9:30 a.m., Mattingly yanked open his office door.

"Are we meeting, or what? In case you forgot, we have a newspaper to put out."

Delilah rolled her eyes. The managing editor's volatility had no effect on her, although Kate suspected she was as anxious about the rumored layoffs as everyone else. It seemed unlikely the senior reporter would lose her job, but she probably made the most and was the oldest person on staff. The paper could save some money if it replaced her with someone less experienced.

"How are the budget talks going?" Delilah asked once everyone had taken a seat around the long conference table in Mattingly's office. "Have you figured out which one of us you're going to fire?"

"No one's getting fired, not today anyway," Mattingly growled. "But I don't need layoffs as an excuse, so I suggest everyone step up their game. What do we got for today?"

Kate gave a brief sketch of the unidentified body story, which would lead the front page. Cowel slid a few printouts of his best shots from the scene over to Mattingly and assured him he had enough variety to include several more on page two. For a moment, Mattingly seemed to forget his near constant dissatisfaction and the gut-wringing budget talks. His eyes narrowed into glittery slits and his usually hard mouth curved with satisfaction.

"This is perfect. Rack sales will be off the charts. The copy desk had better make sure the headline pops. How about 'Fresh corpse in Fish Village,' or 'Early morning murder stuns Fish Village.' That one's a little long. Oh well. We have all afternoon to figure it out."

Delilah went next. The Park Board had a meeting that afternoon and she expected to turn in a story about a fight between two beachfront vendors laying claim to the same small stretch of umbrella and lounge chair real estate. Two weeks ago, the feud exploded into a full-fledged fist fight in front of tourists with cell phone cameras. The resulting footage made it to YouTube and Houston's evening news, not exactly the best ad the tourism bureau could buy.

Ben had an advance story about the trial scheduled to start the next day. A woman faced an attempted murder charge for trying to run over her husband with their beat-up minivan. She claimed it was self defense. He blamed it on the Hennessy they'd been drinking all night and the number of hands she'd lost at Texas Hold'em. The district attorney half expected the man to turn on him and refuse to testify against the old hag, whom he still seemed unaccountably fond of.

Business reporter Jessica Linton had her Junior League profile and a story about a new plastic surgeon enticed to the University of Texas Medical Branch from a much larger hospital up north. Education reporter Krista Chambers' story previewing that week's school board meeting would go on page four.

"OK. One down, six more to go," Mattingly said, his enthusiasm for the next day's paper abruptly gone. "What do we got for the rest of the week?"

Newspapers are voracious beasts. Feeding them can be exhilarating or exhausting, depending on how much news actually happens. The presses run even on slow days, making editors ache for a ten-car pile-up or grisly murder. But some days, an elderly woman's emotional reunion with her long-lost chihuahua is the only thing available.

While the other reporters listed their planned coverage, Kate let her mind wander back to the murder scene. Johnson had been working the case for several hours by now. Surely he had more information to share. But how could she convince him to spill the details, preferably before the afternoon press conference she'd gotten an email about just before the meeting. All the Houston TV stations would be there, which meant they would have the latest details on the six o'clock news before Kate could get them in the newspaper, or up on the web. Her head started to pound as she thought about the possibility someone might beat her to an update on the story.

She owned this story, and as soon as she could get to the police station, she planned to make sure Johnson knew it. She needed him as an ally, not an adversary.

"All right, people," Mattingly said as the meeting wrapped up. "No slacking this week. You'd better write each story as if your job depended on it. Don't give the publisher any excuse to tell me I've got dead wood I can cut from this newsroom."

Dead wood, dead girl. The managing editor's warning conjured up the image of the woman who had drawn her last breath just hours earlier. Her killer had gotten away, but Johnson would unravel the mystery sooner or later. Probably sooner. Kate savored the thought of watching the case unfold, knowing the killer would get what he deserved and the young girl's family would find some peace.

Chapter 3

As soon as the meeting ended, Kate fled the newsroom and headed to the police station, steeled for a fight.

"I'd like to talk to Detective Johnson," she barked into the speaker box that connected the receptionist's bullet-proof glass bubble to the lobby. "Please," she added when the woman's raised eyebrows creased her forehead with incredulous furrows.

"The detective asked me to buzz you back as soon as you got here," she said.

Kate just stared at her, dumbfounded. The receptionist chuckled as she hit the big red button that unlocked the door leading to the back offices.

"Guess it's your lucky day."

"Yeah, I guess so. Thanks."

Kate found Johnson leaning back in the chair behind his desk, elbows on the armrests, fingers spread, tips touching. His thinking pose. She sat down across the desk without speaking and waited. His hazel eyes narrowed in concentration as he focused on a watercolor painting hanging on the far wall. A muddy brown river wound between lush green hills. It exuded a sense of peace, but today it didn't seem to offer Johnson any.

Kate once had a veteran reporter tell her cops were a lot like criminals. They craved power and considered themselves superior to "normal" people. They chose badges over ski masks only because their egos demanded public praise. But something else drove Johnson—a genuine belief in right and wrong. He could have stepped straight out of one of the cheesy 1950s Westerns her dad loved so much, white cowboy hat in hand.

After several minutes, he let out a deep sigh and leaned forward. Kate slid her pen from the top spirals of the notebook balanced on her knees.

"She didn't have an ID on her, so we're looking at a Jane Doe until someone comes to claim her," he said without any introduction. "I know all the Houston TV stations will be at the press conference. If you promise not to post a story until after it's over, I'll give you a preview. I would hate for the big city guys to beat you on the details, especially since you were first on the scene and all."

Kate's exultant and grateful smile froze when Johnson held up one cautionary hand.

"Things could change between now and then. We have officers canvassing the neighborhoods to see if anyone has an idea of who she is. If we hear anything, I'll let you know, but it might not be until the press conference. So you have to be there."

"I wouldn't miss it," Kate said, all traces of the grin gone. "Thank you."

"Mmmmm..." Johnson said, eyeing her through narrowed lids, like he was trying to figure out whether he had made a good decision.

Kate didn't break his gaze, hoping that made her look trustworthy.

Johnson gave her a more detailed description of the girl than she had gotten that morning. He also told her about the girl's dying words.

"That's a juicy detail to release so soon," Kate said.

"It is. We're hoping it might lead someone to come forward. If they knew she died with an apology on her lips, maybe they'll be willing to offer forgiveness."

"Assuming she did something wrong," Kate said, instinctively jumping to the dead girl's defense.

"I'm not saying she did. But her last thought in this life prompted her to apologize for something. We just want the people who love her to know that. Maybe it will encourage them to tell us what she had going on in her life that led to this."

Johnson leaned back in his chair and glanced again at the painting. "Guilt can be a powerful motivator," he concluded with a sigh.

Kate winced. She knew that all too well. On her last day in college, her newspaper adviser had urged her to set aside the only driving force she'd known since high school. They'd just learned the Texas Rangers were opening an investigation into Templeton Mental Hospital, based on her stories. "You've done your part. Stop chasing ghosts and move on," he'd told her. Guilt eventually gave way to an almost manic desire for justice. It didn't feel much different.

Shaking off the memory, Kate stood up to go as Johnson tucked his notepad back into the top drawer of his desk.

"Thanks again," she said, turning back at the door to his office. "And don't worry. I know you'll figure out who did this."

Johnson gave her a slight smile and nodded. As she walked back down the hall, Kate took a deep breath. A satisfying sense of accomplishment settled over her, easing the tension lodged between her shoulder blades. For the first time in six months she felt like she'd broken through the husk of Johnson's professional shell.

She stopped for a celebratory burrito on her way back to the office. While she ate, she looked through all her notes one more time, mopping grease from her lips every few pages. When Lewis got back from lunch, she caught him up with what she knew. Only one headline made sense. Lewis agreed and promised to take it to Mattingly while she wrote.

By 4:30 p.m., the story was written, edited and on the page, with a shorter version prepped for the web. Kate would call after the press conference if anything changed. Mattingly hadn't taken a swig from his Maalox bottle all afternoon. He even told her she'd done a good job persuading Johnson to spill his guts early. She didn't bother telling him the detective volunteered. It had been a good day.

~ ~ ~ ~ ~

When Kate pulled up in front of the police station fifteen minutes later, she counted six satellite vans in the parking lot. Reporters and camera men already clogged the lobby, chatting guardedly to see whether anyone knew something the others didn't. Kate nodded to the *Houston Chronicle* reporter standing at the back of the room, ready to break for the door as soon as the press conference ended. He would have to bang out a story at a nearby coffee shop and email it to his editor within 30 to 45 minutes. Kate couldn't help but smile as she thought about her carefully written, well-vetted story already cozy on the front page.

The police department's PR flak stepped up to the microphone a few minutes after 5 p.m. He thanked them for coming, gave them the spelling of Johnson's name and asked them to hold questions until the end.

Kate felt a flutter of excitement as Johnson took his place behind the podium. He wasn't what anyone would call photogenic. Tall to the point of being gangly, with sandy tan hair and unremarkable features, Johnson didn't look the part of a crusading crime-fighter. But he exuded a calm assurance that compelled people's trust. Anticipation that justice would soon be served spread warmth from Kate's heart all the way to her toes. Johnson would not let whoever did this get away with it.

When Johnson recalled the victim's last words, his voice caught just slightly in his throat. Camera shutters exploded in machine gun bursts and reporters scribbled furiously into notebooks. Goosebumps spread down Kate's arms.

"The officers who spent the afternoon knocking on doors and talking to community leaders haven't found any leads on the girl's identity," Johnson said as he wrapped up his presentation. "The Galveston Police Department encourages anyone who has any information to come forward."

After twice repeating the number to a hotline set up to take tips, Johnson opened the floor for questions. Kate listened carefully to her competitors' queries, to make sure she hadn't missed anything. She had to admit the investigation wasn't off to a promising start. Maybe she would have to write a few more update stories than she first expected.

But Johnson seemed equally confident the killer would soon be in custody.

"We will find out who did this and why," he said. "We will find someone to take this girl home."

'Lo siento'

Unidentified victim's dying words stump investigators

By Kate Bennett

The woman who died early Monday in the front yard of a Fish Village home uttered an apology with her last breath, giving police their only clue to her identity and who might have killed her.

As the pink rays of first light streaked over the island's East End, someone shot the unidentified woman in the stomach and escaped without being seen. Frank Harper, who lives in the 200 block of Barracuda Drive, heard a single gunshot as he made coffee at about 6:15 a.m. When he came out to investigate, he found the woman on his front lawn, gasping for air and bleeding to death.

Although she didn't acknowledge Harper's presence or appear to speak to him, he clearly heard her say "Lo siento" just before she died, according to Galveston Police Det. Peter Johnson. The phrase is Spanish for "I'm sorry," and police hope it will encourage someone who knows her to come forward.

Harper, who is not a suspect in the case, did not know the victim, nor did any of his neighbors. Officers who spent the afternoon interviewing community members and talking to area residents found no further clues about who she is or why she was in Fish Village at that hour.

"We are just beginning this investigation, and we are confident that we will find whoever did this," Johnson said Monday afternoon. "But the first step is to find out who this girl is."

Johnson described the victim as a Hispanic woman in her late teens or early 20s with long black hair and brown eyes. She was wearing jeans, a white polo shirt and well-worn tennis shoes. She didn't have a bag or purse with her and her pockets were empty. Although she could be a Galveston resident, she might also be a visitor, making it even harder to find someone who knows her.

Fish Village residents who gathered just outside the yellow crime scene tape shortly after the shooting said they couldn't remember the last time anyone had been murdered in the neighborhood.

"It's just so shocking," said Melanie Hurst, who lives two houses away from where the victim died. "I had just turned on 'Good Morning America' when I heard a loud popping noise and then the sound of tires screeching. But when I looked outside, I didn't see anything. I thought it might have been someone's car back-firing."

Hurst, a surveyor for the U.S. Army Corps of Engineers, was the only neighbor who heard a vehicle. But several people heard the gunshot.

"I would recognize that sound anywhere," said Paul Gaines, a former U.S. Army medic who now works for the University of Texas Medical Branch and lives across the street from the crime scene. "It was definitely a single gunshot, probably from a semi-automatic pistol."

Police declined to say what kind of weapon the killer used.

Mayor Matthew Hanes, who has asked for regular updates on the investigation from Police Chief Sam Lugar, said he had complete confidence in investigators' ability to find the woman's identity and her killer. He also urged islanders and visitors to remember violent crime happens rarely in the city.

"Galveston is a safe place," he said. "We know that such violence almost never happens between strangers. No one needs to worry that we have a crazed killer on the loose looking for another victim. Once we know who she is, what happened here will make much more sense."

Harper, who called 911 immediately after the victim spoke, still appeared visibly shaken as police officers tramped through his yard, peering behind azalea bushes and stomping on the red and white impatiens in his front flower beds.

"I still can't believe it," he said. "Never in a million years would I expect to have something like this happen here, to me."

Harper, an engineer with the Corps, moved to Fish Village in 1987. Since then, he's only called the police a few times. Once, vandals knocked over his mailbox. Another time, tourists wandering up from the beach stopped to urinate on his oak tree. But he never felt unsafe, until now.

"It just makes you think," he said. "If something like this could happen here, it could happen anywhere."

Chapter 4

Two days later, Kate sat in front of Mattingly's desk, squirming under a barrage of criticism.

"It's been two days, and you still have nothing new on the murder investigation? What the hell is going on here?" Mattingly yelled. "Everyone wants to know what happened and who this girl is. Do you really believe the police have nothing to tell us?"

"I don't know," Kate said miserably. "I've worked every single source I have in the department. They all say the same thing—the case went cold right from the start."

"This is a disaster," Mattingly growled, yanking open a desk drawer and pulling out a bottle of Maalox. "I pay you to get information, and I've got nothing. Better yet, the publisher thinks we dropped the ball. Everyone in his Rotary Club asked him about the case yesterday. He had to say he didn't know anything. The head of the newspaper doesn't know anything about the story everyone's talking about! That's not exactly good advertising."

Kate stared at her hands, knotted into a tight ball in her lap while Mattingly twisted off the cap on the Maalox bottle and took two noisy gulps.

"I want you to go to the police department right now and tell Johnson he'd better spill his guts on this investigation or we're running with a story about his complete incompetence. Put the screws to him."

"But I've got that warehouse ribbon cutting to cover in an hour," Kate protested, her shoulders tensing into throbbing knots at the thought of confronting the detective.

"I don't care," Mattingly barked. "Do both. No excuses. This is what it means to do more with less, as the publisher likes to remind me. In case you've forgotten, he's gunning for someone's job. It could be yours. Don't give him any more reason to tell me we can run this newspaper with one less reporter. Go."

Kate stood up and walked back to her desk without saying a word. Her head had started to pound in rhythm with her heart. She understood Mattingly's frustration and the pressure he was under, but he was being too harsh. Kate also expected the investigation to be further along by now, but it had only been two days. Was that really enough time to catch a killer when they didn't even know the victim's name?

~ ~ ~ ~ ~

Kate squared her shoulders and steeled herself for a confrontation as she walked into the police station. When the receptionist saw her, she smiled and then glanced around quickly before motioning Kate over to her glass enclosure.

"They still don't have any leads," she whispered, her mouth pressed close to the microphone that projected her voice through the partition. "They've gotten tips on the hotline, but nothing's panned out so far. The other officers say Johnson thinks the girl must have been involved in something really bad, something so bad her relatives are afraid to even claim her. The other theory is that she doesn't have any relatives close enough to claim her, or to even know what happened. It's possible her killer was the only one in the area who knew who she was."

"Thanks," Kate said, her eyes darting around the foyer to make sure no one was watching, or listening. "I really appreciate it. Is that it? I mean, do you think Johnson knows more than he's letting on?"

"I doubt it, but I guess it's possible. If you're going to go talk to him, be careful. He's already snapped at a few of the officers this morning. And I thought he was going to get into a shoving match with one of the other detectives in the break room. He's wound up so tight I'm surprised his head hasn't popped off."

Kate nodded and headed toward the door leading to the back offices. On the drive over, she'd considered how best to approach the detective—pleading, threatening, wheedling. She finally settled on indignant purveyor of public accountability.

"Hey," she said as she marched into his office and sat down in the chair in front of his desk. "Just thought I'd stop by and see if you had any news for me."

Johnson's arched eyebrows and pursed lips suggested her abrupt entrance wasn't welcome.

"I told you yesterday I'd call you if I had anything," he said curtly. "Haven't you learned by now I'm gonna shoot straight with you?"

"Sure, unless the chief orders you not to."

"Then I would tell you I couldn't talk, not that I didn't have any information. But at this point, I really don't have any information."

"Look, Johnson, you're one of the best detectives in the department. I just can't believe you really don't have any leads. I know it's only been two days, but earlier this year you had that gang banger's killer arrested within 24 hours."

"That was a different case," Johnson said slowly, every word punctuating his rising frustration. "Sometimes these things take time."

"The public has a right to know how this case is progressing," Kate said, staring at him determinedly. "They are footing the bill, after all."

Johnson slapped his palm down on his desk so hard his card holder, coffee cup and keyboard jumped. So did Kate.

"I told you I'd let you know when I have something worth sharing," he barked. "I don't have anything else to say."

"I think you're holding out on me," Kate said, her hands gripping the arms of her chair so tightly she could feel her nails sinking into the wood. "I need something for tomorrow's paper."

"Out!" Johnson yelled, jumping to his feet and stabbing the air in the direction of his office door. "My job is to catch the killer, not keep your byline on the front page. Next time I do have something to share, don't expect to be the first one to know."

Kate cringed. She'd pushed too far and hurt her chances of getting a scoop if there was one. She briefly thought about apologizing and telling Johnson about her rebuke from Mattingly. But the last thing she wanted to do was look weak, even if she was wrong.

Without breaking eye contact, Kate rose slowly from her chair, spun on her heel and marched out the door. She hoped her raised chin made her look defiant.

~ ~ ~ ~ ~

Fifteen minutes later, the adrenaline spike fueled by her confrontation with Johnson had almost subsided. Her heart settled back into its normal cadence as she pulled up outside a bright metal warehouse that looked out of place beside its rusted and vacant neighbors. The short parking lot radiated with new asphalt that still emitted a faint burning smell. Oleander bushes freshly planted on either side of the driveway swayed gently in the clammy breeze. Two bunches of bright red balloons tethered to the shiny chain link fence surrounding the property bobbed and shuddered.

Business reporter Jessica Linton normally covered openings, but this project had all the makings of a boondoggle. Mattingly wanted more than a fluff piece about it. Kate had already written volumes about developer Eduardo Reyes' request for tax rebates and special permits. Despite the negative press and some vocal opposition from neighborhood groups, the city council approved the deal shortly after the new mayor took office in January. Reyes promised the complex, designed as a short-term holding facility for cargo, would help lure businesses and, more importantly, jobs back to the island. Mattingly had voiced his doubts in at least five editorials during the last six months. But Mayor Matthew Hanes, Reyes' college buddy, supported the project and pushed it through with minimal resistance.

Mattingly often called Reyes the most influential, least accountable person on the island.

Knowing she couldn't put it off any longer, Kate climbed out of her car and started walking toward the warehouse. As she got closer, she could see Reyes making his way across the long loading dock, where island dignitaries had started to gather. His thick chest seemed to swell more than normal. His wavy black hair shimmered with an oil slick's iridescence. Beyond the open roll doors, Kate spotted tables spread with finger foods. Big fans on either side pushed the thick morning air in velvety waves across the small crowd. Kate sighed. She could already feel a trickle of sweat working its way down the small of her back.

Reyes greeted her at the top of the stairs leading to the front door.

"The *Gazette* sent its prettiest reporter," he crooned loudly. "What an honor!"

Kate managed to keep from rolling her eyes as she held out her hand. Reyes took it in both of his and squeezed. It galled Kate to see Reyes gloat over her presence, knowing how vehemently her boss opposed the project.

"If you need anything, you just let me know," Reyes said with a wink, his gaze quickly sliding over her shoulder to the group walking up behind her.

"Matthew! It's a great day for Galveston."

Mayor Matthew Hanes took the steps two at a time and grabbed his friend's hand in a clasp that turned into the back-slapping embrace used only by men who call each other "brother."

Kate marveled at what still seemed like an unlikely friendship, the depth of which she discovered while covering Hanes' mayoral campaign. Reyes and Hanes graduated in the same class from Galveston's Ball High School, but they came from opposite ends of the island's social spectrum. They didn't become friends until college.

Hanes spent 10 years practicing maritime law before running for city council. After two terms representing District 6, he ran for mayor. Reyes financed almost his entire campaign with one fundraiser in Houston attended by most of their law school classmates, who expected as a matter of course they would help fund the political campaigns of some of their number. Despite grousing in the *Gazette*'s op-ed pages about big city lawyers buying the election, Hanes won in a landslide.

His support for Reyes' warehouse project was the least he could do to show his gratitude.

Kate expected Reyes to kick off the ceremony, but it was Hanes who stepped up to the microphone first.

"Thank you so much for coming," he said, gripping the mic stand with one hand and leaning slightly to the side, crooner style. "As my friend here has already said, this is a great day for Galveston."

The audience, mostly elected officials, business owners, Chamber of Commerce members, and people trying to curry favor, clapped enthusiastically. Kate pressed her lips together to keep from smirking. What patsies.

"There were many who said this project would never happen. There were some who said it would be bad for our island. Our friends at the *Gazette* called it a...wait, let me make sure I get this right...a boondoggle. Dontcha just love that word?" with this, he grinned at Kate. A man in a suit standing beside her snickered. "But we knew it would succeed. And Eduardo Reyes never gave up on his dream of bringing jobs back to this city. No one loves Galveston more than my friend, and yours, Eduardo Reyes."

Apparently unable to contain his excitement any longer, Reyes jumped up and clasped the mayor in another "brother" hug. He laughed and feigned shushing motions as the small crowd clapped again. Then he cradled the microphone in both hands and brought it to his face, inches from his full lips.

"Thank you, my friends. Thank you, thank you. We did this together, and I thank you from the bottom of my heart for all your support. When I was a boy, I would listen to my father and my uncles tell stories about the island as she was when they were growing up. Busy, prosperous and full of jobs! That's the dream I've carried with me all these years, and that's the dream I give you today."

While he spoke, two men in khaki overalls stretched a bright red ribbon across the roll door behind him.

"This new warehouse is just a small piece of the puzzle. But I hope it will be the beginning of more good things to come for the city we all love."

One of the men in overalls handed Reyes a pair of large, black scissors. Holding them up, Reyes turned toward the ribbon, pausing just long enough to savor the moment. Then, with an almost menacing slashing motion, he severed the taught plastic, snapping the halves apart. The audience cheered, surging toward the fans and food as Reyes motioned them inside.

Kate scanned the crowd and picked out a few familiar faces. Joe Henry Miles, chairman of the Port of Galveston, pumped Reyes' hand and slapped him on the shoulder. Miles, Mayor Hanes' fishing buddy, shared the vision of Galveston's resurrection, largely because the port would play a big role. Behind Miles, Tim Hammond hovered. As head of the dock worker's union, Hammond threw his support behind Reyes' project, bringing dozens of longshoremen to line the edges of the council chambers during debates on permits and tax incentives. Their presence filled the room with a vague threat, along with the tang of saltwater and sweat. Although their activities today bore little resemblance to the violent lawlessness of 30 years ago, many islanders still viewed them as little more than thugs. The project's opponents always eyed them with suspicion and made a show of leaving the meetings en mass, invoking the protection of the herd.

Kate made smalltalk with a few Chamber of Commerce wags, picking up quotes about how great the new warehouse complex would be for the city. While she dutifully captured another round of breathless hyperbole, her mind wandered back to her conversation with Johnson. His genuine anger almost convinced her he really had nothing to share. But a nagging suspicion prompted her to try the mayor, hoping she could surprise him into revealing something.

"Pretty crazy about this murder in Fish Village, huh?" she asked, catching him while everyone else flocked to the food table. She kept her question purposely vague, hoping Hanes might think she knew more than she did.

"Well, it's baffling, that's for sure," Hanes said. "But the police are doing everything they can, and I'm sure they'll turn up something soon. The important thing we all need to remember is that Galveston is safe. This is an isolated incident, and no one planning a trip to the beach this weekend has anything to fear."

He looked pointedly at the notebook in which Kate had written nothing down. She smiled sweetly.

"Indeed. Well, thank you very much, Mayor Hanes. I'll see you tomorrow."

Despite the ambiguity of the mayor's confidence in the police, Kate was pretty certain he wasn't hinting at, or trying to hide, anything specific. She sighed as she walked back to her car, the mid-morning air heavy as it poured down her throat. Her damp shirt clung to the small of her back. Maybe she owed Johnson an apology after all.

Chapter 5

The next night, Kate sat at the half-moon table reserved for reporters at the front of the city council chamber, eyeing a restless crowd. Dozens of city workers fidgeted shoulder-to-shoulder in the back of the room. Garbage collectors in grimy blue uniforms stood next to accountants in shirtsleeves and ties. The ones in the back stood on tip-toe to peer over those in front, hoping to spot a co-worker who might have saved them a seat in the stuffed-to-overflowing benches. Along the wall, police officers huddled in twos and threes. They hadn't been called in to keep the peace. They were there to remind their bosses the cuts they made affected real people with families to feed and bills to pay.

Hanes wanted to cut 10 percent from the city's expenditures for the following year, part of his pro-business campaign platform. But to do it, he had to take on the police union, which lobbied for, and generally got, a 3 percent pay raise every year. To avoid accusations of inequality, the city council approved the same increase for civilian workers, who didn't have bargaining rights. In addition to freezing salaries this year, Hanes planned to cut pension benefits. The combined reductions would allow the city to cut the property tax rate by a quarter percent, saving the average homeowner about $60 on his tax bill. It wasn't much, but it was something.

"Alright, I'd like to call this meeting to order," Hanes said, giving the wooden block on the desk two good whacks with his gavel. The audience stood obediently to recite the Pledge of Allegiance, the only thing everyone in the room could agree on. After issuing a proclamation recognizing National Hotdog Week and a resolution thanking a Boy Scout troop for cleaning up a neighborhood park, Hanes brought the discussion back to the only item on the agenda most people cared about.

The audience members would have their say first, then the council would take up its debate. Kate didn't expect any surprises. She was pretty sure Hanes had enough votes to push his agenda through. And the council wouldn't approve the budget for another six weeks, giving the mayor plenty of time to win over any holdouts. He didn't usually mind opposition, as long as he had the votes to carry his proposals through. But Kate knew he really wanted a unanimous decision on this one.

The first person to the microphone was a technician from one of the water treatment plants. Dingy baseball cap crushed between his hands, the man cleared his throat and shifted his weight from his left foot to his right foot and back again. His bushy, white mustache twitched as he worked himself up to say his piece.

"My name is José Martinez. I started working for the city when I was 18. I won't say how old I am now, but you can probably tell I'm a long way from a teenager."

The audience laughed, a gentle encouragement that seemed to give the self-conscious man more courage.

"I'm proud o' my job, even though it's not glamorous. It's hot, dirty work. I shovel people's shi--, I mean poop, all day. That's all the stuff you folks flush down your fancy commodes," he said, turning to look at the stone-faced neighborhood representatives sitting closest to him.

"You wouldn't believe some of the stuff I've seen. You peoples is nasty."

At this, the city workers roared with laughter. Kate could see why they picked Martinez to speak first. He flashed a grin over his shoulder.

"Mr. Martinez, we would like to hear what you have to say, but please restrict your comments to the budget proposal," Hanes said, attempting to bring the technician to order with a scowl.

"Here's the thing, Mr. Mayor," Martinez said, after licking his lips and swallowing hard. "We work hard for the little bit o' pay we get. And we're grateful for it, don't get me wrong. But it's not easy making ends meet here. Food's expensive. Rent's expensive. Insurance—it's really expensive. Some of us can't afford it. And what's gonna happen if we get another storm? We're due."

From the audience, a few people murmured "Mmm-hum" and "That's right!" In the front rows, the neighborhood representatives shifted uncomfortably in their seats.

"This tax cut don't amount to much. They don't really need it. But we depend on our pay raise just to keep up. If you take that away from us, our lives is only gonna get harder. We'll keep doing our work. I'll keep shoveling your poop. But it's just gonna be hard. And me and my wife's raising our grandson. He wants to play football next year. How'm I gonna tell him he can't 'cause I can't afford the registration fee? It's just not right. That's all."

Martinez sat down and someone else replaced him. Kate's fingers flew over her laptop's keys, the faint clicking punctuating each speaker's declaration of deprivation and hardship. The homeowners were lucky they had the mayor on their side. Their statements lacked the emotional impact of the employees' appeals. Reining in spending made sense, they said. Maxing out the tax base hurt the city's bond rating and made it harder to borrow money for the big improvements the 100-year-old water and sewer systems needed. The city would never attract more businesses and developments if the taxes kept climbing, they warned.

"You just have to ask yourself what kind of city do you want," said Daniel Price, president of the Silk Stocking District's homeowners' association. He grasped each side of the podium with his hands and stood with one foot forward, as though he were giving a lecture. Kate imagined if she could get close enough, she might be able to hear his starched white shirt crackle every time he moved. "Are we going to stay stuck in this rut, wasting the potential of our little slice of paradise? Or are we going to seize this opportunity and run with it? If we don't get our spending under control, if we continue to let the police union dictate 60 percent of the city's budget, it's going to get a lot harder to live here. Not just for us, but for you too."

Following Martinez's example, he turned around and looked hard at the city worker section of the audience.

"If they have to raise taxes to cover never ending salary increases, we'll all pay. That extra money on your paycheck will only go right back to the city when you pay your property taxes."

Turning back to the council, he jabbed his finger in their direction for emphasis.

"You just remember what you said when you ran for office, not just the mayor, but all of you. You all pledged to cut taxes. Now's the time to make good on that promise. If you don't, I guarantee you someone else will be sitting in your seats two years from now."

Paul Petronello, the head of the police union, was the last to speak, swaggering up the aisle to the microphone almost two hours after the meeting started. He must have known he was fighting a losing battle, but no stranger to the proceedings would have guessed it by his almost nonchalant attitude. Kate decided he was just too proud to let anyone see his cause going down in flames.

"Police officers have a lot of options for jobs in this area," he said. "All of the Houston suburbs in the northern part of the county offer much better assignments. Patrolling neighborhoods with million dollar homes is a lot less dangerous than cruising through the projects. Remember what it was like here in the 1980s? Whole sections of town belonged to drug dealers and gangs. Shootings happened weekly, not monthly."

Out of better options, Petronello played the only card that might make the council members change their minds —threaten a drop in tourism.

"You don't want to go back to the days when visitors feared getting mugged, carjacked, or worse if they got lost in the wrong part of town. But if you cut our pay, a lot of these guys will start looking for other jobs," he said, motioning toward the officers standing against the walls. "Even if you don't think we deserve a decent wage for putting our lives on the line every day to keep this city safe, consider what kind of protection you'll get if the only officers who come here are the ones who can't get jobs anywhere else. We've worked hard over the last three decades to make this city safe. Think long and hard before you throw it all away."

After Petronello sat down, the council took a 15 minute recess. Kate cracked her knuckles and stretched, her back and fingers stiff from hunching over the keyboard for so long. As she made her way through the crowd to the back of the room, she looked for Johnson. She didn't really expect to see him. She'd never seen him at a council meeting. When she asked him about it one time, he admitted he watched them on TV at home. She wondered what he thought of the debate.

Another day had passed since the Fish Village murder and the police still had no leads and no clue about the victim's identity. Kate was certain now she owed Johnson an apology, but she hadn't worked her way up to it yet. She was only doing her job, after all. The police worked for the people, and they had a duty to share what they knew, as long as it didn't hurt the investigation.

But Kate had to admit now Johnson wasn't holding out on her. He really had no news to share. Even so, she told herself her approach was justified. Her tiff with Johnson was just part of the faltering dance reporters had to do with public officials to keep them honest. But the truth was, she hated apologizing for anything. Apologizing put you in someone else's debt, and she hated owing anyone anything. That helped her stay independent, she reasoned. But it also kept her alone.

Kate made it back to her seat just in time to watch the council members file out of the conference room where they spent the recess, grazing on finger foods and fruit platters. Judging by their expressions, the break had fortified them against the emotional pleas they'd endured during the first half of the meeting. Only two of the council members smiled out at the audience. Terrance White represented a district where many of the city workers lived. Julia Escoveda's brother was a police officer, and she had taken large campaign donations from the police union. They were the only two council members Hanes had not persuaded to support the budget cuts.

"As you know, this is just a discussion item," Hanes said after rapping his gavel on the desk. "No decisions will be made tonight. I can't speak for my fellow council members, but I've been moved by what you've said—all of you. I don't want to make life harder for any of my fellow islanders."

Ever the politician, Kate thought.

"But as Mr. Price said, if we don't get our spending under control and end up having to raise taxes, everyone will pay. And higher property taxes will just discourage businesses from moving here. That's the one thing we don't want to do—scare off potential employers."

Hanes leaned forward, his hands clasped in front of him, and looked intently at the audience.

"I'm sympathetic to the police union's position, but they simply can't continue to hold this city hostage with threats of lawlessness. Galveston is very different than it was 20 years ago. The drug dealers and gangs are gone. It's a safe place to raise a family. We deeply value our law enforcement officers and the contributions they make to our safety. But no one needs to live in fear here."

Right, Kate thought. Tell that to the girl laying in the morgue, whose killer was still on the loose.

Chapter 6

Kate woke with a start to the clang of a garbage truck scooping up the dumpster beside her building. She'd quit grumbling about the weekly pickup months ago, but she hadn't yet learned how to sleep through it. She didn't need to look at her alarm clock to know it was about 5 a.m. The garbage truck came at the same time every Tuesday. Normally, she managed to fall back asleep, but today she lay looking at the ceiling long after the truck rumbled down the street.

She stretched her arm out and felt the depression where Brian, her boyfriend of just a few months, had been sleeping an hour earlier. He had only stayed over a few times, and she still wasn't used to waking up to him there. The first night she lay beside him, she never really fell asleep. The memory of his arms around her and his throaty laugh kept dragging her back to consciousness.

Brian had been a surprise. Focused, dependable, easygoing. A doctor. He wasn't the kind of guy she gravitated to. She only said yes the first time he asked her out be-

cause she wanted her ex-boyfriend to see she wasn't fatal-
ly wounded by his defection to a sleek Brazilian waitress.

Brian sent her flowers the next day and called that
night to see if she was free the following weekend. She
said yes because she didn't want to go out alone and
bump into her ex. But by the end of the night, Brian had
started to reel her in. They spent two and a half hours over
dinner swapping work stories. He watched her with intense blue eyes as she railed against the island's vicious
local politics. She laughed so hard she cried when he re-
counted some of the bizarre cases that came into the
UTMB emergency room.

And now? Kate frowned into the darkness. She was
not in love. She had managed to avoid that so far in every
relationship, and she saw no reason to fall apart now.
Love was messy, dangerous and inevitably painful. But
something drew her to Brian. He was easy to be around,
and she felt no pressure from him to give more, do more,
or be more. He seemed to take her in without any expecta-
tions, just enjoying the ride. Most men she'd dated tried to
tame her or break into her emotional fortress. Brian
seemed content for now to walk around the walls, although Kate suspected he was feeling for cracks. She
planned to cut him loose before he found any.

Giving up on going back to sleep, Kate rolled over and
turned on the police scanner sitting on the floor next to the
bed. The light banter scattered across the scratchy air-
waves focused mostly on the upcoming shift change and
breakfast options. Empanadas from the panaderia on

Broadway were winning out over burritos from the taqueria just a few blocks down.

As she had almost every morning for the last two weeks, Kate thought about the still unidentified Fish Village murder victim. The case had gone completely cold, and she had never seen Johnson so morose. The lines creasing his forehead looked like they were becoming permanent. She'd heard of police officers sinking into depression or becoming obsessed over that one case that got away. She hoped Johnson wasn't having an early breakdown.

It had taken her a week to bring herself to apologize for accusing him of keeping information from her.

"Don't worry about it," he'd said, staring at the painting on his office wall.

"Really..." she began, not exactly sure how to convey how sorry she truly was.

After an uncomfortably long pause, he finally looked at her and managed a grimace that seemed intended for a smile.

"It's ok, really," he said. "I know you're just doing your job. And I'm trying to do mine."

The complete lack of progress on the case was eating him alive.

Now another week had passed, and still no tips, no leads, no answers. Kate was just starting to replay the facts of the case in her mind when the scanner crackled to life with a new urgency.

"All units in the vicinity of 54th Street, respond to a 10-54," the dispatcher said in a dispassionate monotone. "The caller says you should look about 10 yards up the alley."

Kate was on her feet and pulling on a shirt before the first unit acknowledged the call. A 10-54 sometimes meant an old lady had died in her sleep. But since old ladies rarely slept in allies, even in Galveston, Kate was pretty sure this call would turn into a good story.

~ ~ ~ ~ ~

The putrid stench of rotting garbage punched the back of Johnson's throat, making him gag as he climbed out of his car. An unpaved alley stretched out in front of him. A pile of old tires, waist-high weeds and overflowing garbage cans broke up what should have been a clear view to the next street. One naked bulb shining over the back door of a rundown house offered the only weak light in the otherwise dark corridor. In a house behind him, a small dog yapped incessantly.

For the last few weeks, Johnson had reviewed the details of the Fish Village murder at least three times every day. He took the thin case file home with him at night, poring over the notes in hopes something new would jump out. The longing to find the killer filled him with a restless energy that had no outlet. He took his dogs for long runs on the beach after work and spent mornings at the police gym, straining his muscles against weights he could barely lift. He fell into bed each night exhausted, but still the nameless victim's vacant stare burned into his mind and made it hard to fall asleep. Her eyes had taken on a hint of accusation that filled his fitful dreams with an unquenchable helplessness. He woke up tired and angry.

He thought this battle was long over. Hadn't he conquered the belief that he needed to right wrongs in order to find peace? He knew the righteousness at the end of that road was a mirage. The water in that desert would never quench his thirst. But his heart still longed to drink anyway.

This morning's call over the scanner had given him a jolt of hope. He assumed immediately the body in the alley was a murder victim. If the cases shared a connection, his stalled investigation might finally get some traction. If they didn't, at least he'd have a new victim who needed justice, something to keep his mind off the other case.

"Let's get some light in there," he yelled.

Three patrol cars had arrived at the scene before him. The driver of the one closest to the alley entrance repositioned his cruiser so the headlights flooded the narrow lane. The body lay about 20 paces in. Johnson pulled a flashlight out of his glove box and walked toward the victim. He had fallen on his side, facing toward the far street. At first, Johnson thought he was lying next to a pothole filled with water from the previous day's afternoon downpour. But when he got closer, he could see the shiny puddle stretching out behind the victim's head was dark red.

"Well, he's definitely dead," Johnson muttered with a shudder.

Shining his flashlight around the body, he could see scuff marks in the damp dirt. It looked like the victim had struggled with his attacker briefly before succumbing to the fatal blow. When Johnson stepped around the body to get a view of the man's face, he saw right away what had killed him. A dark, jagged gash cut across his neck, just below his Adam's apple.

"A slasher. You don't see that too often," said the officer who had followed Johnson into the alley.

The detective nodded absently as he examined the man's clothes—jeans, flip flops and a T-shirt Johnson recognized. The slogan on front declared him a proud supporter of the Ball High football team. At least he probably wouldn't be hard to identify, a relief despite the pain of notifying the family.

Looking back to the street, Johnson could see a crowd already gathering behind the crime scene tape the other officers had stretched across the alley entrance. The sky had started to lighten, and as soon as the inky pre-dawn faded into the pale blue of a perfect summer morning, they'd be able to see everything. Flashing red lights announced the ambulance's arrival. Once they confirmed the death, dispatch would send the coroner. In the meantime, the paramedics would cover the body. Signaling for the officer to stay in the alley, Johnson walked back to the street. He told one of the other officers standing guard to call in reinforcements to help interview everyone who lived nearby and all the people gathered to catch a glimpse of the action. Chances were, someone knew the victim.

Locals referred to the blocks between 57th Street and 39th Street as "Little Mexico." It was a tight-knit community of blue collar families. Most of the houses had peeling paint and bare yards. The cars in the driveways and on the street had shiny rims. On most Sundays, plaintive yet festive Tejano ballads punctuated by wheezing accordions filled the warm afternoons. Officers had walked this very block just two weeks ago, knocking on doors in an attempt to find someone who knew the girl from Fish Village. Now they'd have to do it all over again.

Glancing at the crowd, Johnson noticed Kate, notebook in hand, already interviewing potential witnesses. Her light brown hair was pulled back in a ponytail, accentuating her high cheekbones and grey eyes. Her round face and little, upturned nose made her look soft and girlish, quite a contrast to the determined and often caustic woman Johnson had come to grudgingly admire. Cursing softly, he walked toward her. When she saw him, she cut short her conversation with a middle-aged woman wearing an apron over a garish, hot pink mumu and met him at the yellow tape barrier.

"They're all wondering who it is," she said. "They're half afraid and half hopeful it's someone they know."

Johnson smiled, his first genuine expression of amusement in weeks. He knew exactly what she meant. No one wanted a murder victim in the family. But people who knew someone who died earned an extra, if temporary, measure of importance in the community. They would be at the center of the gossip, sharing details perhaps no one else could. Neighbors would ask them questions at the corner store and the hair salon. They would be pitied almost as much as the grieving family. They had known the victim personally, after all.

"I don't have much to tell you yet, but stick around and I'll see what I can do," Johnson said.

He expected an argument, but Kate just nodded and wandered off to talk to more of the neighbors. The cloudless sky overhead now radiated an almost colorless light, the last gasp of night. About 15 blocks to the east, an orange sliver would just be visible above the muddy Gulf of Mexico. Now that neighbors could see the growing police presence, Johnson expected the crowd of onlookers to grow.

More squad cars pulled up, giving the detective enough manpower to shut off the block and start asking questions. He had just gathered a few officers into a huddle at the alley entrance when he heard raised voices coming from the end of the street. The officer stationed at the corner to keep anyone from entering or leaving the block was arguing with a woman waving her hands wildly and speaking in rapid Spanish. Although he couldn't make out what she was saying, Johnson could hear the urgency and terror in her voice. She looked nothing like the half hopeful gadflies hanging around to see whether they knew the victim. It was obvious this woman carried the crushing weight of the conviction that she did.

Johnson waved at the officer to let her through. His stomach churned with growing dismay as she ran full tilt toward the alley. The crowd parted to let her through. She stopped when she got to the crime scene tape.

"Julian!" she wailed as one of the older women in the crowd put a comforting arm around her shoulders. "Mi Dios! Julian!"

She started to rock forward and backward, tears streaming down her cheeks. The crowd closed in around her, forming a protective cluster. She never took her eyes off the body, now covered with a sheet. When Johnson approached her, the older woman spoke first.

"This is Muriel Costa. Her husband is Julian." At the mention of her husband's name, Muriel Costa let out another loud wail.

"Mrs. Costa, I'm Detective Peter Johnson. We haven't identified the victim yet. What makes you think it's your husband?"

The inconsolable woman just shook her head and moaned. The older woman rubbed her back while she tried to catch her breath. Johnson suddenly had the feeling she was trying to figure out what to say.

"I...I...can't find him," she finally managed. "I don't know where he is, and he won't answer his cell phone. Mi Dios!" she exclaimed, breaking into sobs again.

Johnson hadn't stopped to check the man's pockets for a wallet or identification. He motioned for two of the officers to follow him back down the alley. The paramedics stood a little to the side. At Johnson's signal, they carefully lifted the sheet covering the body, angling it toward the crowd to screen the view. He took a pair of gloves from one of the officers and tugged them on as he crouched down. He pulled a wallet out of the man's back pocket. The leather was shiny and dark with use. Johnson flipped it open and stared at the ID.

The paramedics slowly lowered the sheet when Johnson stood up. Holding the wallet in his hand, he walked back toward the crowd. The tightness in his chest made it hard to take a deep breath. As soon as she could see his face, Muriel Costa began to wail again.

"No, no, no, no, no," she cried, shaking her head and trying to break free from the arms encircling her shoulders.

"I'm so sorry..." Johnson said thickly. He could feel a tingling behind his eyes. His constricting throat cut off the rest of what he intended to say. It didn't seem to matter anyway.

When he looked away from the grieving widow, he caught Kate's eye. She held her notebook up to her face, covering her mouth. Her nostrils flared as her wide eyes absorbed the human tragedy unfolding just a few feet away. He was used to her detached nonchalance. This naked horror was new. Just like police officers, reporters shielded their hearts with a hard shell of cynicism and distance. But sometimes, other people's suffering broke through with soul-shattering force.

As Johnson started to turn away, he noticed Kate wiping the corner of her eye with trembling fingers.

Dock worker murdered

Man found just four blocks from home with his throat cut

By Kate Bennett

Galveston police are investigating the second murder in as many weeks after finding a body in an alley between 54th and 53rd streets early Tuesday morning.

Neighborhood residents identified the victim as Julian Costa, 27, a longshoreman who lived with his wife and three small children about four blocks away.

Investigators say Costa's throat was cut. They have not identified any suspects but are interviewing the man's family, friends, and co-workers in hopes of finding out what he was doing in his final hours.

The victim's wife, Muriel Costa, was among those who gathered at the scene as dawn broke. Although police had not even checked the victim for identification, Costa seemed convinced the dead man was her husband.

Between sobs, she said she had been unable to reach her husband on his cell phone. But she gave no other explanation for how she knew he was dead or where his body would be.

She was too distraught to speak to investigators at the scene. Det. Peter Johnson said he expected to interview the widow in the next few days.

According to neighbors, Julian Costa was a Galveston native who graduated from Ball High School and went to work at the port almost immediately.

"He's a hard worker, and he loves his family," said Violetta Martinez, who lives less than a block from the crime scene and knows the family. "They have a little baby too, pobrecito. And they go to mass regular. What's she going to do, his poor wife?"

Pedro Briones, who went to high school with Costa, said he had never known the victim to be in any kind of trouble.

"He was a nice guy, quiet," Briones said. "That's it. It's a damn shame. I hope they catch whoever did this."

Tim Hammond, head of the dock workers union, described Costa as a hard worker who was good at his job. He did not seem like the type to get into trouble or be involved in anything that would get him killed, Hammond said.

"We will miss him on the waterfront, but I feel most for the family," Hammond said. "This young woman must now raise her three children all alone. That's a very vulnerable position to be in."

Although investigators don't yet have a lead on Costa's murderer, they are likely to have more clues in this case than they did in the island's last homicide. The young woman found shot to death in Fish Village two weeks ago remains unidentified.

Investigators have no reason to suspect the two cases are connected, Johnson said.

"But obviously we will look into that as a possibility," he said. "Nothing is impossible at this point."

Chapter 7

Johnson looked down at his feet and took a deep breath before knocking on the white metal door. The clapboard house, once a soft apricot, had faded to a dingy beige in the unrelenting summer sun and salt-crusted air. The front door had muddy smears just below the knob, at about the height of a five year old. In the flowerbed flanking the porch, Johnson noticed a small red bucket next to a yellow plastic shovel, the kind parents bought their kids to take to the beach. Just a few feet away sat two dark green plastic chairs shaded by the canopy of a big oak tree. He imagined Muriel Costa sitting in one of the chairs, watching her children play after they came home from school. He wondered how long it would be before she could sit there again and smile with genuine joy.

The small boy who opened the door didn't say a word. He just looked up at the detective with a solemn expression, sizing him up. His red shirt and khaki shorts were clean but faded, a sure sign of hand-me-downs. His soft brown hair had a slight wave, and in the back, one piece curled up, sticking out from the rest. On any other day,

Johnson guessed the boy might be mischievous. He held the child's gaze for a few heartbeats before smiling hesitantly. He was about to ask his name when an older woman appeared in the doorway behind him. The detective recognized Violetta Martinez from the previous morning's crime scene. Putting a gentle but firm hand on the boy's shoulder, she steered him back into the house, opened the door wider and motioned for the detective to come inside.

Although the murmur of voices had filtered through the door before Johnson knocked, the room grew silent as he entered. Ten people, mostly women, gathered in the living room, sitting on or gathered around well-worn couches. Out of the corner of his eye, Johnson could see a few more women hovering near the kitchen table, its top already obscured with covered bowls, baskets, and casserole dishes. In the center of the largest couch, the widow hunched, small and fragile. The man sitting next to her, holding her hand, rose as Johnson approached.

"Father Tomás," the detective said, reaching out to shake his hand.

"Detective Johnson, you come to a house in mourning," the priest said. "We are at your disposal. We are just as anxious to catch Julian's killer as you are."

Johnson nodded and looked down at Muriel, who stared at her hands, clasped tightly in her lap.

"Mrs. Costa, I know this is difficult, but I need to ask you a few questions. Is there somewhere we can go to talk privately?"

Glancing up at the priest with what looked to Johnson like apprehension, the widow slowly stood to her feet. Motioning for him to follow, she led him through the kitchen and out the back door. As they passed through the kitchen, the women in the living room resumed their conversations, the murmur of their chatter blending into a soft hum.

Outside, a rusty metal patio table with a glass top almost completely filled the small, sun-bleached deck that stretched half the width of the house. Muriel Costa sat in the chair farthest from the door. Johnson sat across from her. Although it wasn't yet noon, the sun already blazed uncomfortably hot and bright. Johnson wished he could put on his sun glasses but didn't want the widow to think he was trying to hide his expression while he questioned her.

"Mrs. Costa, can you tell me what happened yesterday morning?" Johnson asked gently, hoping to ease her into the interview. "What made you come to that alley?"

Still without looking up, Muriel swallowed and licked her lips. It took her a long time to answer.

"When I woke up, Julian was gone," she finally said, haltingly. Johnson had to strain to catch her husky words. "He usually only left early like that when they had a ship to unload. Otherwise, he liked to have breakfast with us."

She paused and looked up at Johnson quickly. In her lap, she twisted her clenched hands. Johnson focused on keeping his breathing steady. A vague uneasiness seeped down his chest and settled heavy on his stomach.

"I thought he might have gone to the store or something, but the car was still here. So, I tried to call him. He didn't answer."

At this, her voice cracked and her bottom lip trembled. Johnson waited for her to collect her thoughts again.

"By this time, the kids had started to wake up. The baby was crying. I kept thinking he would come back any minute. When he didn't, I started to get worried. Then I heard sirens."

She swallowed again and wrapped one hand around her throat. Nausea gnawed at Johnson's gut.

"I don't know why. I just knew something was wrong. So I called my neighbor to come watch the kids and I ran over to see what was going on. I thought maybe he'd had an accident."

Tears now streamed down her cheeks. Johnson reached into his pocket and pulled out a folded handkerchief. Muriel met his eyes for only the second time as she took it from him. Her glance seemed to hold a question. Was she trying to figure out whether he believed her?

While she wiped her face, Johnson wondered why she assumed something bad had happened to her husband. By all accounts, he wasn't the kind of man who frequently found trouble.

"You didn't think he'd just been called in to work?" Johnson asked.

She shook her head no.

"Do you have any idea what he was doing out so early in the morning?"

It took her longer to respond this time. And just like the previous morning, Johnson had a nagging suspicion she was trying to figure out what to say.

"I don't know. Maybe he went to meet someone. I just don't know."

"Surely he wouldn't have gone to meet a friend at that hour," Johnson prompted. "Maybe someone from work?"

Muriel hesitated.

"Maybe."

"But why would he do that if he would see them later that day anyway?" Johnson asked.

She just shook her head and shrugged.

"Do you know why anyone would have wanted to hurt your husband?"

The widow flinched and started to cry again. She shook her head, but Johnson thought it looked like she wanted to say something.

"Mrs. Costa?"

"No!" she said, shaking her head more vigorously this time. "Everybody loved him."

"What about at work? Was everything ok at the port?"

Muriel looked down at her hands again, clenching and unclenching them in her lap. Johnson's heart started to beat faster. Was that the missing link?

"He liked it there, and the pay was good. But with the new baby, things have been hard, you know? Diapers are expensive. I think he was picking up some extra shifts, doing extra work to bring in a little more money. He didn't say what he was doing. I didn't ask."

Johnson's eyes narrowed.

"Do you think he was doing something off the books?"

She met his eyes this time, her liquid brown stare framed with a web of worry lines.

"I don't know. Julian was a good man. If he was doing anything wrong, he didn't mean to."

With this, she started to cry harder, holding the crumpled handkerchief to her face and moaning softly. While she wept, Johnson wondered what she wasn't telling him. She obviously mourned for her husband. And Johnson suspected she knew more about what he'd been up to than she admitted. If she knew who was responsible for his death, why not say something? Only fear or loyalty would keep her silent. But at least she'd given him enough of a clue about where to look next. He would try to untangle that thread before pressing her any further.

"Thank you, Mrs. Costa," he said as he stood up. His shirt, soaked with sweat, stuck to his back. "I may have more questions for you later, but that's enough for now."

Father Tomás met him when he walked back into the living room. While Violetta went to comfort Muriel, the men walked out the front door.

"This is a sad day, detective," Father Tomás said, his hands clasped behind his back in that oddly contemplative stance peculiar to priests. "I sincerely hope you find whomever did this. Was Muriel helpful?"

"Somewhat," Johnson hedged. He wondered whether Julian Costa would have confessed his misdeeds to the priest, if he had been involved in something illegal.

"Well, I'm sure she'll tell you everything she can. She loved her husband dearly."

"Everything she can, or everything she knows?" Johnson asked, watching the other man's face carefully.

The priest smiled and held out his hand.

"Good luck, detective. God's peace be with you."

~ ~ ~ ~ ~

The windows of the conference room in the Port of Galveston's fifth-floor offices looked over the waterfront, its cranes and warehouses stretching toward the island's East End. Johnson stood inches from the glass, watching an oil rig float slowly up the channel. Sea gulls wheeled across his view every few minutes, their piercing cries joining in a discordant symphony. After talking to Muriel Costa, he'd gone back to the station to type up his notes. The more he thought about it, the less he believed the widow was telling all. Her reticence suggested she knew her husband had been involved in something ill-advised, if not illegal, and suspected he'd been killed because of it.

But Julian Costa was no street thug. Everyone the police had interviewed described him as a loving father, hard worker and good friend. He had no criminal record. Costa's job at the port offered the only connections Johnson hadn't fully explored.

When the door behind him opened, Johnson turned. Joe Henry Miles, the port chairman, already had his hand stretched out as he strode around the conference table.

"Detective! It's good to see you," Miles said, clapping Johnson on the back after shaking his hand quickly and turning toward the man who had followed him through the door. "You know Hammer, of course."

With this, Miles made a barking sound Johnson took for a mirthless laugh. The short, barrel-chested man in front of him grinned and crushed his hand in an unforgiving grasp. Tim Hammond had led the dockworkers' union for 30 years. People started calling him "Hammer" while he was still schlepping cargo on the dock, working his way up the ranks. Johnson had heard he'd spent more than a few nights in jail when he was younger, mostly for brawling. The police reports listed the cause of the fights as "a woman" or "a disagreement over a card game." But Hammond was well-known as the enforcer for his bosses at the union. Every one of his clashes with other longshoremen were designed to deliver a message or mete out a punishment. Hammond helped bring order to the waterfront after a period of constant disputes between competing gangs of workers. He earned a reputation as someone not to be crossed, even by the police.

"Detective, we're happy to help in any way we can," Miles said as the three men sat down at the table. "As Hammer here will tell you, Julian Costa was a good worker. We're sorry to have lost him."

Johnson thought Miles' choice of words odd. He made it sound as though the dead man had decided to leave the port for a job on the mainland.

"Can you tell me a little more about his work and how he got along with the other men?"

"Costa came to the waterfront right out of high school," Hammond said. "He kept his nose clean and followed orders. He was quiet but the other men liked him. He never caused any problems."

"So you don't know of anyone who might have wanted to kill him?"

Hammond shook his head once, keeping his eyes locked on Johnson's face.

"I suspect you're probably looking at a robbery gone bad, or something like that, detective," Hammond said, waving his hand dismissively, as though he'd just solved the case. "If Julian Costa's murder wasn't random, I'm afraid you'll have to look somewhere other than the port for answers."

Johnson tapped the tip of his pen on the notepad laying on the table in front of him.

"So, he wasn't involved in anything off the books, to your knowledge?"

"Detective, nothing happens on the waterfront that I don't know about," Hammond said, punctuating his words with a slight pause for emphasis. "If Costa was involved in anything illegal, it had nothing to do with the port."

"Had he been working extra shifts lately?"

Hammond shook his head no.

"His wife said he was doing something at the port to make a little extra money."

Hammond's eyes narrowed and he pressed his lips together so hard they almost disappeared.

"Is that so?" he finally said. "That's news to me, and like I said, nothing happens out there that I don't know about."

Hammond leaned back and folded his stubby arms across his chest, tucking his hands into his armpits.

"Maybe he was doing something he didn't want his wife to know about, so he told her he was picking up extra shifts," Miles said, breaking into the discussion for the first time. "There are plenty of ways for a man to make a little extra money, detective."

"Mmmmm...." Johnson replied, tapping his pen again. "His wife seemed sure whatever he was doing involved the port."

"Well, maybe that's what he told her. Maybe she believed him, maybe she didn't. Maybe she really knows what he was up to but doesn't want you to find out. You know how secretive women can be."

Miles barked out another mirthless laugh and smacked his hand on the table.

"You just can't trust 'em, detective. You never know what they may be hiding. They're sneaky creatures, women."

Johnson grimaced and bit back his disgust. Miles, a native of New Orleans, had a reputation as a womanizer. When he interviewed for the top job at Galveston's port three years before, Johnson remembered he'd had to explain a few arrests for "domestic" incidents. The *Gazette*'s

Delilah Peters had discovered the candidate's checkered past, and the newspaper demanded answers. Miles had never been charged in the incidents, but he had to admit he'd spent part of one night in jail after a particularly raucous Mardi Gras party ended with his girlfriend getting a black eye. She later claimed she'd tripped and fallen into a table. In Delilah's story, Miles described the incident as "a lot of fun that got a little out of hand."

After he moved to Galveston, the police had been called to Miles' white-columned Victorian in the historic East End neighborhood several times for loud parties. He always got off with a warning, in part because the mayor was usually there to help smooth out the worst of his friend's excesses.

"Well, this woman is mourning her husband and trying to figure out how to raise three children by herself," Johnson said. "I hope she can count on help from the union."

Hammond leaned forward and put his arms on the table.

"Of course," he said. "We'll take care of her. We always take care of our own."

His words pledged protection and comfort, but his tone sounded more like a threat. Johnson wondered what fresh difficulty lay ahead for Muriel Costa.

"Well, gentlemen, I guess that about covers it, for now," Johnson said as he pushed his chair back and stood up. "If I have any other questions, I'll let you know."

"Keep us posted, detective," Miles said, leading the way to the door. "Of course, we'll be following the case with interest. If you find out anything you think we should know, please give me a call."

As he drove back to the station, Johnson replayed the interview. Again he felt like he had more questions than answers. Hammond claimed Costa was not making extra money at the port, but Johnson felt sure he was lying. That could only mean Hammond was involved in whatever scheme the dead dock worker had been caught up in. Like he said, nothing happened on the waterfront that he didn't know about. It had been a long time since a dock worker had been killed over a territorial dispute, but Johnson supposed it wasn't impossible that's what had happened to Costa. If so, the murderer would be difficult to ferret out, unless Hammond chose to give him up. And Johnson couldn't think of any reason for the union leader to do that.

"Damn it!" he said suddenly, pounding the heel of his hand against the steering wheel. Another dead body and no obvious suspects. People rarely got murdered for no reason. What was he missing?

Chapter 8

Johnson spent the next few days interviewing Julian Costa's co-workers, neighbors and friends. No one knew anything about what he was doing in that alley the morning someone crept up behind him and slit his throat. Johnson couldn't discover any connection between Costa and the island's known drug dealers. Nothing about the man's bank account or lifestyle suggested he was bringing in large quantities of extra cash. No one on the waterfront admitted to knowing what might have gotten him killed or who might have wanted him dead. All of Johnson's training and experience told him the murder wasn't random, but every trail that started with Costa's life ended in a dead end.

Four days after the murder, Johnson attended the funeral at Our Lady of Guadalupe Catholic Church to see if he could spot anyone who looked suspicious or out of place. Several hundred people packed the old clapboard building. The Costas' neighbors from Little Mexico filled the pews on the right side. Longshoremen, a few still in overalls and boots, filled the pews on the left. Tim Hammond led a long procession of mourners past the coffin to shake the widow's hand. Johnson couldn't see Hammond's face as he stood in front of Muriel, but he held her attention for a long time, whispering earnestly. He ruffled her oldest son's wavy hair as he walked away.

Joe Henry Miles paid his respects after the longshoremen. The mayor and his wife were with him. It seemed a little strange that the mayor would bother to attend a dockworker's funeral. But like every politician, Matthew Hanes was always campaigning. It couldn't hurt to be seen honoring a member of Galveston's working class. Johnson cringed when Hanes stopped next to his pew on his way out of the church.

"It's been a rough couple of weeks, detective," Hanes said. "I know you want to solve these murders just as much as the rest of us. It's not good for Galveston to have killers running around unpunished. If you need extra resources, you just let the chief know. Things are tight, especially with the budget talks and all, but I'm sure we can work something out. We need to make this a priority, don't you think?"

Johnson could do little more than nod and pretend he hadn't understood the mayor's dig. It had only been four days since Costa's violent death, but his fellow officers obviously weren't the only ones ready to label it another unsolved case. Johnson balled his hands into tight fists as he thought about his co-workers' waning confidence in him. They watched him out of the corner of their eyes when he walked past them in the hallway. Groups gathered over coffee in the break room stopped talking when he walked in, offering only anemic greetings. Few made eye contact. No one asked about the case any more.

Johnson had twice daily meetings with Police Chief Sam Lugar to talk about his progress with interviews and theories. The detective felt certain Costa's death had something to do with his work, but the chief waved off suggestions of anything criminal at the port.

"We have no evidence of anything like that, just the widow's hints he was doing something to make extra money," the chief had told him earlier that morning. "You'd better be damn sure you know what you're talking about before you go accusing anyone at the port of doing something illegal. Everyone in this town will fight you on that one. What a nightmare."

The chief wiped a bright red handkerchief across his dewey brow and swore. Johnson took that as his opportunity to excuse himself. Although he hated to admit it, he knew the chief was right. He had nothing other than a hunch and a grieving widow's suspicions to suggest Costa's death had anything to do with his job.

~ ~ ~ ~ ~

Although he hadn't been satisfied with Muriel's initial interview, Johnson hadn't pressed her for more information. But now, three days after the funeral, he knew it was time to talk to her again.

When he pulled up outside the dingy house, two boys were rolling around in the dirt, pulling shirts and pushing faces. Just as Johnson opened his door and stepped out into the street, the bigger boy, whom Johnson recognized as Muriel Costa's oldest son, managed to get the upper hand on his opponent. Straddling his waist and pinning him to the ground, the older boy pulled his arm back in a windup and prepared to smash his fist into the younger one's face.

"Hey!" Johnson shouted.

The aggressor wheeled around as Johnson strode quickly toward him. He jumped up and ran toward the front door, leaving the younger boy sniveling in the dirt. He scrambled up by the time Johnson reached him, wiping his face with the back of his hand and trying to brush off his dirt-caked shirt.

"You okay?" Johnson asked.

The boy, whom Johnson recognized from the funeral as the Costas' second son, nodded miserably.

"He said papa algo que se hace mal," the child said, spitting dirt-stained saliva onto the ground at his feet. "I tol' him to take it back."

Johnson's heart began to beat faster. Julian Costa's oldest son thought his father had done something bad. Had he overheard his mother talking to someone about what happened? Why else would a child declare his father a bad guy? Before he could ask the child what he meant, Muriel appeared at the door.

"Juanito! Que paso?" she exclaimed, gaping at her dirty child and the detective.

The question provoked fresh tears and a stream of rapid-fire Spanish Johnson couldn't follow. The angry mother barely let him finish before she ordered him inside and slammed the door, leaving Johnson standing alone in the front yard. He hadn't meant to gather information from a child, but he now had more evidence the dead dock worker might have been doing something he shouldn't have. Should he confront Muriel with her son's declaration? Before he had a chance to evaluate the consequences, she opened the door again. This time, she had a baby perched on her hip. As Johnson walked toward the house, she glanced quickly up and down the street.

"Detective, now is really not a good time," she said, looking at him with wide, apprehensive eyes. "The boys have been fighting, and the baby won't stop crying. I can't talk to you right now."

The baby's eyes were red and her nose dripped, but she wasn't crying.

"Mrs. Costa, I understand this might not be the best time, but I need to ask you a few more questions," Johnson said. Although he respected her genuine grief, he refused to let her use it as an excuse to avoid helping him catch her husband's killer.

Glancing one more time up and down the street, the widow turned without speaking and walked back to the house. Who was she looking for? When she didn't shut the door in his face, he followed her inside. Toys littered the living room floor, and only a few covered dishes remained on the table. The mourners had melted away, and

Muriel was finally getting a taste of life on her own. She looked frazzled, weary, and afraid.

"I need to ask you more about those extra shifts your husband was picking up at the port," Johnson said, taking a small notebook out of his front shirt pocket. "Can you tell me more about what he might have been doing? Did he tell you anything about the work? What time of day did he normally take the shifts?"

Muriel stared at him with wide eyes, the tendons on her slender arm sticking out as she gripped the baby tightly to her chest.

"What extra shifts? I don't know what you're talking about," she finally said, haltingly but firmly.

"You don't? You told me you thought he was picking up extra shifts to make a little extra money, to pay for diapers. Remember?"

Muriel shook her head. "No. I never said that."

"You did!" Johnson exclaimed. Shock at her lie squeezing his voice up almost an octave. "When I asked you what he might have been doing, you said you didn't know."

"I don't remember that at all," she said, absently smoothing the baby's scraggly hair.

"Mrs. Costa!..."

Johnson's cheeks flushed. His heart pounded in his ears. He had listened to plenty of witnesses change their stories, but Muriel Costa's about-face came as a complete surprise. For a minute, he couldn't figure out what to say next.

"Mrs. Costa, whether you remember it or not, that's what you told me. And it's the only lead I have to go on. The people at the port tell me your husband wasn't picking up extra shifts, which means whatever your husband was doing was probably off the books. If you can help me figure out what that was, we might be one step closer to catching his killer."

"Please, detective. You don't know what you're talking about. If the union bosses say he wasn't picking up extra shifts, then I'm sure he wasn't. If that's what I said, I must have been confused. I hardly remember anything about those first few days."

Almost convulsively, the woman began to bounce the baby on her knee, the frenetic movement more a sign of agitation than an attempt to soothe the child. After a few moments of silence, she looked up at Johnson with wide, tear-filled eyes.

"Please, detective! I don't want to cause any trouble with the union. I need Julian's pension."

Worry creased Johnson's brow. The widow looked absolutely terrified. He suddenly thought of Tim Hammond's earnest whispering at the funeral.

"Mrs. Costa, has someone said something to you? To scare you? You don't have to be afraid. If you think you're in danger, we can protect you. I can assign an officer to stay with you day and night until we catch your husband's killer."

"No, no, no! You have it all wrong," the widow said, standing abruptly and pacing across the room to the window. "I am not afraid. I do not need protection. And I don't know anything about my husband's work. He was a good man who didn't deserve to die. That's all I know."

When she got as far away from Johnson as the room would allow, she whirled to face him.

"You should be out there trying to catch his killer, instead of coming around here accusing me," she said, spitting the words through her teeth.

Johnson flinched. Her accusation stung as much as it surprised him.

"I'm not accusing you of anything. I'm just asking you questions, and so far, you've been completely unhelpful. Don't you want us to catch whoever did this?"

Muriel bit her lip as she looked out the window.

"It was probably just some homeless person who was either drunk or high or something. They're always hanging around. Maybe one of them asked Julian for money, and when he wouldn't give them anything, they killed him."

"Why didn't they take his wallet then? And what was he doing walking through that alley in the first place?"

"I don't know, detective. I don't know. But I can't listen to this any longer, all these questions and theories. You need to leave now. I've told you everything I know."

Johnson was sure that was a lie. But he hesitated only briefly before he rose reluctantly and followed her toward the front door. As he stepped over the threshold, he turned back to look at her.

"I'm just trying to figure out what happened to your husband. Don't you think your sons deserve to know why he died? They seem to think he did something bad. Is that how you want them to remember him?"

She looked down at her feet as he made his final attempt to get her to cooperate, and he thought for a moment he might have broken through. But as she looked back up, she slowly swung the door closed between them.

~ ~ ~ ~ ~

Kate took a swig from a half empty bottle of beer as she sat in her open window and listened to the deep boom of the cruise ship's horn. It was preparing to pull out of port. From her fourth story loft five blocks from the waterfront, she had a perfect view of the massive boats as they floated by. She liked to watch them leave, their decks and balconies choked with eager vacationers waving goodbye to no one in particular.

It was Saturday, and she'd spent most of the day cleaning and doing laundry. Brian's shift started at noon, so he'd stayed just long enough to cook an omelet and some chicken sausage before heading to the hospital. Kate had never heard of chicken sausage before she met Brian. Her dad ate steaks and hamburgers. Bacon was the only option for a breakfast meat at home. She sometimes wondered what her dad would think of Brian, if they ever met. Brian often talked about his parents and had even suggested Kate meet them when they came to visit later in the summer. He never pushed her to talk about her family, so she never did.

A faint breeze wafted past the window, like the last gasp of a dying hair dryer. Kate's shorts had stuck to the tops of her legs and a trickle of sweat pooled in a crease in her stomach. The cruise ship had floated off the dock now and was moving slowly toward the ship channel. It made almost imperceptible progress at first, but it soon disappeared behind the bank building in front of her apartment, giving one final blast on its horn as it headed for the Bahamas. Reluctantly, Kate slid the window shut and headed for the shower.

While she cooked dinner, she tried not to think about the latest murder and the stalled investigation. Muriel Costa's raw anguish over her husband's death seared her soul. She'd once felt pain that deep, but the sheer shock of it had cauterized her grief and left her numb. She had never given vent to her sorrow. Now it festered under a ragged scar that had never fully healed. Muriel Costa's wailing had threatened to reopen the wound.

But Kate refused to revisit the past. The only thing that mattered was today. And the day after that. And the day after that. If she could spend every day ahead of her exposing injustice and fighting for people who couldn't fight for themselves, maybe the keening in her own heart would finally fall silent.

She popped the top off another beer and wandered over to her bookshelf looking for a distraction. She picked out an old Michael Connelly mystery and settled down in her most comfortable chair. In the background, the police scanner hummed with the chatter from routine traffic stops and public disturbance calls—typical for a Saturday night. A few chapters later, the book slowly closed in her lap and her head rested back against the chair as she dozed off.

When she woke, it was completely dark outside. She could hear shouting and laughing from a group of bar-hopping carousers walking by under her window. She checked her phone—1:20 a.m. As she walked to the kitchen to put her empty beer bottle in the trash, the scanner crackled to life with another call for a loud party. But the address was in the East End, not your usual party-un-til-dawn neighborhood. Kate frowned as her fuzzy brain tried to process the address. When the responding officer requested a few extra cars, in the event of the likely need for courtesy rides, she knew exactly whose house it was.

Fifteen minutes later, Kate stood behind a large oak tree across the street and a few houses down from Joe Henry Miles' white-columned Victorian. Yellow light blazed from every window, and three cop cars lined the street outside. Miles leaned on the frame of the open front door laughing uncontrollably as two officers led Mayor Matthew Hanes down the front steps.

"That's right, Mr. Mayor, go home and sleep it off," Miles shouted, bursting into another round of guffaws when one of the officers urged him to keep his voice down.

"Aw, officer. You sure do know how to ruin a good time," Miles said, slurring his words and swaying slightly as he tried to stand upright. "We were having a good, 'ole time."

"I'm sure you were, Mr. Miles, but it's time to wind it down for the night," the officer said. Kate couldn't see who it was, but she could hear the exasperation in his voice.

"Oh, ahl-right," Miles said in mock resignation. "I guess all good things must come to an end, huh boys?"

Behind Miles, a group of four other men stood in the foyer.

"Are the rest of you going to be OK to get home?" the officer asked. He sounded skeptical, and Kate couldn't blame him.

"Yes, sir, we'll be just fine," said a quiet voice behind the port boss.

"Hammer here will make sure the boys all get home safe, wontcha now?" Miles said, still swaying slightly.

Kate had witnessed similar scenes before. Miles was known for his loud parties. But she'd never seen a more eclectic group staggering out the front door. She recognized Tim Hammond and several other longshoremen, not Miles' usual party crowd. It must have been a men-only party, also unusual for Miles, Kate thought.

"Good night, boys!" Miles yelled as the group of men headed down the street. "This will go down in history as an epic adventure." As he shut the door, Kate could hear uncontrollable laughter echoing through the foyer.

The first time she'd witnessed the police closing down one of Miles' parties, with the mayor bundled into the back of a patrol car for a ride home, she thought she had a great story on her hands. The next morning, she'd rushed into Mattingly's office to tell him to hold a page-one spot. The managing editor had simply laughed.

"No one wants to read about the mayor's private partying," he told her. "Besides, everyone knows he does it. Unless someone gets hurt or presses charges, we're not interested."

Mattingly's nonchalance ruined Kate's whole day. She sometimes still came out to watch the parties break up, if she heard a call come across the scanner. But she usually just listened to the chatter from the responding officers on the radio. She wasn't sure what made her drive out to the East End this time. It seemed like just another party, but the invitees didn't fit the usual mold. What would make the mayor spend an evening with men he normally wouldn't hang out with? It made her suspicious, although she had no definite reason to be.

As she walked back to her car, Kate considered the growing list of unexplained incidents filling up her notebook. Nothing connected them...but their apparent lack of connection to anything.

Chapter 9

Another week went by without any break in the Costa murder case. Kate spent most of her time writing about the city budget battle. Mattingly wanted a three-part series—one story on the mayor's perspective, one on the police and city workers' perspective, and one crunching the numbers to find out whether the cuts would really make any difference to the city's overall financial position. For the last two days, Kate had scoured previous city budgets for the details of past pay increases. Spreadsheet printouts, waded up burrito wrappers and empty soda cans covered her desk. When Mattingly came out of his office and declared the last draft ready for the page, Kate put her head down on a stack of documents and sighed with relief. She couldn't bear to look at one more number.

The next morning, the phone on her desk started ringing less than five minutes after she walked into the newsroom. She considered letting it roll to voicemail. It was Friday, and she was looking forward to an easy day after her long week. When she picked up on the last ring, she was surprised to hear Johnson's voice.

"Running late this morning?" he asked, not bothering to identify himself.

"No, I just wasn't sure I wanted to take a call so early in the morning," she said. The detective sounded almost chipper, and her heart immediately started to beat faster at the thought he might have something to report on one of the two murder investigations. "What's up?"

"Oh, just a little prostitution sting. We netted three johns, five girls and one very belligerent mamasan," he said. "It's not as good as a suspect in a murder investigation, but it's something."

"Wow, okay. It's been a couple of months since you guys did your last sting. I guess it's worth a story."

"Ha! Well, if you want the details, come down to the station. I've got mugshots and bad coffee to make it worth your while."

"Alright, you've got me hooked," Kate said, amused by his attempt at hospitality. "I'll see you in a bit."

After digging an empty notebook out from under one of the stacks of spreadsheets, Kate stuck her head in Hunter Lewis' office to let him know what she was working on. He nodded appreciatively. Readers always liked seeing their neighbors caught with their pants down, so to speak.

Kate smiled to herself as she walked out of the building. A caressing wind, just enough to make the morning feel deceptively cool, lifted her long hair off the back of her neck. It was already starting to look like a very good day. A straightforward crime-fighting story wasn't a bad way to end the week. She might even have time to sit down for lunch somewhere. She wasn't sure her stomach could take another greasy burrito.

When she got to the station, she found Johnson seated behind his desk, reading over reports. He held a steaming styrofoam cup in his hand. An identical cup sat across the desk, in front of the empty chair facing him.

"Wow, you're really rolling out the red carpet. What's the catch?"

Johnson put one hand over his heart, shook his head and let out a short huff of mock indignation as Kate sat down.

"That hurts," he said. "I'm just trying to let you know how much Galveston's finest appreciates their friends at the local paper."

"Right, which means you really want us to play up this story," Kate grinned. "You're just lucky I have nothing better to do today."

"Here I have a beautiful story, all the details tied up in a nice bow for you—I even have pictures—and you still manage to find a way to be insulting. You need to work on your relationships skills."

"Yeah, yeah. So I've been told. What have you got?"

Johnson smiled over the edge of his coffee cup at her, and Kate thought, not for the first time, how charming he could be when he tried.

"We got word of a prostitution operation at the Sand Crab motel, on the seawall."

"Shocking..." Kate rolled her eyes. Everyone referred to the crumbling hotel as "The Crabs," based on its reputation as a public health hazard. The neon sign out front didn't advertise rates by the hour, but several people had assured Kate the women in miniskirts, high heels, and dangly earrings knew what to ask for at the front desk. Rumor had it the manager was making a killing.

"We set up undercover agents to watch the place several nights ago. Last night, we sent one in to … make a purchase."

Kate smiled at Johnson's delicacy.

"What was he buying, detective?" she asked, opening her eyes wide and gazing at him with a look of mock innocence.

Johnson pressed his lips together and stared hard at her for several seconds before continuing.

"He was wearing a wire, so when the mama came in to collect the money, the rest of the team moved in to make the arrests. Three girls in neighboring rooms were … occupied. Two others appeared to be between customers. The mamasan put up quite a fight."

"Had she been picked up before?"

"Yeah, several years ago, but she's kept a low profile since then. She's a legal resident but she's from the Philippines, and she doesn't speak very good English. We're waiting on her lawyer and a translator. I doubt we'll get much out of her. But, and this is off the record, she did say something interesting when they finally got her subdued and cuffed. She claims there's a new operation in town we should be looking for. She said they 'make her look like small fish,'" Johnson said, imitating the woman's broken accent.

"A new pimp in town? That's not exactly big news."

"Maybe not. But digging out that operation will keep us all occupied."

Kate understood what he wasn't saying. Since he had no leads on the murder cases, he might as well do something productive to help clean up the city.

"Well, that's about it," Johnson continued. "But I'm sure you have questions."

Kate spent the next half hour teasing details from Johnson's "just the facts" account and getting the names, ages and hometowns of the Johns. The girls were mostly local, or from Houston, although several of them had never been arrested before. The vacant stares and haggard faces in their mugshots suggested longstanding drug addiction. Kate shuddered at their desolation.

~ ~ ~ ~ ~

Lewis put the story at the top of the front page, a prominent placement Johnson couldn't complain about. Kate's trio of budget battle stories ran Saturday and Sunday. Paired with the publisher's editorial extolling the virtues of fiscal responsibility, it made quite a splash. Mayor Hanes even called to thank Kate for her excellent reporting.

The politician's gleeful praise turned her stomach. But as Lewis reminded her, all she had done was follow the numbers. She didn't set out to make the mayor's case. But the numbers had. Using some basic calculations, Kate determined the city's tax base could not keep up with the current level of spending. Even if the growth rate of the previous decade held steady—and every economic indicator said it wouldn't—the city had to cut expenses or it would be in serious financial trouble.

~ ~ ~ ~ ~

The following week, Kate braced herself for the mayor's inevitable gloating at the start of the city council meeting. Any time politicians earned support from the local newspaper, they bragged about it. On the other hand, negative stories or editorials elicited sharp public rebukes. Kate had squirmed through her share of those.

The council chamber was filled to overflowing once again. City workers scowled and exchanged angry whispers. Neighborhood and business leaders laughed delicately and traded confident smiles. Most people thought the budget vote was a foregone conclusion. Kate started looking at her watch at 6:05 p.m. The mayor ran a pretty tight ship, and it wasn't like him to start a meeting late.

Five minutes later, the door to the conference room opened and the entire council filed out, led by Mayor Hanes. Kate leaned forward over her laptop keyboard and scrutinized each face carefully. The mayor's mouth was set in a hard line, his eyebrows knit tightly together. Several council members looked nervously out at the audience. Two others wore confused frowns. Only Terrence

White and Julia Escoveda, who opposed the budget cuts, looked pleased. They flashed exultant smiles to their watching supporters. Kate's heart started to pound, adrenaline shooting through her veins. Something had changed drastically.

The tension that filled the room just a few minutes before exploded into palpable anxiety. Kate clearly wasn't the only one who had a suspicion something unexpected was about to happen. Although the mayor whacked his gavel on the desk with the same authority as usual, it was completely unnecessary. The room had already gone silent. As they stood for the pledge, Kate frantically tried to figure out what was coming.

After the audience members had taken their seats again, Mayor Hanes pulled his microphone toward him.

"I'd like to say a few words before we get started tonight," he said, pausing to swallow and take a deep breath before continuing. Kate had never seen him look so uncomfortable.

"As you all know, I campaigned on a platform of fiscal responsibility. As the *Gazette* so aptly noted in last Sunday's story, the city cannot continue to spend at the same rate and stay solvent. During the campaign, I suggested breaking the hold of the police union was the only way to cut our expenses. It's a position I've maintained for the last six months."

Almost from a distance, Kate could hear her keyboard clicking at a frantic pace. She was getting every word, but her mind was racing to figure out what Hanes might say next.

"But this last week, I've done a lot of thinking about the kind of place I want this island to be, the kind of city I want to pass on to my children," Hanes continued, his voice breaking just slightly. "While I still believe Galveston is a safe place to live, work, and play, the events of this past month have shown us we cannot take our security for granted. As Capt. Petronello so aptly reminded us during our last meeting, this city has made major strides in the last 20 years. I don't want to see all that progress undone just to balance the budget."

Kate glanced over her shoulder. The mayor's supporters had started to shoot each other alarmed glances. Several of them shook their heads and shrugged frantically in response to unspoken questions.

"I know this is a surprise to everyone in the room," Hanes said. "It's not something I've discussed with anyone until just before tonight's meeting when I informed my fellow council members of what I planned to say. Despite everything I've said previously on the subject, I can no longer in good conscience continue to take an adversarial stance against the men and women we rely on for our protection. I still believe we need to rein in our spending, but I will not do it on the backs of our hard-working employees."

The city workers let out an exultant cheer that ended in a standing ovation. Kate could see police officers in the back of the room trading fist bumps. An angry rumble started to roll over the mayor's supporters. When Hanes didn't gavel the crowd to order, Daniel Price, president of the Silk Stocking District association, stood and pointed a long finger in his direction.

"You liar!" he shouted. "We elected you to get this city's house in order. You had us all fooled. You will regret this!"

"All right now, that's enough," Hanes said, pounding the gavel on the desk repeatedly until the crowd started to quiet. "We can agree to disagree, Mr. Price, but there's no need for threats."

"That was no threat!" Price said angrily. When several of the officers at the edge of the room started to move his way, he waved his hand at them dismissively and stalked toward the door at the back of the room. "This whole thing stinks. You haven't heard the last of us."

The rest of the mayor's now former supporters followed him. Kate slid her notebook out of her laptop bag and slipped out the side entrance.

In the parking lot, a knot of two dozen very angry people had gathered. As Kate jogged over to them, Price wheeled to face her.

"What just happened in there?" he exclaimed, throwing his hands up in the air in an exaggerated gesture of disbelief. "Did you have any idea he was going to do that?"

"None," Kate said. "I'm just as surprised as you are."

As if to acknowledge her statement, almost everyone in the group started talking at once.

"He's a traitor!"

"I bet he planned this all along."

"Who does he think he is, making promises and then breaking them?"

Scribbling fast in her notebook, Kate tried to keep up.

"We're going to get to the bottom of this," Price said. "Something fishy's going on here."

"What do you think it is?" Kate asked, questioning as much for herself as for the quote. "It's not like he's in a tight re-election campaign and needs votes. He won't even run again for another 18 months. The police union didn't give him any election money, so he doesn't owe anyone any favors."

"I don't know," Price said. "Maybe they've got something on him. I wouldn't put it past the union to resort to blackmail."

Several others in the group nodded. Kate heard a few say, "That could be it."

As she headed back inside for the rest of the meeting, Kate wondered whether Price could be right. She doubted anyone in the police department was extorting money from the mayor. But political blackmail was not so far-fetched. Hanes wasn't exactly discreet, especially when he partied with Joe Henry Miles. Someone in uniform could know a secret neither man wanted revealed. But what could Hanes have done that was so terrible he would risk his entire political career and his family's legacy to keep it a secret?

Mayor reverses course

Hanes now says he supports pay raise for police, city workers

By Kate Bennett

In a shocking about-face during Thursday's city council meeting, Mayor Matthew Hanes announced he has changed his mind about opposing pay raises for police and city workers.

Hanes said he still believed budget cuts were necessary but he didn't want the city's staff to bear the brunt of the financial pain.

"I still believe we need to reign in our spending, but I will not do it on the backs of our hard-working employees," he said.

No one in the room seemed to expect the change, not even the people it benefits most. After Hanes finished speaking, city workers let out a loud cheer, and police officers began giving each other high fives.

But not everyone was happy about the mayor's new position, which marks a complete departure from his campaign promises.

"This is a complete betrayal of everything he promised to do," said Daniel Price, president of the Silk Stocking District Homeowners Association. "I don't know whether he planned to do this all along or whether he really had a change of heart, like he claims. Either way, it just stinks."

Price and his allies gathered outside city hall after leaving the meeting in protest. Several of the mayor's former supporters had already started talking about starting a petition to force a recall election.

But Price said he would take a wait and see approach: "The mayor's not stupid, and maybe he knows something I don't. He says he still plans to cut expenditures, so let's see if he can do it. I just don't know where he can make enough cuts to make a difference."

After the meeting, Hanes again pledged to rein in the city's spending, but he admitted he didn't yet have a list of specific line items in the budget that could be cut.

"I'm not sure how we'll do it, but we will do it," said Hanes, who for once looked uneasy and uncertain. "We just depend too much on our staff to risk losing them."

Personnel costs make up slightly more than 60 percent of the city's budget. Reducing the budget by cutting payroll would spread the pain out, making the reductions widespread but not as deep. If the mayor must cut from the other 40 percent of the budget, he will have to dig much deeper than previously planned.

When asked how that would affect city services, Hanes looked troubled.

"I don't honestly know at this point," he said. "All I can tell you is that I'll do everything I can to make this as painless as possible."

Chapter 10

Kate filed her story just after 10 p.m. but she didn't fall asleep for another three hours. She lay in the dark, stared up at the ceiling and searched every memory of the last six months for any sign Hanes had planned to do this all along. She thought back to campaign fundraisers and stump speeches, press releases and private interviews. He had always seemed completely sincere in his plan to stand his ground against the police union. Politicians could not be trusted to be truthful, but their behavior was usually predictable. How had she missed this? Uncertainty left her with an alarming sense of free fall and failure. It was her job to get wind things like this before they happened.

Her cell phone rang at 6:45 a.m., jolting her out of a deep sleep. She managed to answer it on the third ring without looking at the number on the screen.

"What the hell happened last night?" Mattingly screeched. "How did you not see this coming?"

Kate cringed. The managing editor must not have watched the meeting on television and therefore had no idea about the mayor's change of heart until he opened up the paper that morning while eating his probiotic-filled yogurt and sipping his camomile tea. She realized belatedly she should have called to give him a heads up.

"I have no idea," she said lamely.

"Well, you'd better figure out what happened, and fast," Mattingly spat. "I do not like surprises. And I pay you to know what's going to happen in that council chamber. I'd better see you in the newsroom by the time I get there. I want you on the phone, talking to everyone in this city to find out who knew about this and what game Hanes is playing."

Mattingly didn't wait for a reply before hanging up. Kate cradled her head in her hands and groaned. But she didn't have long for a pity party if she wanted to get to the office before Mattingly did. Stumbling to the bathroom, she washed her face and brushed her teeth. She didn't have time for a shower, so she twisted her hair up into a loose knot and wrapped a colorful scarf around her head. It took her another 10 minutes to tug on a pair of jeans and a button-down shirt. She slipped her feet into her favorite flip-flops as she grabbed her computer bag and headed out the door.

On her way to the parking garage down the block, she stopped at her favorite coffee shop and ordered an Americano with three shots of espresso.

When Mattingly stalked into the newsroom at 8:05 a.m., Kate was already on her second phone call. She spent the rest of the morning repeating the same questions: Were you surprised? Did you have any idea the mayor planned to do this? What do you think's behind it? She talked to a dozen of her best city hall sources before lunch, and none of them had any solid clues to offer. She got a lot of speculation and a few conspiracy theories, but nothing solid. She thought about calling Johnson, but he wasn't part of the mayor's inner circle. If the mayor's plan was common knowledge enough for Johnson to know, Kate would have heard about it too.

When Hunter Lewis stopped by her desk a little later to check on her progress, she still had no answers.

"If Hanes really did make this decision at the last minute, there's no way you could have known," he said, tapping his fingers on her desk as he looked at the notes filling her computer screen.

"No one will admit to knowing anything, not even on deep background," Kate said, her voice slightly muffled with exhaustion and despair. "They all seem genuinely surprised."

"What do they think's behind it?"

"Most people said they had no idea. A few suggested it was a brilliant political move to persuade the police union to play along. Three people told me they thought the police are blackmailing Hanes with something he doesn't want made public."

Lewis nodded thoughtfully.

"But no one has any idea what that could be, nothing definite anyway," Kate continued. "And the police union president seemed as surprised as everyone else. If someone is blackmailing the mayor, I don't think it's him."

By the time she dragged herself into Mattingly's office to admit defeat at about 2 p.m., his anger had subsided. Kate knew she had Lewis to thank for deflecting some of the wrath. He had spent about half an hour behind closed doors with the managing editor earlier that morning. Kate couldn't make out what they were saying, but she could tell by Mattingly's raised voice and Lewis' moderated responses that the news editor was trying to soothe the worst of the unreasonable accusations.

Mattingly leaned back in his big leather chair and looked at Kate through narrowed eyes. His scrunched together, bushy eyebrows looked like they were pointing at her.

"The publisher called me earlier and wanted to know why we didn't get wind of this before last night," Mattingly said. "I had to tell him I didn't know, which didn't exactly help make my case for the strength of the newsroom. You just gave the advertising manager an excuse to claim the budget cuts should be made in our department, not his."

"That's not fair!" Kate exploded, anger flushing her face. "I haven't found one person who knew about this ahead of time. If even the mayor's most trusted friends didn't know, how am I supposed to?"

Mattingly fixed Kate with another long stare. She wondered whether he was thinking about firing her on the spot and saving the advertising manager the trouble of making his case.

"This is the damnedest thing I've seen in a long time," he finally said. "We'll just have to keep an eye on him. He's up to something, and eventually we'll figure out what. Write up what you've got and go home. You look like crap."

Kate left his office without saying a word. Two hours later, she had her story approved, and she was headed home. She felt wrung out and hung up to dry. The last two days had been the worst of the whole year, at least so far.

~ ~ ~ ~ ~

After a much needed three-hour nap, Kate showered and dressed for a date with Brian. Her pride still stinging from Mattingly's harsh assessment, she took extra time to dry her hair into shiny waves that hung past her shoulders. Dark eyeshadow, smokey eyeliner, black mascara and a rich pink lipgloss completed her look. When Brian arrived to pick her up, she was sitting at the table, sipping a beer.

"Wow!" he said appreciatively. "Hello, gorgeous." Cupping her chin lightly in his left hand, he kissed her softly.

She couldn't help but smile back. She was definitely ready for a night out. They were headed to a downtown bar to listen to a new bluegrass band starting to make a name for itself along the Gulf Coast. Kate liked the band because some of their songs reminded her of the old country music her dad listened to. Brian just enjoyed live music in general.

By the time they walked into the bar, the first of the early acts was already on stage. Brian spotted a few of his fellow residents at a table near the door, but the pounding drums and whining guitars made it hard to hear what anyone was saying. After he introduced Kate as best he could, they headed to the bar to get their first round of drinks. While Brian leaned in and tried to get the bartender's attention. Kate scanned the rest of the crowd. It didn't take her long to spot someone she recognized, but it was not someone she ever expected to see at a bar on a Friday night. Alone at a table near the back of the room, Johnson sat nursing a tall beer.

Kate motioned to Brian that she was going to talk to the detective while he waited for their drinks. Johnson didn't even look up as she approached. What thoughts kept him so engrossed? She almost had to touch him on the arm to get his attention. When he finally noticed her standing beside him, his unfocused gaze sharpened into a wide smile.

"Well, if it isn't my favorite reporter," he said, raising his voice almost to a shout so she could hear him over the din.

"What are you doing here?" Kate asked, smiling back. "I've never seen you out before."

His laugh had a hard edge. "I just needed a change of scenery tonight. Plus, I like the Tumbleweeds. Is that who you're here to see?"

Kate nodded just as Brian walked up and set their drinks on the table. The two men had met before. They shared an appreciation for Galveston's lackluster but devoted surfing scene and had paddled out to catch a wave or two together. They hit it off right away.

"Hey, man!" Johnson said, standing up and shaking Brian's hand. "Good to see you again. If you guys aren't meeting anyone or anything, you're welcome to join me. Maybe that will protect me from the waitress' pitying looks."

Brian laughed as he pulled out a chair for Kate. "Sounds good to me."

They listened to the next three songs in a companionable silence. When the first band finished its set, they talked about the Tumbleweeds and local music in general. The men swapped surfing stories. Work was the last thing Kate had wanted to think about tonight. But sitting across from Johnson, she couldn't resist asking what he thought of the mayor's mysterious change of heart.

"So is everyone at the station talking about Thursday's council meeting?" she blurted out during the next lull in the conversation.

Johnson raised his eyebrows and shook his head.

"That was all anybody could talk about this morning," he said. "And Hanes isn't wasting any time getting the deal done. He came by the station this afternoon to meet with Petronello and the other union reps. Judging by the handshakes and backslapping I saw as they came out of the conference room, I guess they reached a mutually satisfactory agreement."

"Wow, I had no idea he would move that quickly," Kate said. "He's got at least a month before the council has to vote on the budget. Maybe he wanted to put to rest any speculation he might change his mind again."

"Maybe. But here's the kicker. After he was done with the union reps, he had a meeting with the chief. I figured they were just talking about policing in general, or worse, the stalled murder investigations. I never expected what I heard when the chief called a few of us in to join them."

Kate leaned forward, her eyes focused intently on Johnson's face.

"What did he say?"

Johnson held her gaze for a few seconds, glanced over at Brian and smiled.

"I'm gonna tell you, but it's off the record, okay? I don't want to see this in the paper with my name associated with it. Get it confirmed somewhere else, but you didn't hear it from me."

Kate's eyes were wide now and she exhaled quickly when she realized she'd been holding her breath. Johnson had never offered her anything off the record. Although she'd always hoped to gain his trust, she secretly doubted he would ever tell her anything without the chief's permission. He would need a very good reason to break his fealty to the department's command structure.

"Sure, of course. You know you can trust me. I would never burn you, especially over a beer," she added with a grin.

Johnson nodded grimly. "I know. I just had to say it. So, when we were all in the room with the door shut, the mayor starts praising our work and tells us how much he appreciates what we're doing. He says all his friends were talking about last week's prostitution sting and describes it as a good piece of policing that's helping to clean up the city. But, he says, with the two unsolved murders, and the prostitution bust, the island is starting to look like a hotbed of crime."

Johnson paused to take a long drag on his now warm beer, grimacing slightly. While he continued, Brian signaled the waitress for another round.

"I couldn't figure out where he was going with all this. Then he says he's asked the chief to put a hold on any other stings for a while, at least until we can get through the summer and fall festival seasons. He doesn't want to scare off tourists, you know."

Johnson shook his head in disgust.

"So, I've got to scrap my investigation into this new pimp who's supposedly come to town. If there really is a new operation getting set up, it basically has a free pass. Never mind that this actually makes the island less safe. As long as it looks like nothing's going on, that's all the mayor cares about."

Johnson's words lingered while the waitress set down a new batch of drinks. Kate's mind wheeled with possible explanations.

"Do you think there's any connection between that and his new pact with the union?"

"I don't know," Johnson said. "All I know is that I'm back to working on two dead-end murder investigations. So, cheers."

As he lifted his beer bottle in an ironic salute, Kate vacillated between sympathy and incredulity.

"So that's it?" she finally managed. "You're not going to sniff around and try to figure out what's going on?"

Johnson took a deep breath and shook his head slowly as he exhaled. His hazel eyes glittered as he held her gaze for several seconds before answering.

"I could. But what then? I become a one-man police force? A vigilante? That only works out in the movies. I learned a long time ago that vigilantes start out thinking they're serving others and end up serving themselves."

"But you could say the same thing about any leader!" Kate sputtered. "Who's the mayor serving? What about the chief? What if the orders he's giving you are wrong?"

Johnson took a long draw on his beer and set it down hard. "Then that will eventually become clear, but it won't be because I'm working to undermine him. If he thinks he can't trust me, he'll never listen to me when I say something he needs to hear."

"That sounds like a cop-out to me," Kate said, ignoring Brian's gentle nudge under the table.

"That's because you can't imagine you might be wrong."

Kate's jaw dropped open and she gaped at him in amazement. Indignation flushed her cheeks and she began to stand. But Johnson held up a conciliatory hand and leaned across the table, his piercing gaze pinning her in place just as if he'd grabbed her arm.

"It's not just you. We all think we see perfectly and understand everything we see. We have no idea how narrow our perspective really is until someone else points it out. And if we refuse to listen, our self-assurance turns into hubris. I've seen what kind of mistakes hubris can lead to. I'm not about to make that mistake again."

Kate leaned back in her chair and crossed her arms.

Johnson sighed. "The orders the chief gives me might be wrong. But my assumptions could just as easily be wrong. Yours, too."

Johnson took another drink of his beer as an uncomfortable silence settled over the table.

"Perspective is important," Brian finally said, breaking the tension. "Maybe taking a fresh look at the murders will turn up something you didn't see before. This could be just what you need."

"Could be," Johnson said, looking over at Kate as the second opening act started to take the stage. "Waiting isn't easy. But action without direction is like beating your head against a closed door and saying you tried to open it."

Twanging guitars and pounding drums cut off any further conversation. Kate mulled Johnson's words. What mistake did he want to avoid making again? She tried to picture the self-effacing detective contorted by arrogance, blinded by pride. It just didn't fit. But neither did the willingness to turn a blind eye to injustice just because his boss ordered him to. Johnson might struggle with believing his own eyes, but Kate didn't. The only thing worth trusting was what she could observe and verify. Her intuition rarely led her astray. If you couldn't trust yourself, who could you trust?

Chapter 11

The brush trembled slightly as Esperanza swirled it in the pressed pink eyeshadow. Iridescent flakes floated onto the cluttered table when she brought the soft bristles slowly to her face. She watched in the mirror, as though from a distance, while her hand guided the brush back and forth across her eyelid. The rosy powder couldn't cover the fear and anxiety that hollowed her eyes and pinched at the corners of her mouth. Her lower lip trembled. Her vacant gaze sharpened suddenly into piercing terror. Her throat tightened and she clutched the tabletop with white knuckles, as though it might keep her from drowning in despair. Her face began to turn a dull red, and she had to will herself to take a shaky, shallow breath. These moments of panic frightened her, although they came so often now she was almost used to them. She took another breath. Then another, as the blood slowly drained from her cheeks and forehead. Her nostrils flared as she filled her lungs again, this time more deeply and with determination. Each time the terror ebbed, hope and courage surged in her chest. *We will survive.*

Slowly, she willed her fingers to let go of the table and pick up the brush again. She looked carefully at her face to remind herself where she'd left off. She wished she could put her makeup on without a mirror. She'd grown to hate what she saw. The woman staring back at her looked nothing like the carefree, exuberant girl who left home just a few weeks earlier, longing to make all her dreams come true. Had it really been such a short time? The agonizing days that stretched into unbearable weeks seemed to have lasted a lifetime. At home, the offer of a job in America sounded like an answer to the prayer her mother intoned every morning during Mass. Cleaning rich people's houses seemed like an easy task. Her mother assured her she would soon move on to bigger and better things. Why didn't any of them see it was all too good to be true?

"Do you think tonight will be as bad as last time?" from across the room, her sister's hushed tones spoke more than the question she asked. At home, Gloria's warbling soprano was filled with laughter and innocence. Here it quivered with fear every time she spoke.

Esperanza sighed and met her sister's eye in the mirror.

"I don't know."

She had lost track of the number of times El Jefe brought men to the house. The parties started off small. Just two or three men who ate and drank and talked business before taking the girls back to their bedrooms. That had been bearable. But last time—it must have been a week ago, she lost track of days—El Jefe brought six men with him. They spent the afternoon fishing on his boat. Most of them were already drunk when they got back to the house. None of them wanted to wait until after dinner to get what they'd really come for.

Esperanza swallowed to push down the lump in her throat. Listening first to her sister cry out in pain and then to her softly cry herself to sleep tore at her heart. She had never really known pain before coming to this hell. But no amount of slaps, pinches, or forced intimacy she'd endured compared to the suffocating knowledge that Gloria's agony was her fault. Every time one of the men came for her sister, her muscles tensed, bile rose in her throat, and adrenaline surged from her chest to her limbs, all in preparation for an attack she could never launch.

The first time, she had tried to fend off her sister's molester. The memory still made her shudder. El Jefe easily fought her off, pinning her arms behind her with one hand, her face shoved against the wall, while he punched her in the back and sides with the other. With every blow, he reminded her how powerless she was to save either herself or Gloria. When he finally stopped and let her go, she slid to the floor, gasping for breath. Through tears, she watched him drag her sister into the bedroom, the pounding of her pulse not loud enough to block out Gloria's pleas for mercy. He showed none. When he was done, he came for her. He didn't even bother to drag her into the other bedroom but pinned her down on the living room floor, his heavy body compressing the bruises already forming on her back. She didn't even have the strength to cry out. The only sound was his grunting. When it was over, he told her he'd be back the next day and expected both of them to be in a more cooperative frame of mind.

They spent the next twenty-four hours locked in a room with no food or water. Somewhere outside the door, they occasionally heard a man's voice. It sounded like he was talking on the phone. When they couldn't hear him, they could smell the acrid burning of the cigarettes he smoked one after another. From that day on, he became a constant presence. Later they'd started calling him El Carcelero—the guard. When El Jefe returned that second night, he brought styrofoam containers of food. Esperanza thought about refusing to eat. But it had been days since their last full meal, and she'd been listening to Gloria's stomach growl for hours. She couldn't resist the warm, comforting aroma of enchiladas seeping out from under the lid of the containers he placed in front of them. Her sister opened hers right away and started to eat. Across the table, El Jefe sat down facing them. When Esperanza lifted a trembling hand to open her own container, his fat lips spread into a satisfied and knowing smile.

"You work for me now, and I always take care of my own," he said. "You're hungry? I feed you. Everything you need comes from me. You understand?"

A sickening sense of shame flushed her cheeks as she slowly nodded. She looked at her sister and a wave of helplessness washed over her. Tears trickled down the teenager's face. She didn't even bother to wipe them away.

"Pobrecito," El Jefe had said. "Don't cry. Everything will be ok. Do as I say and you'll want for nothing."

Gloria had looked at him with wide, incredulous eyes. He smiled again.

"I paid for you to come here, and now you must work off your debt," he said. "Once you've paid me back, you'll be free to leave and do anything you want."

"You'll just let us go?" Esperanza had asked.

"Of course. Yes, of course."

Even then, his words rang with the hollow tin of a lie. Esperanza knew they weren't true, but as she glanced at her sister, she realized Gloria had grasped the promise like a lifeline. She clung to it with the innocent hope of someone too young to understand the depths of man's depravity. Esperanza couldn't bear to rip that away too. She'd already done enough to crush her sister's spirit. So she played along, nodding encouragingly every time Gloria talked about what they would do once they were free. But every passing week made her more sure they would never get out from under El Jefe's heavy hand.

The dull thud of a slamming car door and the murmur of men's voices dragged her back to the present. In the mirror, she watched a wide tear gather in the corner of her eye and roll slowly down her thick lower lashes. It cut a track through the blush that dusted her cheekbone, gathering speed over her jaw before careening into her lap.

Three loud bangs on the bedroom door made her jump.

"Get a move on!"

El Carcelero's raspy voice reverberated with the constant threat of violence, even though he'd never laid a hand on either of them. He'd never had to. His simmering brutality, thinly concealed under a veneer of calm, terrified them more than El Jefe's more direct warnings. After that first night, he had assumed an almost fatherly attitude toward them. He brought them nice clothes and perfume. Several days ago, he gave them a box of chocolates. As long as they did what they were told and kept the customers happy, he exuded the munificence only a tyrant could afford. He never bothered Gloria again, but he regularly came to Esperanza. While she squirmed beneath him, he whispered over and over again in her ear, "You. Are. Mine."

"Are you almost ready?" Gloria asked, walking up behind her.

Esperanza looked at her sister in the mirror. Her luminous black hair framed a delicate face dominated by doe-like brown eyes and full red lips. Her heavy makeup couldn't hide her youth. She still looked like the angelic child who had danced around their mother's kitchen singing the traditional folk songs their abuela taught them. Tonight she wore a slinky black dress that hugged her hips and ended about three inches below her backside. While Esperanza watched, she smoothed the fabric down self-consciously.

"I always wanted to wear dresses like this, but Mama would never let us," Gloria said, smiling wistfully. "When we get out of here, I will never wear anything like this again."

Esperanza wondered whether her little sister really believed they would be free one day. She didn't dare ask. Dreams of freedom, no matter how unrealistic, kept them from collapsing under their horror. Esperanza stood up, turned her back on the mirror and wrapped her arms around her sister's slender shoulders.

"You won't have to," she said. "You won't have to."

When she pulled back, big pools of tears filled Gloria's eyes. Esperanza pulled a tissue from the box on the table and gently blotted her sister's face.

"We'd better go," Gloria said, her voice trembling just slightly. "I don't want him to knock again."

Just as the sisters walked into the living room, the front door opened and El Jefe strode inside, leading four men behind him. Through the open door, Esperanza could see the sky beginning to turn the milky blue of evening. The sun setting behind the house threw a pale hue of orange toward the opposite horizon.

"There they are!" El Jefe said, stepping forward to take the sisters by the hand and pull them toward his guests. "These are my beautiful girls, gentlemen. Be nice to them, and they will be very nice to you. Isn't that right, girls?"

With that, El Jefe leaned toward Gloria and kissed her on the cheek. As he turned to kiss Esperanza, he squeezed her butt and whispered in her ear, "Smile, chica linda." Esperanza forced herself to smile, her heart pounding in her ears. It was like this every time they met new men.

She tried to size each one up, carefully examining his clothes, his demeanor, and finally his face. Did he look brutal or kind? Were his eyes hungry or only excited? She had gotten fairly good at predicting which ones wanted to inflict pain and which ones just wanted a good time. Three of the men were new and glanced back and forth between the sisters, their eyes devouring every curve, deciding which one they liked best. Esperanza recognized the fourth one from several previous visits. He only had eyes for Gloria, gazing at her with a mixture of wonder and raw desire. Gloria smiled shyly at all of the men, her eyes lingering a little longer on the man looking so intently at her. The hair on the back of Esperanza's neck slowly began to rise.

"Girls, bring us some drinks," El Jefe bellowed, clapping his hands together and motioning for the men to come into the room and relax on the deep leather couches.

Esperanza and Gloria scurried to the bar that lined the back wall, pulling glasses and bottles out of the cabinets as El Jefe called out drink orders. Two beers, one scotch, neat, and one margarita on the rocks. Their captor would have wine, as always. Esperanza set the drinks on a tray while Gloria went back to the kitchen to get plates of appetizers. After a few drinks, El Jefe would grill the flank steaks now swimming in marinade in the refrigerator.

While the men drank and talked, the girls perched on the arms of the couches, refilling glasses and smiling any time one of them looked their way. Smiling had become just another forced action disconnected from its real meaning, like almost everything else they did. That mask of acceptance was much easier to put on than it had been at first. During the first party El Jefe hosted, Esperanza thought she would never be able to force her face to do what he wanted, let alone the rest of her body. The second time was worse, because she knew what was coming after the smiles and the drinks. After that, she learned to let her body do El Jefe's bidding while her mind retreated to a place of fantasy, and freedom.

When El Jefe stood and walked toward the kitchen to get the steaks, he motioned for Esperanza to follow him. She glanced at Gloria, who smiled reassuringly. Esperanza hated to leave her sister alone with the four men, but she didn't dare refuse El Jefe's order. She followed him to the kitchen where he handed her the pan and then led the way out the side door. The grill perched on the edge of a wide deck that wrapped all the way around the house. While her captor lit the burners and spread the meat out over the flames, Esperanza looked across the water that surrounded them. The coast line here looked so much different than the rocky, jungle-backed shore at home, where azure waves crashed onto sandy beaches. Their domestic prison rose on thick pilings above a muddy, marshy expanse. She was sure the water that lapped just feet from the parking pad under the house wasn't too deep to wade through. Scrub brush hedged the property about thirty feet on either side of the house. But at night, the girls had spotted lights twinkling through the branches. Sometimes, Esperanza thought about making a run for it.

"I know what you're thinking, chica," El Jefe said, putting his arm around her waist and bringing his lips close to her ear. His touch made her stomach turn. "It doesn't look far, but you would never make it. And why would you want to leave? You have everything here you need. Don't you?"

Esperanza's hands balled into fists as he bent down and kissed her neck.

"Hey!" One of the men opened the door and stuck his head out. He swayed just slightly. "I thought you were out here cooking. Looks like you're just having your own private party."

"Mi amigo, I can party whenever I want, if you know what I mean," El Jefe said, giving Esperanza another squeeze and smacking her hard on the backside. "The steaks are almost done, but if you want an appetizer, be my guest. I think Esperanza is getting a little bored. Aren't you, my dear?"

Esperanza swallowed back bile as she looked at the man. Tiny beads of sweat dotted his forehead.

"Well, I can take care of that," he said. "Come here, baby."

As he leaned toward her, he licked his lips.

Chapter 12

While the men ate at the wide, rough-hewn table that sat between the couches and the bar, Gloria and Esperanza stayed on the couch. This was always the most difficult time, waiting for the men to fill their stomachs. As their hunger subsided, their lust grew. Esperanza normally watched them carefully while they ate. If she sensed one might be more brutal than the others, she would rise to meet him when they were done, hoping to deflect any interest in her sister. But tonight, she stared past the table, trying not to think about the one who had just led her back to her bedroom. The spot where he sank his teeth into her shoulder throbbed.

"Esperanza, was it really bad?"

Her sister's barely audible whisper dragged her back to the living room. She tried to smile.

"No, no. It was fine. Don't worry about me."

Gloria's anxious eyes blocked out everything else. She looked so painfully young when she was worried. Esperanza reached out and took her sister's hand. Gloria squeezed her fingers tightly. Before letting go, she glanced over at the men and then leaned toward Esperanza.

"Do you recognize the one who's been here before?" Gloria whispered. "He keeps looking at me. I know they all look, but he's different."

Esperanza nodded and focused on the table. Even as he talked to the other men, the repeat customer glanced toward the girls. He had a narrow, mild-looking face with a soft mouth and blue eyes. His sandy blond hair was cut close but not severely, giving an overall impression of leisure. He stood out from his companions for his lack of intensity. When he caught them looking at him, he smiled. Most of the men leered or beamed wolfish grins at them, but his smile was almost hesitant. He reminded Esperanza of the love-sick teens who gathered in clusters in the town square at home on Saturday nights, hoping for an encouraging glance from the girls who strolled by with their families. Could he have fallen in love with her sister?

El Jefe pushed his plate away and stood, stretching his arms over his head and patting his stomach. When the others stood as well and headed toward the living room, the man the girls had been watching put his hand on El Jefe's arm to hold him back. He leaned toward his host and whispered something urgently in his ear.

"Mi amigo!" El Jefe said, pulling away in surprise. Then, he let out a barking laugh. "I cannot play favorites."

The man leaned in again and whispered something else. Esperanza had to stand now to greet the other men and couldn't see El Jefe's reaction. But she heard him laugh again.

"Bueno, mi amigo. But this kind of access, it does not come cheap."

What did that mean? The man who had taken her earlier collapsed on the couch and groaned.

"I've had my turn already, boys. I'm going to have to let my food settle before I can go again." He grinned up at Esperanza with satisfaction.

"Well, I'm just getting started," one of the others said, reaching out to clasp Esperanza behind the neck. "Come here, beautiful."

His sour breath, as he leaned in to kiss her hard on the mouth, smelled like cigarettes, steak, and beer. She forced a smile and took his hand. She definitely didn't want this one coming for her sister. She would make sure he was too tired for anything else after he was done with her. As she led him toward her room, she heard El Jefe laugh again.

"Gloria, venir aqui," he said.

Esperanza glanced over her shoulder as her sister approached their captor and the man who had watched her all night. He leaned forward just slightly, his hands shoved deep in his pockets. He smiled almost shyly as her sister approached. He knew he could take her back to her room any time he was ready. What more could he possibly want?

~ ~ ~ ~ ~

The red numbers on the digital clock on her bedside table read 2:00 a.m. when Esperanza eased herself onto the edge of her bed and took a deep breath. Her two after-dinner visitors had been mercifully brief, but then the first man had come back, evidently energized by his short nap. He was rough with her, and seeing her wince in pain only seemed to get him more excited. She'd tried hard to look bored until he was finished. But it would probably take days for the soreness to ease. She tried to empty her mind, put it in neutral, anything to avoid replaying the scene.

A tap on her door roused her from her daze and struck her with a pang of guilt. She hadn't seen her sister since right after dinner. She should have checked on her as soon as the men left. Gloria swung the door open just enough for her to slip in and then shut it quietly behind her. El Carcelero didn't like them to stay up late and would sure-ly tell her to go back to her room if he heard them. Esper-anza tried to smile as her sister climbed onto the end of the bed and sat cross-legged, pulling a pillow onto her lap. She used to do that at home when she wanted to talk about something important. But it had been a long time since they'd had an easy, relaxed conversation.

"How was it?" Gloria asked quietly. "I'm sorry you had to take the other three."

Esperanza frowned. She hadn't realized it until now, but all of the men except the one so enamored by her sister had come to her.

"You only had one?" she asked. "That's good. But what happened?"

"El Jefe called me over and told me the man wanted me all to himself tonight. I was surprised, but of course I didn't argue. I was kind of relieved, but I didn't think about what that would mean for you. I'm sorry."

Esperanza's throat tightened as her baby sister apologized for something she never should have had to endure in the first place. Guilt gnawed at Esperanza's heart every day her sister didn't blame her for getting them into this horror. But she could never bear her sister's anger, no matter how much she deserved it.

"It doesn't matter," Esperanza said, reaching out to squeeze Gloria's hand. "I'm fine. Tell me about this man."

"He's different from the others. Almost tender, at first, like a lover. He told me his name, Jim, and he said he hated the thought of me being with anyone else."

Esperanza stared at her sister in surprise. The men never bothered to introduce themselves. And they certainly never got possessive. A kernel of worry took root in the pit of her stomach. What was this man playing at?

"When he was done, he just wanted to talk," Gloria continued. "He told me he'd never done anything like this before but his wife no longer made him happy."

Esperanza snorted. She suspected most of the men El Jefe brought to the house had wives at home. But she doubted many of them bothered to blame their wives for their behavior. They wanted what they wanted, so they took it. Why did this man need an excuse?

"Was he kind to you?"

Gloria nodded. "If I have to do this, I would much rather it be with someone like him."

Her sister's words felt like a punch in the stomach. *If I have to do this.* How had they reached a point where the lesser of two evils seemed like a blessing? Would there ever be a time they didn't have to do this?

Gloria yawned and smiled sleepily. Esperanza squeezed her hand again.

"Go to bed, chula. It's late."

"Don't you want me to help you change the sheets?" Gloria asked as she stood and stretched. They never went to sleep on the sheets the men had defiled. "I've already done mine."

"No. I'll do it. Go, sleep now." Esperanza gave her sister a quick hug, kissed her forehead, and watched her slip out the door.

~ ~ ~ ~ ~

The next morning, Esperanza got up as soon as she heard the birds tuning up outside her window. She hadn't slept well. She couldn't stop thinking about the man who seemed so obsessed with her sister. When Gloria talked about life after this hell, her fantasy always began with El Jefe setting them free after they paid off their debt. Esperanza was convinced that would never happen. He would never let them go willingly, at least not as long as they were making him money. On the few occasions she dreamed of freedom, she always assumed they would escape, somehow slipping out the front door and down the

stairs undetected. They would run down the long driveway to the road and pray someone drove by.

Never in a million years did she think her sister's sal-
vation might come through one of El Jefe's customers.
But she sensed an opportunity. What if this man really did
fall in love with Gloria? What if he wanted to make sure
he was the only man she ever saw? Could he convince El
Jefe to let her go? He would probably want something in
return, but this man looked like he could afford it.

While she made coffee, she dreamed about securing
her sister's freedom. She imagined Gloria in her own
apartment, free to do what she pleased. Of course, it
wouldn't be true freedom. She would still be at a man's
mercy, but it would only be one man. And it would be a
man who cared for her, maybe. Perhaps one day she could
find a way to truly escape.

She carried a cup of coffee into the living room, where
El Carcelero sat on the couch, watching TV. He took it
from her without looking away from the screen. He had a
room in the back of the house but she didn't think he slept
there often. During their first few weeks there, when she
still thought escape might be possible, she peeked out her
bedroom door several times during consecutive nights.
Each time, she could see him standing on the deck, leaning on the railing. The orange embers at the end of his
cigarette glowed like a tiny warning. He was a constant
presence then.

Now he only came by every few days. She'd heard
him talking to El Jefe about other girls. More unsuspect-

ing women lured from their homes with false promises of honest work. Just like her and Gloria. But it didn't sound like they hosted parties for El Jefe. They met men at a hotel. She shuddered to think about how much worse that would be.

When El Carcelero left their prison, an older woman took his place. She barked orders at the girls while they cleaned the house and supervised them when they prepared meals in the kitchen. Her harsh words were tempered only by her occasional exclamations over their beauty. She brought them makeup and clothes, painted their nails, cut and styled their hair. Esperanza felt like a life-sized doll during their "fashion" sessions. She thought the woman might have taken pity on them. She was old enough to be their mother. But the care she took over their looks never made its way into her heart. One day, after putting Gloria into a deep purple dress that set off her caramel skin and her shiny black hair, the woman had stepped back and smiled with satisfaction.

"Like an angel," she had said. "A dirty, fallen angel." Then she cackled, witch-like, when Gloria started to cry.

Esperanza shuddered as the scene rolled across her memory. They'd known nothing but savagery since they arrived. This man who had such an unusual interest in her sister was the first person to show them any kindness in months. Of course, it was a self-serving kindness, but at this point, she would take it. Now she just had to figure out how her sister could use it to her advantage.

When Gloria woke up, Esperanza scrambled some eggs with bell pepper and onion and set a package of tortillas on the table. El Carcelero took his plate out to the deck, where he could smoke in peace. El Jefe didn't allow smoking in the house. When he was out of earshot, Esperanza smiled at her sister.

"I've been thinking about this man," she said, pausing as she suddenly had second thoughts about what she planned to say.

Gloria looked at her expectantly, her eyes showed no sign of suspicion or unease. Knowing her sister trusted her completely made Esperanza even more uncertain about her suggestion. Gloria wouldn't even be here if it weren't for her. What if she put her in even more danger, or perhaps worse, prolonged her captivity? She stared at the teen so long without saying anything that Gloria finally reached out and touched her cheek.

"What is it? Are you okay?" she asked.

Esperanza nodded and smiled again, wistfully this time.

"Sometimes I just can't believe we even have to talk about these things," she said, her eyes filling with tears. "Lo siento." She could feel the familiar terror rising in her chest, making it hard to breathe.

Gloria reached out and took her hand, squeezing it so tightly the tips of Esperanza's fingers turned red.

"Don't," Gloria said. "It's not your fault. I chose to come. You didn't know what was waiting on the other side of that journey."

Esperanza clung to her sister's hand until the wave of panic ebbed. When she could take a shaky, deep breath again, she pulled Gloria's hand to her face and kissed it.

"Te amo, para siempre," Esperanza said.

"Me too," Gloria whispered.

Silence lingered between them for a few minutes. Esperanza made up her mind and pushed her plate of cold eggs away.

"This man, what if he could persuade El Jefe to let you go? He said he didn't want you to be with anyone else. What if he could make that happen?"

Gloria's eyebrows arched over wide, surprised eyes. "You mean if he paid off my debt?"

Esperanza cringed, even as she nodded encouragingly. She was sure it would take much more than her sister's supposed debt. The question was, would El Jefe be willing to set a price and would the man be willing to pay?

"If he did that, what would happen then?" Gloria asked quietly.

Esperanza looked down at her hands, curled into a ball in her lap. She swallowed hard before looking her sister in the eye. "If he paid for your freedom, you would not truly be free, at least not at first."

She held Gloria's gaze for a few minutes before the teen looked away.

"It wouldn't be freedom, but at least it wouldn't be this," Gloria finally said.

"And if he truly cared for you, and thought you went with him willingly, he probably wouldn't treat you like a prisoner. You would be like his *amante*, his mistress."

Gloria grimaced and Esperanza let her think without interruption. The teen finally sighed, a sign of resignation that tore at Esperanza's heart.

"That might not be so bad," she said, her voice quivering just a little. "Maybe, eventually, he would let me go home to see mama."

Esperanza nodded and swallowed against the lump rising in her throat. If Gloria could go home, what would she tell their mother, who thought her oldest girls were living the good life in America?

"What should I do?" Gloria asked.

"The next time he comes, make him feel like you're glad to see him. Have you told him how we got here?"

Gloria shook her head no.

"Figure out a way to tell him. Make sure you mention the debt. Tell him you have to keep seeing the men El Jefe brings here until you've paid off your debt."

"What do I say if he asks me how much I owe?"

"Tell him you don't know. You don't. But he's a businessman. He knows how to negotiate. If he tells El Jefe he wants to pay off your debt, they can work out between them how much you still owe."

They sat in silence for a while. Esperanza watched her sister's face closely as she thought through the possibilities. The shadows deepened and eased as she wrestled with her decision. After about five minutes, it looked like she was ready to embrace the unexpected opportunity to escape her living hell, until her eyes suddenly snapped wide open with a look of alarm.

"What about you?"

"I'll be fine." Esperanza tried to smile reassuringly. "As soon as I pay off my debt, I'll find you."

This would be the most difficult obstacle to overcome. She didn't believe for one moment that El Jefe would ever let her go, but she had to persuade Gloria they might be reunited one day. It was possible, if their plan worked, that she would never see her sister again. Esperanza could only live with that possibility if her sister really had a chance at a better life. But Gloria loved her fiercely. She would only go if Esperanza could persuade her it would be best for both of them.

Esperanza leaned across the table toward Gloria and took both her hands. "If I know you're safe, all of this will be so much easier to bear. And maybe you can persuade him, after a while, to ask El Jefe to set me free too. If he thinks you love him, there's probably nothing he wouldn't do for you."

A wide smile lit up Gloria's face and a rush of relief made Esperanza almost lightheaded. Her sister had grasped the lifeline. But could she convince this man to pull her out of El Jefe's sea of despair?

Chapter 13

The next four weeks passed uneventfully as August drew to a close. The furor over the mayor's political bombshell had started to blow over, and Kate found herself stuck in a rut of summer season stories—hotel and motel tax revenue was rising, sunburned tourists thronged the beaches every weekend, and no dead bodies or prostitutes showed up to break the magical spell of sun, sand, and surf. Kate wasn't sure who seemed more satisfied at public appearances, the Convention and Visitors Bureau director or the mayor.

But every headline about Galveston's trouble-free summer grated on Kate. She felt like an unwilling conspirator in what seemed like a city-wide cover up. She knew crime was going unpunished. Murders remained unsolved. She felt like storm clouds were gathering on the horizon but she was the only one who could see them.

She still marveled at how Hanes had managed to finesse his way through the shock and anger over his new support for the police union. Kate thought for sure she'd be covering a recall election by now. But Hanes, with his trademark charm and lawyer's knack for persuasion, managed to win over or at least mollify his most vehement critics. She'd even heard from a source who worked at the country club that Hanes had played a round of golf with Daniel Price last weekend.

Today was her turn to work the Saturday rotation. She'd already been out to East Beach to cover the annual sandcastle building competition. Now she sat in the cool, cavernous newsroom waiting for word from the copy desk that her story was okay so she could go home.

A little before 4 p.m., she heard the front door scrape open and Delilah Peters stalked into the room.

"Hey," Delilah said when she made it to her desk and sat down with a "humph."

"What are you doing here?" Kate asked, swiveling around in her chair to face the senior reporter. "Do you have a story you need to finish for tomorrow?"

"No, but I wanted to get some work done on this beachfront property dispute case I'm covering. I've got a lot of legal documents to wade through. Ben kept interrupting me at home, so I just decided to come to the office for some peace and quiet."

Kate smiled at the thought of Ben hovering over Delilah, offering to help interpret the court filings.

"So, how's your detective these days?" Delilah asked as she pulled her laptop and a stack of documents from her bag. "I haven't seen his name in print in about a month."

Kate winced. Almost from the moment she wrote her first crime story, Ben had made jokes about her relationship with police officers, especially Johnson. Delilah had picked up the habit. Normally Kate brushed off their crude references, but these days they chafed the raw feelings left by her last substantial conversation with the detective.

She's mostly avoided him since that night at the bar. She still couldn't believe he intended to drop the prostitution ring investigation. She kept hoping she'd hear about an unexpected bust or a quiet arrest. Anything to redeem him.

Delilah raised an eyebrow and Kate realized she still hadn't answered her question.

"Sorry, I was just thinking about the murder investigations," she said. The answer sounded lame even to her ears. "He's still working them, I guess. The chief also has him running the summer citizen's police academy, and he's working on the new neighborhood policing plan. It's probably about time we did a story on that."

"Well, he's lucky he kept his job after racking up two dead bodies and not one lead. He never struck me as incompetent, but it's hard to believe he had absolutely nothing to go on."

Kate bristled in Johnson's defense and realized she hadn't completely lost faith in him. She knew he'd given those investigations everything he had. Even the best police departments had cold cases. No matter how much he frustrated her, Kate refused to blame him for the unsolved murders. But she wasn't interested in rehashing the investigation with Delilah, so she just shrugged.

Her phone rang just as she was about to change the subject. The copy editor told her the sandcastle story was ready to go and she could take off if she wanted to.

"All right, I'll leave you to your legal briefs," Kate said as she stood up and stretched her arms over her head. "I'm out of here."

"Hot date tonight?"

"Sort of. Brian needs his monthly Frank's fix."

"Must be nice to date a doctor," Delilah smirked.

"It has its advantages," Kate said as she scooped up her computer bag and headed for the door.

Francisco's, or Frank's as the locals called it, was one of the nicest seafood restaurants on the island. It had been around since the 1950s, run by an Italian family that washed into Galveston on the illegal gambling wave that swept a brief period of fame and fortune back to the waning beach town. In those days, mobsters came in from the Northeast to enjoy the tables and the Texas hospitality. Even Frank Sinatra had come to play the famous Balinese Room, which stretched out from the seawall for hundreds of feet on what now looked like rickety piers. The long building was designed to give the gamblers in the farthest room time to pack up their card games if police decided to raid the joint, which they regularly did.

With its grand piano and tuxedo-clad waiters, Francisco's retained some of the old Rat Pack ambiance. Kate would only have been able to go there for very special occasions, after saving up for weeks. But Brian grew up eating there regularly, every time his family came to town for a visit. He thought nothing of blowing $100 on a nice dinner.

"If Mattingly asks me who I think he should get rid of in the layoffs, I'm nominating you," Delilah said, laughing. "Then you can quit fooling around with work and start your cushy life as a doctor's wife."

Kate held out her left hand and saluted Delilah with her middle finger as she walked out the door. For a moment, the horror of becoming a housewife flooded over her, sending shots of panic through her chest. Brian had never said that's what he wanted in a wife, but why wouldn't he? He certainly wouldn't want to marry someone who worked odd hours and slept with a police scanner next to the bed. Not that she wanted to get married. But Brian surely did, at least eventually. Would he figure out she wasn't the right person to fill that role before she got tired of him and moved on?

~ ~ ~ ~ ~

The plaintive notes of "Summertime" floated over the smell of roasting garlic and butter-soaked shrimp when Brian and Kate stepped through the restaurant's doors a few hours later. They'd had to wind their way through a crowd of hungry tourists clustered outside, but Kate knew they wouldn't have to wait for a table. The maître d' greeted them by name and ushered them to a spot near the back of the dining room.

After dropping the crisp, white napkin in her lap as nonchalantly as possible, Kate ran her fingertips along the bottoms of the silverware set in front of her. Six pieces, not counting the butter knife placed across the small plate to her left. She'd needed every bit of self-control learned through years of difficult interviews not to let her anxiety show the first time Brian had brought her here. She'd had no idea which fork to pick up first.

Across the table, Brian smiled at her. Did he know how uncomfortable she'd been that first time or how uneasy she still was in the opulent surroundings? The nicest restaurant she'd been to growing up had checkered tablecloths and stiff metal chairs. It served shrimp too, but Kate was pretty sure they came straight out of the commercial version of the grocery store's frozen food section.

Before they had a chance to pick up their menus, a dark-haired waiter whose chipped teeth looked out of place with his starched white shirt and black jacket strode over to their table.

"Ah, my favorite couple—Lois Lane and the doctor who leave big tip!" he said, bowing toward Brian slightly. Their regular waiter's clipped English and corny jokes always made Kate laugh.

"Slava!" Brian said with a grin. "We missed you last time. They sent us some clumsy oaf who didn't know what kind of wine went with scampi."

"Yes, I had cold. Very bad cold. How I get cold when it's so hot, I don't know. Better now."

"You should have come to see me," Brian said. "I would have taken care of you."

Slava just smiled and motioned to a bartender hovering about 10 feet away.

"You like this," he said, holding out a glistening bottle of white white. "Not too sweet. Go well with the seared scallops you like so much."

Brian looked at Kate, who gave a slight shrug. She knew enough about wine to avoid anything pink and bottles with screw tops, unless her bank account was getting low. She always let Brian order the drinks when they were out.

"Sounds good to me," Brian said. "Let's have it."

While the waiter opened the wine, they studied the specials.

"No exciting news this week," Slava said as he poured the pale liquid into Kate's glass. "No dead bodies. But the police, I think they taking time off."

"What do you mean?" Kate asked.

"Last month, they do big bust at bad hotel. Girls, men, you know? This month, no bust."

"Well, maybe there aren't any more girls to bust," Brian said.

"No, no, no!" Slava insisted as he set the bottle down in an ice-filled bucket on a stand next to the table. "Girls in my hotel. Something funny going on. Do they investigate? No."

"What do you mean, girls in your hotel?" Kate asked, lowering her voice just a little. "Do you think someone's running a prostitution ring out of the place you're staying?"

"Ya! For sure. We never see girls, but men come and go all night. Some other students from Ukraine have room nearby. They tell me, so I go see for myself. When I call police, they do nothing."

"Hmmmm...." Kate said, her eyes narrowing as she thought about the mayor's orders to the police chief. "Do you think they believed you?"

"I don't know. All I know is men still come and no police. Is no good." Slava suddenly seemed to remember he had other tables to wait on. "I come back," he said as he strode toward the kitchen.

"I wonder what that's all about," Brian said. "Do you think they blew off the report because Slava's the one who made it?"

"I don't know," Kate murmured, chewing on her bottom lip.

Slava was one of about 200 exchange students who came to the island each year to work in hotels and restaurants and get a taste of America. Most of them came from Eastern Europe or Asia, and they often got treated no better than illegal immigrants. Landlords charged exorbitant rents. Employers made them work much longer hours than they expected when they signed up for the program. If the police turned a blind eye to their complaints, about anything, it wouldn't be surprising.

"Maybe you should talk to Johnson about it. I know he said they wouldn't be doing any more stings, but maybe they could increase patrols in the area, make the pimp move on."

"Yeah, or maybe I should check it out for myself and write a story about how the cops are ignoring reported criminal activity right in the middle of all the tourists," Kate said, absentmindedly pulling apart a roll as she envisioned possible front page headlines.

"Poor Johnson. You're going to hang him out to dry."

"I am not!" Kate said, trying to ignore the sinking feeling that Brian was right. "Besides, maybe a little publicity will force the mayor to change his mind. That would qualify as helping Johnson out." And maybe that would finally push him to do something, she thought.

"Right," Brian said with a grin, just as Slava came back to take their order.

By the time they finished dessert, Kate had enough information to start doing a little investigating on her own. Her heart started to thump as she thought about sinking her teeth into a really good story. It had been too long.

As Brian led her toward the front of the restaurant, an unmistakably smarmy voice warbled from a table just ahead. When Brian stopped to let a waiter carrying an overloaded tray pass them by, Kate looked over and caught Eduardo Reyes looking at her.

"Well, well, well," he said, wiping his fat lips with an already soiled napkin. "I didn't know they let reporters in here. Guess I need to have a little chat with the management."

He guffawed and slapped the table with his palm. An empty wine bottle tottered precariously near the edge. Reyes' dining companions, two men Kate didn't recognize, also laughed loudly. Between them, she spotted another almost empty bottle.

Brian stepped closer to the table, just a few feet from Reyes and too close for the older man to get up gracefully from his chair. As he towered over him, Brian held out his hand.

"I'm Brian Dougherty. You must be Eduardo Reyes. Kate's told me a lot about you."

Reyes seemed surprised at the younger man's audacity. He tried to scoot his heavy chair back so he could stand but gave up when it got caught on the carpet. Kate tried to smother a smirk.

"Nice to meet you," Reyes finally said, giving Brian's hand a perfunctory shake. "I hope you kids enjoyed your meal. This is one of the best restaurants on the island. Special occasion?"

"No, we come here about once a month," Brian said, circling Kate's waist with one hand and drawing her closer to the table.

Reyes raised his eyebrows just slightly and turned his eyes on Kate. "Well, Miss. Bennett, you've had a quiet few weeks. It's nice, no? I like it when things run smoothly on my island."

"It's definitely been uneventful," Kate said. "But you never know, looks can be deceiving."

"Do you know something I don't?" Reyes asked, barking out another laugh. "I see no storm on the horizon. The skies are clear," with this, he waved a hand toward the restaurant's floor to ceiling windows that framed a perfect view of the gulf.

"They are for now," Kate said.

"Well, we'd better leave you to your dinner," Brian interjected before Reyes could reply. "Nice meeting you."

With his arm still around Kate's waist, Brian swept them out of the restaurant.

"What an ass," he said when they were out of earshot of anyone who might have seen them talking to Reyes. "It's hard to believe he's the patron saint of Galveston."

"Well, believe it," Kate said, her mouth twisted in disgust. "Did you catch the reference to 'his' island?"

"Oh, yeah. Nice touch. And he seems to be enjoying the peaceful summer as much as the mayor."

Kate pondered that as Brian drove back to her apartment. Matthew Hanes basically owed his election to Reyes. What were the chances he had taken such a drastically different position on police and taxes without his friend's blessing? Or better yet, at his friend's direction.

Kate had always assumed calling a truce with the police union was the mayor's idea. But what if it wasn't? She had never found a good explanation for what prompted the change. Maybe that's because it was never about the mayor in the first place.

But what interest could Reyes possibly have in meddling with police business?

Chapter 14

Kate slept until almost 10 a.m. the next morning. She didn't even hear Brian leave before dawn for his shift. After throwing on running shorts and a T-shirt, and scraping her tangled hair into a ponytail, Kate headed for the coffee shop with a newspaper tucked under her arm—her Sunday morning ritual. The sun was already blazing when she emerged from the cool shadow of her building's foyer onto the shimmering sidewalk.

She walked slowly, watching families and people with dogs trudge past. She waved to a few fellow downtown residents she recognized. After eight months at the paper, she rarely went anywhere she didn't see someone she knew, or who knew her. She had enjoyed her first few months of anonymity, when she could run to the grocery store at midnight in her pajamas. The last time she did that, she ran into the mayor's wife, who was buying Tylenol to soothe a sick child. So much for anonymity.

Despite the sultriness, the Sunday morning regulars already filled the tables outside the coffee shop. Kate raised her hand in a salute but didn't stop to chat. After picking up her order at the counter, she slipped into an armchair in the back of the shop, well away from the bright sun streaming through the front windows. Unfolding the newspaper, she scanned the headlines, looking for something to absorb her attention. But she couldn't concentrate on any of them. All she could think about was Slava's story about the prostitutes at his hotel.

If he was right, and Kate could prove it, she would have a great story on her hands. The police chief would have to explain why his officers weren't doing the normal prostitution stings. And the mayor would be forced to admit everything on the island wasn't as picture-perfect as he wanted people to believe. At best, he was trying to cover up a potentially serious problem to protect the island's image. At worst, he had a specific reason for wanting to let the pimps work uninterrupted. Either way, Kate's stomach churned at the thought he might get away with it.

And besides, she had to renew Mattingly's faith in her. Fear over her fate in the looming layoffs had started to keep her up at night. She did not intend to be the one cut out of the newsroom when the axe finally fell.

As she folded up her mostly unread copy of the paper, Kate popped the last bite of her muffin into her mouth and stood up. Despite the blistering heat, this afternoon seemed like the perfect time to do a little hotel reconnaissance.

~ ~ ~ ~ ~

An hour later, Kate wheeled her bicycle out of the storage closet off her building's foyer. If she was going to work on Sunday, she figured she might as well get some exercise too. Plus, the limited parking on the seawall would be full of SUVs disgorging screaming kids and parents already looking harassed after the 45-minute drive from Houston. It took her just 15 minutes to pedal the 3 miles up 21st Street to the beach.

About a dozen blocks to the east, The Clipper Motor Inn sat wedged between newer hotels that offered guests breakfast, beach towels, and complimentary cocktails at check-in. The Clipper's most notable amenities were its vending and ice machines, both occasionally full. Kate guessed the hotel had been built in the early 1950s. Its two stories surrounded two sides of a rectangular swimming pool, forming an "L" that offered most guests an unobscured view of the Gulf of Mexico. In its heyday, it was probably one of the most sought-after hotels on the island. Kate could imagine children splashing in the glimmering swimming pool while moms in high-waisted bikinis and big sunglasses sipped lemonade and read *Life* magazine.

But today, the pool was deserted, the chain-link fence around it and the water's unmistakable green tinge both screamed "Keep Out." A sign hanging askew from one hook outside the manager's office advertised rooms for $59.99 a night. Heat radiated from the fissured parking lot. The Clipper was a step above the Sand Crab, where Johnson's officers had made their last prostitution ring bust, but only slightly. Kate remembered cringing when Slava mentioned he and several other student workers stayed there. But they got a good weekly rate, and it was close to most of the places they worked. Despite Slava's current claims, it wasn't the kind of place known for catering to illegal activity.

Kate pedaled up to a concrete bench across the street from the hotel and sat down, rolling the bike out of the way of tourists walking, riding or rollerblading down the wide seawall. A steady breeze coming off the water wafted the stench of dead fish and rotting seaweed. After 10 minutes, Kate had to wipe her forehead with the sleeve of her T-shirt to keep sweat from running into her eyes. After another 20 minutes, she couldn't tell whether her arms were soaking up the heat or radiating it out. And not one car or person had come in or out of the hotel's parking lot. Staking out the hotel in the middle of the afternoon suddenly seemed like a foolish waste of time.

Pursing her lips in frustration, Kate stood up and stretched. At the corner of the building, outside the manager's office, she spotted a soda machine. It couldn't hurt to take a closer look and get something to drink while she was at it. She walked her bike across the four-lane boulevard during a temporary break in the traffic. While she fished for change in her saddle bag, an emaciated woman shuffled around the corner.

"Hey there, darlin'. Got any change to spare?" she asked in a low, raspy voice.

"Well, that's what I'm looking for. I was going to buy a drink. Want one?"

The woman's almost toothless smile dissolved into what Kate guessed was her usual glum expression when she realized she wasn't likely to get much more than a soda and a few coins. But she nodded anyway, setting down the bag she was carrying and taking out a dingy washcloth to wipe her face. Her wrinkled and gaunt cheeks and neck made her look well over 50. The scabs on her thin arms and her missing teeth suggested a meth addiction. Her skin, probably once a rich ebony now looked almost grey. Kate suspected she might be as young as her mid thirties.

"What would you like?" Kate asked as she pulled a handful of coins from her bag.

"Coke, whenever I can get it," the woman rasped, cackling at her own joke.

Kate fed the coins into the machine and two bright red cans already sweating rolled down the chute. She popped the top on the first one and handed it to the woman.

"And here's the rest of what I have on me. It's not much, but you're welcome to it." The woman nodded as Kate dropped a few dimes, a couple of quarters and half a dozen pennies into her hand. After she slipped the change into the pocket of her shorts, the woman glanced into the hotel parking lot.

"Slow today," she said.

"Is it normally busy?" Kate asked.

"Most days, but not this early. Too hot today. No one wants to come out and play. Course, I'm not playing much these days anyhow."

While she talked, the woman nervously picked at the scabs on her arms. Kate watched her with a mixture of revulsion and pity. It was hard to tell, but she might have been pretty once. Meth, cocaine, and whatever other drugs she could get her hands on had wiped away any trace of appeal. Kate guessed she turned most of her tricks just to get the next fix.

"Do you work around here?" Kate asked, after considering how to phrase the question.

The woman looked at her sideways for a few moments before answering.

"Used to. Used to be plenty business 'round here. I had a special arrangement with the management, if you know what I mean. But now, new girls in town. Miss Kitty's not welcome here no mo'."

"New girls, huh? That's rough." Kate wasn't sure it was exactly appropriate to offer condolences for a prostitute's drop in business.

"Uh huh. And they's organized too. Some young muchacho's running the show. He's real mean. Roughed me up once when I told him he had no right to chase me outa my own block. Said it was his block now. Didn't used to be that way. All us girls looked out for each other. We had enough customers to share. Things a' changed."

"So this ... muchacho ... and his girls, they work out of this hotel?"

The woman suddenly spun toward Kate with a fierce glare. "Who's askin'? Why you wanna know? You a cop or somethin'?"

"No! I was just curious, that's all." Kate cursed to herself for not being more tactful.

"Huh. That'll get you in trouble, girl. People gets suspicious 'round here. Don't you go askin' too many questions."

"Sorry," Kate offered meekly, lapsing into silence and looking down at her feet while the woman continued to stare at her.

When she sensed the woman's gaze had shifted, she looked up again. Her companion was staring absently out over the Gulf. She was scratching at both arms now and one eye had started to twitch slightly. She must have been well past her need for another fix.

"I s'pose you don't mean no harm. Nobody mean no harm. I don't mean no harm. No harm."

The woman's voice had taken on a dream-like quality Kate recognized from her childhood. It always meant a psychological tide was about to turn.

"But the men in white, they mean harm!" the woman hissed, turning slowly to face Kate with wide, vacant eyes. "They take you down, lock you away. They's always after me."

She looked furtively over her shoulder, and Kate knew she was lost inside her own fantasy.

"You look out, you hear? I can't stay here. Can't stay here."

With this, the woman snatched up her bag, threw down her empty coke can and shuffled off the way she had come, down a side street with alleys that often sheltered the homeless. Kate's chest tightened as she watched the woman go, overwhelmed by a sadness too deep for tears. She had run into her fair share of the mentally ill during her time on the island, but it never got easier to see their suffering. It seemed so completely hopeless. They either couldn't afford medication or just didn't want to take it. So they took street drugs to self-medicate. The women turned tricks for drug money. And they always ended up like Miss Kitty, with periods of sanity punctuating a reality saturated with mania, depression, or hallucinations.

Kate sighed as she picked up the discarded can, wheeled her bike around and headed for a trash bin half way down the block. Despite her apparent schizophrenia, Miss Kitty's story about the new girls seemed believable. Kate was pretty sure she was trying to say they worked at The Clipper. It corroborated Slava's account.

A flutter of excitement began to drive away the sadness that had consumed her moments before. The afternoon hadn't been a waste after all. She had enough information to start working on a story that would blow the lid off the mayor's plan to cover up, or at least ignore, criminal activity. A thrill of electricity sent a tingle from the back of her neck all the way to her finger tips. He was up to something he didn't want people to know about.

Now Kate just had to figure out how to prove it.

Chapter 15

The patter of running water in the shower greeted Kate when she opened the door to her apartment. Brian's keys sat on the kitchen table. Surprise and hesitation left her standing in the entrance, unsure what to do. She hadn't realized how comfortable their relationship had become. When he walked out of the bathroom with a towel wrapped around his waist, she considered telling him she needed some space.

"I let myself in with the spare key. Sorry," he said, keeping his distance as if he knew he was wading into deep water. "I called you, but you didn't pick up. I wanted to be sure I caught you before you made plans for the night. I promise I won't make a habit of it."

"Well, if you promise..." She suddenly wasn't sure what she wanted to say. She didn't want him to stay. But she didn't want him to go either. "What do you have in mind for tonight? Whatever it is, I'll have to clean up."

Brian smiled. "Looks like you've been to the beach. I hope you have some aloe vera."

Kate glanced at her arms, which had started to glow a soft pink.

"I was on a stakeout," she said, purposely leaving out the details.

"Interesting." He drew out the syllables in inquiry but stopped short of asking more. "So, are you up for a little religious reconnaissance tonight?"

Kate rolled her eyes.

"I ran into Uncle Bobby this afternoon. He was visiting someone in the hospital and stopped by the ER to hunt me down. I haven't seen him in about a month, and he insisted I come to church tonight. I couldn't say no."

Bob Gage pastored Galveston's First Baptist Church and had been friends with Brian's parents since Brian's father was a medical student. He was Brian's godfather, and usually managed to guilt him into coming to church every time he saw or talked to him. Brian grew up in church and took the pastor's gentle prodding in stride. After his last visit to church, Brian admitted he had a lingering sense of guilt over his lapsed spiritual condition. Kate guessed he accepted his godfather's invitations as a form of penance. She had gone with him several times, but only when he begged. Churches were for weddings and funerals, as far as she was concerned. And even those made her squirm.

She was about to tell him no when she remembered that one of the church's deacons worked with the island's homeless population. He probably knew Miss Kitty and might be able to tell Kate whether he'd heard any of the other prostitutes talking about the new girls in town. She smiled at the prospect of some true reconnaissance.

"Let me just jump in the shower," she said. "I'll be ready in half an hour."

Brian's eyebrows rose in surprise, confusion filling his wide eyes. But he smiled back and waved her toward the bathroom door.

~ ~ ~ ~ ~

A small crowd had already gathered in the church's chapel when Brian and Kate walked in the back door. The pastor spotted them right away and strode down the aisle to meet them.

"You came!" he boomed in a deep voice Kate always thought had dictated his career choice. He was destined to become either a radio announcer or a preacher. While still grasping his godson's hand, the pastor turned to Kate.

"It's always good to see you. After all the excitement you had last month, you must be getting a little bored at the newspaper. I never thought the mayor would worm his way out of that one."

Kate smiled. Next to God and his congregation, Bob Gage loved local politics best. He'd served on the school board in the early 1990s and still couldn't get enough of the machinations that turned the wheels of local government. He'd told her once it served as a good reminder of the pervasive nature of original sin. She'd had to research what that meant. She decided later that was probably his intent.

"It's definitely been a slow few weeks," she said, glancing around to see if she could spot the deacon she wanted to talk to. "But you never know what might be coming up. The news has a way of surprising you."

"That's because people make the news," Gage said, winking at her. "So I guess nothing should surprise us, eh?"

The chords of the service's first hymn saved Kate from having to reply. Gage left them to return to the front of the chapel, stopping to shake a few hands as he made his way up the aisle. While the rest of the congregation stood to sing the first stanza of "'Tis so Sweet to Trust in Jesus," Brian led Kate to an almost empty pew halfway up the room. An elderly woman in a pillbox hat patted Kate's arm as she slipped in beside her.

The words and notes of the hymnal Brian held open in front of them blurred as the familiar tune began. She recognized it from her mother's funeral. Nausea churned in her stomach, and black spots swam before her eyes. She clutched the back of the pew in front of her. How could anyone trust in a God who allowed suffering and evil to rage unchecked? If such a God existed, his cruelty knew no bounds. Kate preferred to think of God as a myth desperate and weak people clung to because they couldn't face the reality of life's meaninglessness.

She made it through the next four hymns with gritted teeth. Her rising indignation and hostility to the words that rang out around her made her dizzy. When the last note finally sounded, she sat stiffly back in the pew and tried to tune out the sermon. Gage preached from the Book of Matthew and talked about how much Jesus loved "the least of these." Kate thought about Miss Kitty and her mother. The closing hymn, "I surrender all," went on for five stanzas while Gage, singing at the top of his lungs, waited at the front of the chapel for someone to join him. No one did. Kate tapped her foot with impatience through the entire hymn and sighed with relief when the pastor raised his hands to offer the benediction.

At the end of the service, the small congregation migrated into the fellowship hall next door for coffee, punch, and cookies—a Sunday night tradition. Brian had given his arm to the little old lady sitting next to Kate, leading her to the refreshments and offering to get her something to drink. While he stood in line to fill up three cups, Kate spotted the deacon, caught his eye, and smiled. She had interviewed David Lyons several times for stories about homelessness, and as she hoped he would, he ambled over to say hello.

"I met someone you probably know this afternoon," Kate said. "She called herself Miss Kitty."

"Ah, yes. She's a regular. Been around the island for as long as I can remember."

"She was telling me that things have been particularly tough in recent months."

"Oh? I know someone roughed her up a few weeks ago. Did she tell you about that? We had to take her to the clinic to get a few stitches."

"She did mention it, although she left out the part about the stitches. Do you see that kind of thing a lot? It seems a little excessive."

"Everything about life on the streets is excessive, unfortunately. They're not normally violent, but sometimes they get into fights about the most random things. One time, I had to break up a brawl between two older men who were arguing over who should get to rummage through a particular trash can. So, you never know."

"But Miss Kitty said it was a pimp who roughed her up, someone new in town. Did she mention any of that to you?"

"She didn't give us any specifics about what happened. She refused to let us call the police, even though I certainly think she had grounds to press charges. And we would have stood by her through the process. But she didn't want to bring attention to herself, and we didn't push. It's not always good to push someone to do something they don't want to do, even if it's the right thing to do."

"Do you think she might have been scared to report what happened?" Kate asked. "Scared of the guy who attacked her, I mean, not just of the police."

"It's possible," Lyons said. "She did seem pretty paranoid about the whole thing, but she often talks about people coming after her. I didn't think anything of it."

"Yeah, toward the end of our talk she started telling me about the men in white."

"That's one delusion we hear from her a lot. It probably has some basis in her visits to the mental hospital, but it's hard to know for sure. Sometimes the delusions are all manufactured."

"So she's definitely schizophrenic?"

"And bipolar. It's a bad combination. When she's on her meds, she's completely rational, and she'll talk about trying to go home and see her family. But as soon as they release her from the hospital, she stops taking her meds and reverts back to life on the streets. It's the same cycle we see over and over again with most of the people we serve."

"But do you think there's any truth to what she says?" Kate asked, her confidence in her source waning.

"I think there's a kernel of truth to everything she says. It's just a matter of figuring out which kernel it is."

Brian interrupted their conversation when he handed Kate her cup of coffee and shook hands with the deacon.

"It looks like Kate's pumping you for information," Brian said, flashing Kate a knowing grin.

"Oh, I don't know. Were you?" Lyons asked with a quizzical smile.

Kate appreciated his discretion. "Not really. We were just discussing topics of mutual interest."

Brian sighed and shook his head. Kate wondered whether he realized why she'd put up so little resistance to coming to church.

"I did have one other question for you though," Kate said. "Have you heard anyone else talking about this guy? I mean, anything that might lead you to believe he's real?"

Lyons paused and pursed his lips before answering. "Not that I can think of. But I have noticed a certain level of tension on the streets when we're out talking to people. It's not anything definite I could put my finger on. It's just a feeling. I realize that's not very helpful."

"No, it's fine," Kate said. "I appreciate your insight, as always. Thanks for your help."

When Lyons wandered off to go talk to someone else, Brian took Kate's hand and pulled her toward where Gage was standing near the door.

"I'm starved," he said. "Let's go get some dinner. Unless, of course, there was someone else you needed to interview?"

Kate grinned. "Nope. All done. We can go now."

After promising Gage he wouldn't wait so long before coming back to visit, Brian led Kate out the door and down 23rd Street toward her building, just a few blocks away. The sun had sunk below the skyline, offering some relief from the blistering heat. They walked mostly in silence, with Kate preoccupied by what Lyons had said. She still had no confirmation that this new pimp even existed, just the suspicions of a waiter with a bent for sensationalism and the claims of a delusional crackhead.

Brian didn't interrupt her thoughts, a level of self-control that endeared him to Kate more than almost anything else. Most men would push and prod, trying to figure out what they didn't know. They couldn't stand to be left in the dark. But Brian never pushed. He almost always waited for Kate to come to him. A hint of her earlier uneasiness fluttered in her chest. She refused to fall in love with him. The flutters turned into a full-fledged throb when she realized she was dangerously close.

When they got back to her apartment, Brian offered to make mushroom and onion omelette and a salad. While he started to cook, Kate opened a bottle of pinot noir and finally told him about her unproductive stakeout, Miss Kitty, and her suspicions.

"If this woman can be believed, her story corroborates what Slava told us," she said. "Now I just have to figure out whether any of it's true."

"I don't suppose you could just go talk to the hotel manager," Brian said, his back to her as he swirled the eggs in the pan.

"And tip him off?" Kate scoffed. "Not likely. There's no way he doesn't know what's going on."

"I wonder who owns the hotel. This could be a big scandal for them when the story breaks."

"I don't know," Kate said, draining her glass as she got up to set the table. "But I'll find out. In the meantime, I think I need to plan another stakeout. I wonder whether Slava would introduce me to the friends who told him about this in the first place."

"I think Slava would do anything for you," Brian said with a grin, sliding the omelet out of the pan and onto a plate. "Just be careful, okay?"

Kate rolled her eyes. "I don't even think my editors would tell me to be careful."

"Well, they have less of a vested interest in your well-being than I do." Kate's heart stuttered in dismay. Brian definitely had grown too close for comfort. She smiled weakly.

While they ate, Brian told her about some of the patients he'd seen that day. The backyard grilling accidents and home improvement mishaps were pretty standard fare for a Sunday. He'd seen one little boy with a marble stuck in his nose, also not unusual. But the prize for the most interesting case of the day went to a fisherman with a long and very sharp lure embedded in his backside. After a few too many beers and too many hours spent standing on the pier, he'd gotten confused about which way he was supposed to cast his line.

"He brought the fishing pole and his tackle box with him into the ER," Brian said, laughing. "He wanted us to be sure not to bend the lure when we took it out. It was one of his best ones."

"Did he drive himself to the hospital? How could he even sit down?"

"None of us could figure it out. Maybe it didn't hurt that bad. It was in there pretty deep. He went home with stitches."

"But did the lure survive?"

Before Brian could answer, a siren started to wail outside the window. Kate listened as it faded in the direction of the seawall. She was about to pour another glass of wine when she heard another siren start up a few blocks away, in the direction of Fire Station 1. Soon she could hear yet another siren wailing in the distance. When she turned on the police scanner, it immediately crackled to life with chatter about something happening on the beach. Kate listened until she heard one of the officers say there was no need to send an ambulance. She was about to turn off the scanner when he spoke again.

"This one'll go straight to the coroner. Go ahead and call them out. Tell them to pull up in front of The Clipper. You can't miss us. We've got quite a crowd gathering."

A jolt of surprise shot through Kate as she ran to grab her notebook and her keys. That was right where she'd been just a few hours before. A spasm of panic gripped her throat. *Miss Kitty*. The new pimp had roughed her up once. Had he come back to finish the job?

Chapter 16

Johnson had already settled into his recliner with a well-worn copy of C.S. Lewis' *The Problem with Pain*—his Sunday night ritual—when his scanner went off. The dispatcher said tourists out for a late evening stroll had spotted what they thought was a body on the rocks at the base of the seawall. At first, Johnson guessed it was the man who went missing in the surf the day before. Often drowning victims took a little while to float back to shore, if lifeguards couldn't find them right away. But when the responding officers radioed back to dispatch, Johnson slammed his book closed.

"No need for an ambulance."

"10-4. Do you need additional units on scene?"

"Better go ahead and roll out the lieutenant and one of the detectives."

"10-4. Anyone else?"

"This one'll go straight to the coroner. Go ahead and call them out."

Johnson's cat, an aged tabby more crotchety than any old woman he'd ever met, protested loudly when he scooped her off his lap and stood up, setting her back down in the chair. She continued to yowl as he tugged on his shoes and clipped his gun to his belt. His three dogs, pit bull mixes rescued from the animal shelter, looked on half expectantly, their big brown eyes rolling between their master and the hook where their leashes hung by the door.

"Not this time, fellas," he said as he pulled the door closed behind him. "This time, it's work."

Johnson lived in an elevated row house about four blocks from the beach on 12th Street. From his front porch, he could see red and blue lights flashing on the seawall. He briefly thought about walking but decided he'd better get to the scene before the lieutenant, if possible. After two dead-end cases—or botched cases, as some of his colleagues called them—he wanted to be ready to field a barrage of questions when his supervisor arrived.

Johnson couldn't see anything at first when he pulled up behind the two other units lined up along the street. A crowd of tourists, some eating ice cream cones, had gathered on the sidewalk, craning their necks to see what was happening on the sand below. He had to push his way through them to get to the long flight of concrete steps carved into the wall. It almost looked like they were daring each other to be the first to attempt a descent to get a closer look.

"Hey, man!" a shirtless teen in board shorts and flip flops called out. "What's going on down there?"

"That's what I'm here to find out," Johnson said. "Give us some room to work, folks. Unless you want to spend the rest of the night sitting in the county jail, you'd better not try to set foot on this beach."

Below him, Johnson spotted two uniformed officers standing next to a rock groin that stretched out into the water from the base of the wall, 16 feet below the street. They talked and laughed quietly, not even making an attempt to canvass the scene for evidence. Plastic bottles, seaweed and cigarette butts—the detritus of another successful summer weekend—littered the thin strip of sand. And about 12 feet from where families had splashed and sunbathed the afternoon away, a body lay splayed on the sharp granite boulders.

She was on her stomach, with her head turned slightly to one side. Her short, frizzy hair lifted gently off her exposed cheek each time the wind puffed a saturated gust across her face. Her arms were stretched out on each side, almost as though they had tried to break her fall but crumpled under the force of the landing. A thin line of blood ran out of the corner of her mouth.

Johnson felt the familiar ache tighten his chest. He saw the evidence of human brokenness every day. But he never got over the feeling that it shouldn't be like this. Another senseless death made the world a little bit darker.

"Hey boss, looks like we've got a jumper," one of the officers called out when Johnson got close enough to hear them over the steady swoosh of the low surf.

"It's like Papa Doc all over again, except there's no wheelchair and no half empty bottle of Jim Beam," the other one said with a laugh.

Papa Doc was a well-known homeless man who panhandled along the seawall, playing on the sympathies of visitors who just wanted to enjoy a day of fun without being reminded of others' suffering. After a diabetes-related amputation confined him to a wheelchair, he almost doubled his daily haul. He usually made enough to get a hotel room at least once a week, and keep himself supplied with his favorite bourbon. Last winter, an early morning jogger found him at the base of the seawall, his wheelchair and a broken bottle about 5 feet away. The official report said he likely passed out and rolled off the edge accidentally. But many officers, who knew him pretty well after talking to him every day during patrols, thought he might have decided he'd just had enough.

Johnson just grunted as he scanned the rocks. A few feet away from one of the woman's outstretched arms he spotted a bag wedged in a crack.

"Did you look through her bag for an ID?"

"Naw, no need. We know who she is. Goes by Miss Kitty, but I think her real name's Sharneece something. We've hauled her in enough times. She's in the system."

The name didn't ring a bell, but Johnson had never patrolled the seawall and only knew the prostitutes his undercover teams rounded up in sting operations. Those girls usually moved on to another city to start over, or pick up where they left off.

"Did she work this area?"

"Used to, but she hasn't been regular for a while. We mostly bust her for drugs now. She's crazy as a loon and almost always high."

Johnson looked back at the broken body. Even if she spent her whole life crazy and high, she didn't deserve to die like this.

Up on the seawall, the crowd had grown as more people stopped to see what was going on. Johnson was about to tell one of the officers to ask them to move on when a woman broke through the front and started purposefully down the steps.

"Hey! You're not allowed down here. Get back on the sidewalk," Johnson yelled.

When she paused half way down and looked up, he recognized Kate. Throwing up his hands in frustration, he strode toward her as she continued her descent.

"The scene isn't secure. You can't be down here. Stop. Right. There!"

Although she did stop on the last thin slab of concrete, Kate's whole body strained toward the victim, her eyes wide and her mouth twisted and gaping.

"Johnson, I know her. I know who that is! I just talked to her this afternoon. What happened?" Kate's question came out in a high-pitched whine, more of an appeal than a request for information. Her chest heaved haltingly and Johnson could count her rapidly beating pulse in the vein raised in the center of her forehead. He'd never touched the reporter before, but he reached out now and grasped her forearm gently but firmly with one hand.

"Kate. Take a deep breath. It's okay. It looks like she jumped. It's happened before."

"Jumped?" Kate squeaked, looking him full in the face with such unveiled horror that he tightened his grip on her arm instinctively.

"Probably. Look, she was a drug addict with mental health issues. Maybe she was trying to commit suicide, or maybe she just got a bad batch of whatever and thought she could fly."

"But…" Kate looked back at the sidewalk more than one story above them and slowly turned toward where Miss Kitty's broken body lay draped on the rocks. Johnson followed her gaze. "That's so far. Do you really think she could have made it that far by jumping?"

Johnson released Kate's arm and put both hands on his hips as he judged the distance for the first time. He had to admit she had a point. It definitely looked like the woman had help reaching her final destination. But who would want to throw a washed up prostitute off the seawall?

"Look, I don't know at this point. I really just got here. Give me a chance to look around, and I'll tell you what I think once I have more information."

"Okay, but listen. I talked to her this afternoon, and she told me the same thing the mamasan from your last sting said—there's a new crew in town. And they're enforcing territories. Someone roughed Miss Kitty up a few weeks ago. I got that confirmed by David Lyons with Last Hope Ministries. It was so bad she had to have stitches."

Johnson frowned and pressed his lips together. His simple suicide was starting to turn into a complicated mess.

"Listen! Something's not right here," Kate insisted. "There's no way that woman threw herself off the seawall. I just talked to her this afternoon!"

Johnson wondered whether Kate's certainty stemmed from her conviction about the dead prostitute's state of mind or a desperate desire not to have been one of the last people to see her before she took her own life.

"If she did do this herself, there's no way you could have known it, Kate. She might not even have known it herself at the time you talked to her. You just never know with someone so tortured. Do you hear me?"

Kate nodded slightly. When she turned to walk back up the steps, Johnson thought he caught the glistening trail of a tear running down the side of her nose.

"I'll wait for you up there," she said, without looking back.

The vice already squeezing Johnson's heart tightened by another turn as he watched her trudge slowly back up the steps. He had never seen Kate so involved in a story before. Reporters, like police officers, kept a professional distance, often joking about the victims and circumstances surrounding even the most grisly murder scenes. It was the only way to stay sane, inundated by so much depravity day in and day out. Why was Kate taking this woman's death so personally?

While he waited for the lieutenant and the coroner to arrive, Johnson walked around the body looking for anything that might indicate a murder. Stepping gingerly across the jagged boulders, he looked carefully into each crack. Small crabs and three-inch-long roaches scurried out of the glare of his flashlight. He spotted a few stray socks, several beer bottles, crushed cans, tangled fishing line, one dead fish and dozens of cigarette butts. A few of them looked fairly fresh, but they weren't very close to the body. Of course, they could have been flicked from above by someone standing on the seawall. If she had been pushed, would her killer have stood there long enough to finish a cigarette, risking getting caught? That would have taken some nerve.

When Lieutenant Mark Jarrell marched down the steps, looking annoyed at having his Sunday evening interrupted, Johnson gave him a rough sketch of what they knew, which wasn't much. Jarrell rolled his eyes when Johnson pointed out the distance of the body from the seawall and suggested she might have been pushed.

"Do yourself a favor, detective. Unless you have a really good reason to label this a murder investigation, leave it alone. You have a dead prostitute that no one's going to miss and two unsolved murders in your file already. How likely is it you'll find whoever did this, if it even was a murder? Unless the coroner finds something suspicious, no one's going to question this as a suicide."

Johnson stared hard at the body while the lieutenant marched back up the steps to go home to his family. He was right, no one would miss her. But police didn't pursue and punish killers based on the victim's value to society. Anyone who snatched someone else's life from the hand of God deserved justice. The unsolved murders weighed on his conscience, not because his colleagues thought he'd bungled the investigations but because the killers might never pay for their crimes. His only comfort came from knowing they wouldn't escape eternal justice.

After he watched the coroner peel Miss Kitty off the rocks, Johnson slowly climbed the steps back to the sidewalk. Most of the crowd had moved on after the coroner drove away. Johnson found Kate sitting on a concrete bench about 30 feet from the top of the steps. Behind her, the lights of the The Clipper hotel glowed a dirty yellow. He sat down next to her and let silence hang between them for a few minutes. He still wasn't sure what he wanted to say.

"You don't think she was murdered, do you?" Kate asked accusingly.

"I don't know. There's just no way to tell at this point. She could have been pushed or she could have jumped. We'll have to see if anyone comes forward to say they saw something suspicious."

Kate snorted. "How likely do you think that is? And when no one does, what then?"

Johnson watched three waves roll ashore before answering.

"Then I don't think we'll have any choice but to classify it as a suicide."

Kate whipped around to face him, her eyes narrowed into glittering, angry slits. "What about whoever roughed her up several weeks ago? What about this new prostitution ring everyone's talking about? What if someone saw her talking to me and didn't like it?"

"Based on what, Kate?" Johnson asked, as gently as he could amid his own mounting frustration. "We have no proof that there is some new gang in town, and even if there is, pimps don't normally go around killing people. The last thing they want to do is draw attention to themselves."

"But what if they thought someone was starting to take notice of them and they wanted to continue operating under the radar? What if they killed Miss Kitty because she knew too much about them and they knew no one would look closely into her death?"

"I am going to look into it, I'm just not starting from the assumption that she was murdered, when I have no evidence to support that."

"No evidence," Kate sneered. "That sounds familiar."

Johnson recoiled as though she'd slapped him. Her accusation lodged between his ribs like an arrow on fire. The heat of her anger, mixed with his own, slowly spread down his abdomen and arms until his stomach was a hard knot and his fingers throbbed. He smacked the palm of his hand on his thigh.

"Damn it, Kate."

Before he said anything else, Johnson shoved himself off the bench and jogged to his car. He never looked back as he gunned the engine and rocketed into the empty street. As he drove past The Clipper, he spotted a man standing on the second floor walkway, leaning on the railing. The end of his cigarette glowed red in the darkness.

Homeless woman found dead at base of seawall

Investigators have ruled the death a likely suicide

By Kate Bennett

Galveston police officials have identified the woman found dead at the base of the seawall Sunday night as Sharneece Willis.

Tourists out for a late-night stroll spotted the body at about 11:30 p.m. Willis, 45, was laying face-down on the granite boulders between the wall and the beach.

Galveston County Coroner Trevor Ostermeyer said her neck was broken, suggesting she likely died immediately. Ostermeyer is still waiting for the results of toxicology tests, but Willis was a known drug user with multiple convictions for possession.

"I won't be making a final determination until I get all the test results back, but at this point, I see no evidence of foul play," Ostermeyer said. "She wouldn't be the first homeless person who fell, or jumped, to her death."

About a year ago, a homeless man was found under similar circumstances. Officials believe he fell asleep in his wheelchair without setting the break and rolled off the wall onto the rocks below.

David Lyons, director of Last Hope Ministries, said Willis had lived in Galveston for about 20 years. Lyons is working with police officials to try to contact her family in Louisiana.

"It's just a shame," Lyons said. "She was a good woman, with a good heart. But she was haunted by a lot of demons."

Chapter 17

It had been four weeks since Esperanza and Gloria made their plan to escape. But they'd had no chance to put it into action. Jim hadn't visited again, and Esperanza had finally come to accept that they'd lost their opportunity. It had been a hard blow to absorb, harder than every slap El Jefe had laid across her cheek. The fledgling hope that filled her heart died an agonizingly slow and painful death.

She'd tried to keep Gloria's hope alive through the first two weeks. But eventually she had to admit to her baby sister that the whole scheme had been as foolish as their dream of making a good life for themselves in America. Gloria had accepted her sister's assessment with calm resignation. But Esperanza heard her crying that night after they'd gone to bed.

The last week had passed uneventfully. Even El Jefe skipped his usual weekly visit. After they cleaned the house and cooked their meals, the girls had nothing to do but watch TV or flip through the fashion magazines El Jefe had left the last time he stopped by. They were always several months old, which made Esperanza think he picked them up after his wife discarded them. Although he wore a flashy gold band set with diamonds on his left hand, he never mentioned his wife. Esperanza wondered whether she knew what went on at his cabin perched above the marsh.

The girls were curled up on the couch, absorbed in a Spanish language telenovela, when they heard tires crunching on gravel. Esperanza jumped up when she heard two car doors slam in rapid succession. El Jefe never brought anyone with him to the house during the week. El Carcelero came in from his perpetual perch on the deck, stubbing out his cigarette against the door frame as he bared his teeth in a menacing grin.

"Looks like you've got a visitor," he said before slipping down the hall to the back door.

Esperanza heard a brief murmur of conversation before El Jefe opened the front door. Trailing right behind him was the man who had occupied so much of the sisters' thoughts and discussions during the last few weeks. Relief flooded through her. He'd come back! She glanced at her sister. Gloria's smile radiated a joy that should have been completely out of place given the circumstances. But Esperanza understood. Hope had been reborn.

"Ah, mis chicas guapas! You are a sight for sore eyes at the end of a long day," El Jefe said appreciatively. But his smile quickly faded as he looked them over from head to toe. A surge of alarm coursed through Esperanza. They were wearing jeans and T-shirts. Neither had on any makeup. He normally didn't care what they looked like when he visited them alone. But he always wanted them to look their best for the customers.

"Perhaps I should have told you I was coming, so that you could have made yourselves a little more presentable. But I bumped into our friend here unexpectedly and he insisted on joining me."

"I think they look wonderful," Jim said, smiling his hesitant, love-sick smile.

"Bah, mi amigo! As long as you are satisfied." El Jefe threw himself down on the couch and sighed heavily. "Esperanza, come here and help me forget my cares." He patted his lap.

Esperanza willed her reluctant legs to carry her towards her tormentor. When she sat down on his wide thigh, he wrapped his arms around her waist and pulled her face toward his. He left a trail of gentle kisses down her neck and across her collarbone. She tried to still her anxious breath as she waited for the rebuke she was sure would come. When he pinched her hard in the stomach, it was all she could do to keep from crying out.

"Make sure you don't embarrass me again by not being ready to receive guests," he whispered as he kissed her behind the ear. "You're lucky he's so besotted with your sister."

Esperanza followed El Jefe's gaze across the room to where Jim had sat down next to Gloria on the couch. He had taken her hand and was gazing into her face as he talked to her. It looked like he was telling her about his day. The teen was smiling encouragingly, looking at him as though she found every word fascinating. Esperanza smiled with a glimmer of satisfaction and relief to see her sister playing her part so well. But the performance only made her hatred for their captor burn that much hotter.

"Get me a drink, chica," El Jefe said as he stood up, pushing her off his lap. "And bring it back to your room."

Esperanza continued to watch her sister and her admirer while she uncorked a new bottle of wine and poured the garnet liquid into a bowl-like glass. Jim's long absence had apparently done nothing to dim his infatuation. Esperanza strained to hear their conversation.

"So it was a long day," he said. "And all I could think about was coming down here to see you."

Gloria smiled, fixing him with her luminous eyes.

"God, you are so beautiful," the man said, bringing her hand to his mouth and kissing it fervently. "A beautiful angel."

Esperanza didn't dare linger longer and risk El Jefe's wrath. As she walked down the hallway, she heard Jim say hesitantly, "Do you think we could..."

She shook her head in amazement at his almost gentlemanly manner. If she didn't know better, she might think they were courting. She hoped fervently her sister could convince him to rescue her.

When Esperanza opened the door to her room, El Jefe scowled up at her from the middle of her bed. He was propped up on her pillows, nestled under the covers. His clothes lay in a pile on the floor.

"What took you so long?" he barked. Esperanza flinched and he chuckled. "Don't worry, putita. I won't bite. Come here and make me forget all about it. You know how cranky I get when you keep me waiting."

~ ~ ~ ~ ~

El Jefe left, with Jim reluctantly in tow, several hours later. Esperanza waited until she heard the tires of their car crunching on the gravel drive before she knocked softly on her sister's door and slipped inside the room. Gloria sat on the chair in front of her dressing table, gazing into the mirror. Esperanza sat down slowly on the end of the bed, trying to read her sister's vacant expression. Had something gone wrong? She was starting to get really worried when Gloria met her eyes in the mirror.

"I think it just might work," she said, amazement reverberating through her hushed tones. "I told you I would try, but I didn't really believe I could do it."

Esperanza's heart started to thump with hope as Gloria swung around in her chair and fixed her wide, innocent eyes on her sister's face.

"You should have seen him! After he was finished, we lay in silence for a while. Then he asked me what I was thinking. I couldn't have asked for a better opportunity. I told him everything, just like we'd talked about."

Esperanza wanted to jump up and shout with relief. Could this really be the beginning of the end of her sister's torture?

"What did he say?"

"Nothing, for a long time. But he looked really worried. He frowned a lot. It scared me, and I finally asked him if he was mad at me." Gloria paused and shook her head at the memory. "He put his hand on my cheek and said, 'Never!' Can you believe it?"

Esperanza started to bounce up and down on the bed, her lips curling into an involuntary grin. This man was even more obsessed with her sister than she had imagined. Could it really be this easy?

"And? Then what?" she prompted.

"He said, 'I had no idea.' I really believed him. Is that stupid?"

"No. I'm sure El Jefe hasn't told the men how we got here or why we never leave. Not that most of them would care."

"Don't be mad, but I didn't ask him about paying off my debt and taking me with him. I didn't want to go too far, too fast."

"No, of course that's right. You do it when you think the time is right. Did he say why he hadn't been here in so long?"

"Yes, he said he'd been away on a business trip and then had some other things that kept him from coming. The way he said it made me think it was something with his family."

A shadow crossed over her sister's face and Esperanza wondered whether they were making a huge mistake. They were hanging their hope on a man who was unfaithful to his wife and regularly abandoned his family to spend time with a woman he paid for intimacy. He was not a man anyone should trust to keep his commitments.

But what choice did they have?

"There's something else." Gloria said. She tucked her fingers under the collar of her sweatshirt and pulled out a thin gold chain with a heart-shaped pendant floating on the end. "He gave me this. He said that's why he wanted to see me tonight. He bought it today and couldn't wait to give it to me."

Esperanza shook her head in amazement.

"I can't believe it went so smoothly," Gloria said. "Maybe it was too smooth." The teen rested her chin on her arm, draped over the back of the chair, and began chewing on her lower lip.

"No, no chula. Don't think like that. You did really, really well. Now we'll just have to wait and see. Did he say when he was coming back?"

"No. He just said he would see me soon. And he kissed me so tenderly... If he's always like this, I think I could easily learn to live with it. He's so different than the others."

Esperanza nodded but didn't say anything else as heavy footsteps came down the hall. She jumped when El Carcelero pounded on the bedroom door.

"Time for bed. Lights out. Now." His growl left no doubt that he would enforce his curfew with his fists if he needed to.

Esperanza sprang up, gave her sister a quick, tight hug, and slipped out the door.

Chapter 18

Two days later, Kate sat hunched over her desk, clicking the top of a ballpoint pen rhythmically as she stared at nothing. Every time she closed her eyes, she saw Miss Kitty's broken body. She refused to believe the woman killed herself. She had no evidence to prove otherwise, but a gnawing certainty in her gut told her Miss Kitty's death was just one piece of a much bigger puzzle. She couldn't figure out whether Johnson didn't want to see it or simply refused to because he didn't think he could do anything about it. No one in the police department or city hall wanted another unexplained dead body spoiling the idyllic summer. Either way, Johnson seemed content to let it go. Kate couldn't.

"What are you so morose for?" Delilah Peters asked, sauntering over to Kate's desk and stepping into her vacant stare. "Did you find out something about the layoffs the rest of us should know?"

Kate sighed as she looked up at her co-worker. The crows feet around her usually bright hazel eyes seemed to have deepened in the last few months. Fear over the newspaper's future weighed heavily on everyone. The never-ending budget haggling only made it worse. At this point, most of the reporters just wanted the axe to fall so the uncertainty would end.

"No, it's not that at all," Kate said. "I'm just trying to decide what to do about a story. At least I think it's a story."

"What does your gut tell you?"

"I'm sure there's a story there, I'm just not sure how to dig it out."

"Well, if it's a good story, it's worth pursuing. Any chance you'll get scooped on it? Is anyone else sniffing around?"

"No, it's not even on the radar. That's part of the problem. No one else seems to think it's a story."

"I would trust your gut before I would trust everyone else," Delilah said, smiling. "The best stories are the hardest to dig out. If it turns out to be a huge scoop, it might keep you from getting fired. If it's a bust, at least going after it will keep you distracted from this mess. It's a win-win situation."

"You're right," Kate said, grimacing. "I could use the distraction. Now I just have to figure out where to start."

Across the newsroom, Delilah's phone started to ring. "Start where you left off," she said as she scooped up the receiver and cradled it between her ear and her shoulder.

Kate thought about Miss Kitty again. She said she used to have a special arrangement with the management at The Clipper, until this new pimp came in and took over the territory. And Slava was convinced someone was running a good-sized prostitution ring out of the hotel. But that wasn't enough to start asking questions. She needed to see it for herself.

~ ~ ~ ~ ~

The lunch crowd at Franks had dwindled to just a few tables when Kate walked in and asked to speak to Slava.

"But you're too late for lunch and too early for dinner," the waiter said as he came out of the kitchen and walked around the long mahogany bar toward her, wiping his hands on a towel. "And where is the doctor?"

"I'm not here to eat. I came to ask you for a favor." A shiver of unease crawled up Kate's neck. She suddenly realized she could be dragging her friend into a dangerous situation.

"Favor from me?" Slava put his hand over his heart, eyes wide and forehead crinkled with genuine surprise. In his starched white shirt and crisp black pants, the effect was comical. Kate couldn't help but laugh.

"Yes, you. Remember what you told me last time we were here about the girls at the hotel where you're staying?"

"Ah, yes. Girls. Men. All night." Slava waved one hand in the air as though to say that told the whole story.

"I'd like to see them for myself. Do you think your friends would let me spend a few hours tomorrow night in their room? If I peek through the curtains I should be able to watch what's going on without being seen, right?"

Slava clasped his hands together in front of him and took a few steps closer. His wide eyes now gleamed with conspiratorial anticipation.

"Like stakeout?" he asked in a hushed whisper. "You want to make stakeout and catch these men?"

"Well, yeah, like a stakeout. But all I want to do is watch, for now. Then I'll have to figure out what to do once I have a better idea of what's going on."

"Okay, okay. Just watch now and write big story later." Slava's enthusiastic grin told Kate she had an ally.

"Something like that."

"Come tomorrow. Meet me here after dinner. We can go to the hotel and I'll introduce you to my friends."

"Don't you need to ask them first? Maybe they won't like it."

"I ask them. But they do it, because I ask. They're good girls."

"Thanks, Slava. I owe you, big time."

"No big time, big tip!" Slava laughed as he held the door open for her and waved goodbye.

~ ~ ~ ~ ~

Close to midnight the next day, Slava ushered Kate around the end of The Clipper farthest from the seawall. His room was around back and faced the alley that ran behind the building. About seven of the less-than-desirable rooms housed students visiting the island for the summer. Slava nodded to a few as they walked past, but they didn't stop to chat.

Four Ukrainian girls shared the only room occupied by students in the front of the hotel. Although they could see a slice of the pool and the beach beyond, the angle of the fence bordering the property cut off most of the view. That was probably why the manager set this room aside for the students. And while they had an obstructed view of the Gulf of Mexico, they had a full view of the rest of the hotel and the parking lot. Kate immediately understood why they noticed the unusual nighttime activity so easily.

The girl who opened the door had dark hair swept back into a ponytail and bright blue eyes accented with heavy black eyeliner. She motioned them inside and quickly shut the door to keep out the bugs swarming around the light outside. Three other girls sat or sprawled on the room's two double beds. The TV was on low and the bathroom's fluorescent light cast an institutional pall over the room. Empty yogurt cartons, soda cans, and pizza boxes littered the top of the dresser. Eyeshadow compacts, lipstick, brushes and perfume bottles covered the bathroom counter. Kate wondered what impressions of America the girls would take home with them after spending four months in a cramped and inhospitable hotel room.

"Anna, Iryna, Vira and Nataliya," Slava said, pointing to each girl in turn. "Ladies, this is Kate."

The girls smiled a little shyly and eyed Kate with open curiosity. She shifted uncomfortably and looked at Slava a little self-consciously.

"Good, okay. I leave you now. Anna take good care of you."

After Slava shut the door behind him, Anna motioned Kate to a round table by the window. She picked up a trashcan and swept empty styrofoam plates, cups and plastic containers into it. With what Kate took for an apologetic smile, Anna pointed her to a chair on the far side, next to the heavy orange curtain covering the window.

"If you sit there, you can look behind curtain and see whole hotel."

"Thanks. I really appreciate you letting me borrow your window," Kate said, the awkward situation adding to her unease.

"No problem. Slava say you catch bad men. Good."

"We'll see," Kate said, smiling at Slava's assurance. "I just want to watch for tonight to see what's going on.

"No problem. You watch. You see."

Kate leaned to her right and rested her head against the wall, peering around the edge of the curtain to look along the length of the sidewalk fronting the long wing of the hotel. She had a clear view of both floors of the L-shaped building's shorter wing, about 30 yards away. A halo of light edged almost all the windows. Nearly full occupancy on a weeknight, even in the summer, wasn't bad. Of course, the hotel offered pretty cheap rates.

To her left, the girls picked up whatever they had been doing before Kate and Slava came in. Vira, who had a spiky crop of bleached blonde hair, turned up the volume on the TV and laid down on the bed closest to Kate, her head resting on a stack of pillows near the end. Iryna and

Nataliya, perched on the other bed, picked up their interrupted conversation. Anna walked to the bathroom and started to wash her face.

While she kept most of her attention focused on the widow, Kate stole glances into the room every few minutes or so. No matter which way she looked, she was on the outside looking in on someone else's life. The girls pretended she wasn't there, not even bothering to retreat to the bathroom when they stripped off their work clothes and wiggled into shorts and T-shirts as they got ready for bed. Kate had never felt more invisible.

On the outside, she watched a couple ride up on a motorcycle, a six-pack of beer sandwiched between them. Kate couldn't hear what they were saying, but she could guess at the gist, based on the way the woman pressed up against her companion and he slapped her wide butt. They disappeared into a room a few doors down. Another couple drove up about 15 minutes later. Judging by their stoney faces and the distance they kept between them, they weren't having a good night.

After that, no one stirred in the parking lot or along the open corridors for another hour. Kate's mind wandered over the events of the last few months. So many unexplained, seemingly unconnected events. She traced a line between the murders of Julian Costa and the unidentified girl in Fish Village, Miss Kitty and the new prostitution ring. Over all hung the mystery of the mayor's sudden cozy relationship with the police union. She ran over the details of each case again and again until they blurred into a single, nonsensical plot. Behind her, all of the girls except for Vira had climbed under the covers and settled in for the night.

By 1:30 a.m., Kate was about to give up and go home, concluding this new prostitution ring was a figment of several overactive imaginations, when a lone man emerged from the stairwell at the far end of the hotel's second story and knocked at the first door. Almost immediately, it opened a crack. The visitor went inside and the door closed. A few minutes later, a different man emerged, closed the door behind him and wandered to the end of the walkway. He lit a cigarette and leaned against the railing.

A shot of adrenaline streaked through Kate's chest. She sat up straight and pressed her cheek into the wall at the edge of the window. She put a hand over her mouth as though from that far away the man might hear her breathing.

"What is it?" she heard one of the girls whisper.

Glancing quickly inside the room, Kate saw Vira looking intently at her from the edge of the bed, her pale face framed by the glow of the TV. In a low voice, Kate briefly explained what she had seen, her eyes darting back every few seconds to the man with the steadily glowing cigarette. Vira nodded knowingly.

"That's what we see too, almost every night."

"Does it always start this late?"

Vira nodded, switched off the TV and came to stand behind Kate at the window.

"First customer of the night. Busy now, until dawn."

"How long has this been going on?"

Vira shrugged as she moved back around to her side of the bed and climbed under the covers.

"Three weeks."

About 15 minutes after he arrived, the visitor came out of the room and walked up to the man at the railing. He handed him something and headed back down the stairs. As the first man took one last drag on his cigarette, he glanced at whatever was in his hand and stuffed it in his pocket. After dropping the cigarette butt and grinding it out with his foot, he stepped back into the room.

For the next four hours, the routine repeated with a dozen other men. The visitors never stayed outside for more than a few minutes, either coming or going. Some went into the first room. The pimp took others to one of three rooms down the landing. Each time a door opened, Kate tried to catch a glimpse of what was inside. But all she could see was the soft yellow glow of a muted light.

The last customer came at about 5:30 a.m. Kate wondered sleepily whether he was on his way to work or just getting off his shift. When no one else appeared, her heavy eyes slowly closed and she drifted into a dreamless sleep, her cheek still pressed against the wall.

She woke with a start 45 minutes later when the girls' alarm clock erupted with an incessant beeping. Disoriented, Kate sat up and rubbed her eyes. It took her a minute to remember where she was. On the bed closest to her,

Anna sat up and stretched, slapping the snooze button with annoyance.

"Busy night?" she asked, her voice still thick with sleep.

Kate nodded. "Thirteen men."

"That's bad. Very bad. Now you write story."

"Now at least I know it's really happening," Kate said, smiling sleepily but with muted satisfaction. "I have to talk to my editor about a story."

"He want story," Anna insisted. "Is good story."

"I hope so," Kate said. Determination to convince Lewis drove away the last of her cloying sleepiness. "I really hope so."

Chapter 19

The horizon glowed faintly when Kate left the girls and walked quickly to her car, parked in the back of the hotel near Slava's room. She didn't see anyone and hoped no one saw her. She had slowly begun to realize during the long hours of her night watch that she was dealing with a very dangerous situation. If Miss Kitty had been murdered because someone saw her talking to a reporter, knowing she could reveal at least some details about the prostitution ring, the person or people running the show would do anything to keep their operation a secret. Kate thought about Miss Kitty's broken body crowning the granite boulders and the cigarette-smoking man who waited for the girls to turn their tricks so he could take the johns' money. Was he at the top of the food chain or was someone else giving him orders? Either way, Kate wouldn't want to run into him alone on some side street.

She managed to stay awake long enough to drive back to her building and trudge up the stairs to her apartment. But as soon as she collapsed into bed, she fell instantly asleep.

Three hours later, she groaned when the alarm beeped. She could use at least two more hours of sleep, but she needed to get to the office and tell Lewis what she'd discovered. She wished she could just run with a story for tomorrow's paper, but she didn't have enough information. The challenge would be finding out more without tipping off the pimp or his bosses that she knew what they were up to. She also had to consider how far she wanted to go before telling the police what she'd seen. If the chief decided to move forward with a sting and a bust, despite the mayor's request, she would be left with another run-of-the-mill prostitution round-up story. As it stood, she had enough to say the police had ignored complaints about the operation. But could she prove the mayor was behind the curtailed prostitution investigations?

~ ~ ~ ~ ~

Kate stood in the doorway to Hunter Lewis's office for almost a minute before the news editor stopped his frenetic typing and looked up at her over his laptop screen and his horn-rimmed glasses. He always spent Wednesday mornings working on his weekly editorial. He hated to be interrupted.

"Sorry, but I need to run something past you. It can't wait."

"Five minutes," Lewis said, pulling off his glasses, leaning back in his chair and lacing his fingers behind his head.

As briefly as she could, Kate told him what she had discovered, starting with the claims made by the mamasan Johnson's team busted a month ago and ending with what she'd seen early that morning. By the time she got to Slava's claims about the police ignoring his reports, Lewis was leaning forward over his desk, staring at her intently.

"Why not just take this to the police?" he asked when she was done. "Just ask Johnson why they haven't done anything about it."

"Well, that's the thing. I know why they haven't done anything about it, but I don't have it verified on the record. After the mayor inked his new pay-raise deal with the police union, Johnson told me he met with the police chief, who then called the detectives in for a private pow-wow. The mayor asked them to put any more prostitution stings on hold until after the summer and fall festival seasons are over. He told them all the news about recent criminal activity, even if it involved getting offenders off the streets, didn't make Galveston look like the safest place to visit."

Lewis leaned back in his chair again and let out a low whistle. "So, what we've got here is a scheme to gloss over criminal activity just to please the Convention and Visitors Bureau."

"At the very least, yes," Kate nodded. "But there's something else. I rode my bike past The Clipper on Sunday afternoon, just to get a sense of the place, and I bumped into that homeless woman who died later that night. She said the same thing about the prostitution ring.

Anyone could have seen her talking to me. The police say they have no evidence she didn't jump, or fall, off the seawall. But what if she was pushed? What if someone didn't want her talking to a newspaper reporter?"

Lewis crossed his arms on the desk and chewed on his bottom lip before answering. "Did you mention that to Johnson?"

"Yeah, but he thought it was a little far-fetched. Both he and the coroner said they found no evidence of foul play. And with two unsolved murders already on the books, Johnson's not eager to take on a third. Without any evidence, there's no reason to suspect it wasn't just a co-incidence that she talked to me that afternoon. I just have a hard time believing that."

"Well, we can't print something just because you be-lieve it's true. Once all this comes out, you can ask about it again, but if we still don't have any evidence that points to a murder, that's not part of this story. You'll just have to drop it."

Kate shifted uncomfortably in her chair and let her eyes wander over the journalism award plaques covering the wall behind Lewis' desk. He was right, but letting it go amounted to saying she didn't care about what hap-pened to someone who didn't deserve to die, whether by her own hand or otherwise.

"So, what do I do now?" she finally asked when Lewis didn't say anything else.

"First, you need to talk to your buddy Johnson and see if you can persuade him to go on the record about that meeting with the chief and the mayor."

Kate cringed when she thought about her last exchange with Johnson on Sunday night. She wasn't even sure he would want to talk to her, let alone cooperate for a story that might get him in trouble.

"Then, you've got a city council meeting to cover tomorrow, right? Why don't you just ask the mayor whether he's heard any complaints about a prostitution ring running out of a seawall hotel. See how he reacts and what he says. And go back and talk to those girls at the hotel. Get them to tell you what they've seen and how long it's been going on. That, combined with your own observations will be enough to tie the story together."

"Don't we need to give the chief a chance to comment?"

"Yes, but I want that to be the last thing you do. Let's see if we can prove he's not doing his job at the mayor's request. Then we'll see what he says about that. If you show your hand too soon, he could just order a bust. That would leave you with no story at all."

~ ~ ~ ~ ~

Kate spent the rest of the day writing a piece for the next day's paper previewing the council meeting. The budget vote wasn't scheduled for another week, so the only interesting thing on the agenda involved a discussion about where to spend the reduced infrastructure improvement funds. Neighborhood groups were vying for money to fix their potholes and leaky water lines. It would make for good public theater, the kind of thing Kate normally reveled in covering. But nothing except the prostitution story could hold her attention now.

She called and left messages for Johnson twice that afternoon. When he didn't call her back, she began to lose some of her nerve. He obviously didn't want to talk to her. She'd never convince him to risk his job to give up the police chief and the mayor. She thought about sending him an email apology and begging him to see her, but she knew he would instantly see her apology wasn't sincere. She refused to grovel just to get information, even though she knew her parting jab on Sunday had been a low blow. And probably unfair. But she wasn't sorry for pleading a dead woman's case.

In the end, she decided to appeal to Johnson's sense of justice.

~ ~ ~ ~ ~

The next afternoon, about an hour before the city council meeting, she called the police department receptionist to make sure Johnson was at the station. When she walked through the front door, her co-conspirator behind the front desk buzzed her back without asking any questions. Johnson was sitting at this desk reading through reports. She sat down in one of the chairs across from him before he had a chance to tell her not to.

"Look, I know you don't want to see me, but I have something you need to hear."

Johnson didn't stop her when she paused to take a breath, so she plunged ahead.

"Someone I know who's staying at The Clipper told me about some suspicious nighttime activity that matches what we've already heard about. I went there the other night to see for myself. Thirteen men stopped by four rooms between 1:30 a.m. and 5:30 a.m. for about 15 minutes each. They weren't delivering pizza."

Kate smiled weakly at her attempted joke. Johnson didn't smile, but he was watching her intently.

"I'm working on a story, and I need to know whether you can tell me anything about the lack of prostitution stings in the last month. My friend at the hotel claims he's called to report all the after-hours traffic, but no one's looked into it, as far as he knows. I want to know why."

Johnson pursed his lips and looked at her through narrowed lids. Kate held her breath.

"Give me time to think," he finally said. "I'll call you."

Kate exhaled in a rush and nodded. Maybe she hadn't alienated him forever. Standing to go, she met his eyes one last time. She doubted she could convey her appreciation with just a look, but she hoped he could read a "thank you" somewhere in her steady gaze. When he pulled up one corner of his mouth in a lopsided, if slightly anemic smile, she figured he'd gotten the message. She flashed him a brief smile of her own before turning and walking out the door.

~ ~ ~ ~ ~

The council meeting dragged on more than usual as Kate watched the minutes tick by on the clock in the corner of her laptop screen. She fidgeted in her chair, tapped her fingers impatiently on the table when she wasn't typing and tried unsuccessfully to focus on what the pleading homeowners had to say about the projects in their neighborhoods that needed to get done in the next year. Kate was pretty sure they all needed to be done, and might have if the mayor hadn't caved on the police pay raises. But now that the council members had to balance the budget on the backs of other departments, they only had enough money to fund the most pressing projects. Old women came to the microphone to bemoan potholes they didn't see until it was too late and they had a flat tire. Parents held up pictures of dilapidated playground equipment they feared might collapse under their children. At least a dozen people complained about frequent flash flooding caused by a drainage system clogged by decades of trash and sand.

An hour and a half after the public comment session started, Mayor Matthew Hanes gaveled the meeting into a 15 minute recess. Kate willed herself not to approach him right away, watching instead as he worked his way through the crowd. She followed him toward the back of the room at a discreet distance while he shook hands and held court. Everyone seemed to have something to say to him. When he finally pushed through the back door and into the quiet foyer between the council chamber and his office suite, Kate was right behind him.

"Mayor Hanes, do you have a minute?"

Kate thought she saw the mayor heave a frustrated sigh, but when he turned to face her, his normally diplomatic smile plastered his face.

"Of course. What can I do for you Miss Bennett? I only have a few minutes before we need to head back."

"This won't take long. I just wanted to ask you whether you've heard any complaints in the last few weeks about a prostitution ring operating out of one of the hotels on the seawall."

Hanes took a step back, his smile melting.

"No, I haven't. And I'm sure I would have if something were going on. People are hardly shy about complaining, as you know. Why do you ask?"

"Well, we've gotten a few phone calls at the paper, and I was just wondering whether you were hearing the same thing we were."

Hanes, who had at first looked annoyed by her questions, now placed his hands on his hips, dropped them to his sides and finally crossed his arms in front of his chest. He pressed his lips together and frowned before answering.

"I haven't heard a thing. And I'm sure I would have, if anything were going on. For one thing, the police chief would have told me. He keeps me apprised, you know."

"Well, I suppose he may not know. I had heard the police were focusing on other things this summer."

"What other things?" he said sharply.

Kate shrugged.

"I assure you I have no idea what you're talking about," Hanes said, backing toward his office. "The police are tasked with keeping this island safe, and they are doing a damn good job of it, as far as I can tell. But of course we need to address people's concerns. I can promise you I will look into it. Now if you'll excuse me..."

Kate didn't bother trying to stop him. She doubted he would give her anything useful at this point anyway. She couldn't tell whether he had heard about the prostitutes on the seawall, but he definitely didn't like the suggestion that the police might not be doing their job.

By the end of the 15 minute recess, all of the city council members had returned to their seats. But the mayor, normally a stickler for staying on schedule, hadn't returned. Five minutes later, he yanked open the back door to the chamber and strode up the aisle. He'd ditched his suit coat, his tie was loose and his hair looked mussed, like he'd been running his fingers through it. He banged the gavel down with unnecessary force, startling several people in the audience.

"Ladies and gentlemen, my apologies. I had to make a phone call that took longer than expected. I did not mean to keep you waiting. Next agenda item, please, madam secretary."

A phone call.

While the city secretary read the next item on the agenda in her usual monotone, Kate's head spun with possibilities of who the mayor might have called. Whomever he'd talked to, it didn't look like the conversation had gone the way he wanted. He hadn't acted like he'd been on his way to make an important phone call when Kate caught up with him in the foyer. Did that call have anything to do with what she'd told him? If so, the police chief seemed like the most likely candidate. And if he'd told the chief to send some officers over to the hotel to check things out, Kate could kiss her big story goodbye.

She hadn't planned to go back to the hotel until the next night. But if she had any hope of getting ahead of a police raid, she had to go now.

Chapter 20

As soon as the meeting ended, Kate stuffed her laptop into her bag and dashed to her car. While she drove toward The Clipper, she punched Johnson's number into her cell phone. She would tell him what she knew in hopes he would let her know if the chief ordered some kind of surveillance. If the police saw what she'd seen, they'd move in right away to make arrests.

She got his voicemail.

"Hey. It's Kate. I'm just leaving the council meeting. I asked the mayor a few questions about the hotel, just to get his reaction. He said he'd never heard anything about it. But after we talked, he went and made a phone call that made him late to rejoin the meeting after the recess. He looked really flustered. I think he might have called the chief to tell him to have you guys check it out. If you hear anything, can you call me? Please?"

Kate parked in the same spot she'd used the night before, near Slava's room. She cursed softly as she looked down the passageway to the front of the hotel. It hadn't seemed so dark with the confident Ukrainian by her side.

A tremor of fear rumbled through her. She shook it off and snorted derisively. "Chicken. What are you scared of?"

With one more shake of her head, Kate opened the car door and grabbed her notebook out of her laptop bag. As she slammed the door closed, the dense night air swallowed the dull thud. Kate took a deep breath and strode toward the walkway that skirted the side of the building and led to the front of the hotel. Her heart hammered in her ears. Each shallow, rapid breath puffed into the abyss in front of her. Her determined walk quickened to a slow jog. After about fifteen steps, she could see the light outside Slava's friends' room glowing faintly ahead. She sighed out a low laugh and slowed her pace.

"Nothing to be afraid of," she told herself as she prepared to round the corner.

The blow came from her right. She never saw a thing. It knocked her into the building, the rough concrete tearing into her shoulder. The air rushed out of her lungs as strong hands grasped her elbows and pinned her arms behind her back, pressing her face-first into the wall.

"Are you sure about that, chica?"

Terror burst through her stunned surprise. She yelped. The man grabbed her hair and slammed her head into the wall. A starburst of pain radiated across her forehead. She gasped and whimpered.

"Silencio! Don't make a sound or you'll regret it."

The tang of stale cigarettes clung to every word he spat in her face. Kate's stomach heaved. The man pressed himself up against her, sliding his hand down her side and squeezing her butt. When she tried to struggle, he tightened his grip.

"Feisty. Mmmmm... Me gusta!" He gyrated against her.

Fear surged in her chest. Why hadn't she called Slava to tell him she was coming? Despair constricted her heart. No one knew where she was.

"Too bad I don't have more time. We could have some fun, no?

Blood pulsed across her temples. Her head throbbed. She tried to twist her arms free. He tightened his vice grip on her wrists, crushing them together.

"Be still or I'll break your arms."

Kate stopped struggling and closed her eyes against the nausea burning up her throat.

"You been sniffing around. My boss don't like it. If you know what's good for you, you'll stop. Got it? You and your little friends."

The pimp! Kate's eyes flew open when she realized who her attacker was. How did he know about her investigation?

"Got it?" He pressed her harder into the wall, scraping her face on the stucco.

Kate nodded once, clenching her teeth as she felt a warm trickle make its way down her cheek.

"Bueno, chica. Bueno. You don't want to see me again, no?" He made a clicking noise and squeezed her butt again.

When he loosened his grip, relief flooded through her. But before she could turn around, he punched her in the back, just below her rib cage. She gasped as a sharp pain knifed through her. Her head swam. She only had a vague sense of his retreating footsteps as she crumpled to her knees.

Black spots obscured her vision and she retched, coughing and gagging against the pain.

She took a few ragged gasps and tried to stand. But her legs trembled uncontrollably. She fell back against the wall.

"Help!" She wailed, helplessness lashing her to the ground. "Somebody help!"

A door scraped in the distance.

"Did you hear that? Where did it come from?" Kate recognized Anna's clipped accent.

"Here! I'm here."

Tears of relief filled Kate's eyes when Anna burst around the corner with Vira right behind her.

"My God!" Anna rushed to her side and knelt down. "What happened?"

"The pimp..." Kate rasped. "He came out of nowhere."

"Call 9-1-1," Anna said over her shoulder to Vira, who spun around and ran back toward their room.

Kate's side ached with every breath. She grimaced and Anna reached out and squeezed her hand.

"Is okay. They be here soon."

Kate nodded and tried to take a deep breath. Anna and the scene behind her pitched and rolled. Kate closed her eyes and struggled against the waves of dizziness paralyzing her mind.

"How bad he hurt you?" Anna whispered. "Did he..."

She didn't need to finish. Kate knew exactly what she was asking. Every woman's worst nightmare. She shook her head.

"Thank God! The rest will heal."

Kate smiled weakly. As her fear subsided, some of the pain did too. Anna squeezed her hand again. Vira reappeared carrying a bottle of water. Kate took it gratefully and brought it shakily to her lips.

"I call Slava too. He be here soon."

Kate groaned, suddenly realizing the amount of attention she was about to endure. She was the story now, a reversal of roles no reporter wanted. Sirens wailed in the distance.

~ ~ ~ ~ ~

Johnson bounded down his front steps and yanked open the door of his cruiser. He rarely used his siren but he flipped it on as he gunned the engine and headed toward The Clipper. He'd just finished listening to Kate's voicemail when he heard the call go out over the scanner. The dispatcher said a woman had been attacked. But she didn't say how bad.

Dread filled his chest with every breath. Based on what Kate told him earlier that afternoon, it seemed likely the victim was a prostitute. But he couldn't shake the nagging fear Kate had returned to the hotel to finish her reporting. What had she gotten herself into?

When he pulled into the parking lot, red and blue lights already strobed off the hotel's dingy facade. Guests had started to gather outside their doors to see what was going on. Another officer stood outside the last room on the bottom floor, talking to three young women. Johnson was headed toward them when he saw one of the paramedics round the corner.

"Detective," the man said with a nod. "Looks like the local media's tired of just reporting the news. They're trying to make it now."

Johnson flinched, the medic's words hit him like a sucker punch to the back of the head. Fear spiked up his spine and circled his neck in an invisible choke hold. For a moment he couldn't breathe. All he could do was stare at the man in front of him.

"She's pretty banged up, but I don't think it's anything serious," the medic continued. "She'll get an interesting story out of it, that's for sure."

Johnson's breath burst through his lips in a rush. *She was going to be okay.*

"Can I talk to her?"

"Go right ahead. She was a little woozy when we first got here, but she's starting to snap out of it. I'm just going to get the stretcher. She said she didn't want to go to the hospital, but I'm not giving her a choice. I think she at least needs a CT scan."

Johnson's brow furrowed with renewed worry. He walked past the officer interviewing the three women, giving only a short wave before stepping into the dark passageway. His stomach dropped when he saw Kate sitting on the ground, the other medic kneeling beside her. To the side, a woman and man stood watching.

"Ouch!" Kate said as the medic applied a gauze pad to her bloodied forehead.

"Gotta get it cleaned out," the medic said firmly.

Kate winced again and glanced up. Johnson caught her eye and smiled, then shook his head. Relief seeped from his head to his toes in a flood of warmth. She looked like she'd gone a round with Galveston-born boxing legend Jack Johnson, but she was alive. The tension that had cinched his neck and shoulder muscles when he heard the call go out over the scanner started to ease.

Kate grimaced. "If you're about to lecture me about safety, now's not a good time."

"No lecture. Not yet anyway." He squatted down next to her. "I'm just relieved it's not worse."

"Yeah..." She met his eye and then quickly looked away, but it was long enough for him to see her lingering fear.

"Want to tell me what happened before they whisk you off to the hospital?"

"I told them I don't need to go! Will you back me up on this? I need to be here so we can go over everything, and I can get interviews for my story."

"The story can wait," Johnson said, exasperation making his words a bit more forceful than he intended. "I think you've still got the exclusive here."

Kate rolled her eyes.

"So, what happened?"

"Some guy ambushed me as I was walking around the end of the hotel on my way to Anna's room." Kate glanced up at the young woman standing nearby, her arms crossed and her forehead creased with worry. "He told me his boss didn't like me sniffing around their operation. He said I'd better stop or I'd regret it. That's it."

A flash of anger blurred his vision. If he'd taken Kate's tip more seriously, staked out the hotel himself, she wouldn't be sitting there in a crumpled, bloodied heap.

"I hear her calling for help," Anna broke in. "That's how we find her. When Vira go to call police, she see man dragging girls out of rooms at end of hall. Four of them. They leave in a hurry."

"Did you get a look at his face?"

"No. Is too far," Anna said. "Too dark."

He looked down again at Kate. Under the bandage on her forehead, her eyes flashed with determination.

"Did you get a look at him?"

Kate shook her head. "He was behind me the whole time."

"What about his voice? Did it sound familiar?"

"No. I'm pretty sure I've never met him before. About all I can tell you is that he stank like stale cigarettes. Big help, huh?"

"It's alright. You're doing great."

Before he could ask another question, the medic pressed something to Kate's tattered shoulder. Her eyes bulged and her mouth formed a silent "Oh!" of surprise and pain. Johnson winced in sympathy.

The man standing next to Anna made a disapproving clicking noise. "This would not happen if you investigate when we call you."

Johnson's cheeks flushed. The guy was probably right, but that didn't make it any easier to hear.

"That's Slava," Kate said through gritted teeth. "Slava, this is Detective Peter Johnson. He's one of the good guys."

Johnson smiled. Slava snorted.

"They can tell you about as much as I can about what was going on here," Kate continued. "Slava's the one who told me about it in the first place. I'm sure the guy who attacked me is the pimp. I have no idea how he found out I was watching him."

A kernel of worry lodged in Johnson's gut. Something wasn't right. How did the pimp know Kate would be there?

"Maybe he saw you leave the other day. Maybe he's got someone keeping watch. We'll talk to the other guests and see if anyone saw anything."

"And the manager," Kate said. "He's got to know something. There's no way he didn't know all this was going on right under his nose."

Johnson nodded and stood up. The first medic had returned with the stretcher.

"Time to go," he said. "The sooner we get you to the hospital, the sooner you can get out."

Kate rolled her eyes again. "Fine. But I'm calling Doug Cowel so he can get over here and get some photos."

"Kate..." Johnson started to protest.

"What? You're going to get into those rooms, aren't you? There's got to be evidence in there!"

Johnson hesitated. The police chief wouldn't like it. But he had ample cause to search those rooms. And if he didn't, he had no chance of catching Kate's attacker. He refused to sacrifice that opportunity to the mayor's public relations campaign.

"Of course I am," he said.

Kate grinned as the medics strapped her onto the stretcher.

"This is going to be a good story. And it needs photos." She pulled her cellphone out of her back pocket. "I'll be back as soon as I get the all-clear. I'll expect a full, on-the-record accounting of everything you find."

Johnson shook his head and chuckled. When Kate disappeared around the corner, he turned to Anna and Slava.

"Can you guys tell me when all this started?"

"About three weeks ago," Anna said. "One night we stay out late, me and my roommates. When we come home, we saw man knock on door closest to stairwell and go in. Another man come out. About 15 minutes later,

Slava come to check on us, to make sure we get home okay. While I talk to him outside, I see man come out of room and go down stairs. I thought it strange. How you say? Suspicious. So I went back inside and watched out our window. Men come all night."

"When Anna tell me this, I say we must call the police," Slava jumped in. "America is civilized country. I think, police will not let this happen. But after I call, no one come. So, I call again. Still, no one come. After that, I say, the police are not interested. And I stop calling."

"But the men keep coming," Anna said. "It's like that almost every night."

"Why you no come investigate?" Slava demanded, his voice rising. "If you come investigate, Kate would not be at hospital right now."

Johnson sighed. "I know. And if I'd known about it sooner, I would have investigated. But I just found out about it this afternoon."

"But we call!"

"I know, I know. And I'm going to find out why no one responded. I don't have an answer for you right now. But I will get one."

"Da," Slava huffed. "Police in Ukraine ignore stuff like this all the time. You know why? Corruption. Some-one always using police to hide their crimes. We thought America different. Is no different."

Johnson gritted his teeth in frustration. Corruption? The police chief called off the prostitution task force to avoid bad press. It was a bad policy decision, but until now, Johnson thought that was all there was to it. The mayor didn't want to scare visitors away at the height of tourism season. But now he wasn't so sure. Was there more at stake than protecting the island's family-friendly image?

Chapter 21

Kate cringed as the medics wheeled her into the emergency room. The bright lights stabbed her eyes, making her head throb.

"Twenty-six-year-old female, with lacerations to her head and shoulder," the medic said to the nurse who met them. "She's also got a contusion to the back and one to the head. Possible concussion."

"All right. Let's get you checked out." With a bright smile, the woman led them around the central desk to the patient areas partitioned with light blue curtains. Kate closed her eyes and willed them to move faster. What were the chances she could get in and out without being spotted by someone she knew?

"Kate?" Her eyes popped at the sound of Brian's familiar voice, laced with worry. "What happened?"

"Hey." She smiled weakly. Her cheeks flushed with embarrassment. She'd forgotten he would be at work that night. "Would you believe I tripped and fell?"

"No, I wouldn't." He crossed his arms and scowled.

The nurse looked uncertainly between the two of them.

"I'll get Dr. Simon," Brian said.

When he walked away, the nurse raised an eyebrow at Kate.

"You two know each other?" she asked as she pulled a blood pressure cuff from it's holder on the wall.

"Something like that."

The nurse didn't say anything else as she took Kate's vital signs and typed notes into the computer next to the bed.

"Okay. The doctor will be here in just a minute."

Kate nodded as the nurse disappeared behind the curtain. A few moments later, Brian ducked inside the fabric partition. Furrows of concern creased the space between his eyes. He pressed his lips together as he looked down at her. Irritation needled the back of her neck. She didn't want him to make a big deal about it.

"What happened?"

"I went back to the hotel to interview Slava and his friends, and the pimp ambushed me. I have no idea how he knew I was on to them. Anyway, it looks worse than it is." She glanced at her shoulder. "It's just a few scratches really."

"A few scratches? I think it's a little more serious than that."

"It's not. Really, I'm fine. It's not a big deal."

"Kate, he could have killed you."

She sighed. The terror she felt during and immediately after the attack had faded. Brian was right, but she didn't want to think about how much danger she'd really been in.

"He wasn't trying to kill me, just deliver a warning."

"Which I'm sure you won't heed."

Kate gritted her teeth. "I'm just doing my job, okay? I wasn't trying to get attacked."

"I'm pretty sure your job does not include taking unnecessary risks."

"Don't tell me how to do my job."

"I just want you to be more careful." He took her hand and looked at her intently, his eyes searched her face. "You're... I..."

The curtain around the bed rustled. On the other side, the nurse rattled off the basics of Kate's injuries.

Brian sighed. Leaning over her, he pressed his lips firmly to the uninjured side of her forehead. Then he turned away without saying another word and held the curtain open for the other doctor. Kate stared after him as he disappeared behind a veil of blue.

She was pretty sure she knew what he was about to say. He'd been dancing around it for weeks. He was forcing her to make a decision. If she couldn't love him back, she'd have to let him go.

~ ~ ~ ~ ~

Almost three hours later, Kate walked through the emergency room doors to a waiting taxi. Dr. Simon had cleared her to leave but warned her to watch for signs of a concussion. Thankfully none of her cuts required stitches.

She'd talked briefly to Brian before leaving. But everything unsaid between them choked out all but the most basic conversation. She finally told him she'd call later.

When the taxi dropped her off outside the hotel at 2:45 a.m., Kate counted five cop cars in the parking lot. People still thronged the landings on both floors. The doors of all four rooms once occupied by the prostitutes stood open. Doug Cowel had staked out a spot behind one of the police cruisers, shooting with a long lens into one of the open rooms. When Kate walked up behind him, she could see why he chose that angle. The light pouring out of the door into the darkness perfectly illuminated two officers digging with gloved hands through the trash can.

When he turned around, the photographer let out a low whistle. "That is gonna hurt in the morning. I called Lewis on my way over here and told him what happened. He's pretty worried. I told him it sounded like you were going to make it, but I think he was momentarily gripped by the terrifying prospect of having to replace you."

"Whatever," Kate huffed. "That would just save them from having to fire someone."

Cowel grinned. "Seriously, you should call him when it gets a bit later, let him know you're alive."

"I will. I've got to tie up all the loose ends here first. What'd I miss?"

"Lots of interviews and evidence bagging. Looks like they got some good stuff from those rooms. And they hauled someone away in handcuffs. I think it was the manager."

"I hope they put the screws to him," Kate said, finger-ing the bandage on her forehead. "There's no way he was clueless about all this."

"You should go find Johnson. He keeps asking whether I've heard from you. He was over that way when I last saw him." Cowel jerked his head to the left, toward the opposite end of the hotel.

As she made her way around the fenced-in pool, Kate spotted the detective talking to a group of other officers. She hung back until he was done. When he turned around and saw her, she couldn't resist flashing a triumphant grin.

"I told you I'd be back."

"You should be home, in bed. There's nothing here that can't wait until morning."

"And miss all the excitement? Not a chance. Besides, I had to get my car."

Johnson shook his head. "Right. Your car. I suppose you want an update on what we found?"

"You bet."

"Well, it's obvious what was going on here. We've found used condoms in the trash cans, and the sheets in one of the rooms are gone. So much for housekeeping. Other guests said they noticed the same suspicious activi-ty you did. But your young Ukrainian friends are the only ones who said they called the police. I think you know just about everything else."

"What about the manager?"

"He claims he knew nothing and saw nothing. He said the people who rented those rooms paid in cash, one week at a time. When we asked him if it was the same people each time, he said, 'No. I don't know. No.' Then he said he wouldn't say anything else without his lawyer."

"He has a lawyer?"

"Evidently. He's obviously lying. He had to have known what was going on. There's no way to get up those steps without walking past his office. But if he continues to play dumb, I don't know that we'll be able to charge him with anything. We need someone to come forward and give us evidence that he was cooperating with the pimp, but I doubt that's going to happen."

Kate thought fleetingly about Miss Kitty.

"I need an official response about why you guys didn't respond to the calls."

Johnson paused for so long Kate thought he wasn't going to answer.

"I think I'd better let the chief handle that one," he finally said, turning to look her in the eye. "But if I were you, I would ask him why the prostitution task force members have been assigned to other projects for the last month when they seemed to be on such a roll after the last sting operation."

"That's the best you can do?"

Pressing his lips together in a thin line, Johnson nodded. "For now, it is. I'm sorry."

Kate tapped her pen on her notepad and contemplated whether she should play the guilt card to try to goad him into saying more. Johnson had a keen sense of right and wrong. If he thought someone in the department was covering up illegal activity, especially after she was attacked, he would expose them, even if it meant losing his job.

"It doesn't bother you that the mayor's request, or order, or whatever it was, made all of this possible?"

"It does! Especially after what happened to you. I just haven't figured out yet whether that was his intention. I don't think it was. He just wants to keep tourism up as much as possible. That might be short-sighted and naive —"

"And shady and self-serving—"

"But it's not criminal."

"There's not a little part of you that thinks this is all a bit too tidy?"

Johnson sighed. "Yes. But I learned long ago not to trust my gut exclusively. I have to have evidence to back up my suspicions. I have absolutely no evidence that anything more than poor decisions was at work here."

"Did the chief call anyone after the mayor called him during the council meeting?"

"Not that I know of. If he did, I never heard about it. We're only here tonight because you got attacked. The lieutenant said he would call the chief himself when it got a little closer to 6 a.m. I'm sure he'll stop by shortly after that. You can ask him yourself when he gets here."

Kate rolled her eyes.

"You know, it's entirely possible the mayor's phone call had nothing to do with what you asked him," Johnson said. "Or, maybe it did but he called someone else. Maybe the city's PR flak?"

That was possible, of course. But why would he come back to the meeting looking so flustered? Kate sighed.

"Anything's possible," she said. "But in the absence of evidence, I tend to lean toward what's probable."

"Well, just be careful. Even what's probable can turn out to be wrong. I've got to go check on my guys. You should really go home. But I suppose you're going to stick around to talk to the chief?"

"Do you really need to ask?"

Kate spent the next hour interviewing other hotel guests and watching investigators pack evidence into paper bags. By 4:30 a.m., she could barely keep her eyes open. Deciding she could risk missing the chief's arrival, she drove down the seawall to a coffee shop that had just opened. The barista looked as bleary eyed as Kate felt, but she managed to concoct a vanilla latte with two extra shots of espresso and bag three of the gooiest looking pastries in the case. Kate figured the sugar and caffeine would counteract the drowsiness of the pain meds and keep her coherent until at least 9 a.m.

She drove back to the hotel parking lot and sat in her car with the windows down, eating her breakfast while the damp morning air coated the inside of her windshield with salt-crusted condensation. Her head had started to throb again and her shoulder ached. Now that the burst of energy that had carried her through the last six hours had worn off, she was starting to feel the crushing weight of disappointment. Not only had she been attacked, her juicy scoop had slipped through her fingers. Flares of frustration licked the inside of her chest as she thought about the missing pieces of the puzzle. She would never get a confirmation that the mayor had called off prostitution stings for the rest of the year. It might not be criminal, as Johnson had pointed out, but Kate was sure Hanes hadn't done it for the city's benefit. All he cared about was maintaining his image.

Police Chief Sam Lugar's unmarked cruiser pulled into the parking lot a little after 6 a.m. Kate watched him get out and stride over to where one of the lieutenants and several detectives, including Johnson, stood in a semi-circle. She gave him five minutes to get his bearings before she got out of the car and made her way toward him. The other officers stopped talking as she got closer, prompting Lugar to look over his shoulder and see her when she was still about 10 feet away. His narrowed eyelids and pursed lips told her he was as unhappy to see her as she expected him to be.

"Morning chief. I have a few questions when you have a moment."

"I'm still trying to get a report from my men, Miss Bennett. I can't really tell you anything until after I hear it from them."

"Fair enough. But since I was here when the whole thing went down, I don't think I have any questions for you about that. I want to talk to you about what led up to this."

Lugar's nostrils flared. Kate had struck the right chord. She wanted him angry when she talked to him. He was more likely to let something slip if he was battling to keep his emotions in check.

"Fine," he snapped as he waved over one of the junior officers hanging around the edge of the parking lot. "Sanders, please escort Miss Bennett over to my car and be sure she waits there until I'm ready to talk to her."

Kate smirked at him but followed Sanders without complaint. Fifteen minutes later, Lugar joined them, waving the officer back to his previous post.

"Now, Miss Bennett," Lugar said, his voice dripping with condescension. "What was it that you wanted to ask me?"

"How did your prostitution task force miss this operation? Especially when several guests here said they called to report suspicious activity. It almost looks like you guys went out of your way to ignore what was going on here."

Lugar crossed his arms tightly in front of his chest and glared down at her. "I can assure you that is not the case. I don't know about these calls people claim they made. Oftentimes people say they called the police after the fact, because they want to get attention. Nine times out of ten, they never called. I'm not saying that happened here, but it's a distinct possibility."

"Well, I suppose it would be easy enough to check the 9-1-1 logs."

"You're talking about a lot of records. I wouldn't say looking for one call, or even several calls, is easy."

"But surely, if you're going to suggest someone is lying about something like this, you would check."

"Miss Bennett, I hardly see how this is relevant."

"Your task force, the one you established to clean up crap like this, was on a roll about a month ago. But ever since then, those officers have been assigned to other duties. Why? They obviously hadn't eradicated prostitution from the island. So why call them off the job?"

"Who says they were called off the job?" Lugar almost shouted, sweat beading up on his forehead. "I don't know where you're getting your information, Miss Bennett, but no one's been called off anything."

"Then why didn't they find out about this until someone attacked me? Everyone's gotten away—the pimp, the girls, the johns. And your guys are standing around scratching their heads like they had no idea what was going on right under their noses. How did that happen?"

"That's enough!" Lugar thundered. Out of the corner of her eye, Kate could see several of the detectives stop talking and look over in their direction. "How I direct my men is my business, and I don't have to justify anything to you. But in the middle of summer, I do not have the extra manpower to cover every square inch of this island. We do the best we can with what we have. The task force members were reassigned temporarily to cover other things. And as you yourself said, we've busted up some sizable operations in the past. If this group has the balls to set up somewhere else, I promise you we'll nail them."

"I can't quote you saying 'balls,' chief. This is a family newspaper."

"We're done here."

Police raid uncovers prostitution ring

Pimp and girls escape, but evidence points to a well-organized operation at a seawall hotel

By Kate Bennett

Galveston police have uncovered a prostitution ring operating out of The Clipper hotel. Based on witness accounts, they believe at least four women and one pimp were involved, but none of them were at the hotel at the time of the early-morning raid.

Although the rooms once used by the operation were empty, guests and short-term residents had plenty to say about what once went on behind closed doors on the second floor of the crumbling motor inn on Seawall Blvd., between 14th and 15th streets.

"Men came in and out all night," said Slava Yelyuk, a Ukrainian student staying in Galveston through the foreign student worker program. "We knew something bad was going on."

Although Yelyuk and several other hotel guests previously reported to the police suspicious activity that suggested a prostitution ring, detectives had not launched an active investigation.

This morning, Police Chief Sam Lugar said he had not heard any reports of 9-1-1 calls made about prostitution at the hotel. He emphatically denied the police had ignored the calls. Although the department has an active prostitution task force, Lugar said the officers had been reassigned for the summer, to cover additional policing needs along the beach front and other areas frequented by tourists.

When hotel guests didn't get a response from the police, they called the *Gazette*. Reporters conducted their own investigation. Observations made during the last few days corroborated the guests' claims.

Early Wednesday morning, the *Gazette* witnessed 13 men visiting four rooms between 1:30 a.m. and 5:30 a.m. Before going into the rooms, they stopped and handed something to a man waiting outside. They each stayed about 20 minutes.

Although the alleged pimp and the girls were gone when officers arrived at the hotel, investigators discovered enough evidence to confirm a prostitution operation, Det. Peter Johnson said. The sheets had been removed from one of the rooms, but the trash cans were full of used condoms, tissues and paper towels.

In one room, officers found a makeup bag one of the girls evidently left behind. It contained lipstick, mascara, eyeshadow and brushes, but no identification. Investigators will send the items to a lab to be processed for DNA evidence, Johnson said, but the chances of finding a match to someone already in the system are slim: "Chances are, we may never know who these girls were or where they came from."

The hotel manager may offer the best chance to get information about the man and the girls, but he's not talking. Ricardo Peña, 27, is in police custody but has refused to answer any questions without his lawyer present. As he was taken into custody, he said he had no idea that anything untoward was happening in the hotel. But his office sits at the base of the stairs all the men used to get to the second-floor rooms. Hotel guests say it is unlikely the manager didn't notice the unusual traffic.

"If we thought something strange was happening, how could he not know?" asked Jason Bevins, who came to Galveston for a week to go deep-sea fishing. Bevins and his wife said they suspected prostitutes but didn't call the police. "I guess we just figured it was none of our business, you know? I mean they are consenting adults, and all."

But Lorraine Hopper, visiting the island with her mother and two sisters for a girls weekend, didn't take the situation so lightly: "I don't care what anyone says, this kind of thing is not right, consenting or not. Plus, how do we know those poor girls weren't forced to do it?"

Chapter 22

Kate sat at her desk, pinned to her chair by dazed exhaustion. She knew she should get up and go home, but she wasn't sure she could even walk as far as the newsroom's front door. The web editor had posted her story almost an hour ago, about the time her latte, sugar, and adrenaline rush wore off. Even though it didn't turn out to be the scoop she longed for, Mattingly and Lewis were pleased. The *Gazette* had the story before anyone else, with details only Kate could provide. In the news business, you couldn't ask for much more than that.

"Just let Haviland Bells try to tell me I can do more with less in this newsroom," Mattingly crowed, holding aloft a half-empty bottle of spring water. "You can't get this kind of dedication and persistence from stringers and interns. Boots on the ground! That's what we need more of if this newspaper is going to survive. Good work, Bennett."

Kate smiled weakly. Mattingly's praise helped soothe the ache left by the story she knew she could have had, if circumstances had worked a little more in her favor. If it helped the managing editor save a newsroom job in his ongoing battle with the publisher, it was worth it.

"Look who's kicking ass and taking names," Delilah said when she and Ben walked in the door. She stopped short when she saw Kate's bandaged forehead and cheek. "Whoa! I thought you got them, not the other way around. What happened?"

"Turns out my clandestine operation wasn't so clandestine after all," Kate said. She wanted to laugh but her head hurt too much.

"Does it look worse than it is?" Delilah looked genuinely worried.

Tears pricked the back of Kate's eyes. "It is. Really. It's nothing a long nap and the maximum dose of Advil won't fix."

Delilah arched an eyebrow. "Well, I'm not sure it was worth whatever you had to go through to get it, but it's a hell of a story."

"Yeah, great work, kiddo," Ben said, with more sincerity than Kate had ever heard from him. "You made the police chief squirm. That always makes for a good day."

"What's your follow-up going to be?" Delilah asked. "Do you think you can find out who's really running that ring?"

"I don't know," Kate said, letting out a long sigh. "The police have the hotel manager in custody, but he's already lawyered up. Unless he starts talking or another witness comes forward, this whole thing may be a big dead end."

"What about the hotel? You know who owns it, right?"

"No. I've been meaning to look that up, but I just got focused on the investigation. I can look it up in the property records database right now."

"Don't bother. I can tell you who it is," Delilah said, a wide smile of satisfaction spreading across her face. "Eduardo Reyes."

"What?!" Kate screeched, so shocked she jumped up from her chair. A surge of dizziness sent her head spinning and she quickly sat down again. "Are you sure?"

"Positive. I wrote a story about it several years ago when he bought it. Wasn't exactly big news at the time, but the Chamber of Commerce types got all excited because they thought he would tear it down. They expected Reyes to either develop the site himself or sell it to someone who wanted to build another fancy hotel. There was even some talk of him doing a deal with the city to put in a parking lot and some green space. But nothing ever came of that. It's been business as usual at The Clipper ever since."

"I'd forgotten all about that," Lewis said, emerging from his office. "Kate, you should put in a call to his office and get a comment for the print version of the story. Pressure him to give you something about the manager. How long has he worked there? What does Reyes know about him? Does he report directly to Reyes about the hotel's operations or does Reyes have someone else handling whatever day-to-day decisions need to be made?"

"And most importantly, ask him what he thinks of his hotel dragging his precious island through the gutter,"

Delilah said. "If you can add Reyes to the list of people squirming over this, you will have had a very good day indeed."

Kate's heart thumped, and her hands tingled as the adrenaline and blood coursing through her veins gave her a burst of energy. The pounding in her head made it hard to think clearly. Was it possible that Reyes knew exactly what was going on at his hotel? He'd never admit it, but could he have given the pimp his tacit approval for the prostitution ring? Could he be getting a cut of the profits? Could he even be the one calling the shots?

Kate took five deep, measured breaths before she picked up the phone. Her fingers trembled with excitement as she dialed the number listed for Reyes in her contact database. The law firm's receptionist patched her through to his assistant, who said she didn't know if he was in yet but would check. Kate's grip on the phone tightened as the seconds ticked into minutes. She could hear the blood whooshing in her ears, louder and louder as the silence on the line dragged on. When she heard the click signaling someone had picked up the call, she started so violently she almost fell out of her chair.

"Miss Bennett, it sounds like you had a rough night," Reyes' voice oozed through the receiver. "Shouldn't you be at home, recovering, instead of bothering me? I'm a very busy man."

"Who happens to own the hotel at the center of the island's latest prostitution scandal. Surely you had to know I would be calling, sooner or later."

Reyes barked out one of his mirthless laughs. "I don't spend much time thinking about what you might or might not be doing, Miss Bennett. I hope that doesn't crush your ego."

Anger burned in Kate's chest like a bad case of indigestion. "This is not about me. This is about you and what you knew about a prostitution ring operating out of your hotel."

"Well, I can guarantee you I had no idea criminals were using my property as a base of operations. If I did, I would have turned them over to the police myself."

"What about the manager? What can you tell me about him? It seems very unlikely he didn't know what was going on."

"I don't know the man personally. As you can probably imagine, I have too many business operations to oversee them all myself. I'll have to talk to the person I have in charge of the hotel and see what he has to say. But I can pretty well guarantee he had no idea what was going on either. I don't hire people who condone or get caught up in illegal enterprises, Miss Bennett."

"So what you're telling me is that no one associated with you knows anything about any of this. It sounds like someone's not doing a very good job of keeping an eye on your assets."

"Print that and I'll slap you with a defamation suit so fast you'll be looking for another job before the end of the week. Now, Miss Bennett, I have more important things to do with my morning than entertain your uninformed questions. Have a good day."

Reyes hung up. Kate's face burned with anger and indignation.

"That sounded entertaining. Get anything useful?" Delilah asked. Everyone in the newsroom had been listening to Kate's side of the call.

"Nothing, of course. What an ass! He threatened to sue me for defamation. I don't care how much he denies it. I'll never believe he had no idea what was going on."

"Bennett!" Mattingly yelled from his office. "I just got off the phone with the mayor. He's called a news conference for this afternoon. He's breathing fire over your web story. Claims it makes the city look bad and sends the wrong message about police and safety. I'm sure he'll come at us with both guns blazing."

"He's just on the defense because Kate's going to nail him to the wall," Delilah said.

"That's all well and good, but we can't connect dots we don't have," Mattingly warned, striding across the newsroom to stand in front of Kate's desk. "You be extra careful, you hear? You'd better be able to back up every word of that story. I don't mind listening to the mayor whine, but I do not want to have the publisher tell me I have to cut staff so he can pay our legal bills."

Kate's mouth had gone completely dry, so she just nodded in reply. How had her victory from an hour ago evaporated into veiled threats that clung like a stubborn midday fog to her head? She was beginning to realize how Mattingly ended up with ulcers and anxiety attacks. Sometimes, being a reporter felt more dangerous than walking blindfolded through a minefield.

~ ~ ~ ~ ~

Johnson sat alone in his office trying to process everything he'd learned in the last 24 hours. His throat tightened when he thought about Kate's battered face. He should have been there for her, no matter what orders he'd gotten from the chief. He'd vowed never to let his own bias blind him again. Kate called that an excuse for inaction. That's not how it started. But was that what it had become?

Johnson had been disappointed when the chief called off prostitution stings at the mayor's request. He thought it was short-sighted and unnecessary. But he tried to take a long view of the situation, knowing his officers would eventually get another crack at the operations. But in the meantime, how many women had suffered abuse at the hands of the man selling them, and the men who bought them? Waiting could create just as many victims as plowing ahead without having permission.

About 30 minutes later, the chief called an emergency meeting. Johnson walked down the hall to the conference room with a growing sense of dread.

"The mayor's called a news conference for this afternoon," Sam Lugar said once the investigators and senior officers had taken their seats. "As you all know, I postponed prostitution stings earlier this summer to give us a little break from the crime news that filled the newspaper several months ago. Obviously, the mayor does not intend to talk about that at his press conference."

Lugar, who stood at the front of the room, paused to lean over the conference table, planting both hands in front of him and resting his considerable weight on his rod-stiff arms.

"But I have to explain why we haven't been actively pursuing sting operations for the last few months. I've already had a very unpleasant chat with a reporter from the *Gazette* this morning. As I told her, and as I plan to say at the press conference, my staffing decisions were driven by a need to reallocate resources during the heavy summer tourism season. Our top priority is to ensure the safety of our visitors and residents, and that requires increased patrols and a more visible police presence in all the obvious places. We do not have the manpower for special operations in the summer."

He paused again to look slowly around the room, making sure he had every officer's attention.

"That's my message. That's the department's message. And that's the only message I expect to hear any of you sharing with your family, your friends, your neighbors, and strangers who stop you at the grocery store. If you get any calls from anyone in the media, tell them you cannot comment and direct them to the city's public information officer. Are we clear?"

A murmured chorus of "Yes, sir," reverberated around the room. Johnson swallowed hard. Lugar was lying through his teeth. Most likely to save his job. If he crossed the mayor, he wouldn't last long at the head of the department. It was petty, and arguably despicable. But was that all the chief was trying to protect?

Johnson knew from the moment he put on a uniform he would eventually have to take an order he disagreed with. It was part of the deal he'd accepted when he joined the force. He'd learned firsthand the futility of vigilante justice. And he'd vowed never to put himself in that position again. But somehow that hadn't seemed like enough protection. He needed someone else to call the shots so he wouldn't have to. He still didn't trust himself to make the right decision.

But what if the person giving the orders couldn't be trusted either?

~ ~ ~ ~ ~

Several hours later, Johnson stood on the seawall watching as television satellite trucks pulled up and reporters jumped out, some with microphones already in hand. Kate and Doug Cowel had staked out spots at the front of the crowd gathering for the mayor's news conference. Despite the oppressive heat, Kate had both hands wrapped around a giant cup of coffee. Her ponytail hung limply on her shoulders, and dark circles had started to form under her usually piercing blue eyes. She looked absolutely shattered.

At 3 p.m. on the dot, Mayor Matthew Hanes stepped out of an SUV parked at the curb near where city workers had set up a podium. Lugar climbed out after him. Some of the more senior officers gathered on either side of the podium, part of Lugar's choreographed demonstration of solidarity. Johnson and some of the other detectives and officers, many of whom had responded to the early morning call, hung behind the gaggle of reporters grouped in front of the podium.

"As you know by now, in the early morning hours, Galveston police officers responded to a call at The Clipper Hotel," Hanes began. The clicking of Cowel's camera shutter punctuated every third word. "A woman was attacked by a man thought to be operating a prostitution ring out of several rooms at the hotel. Based on eyewitness accounts and evidence found at the scene, it looks like the ring included four women and one pimp."

The mayor paused to look slowly around his audience. Every time he listened to Hanes speak, Johnson pictured him in front of a jury. He had a lawyer's cadence and flare for the dramatic.

"Prostitution is not new in Galveston," Hanes continued. "Many of you have heard the stories of our historic red light district. Of course, that was a long time ago. But our fine officers have continued to pursue those involved in the world's oldest profession, with great success, I might add. As our sometimes friends at the *Galveston Gazette* noted in this morning's story, we have a prostitution task force, but it was not investigating the operation at The Clipper. But the *Gazette* was wrong, dead wrong—

and I can't emphasize this enough—to suggest any ulterior motive for the task force's inactivity."

Hanes paused again and fixed Kate with a withering stare that lasted several seconds longer than it needed to, even to make a point. Johnson's eyes narrowed. Standing at the back of the crowd, he couldn't see Kate's face, but it looked like she met the mayor's gaze without flinching. *Atta girl. Give it right back to him.*

"In a minute, I'm going to turn the microphone over to Police Chief Sam Lugar, who can explain our staffing situation during the summer, when the safety of our visitors, as well as our citizens, is our top priority. But the main thing I want to communicate to our friends in Houston and elsewhere in the state is that Galveston continues to be the closest, most enjoyable and most economical vacation spot in Texas. Once you walk our beaches, you won't want to go anywhere else."

For the next five minutes, Lugar spun his carefully crafted lie. Johnson sighed. Kate was right to be angry about the way this went down. And he understood her frustration at not being able to lay the blame at the mayor's feet. But maybe it wasn't as big a lost cause as she thought. Neither the chief nor the mayor wanted something like this to happen again. They might not reactivate the task force, but Lugar surely would increase patrols around the island's hotels. Officers would keep a much closer eye on known hot spots and potential retreats for other prostitution rings. Johnson doubted this pimp would make another appearance any time soon. But if he did, he wouldn't go unnoticed for long.

And Johnson had one more hand to play before this case folded. Ricardo Peña sat in a holding cell back at the police station. He already had a lawyer with him, but maybe Johnson could persuade him to give up the pimp. If the district attorney took a hard line and threatened some serious charges, Johnson would have something to bargain with.

Would Peña take the bait?

Chapter 23

Several hours after the press conference, Johnson leaned against a wall at the front of the county jail, his arms folded across his chest. The bright daylight that had scorched the island with another day of record-breaking heat had softened into a heavy twilight. The thick humidity, unbroken by the usually steady sea breeze, made it hard to breathe. Or maybe he was just too tired to inhale deeply enough. If he closed his eyes, he had no doubt he would fall asleep where he stood. His 1 a.m. summons to The Clipper had a lot to do with it. But the crush of another investigative disappointment didn't help.

Through the jail's bullet-proof glass doors, Johnson watched two men stride purposely toward freedom. Ricardo Peña, the hotel manager, kept his eyes on the ground in front of him. Xavier Sepulveda, one of the island's mid-level defense attorneys, looked triumphantly ahead. Peña had refused to talk from the moment of his arrest, although he never asked for his phone call. He hadn't been at the police station for much more than an hour when Sepulveda arrived. Johnson guessed they must have had an agreement that if anything happened at the hotel, the lawyer would come to the police station right away. That only confirmed Peña's complicity in the operation. But the district attorney said the case would be hard to make on the evidence they had, which was all circumstantial.

Johnson wanted to hold Peña for the full 72 hours allowed before they had to charge him. Even Lt. Jarrell backed him up on that. But Lugar told them to cut the manager loose. There was no reason to keep asking Peña questions his lawyer wouldn't let him answer. Now Johnson had to watch his best chance of getting information about the prostitution ring walk out the door.

"Have a good evening, detective," Sepulveda said, flashing a self-satisfied smirk as he and Peña walked by. The hotel manager glanced up furtively and picked up his pace, as though making eye contact for too long might land him back behind bars.

After the two men climbed into Sepulveda's shiny black Lexus and drove out of the parking lot, Johnson pushed himself off the wall and trudged back into the building. The hallways leading back to the police station, housed on the other side of the massive justice complex, blurred into a mix of passing faces and hollow footsteps. All Johnson could think about was going home and falling into bed. But when he got back to his office, he found a note from the receptionist waiting on his desk: The chief wants to see you before you leave. Johnson groaned. His head started to throb.

Johnson dragged himself down the hall and knocked on the chief's open door.

"Have a seat, detective," Lugar said. "And go ahead and shut that."

Johnson's chest constricted as he swung the heavy door shut and heard the latch click.

"It's been a long day," Lugar said, picking up a pen and twirling it in his fingers as he sat hunched over his desk, fixing Johnson with a weary stare. "Long summer, really. And you've had it worse than the rest of us."

Johnson had no idea what to say or where the chief's monologue was headed, so he just nodded.

"I know these cases weigh heavily on you, perhaps more than the other detectives. You're one of those rare officers who never seems to lose that wide-eyed devotion to pure justice."

Lugar sighed heavily and looked down.

"I'll admit, I envy you that."

Still lost for words, Johnson searched the deep lines around Lugar's eyes and across his forehead for clues about whether this was a long windup to a sharp rebuke or a rare pep talk.

"Unfortunately, few cases are as black and white as we would like. Take this prostitution ring, for example. The pimp got off scott free, and the hotel manager almost certainly will too. I have no doubt he knew exactly what was going on in those upstairs rooms. And I'm sure he was getting his piece of the pie. But that will be almost impossible to prove, and the DA will never try a case he can't win this close to an election."

Johnson felt like a boxer pummeled into a corner by a dominant opponent. He knew the chief's analysis was right but his heart struggled to accept it. Lugar stared at him as though demanding an answer before continuing. Johnson swallowed.

"I know," he finally said, his voice croaking as though he hadn't had anything to drink all day.

"Further complicating things is the latest detail your friend at the *Gazette* dug up," Lugar continued. "Did you see the latest version of the story they posted online after the news conference?"

Johnson shook his head, his mouth suddenly so dry he feared any words would catch in his throat.

"Turns out Eduardo Reyes owns The Clipper. He denies even knowing the hotel manager personally, which I guess isn't that hard to believe. But I've already gotten a call from the mayor. He said if we don't have the evidence to press charges against Peña, or anyone else, he wants us to drop the case."

Johnson's heart started to pound, sending blood surging into his cheeks. Lugar held up his hands in a conciliatory gesture.

"I know, I know. It's not the mayor's call to make. But I understand where he's coming from. If we keep chasing this, the newspaper will keep writing stories about it, and that's not going to make any of us look good."

"Since when was anyone's image our top priority?" Johnson demanded.

"That's just the political reality, I'm afraid." Lugar leaned back in his chair. His hard stare now came through narrowed lids. "And I know you know that. What good does it do us to piss off the mayor and his biggest supporter by pursuing something we know we can't ever make stick anyway? That's just a complete waste of aggravation all the way around."

Johnson held the chief's gaze for several seconds. Lugar sighed heavily.

"For what it's worth, I don't like it any more than you do," the chief said. "I still remember how it felt the day I graduated from the Academy. All I wanted to do was put bad guys behind bars. But it didn't take long for me to realize law enforcement is a little more complicated than that."

Lugar sat forward again, leaning over his elbows on the desk. His eyes never left Johnson's face. Suddenly Johnson realized he was about to get a direct order that would be very hard to obey.

"You need to let this one go," Lugar said. "We win some and we lose some. Put this one in the loss column and move on. Sometimes that's all we can do."

Johnson searched for an argument that would change the chief's mind. Lugar was right about the lack of hard evidence. Without that, the investigation was closed. But if he could find a new thread to follow... Johnson's thought trailed off. He was about to plunge headlong into an abyss he had vowed never to even look into again.

But what if he was careful? Only looked for evidence, presented what he found, and let the chief decide whether it was worth pursuing? Maybe he could keep himself from falling over the edge.

He thought of Kate sitting on the ground, blood dripping down her face. His heart constricted. He knew he had to try, no matter where it led him.

Lugar was still staring at him. Waiting for a response. Johnson cleared his throat and sat up a little straighter in his chair. He wouldn't give up without a fight. But the chief didn't have to know that until he had something more concrete to share.

"Yes, sir," he said.

"Good. Now go home and get some rest. Tomorrow's a new day."

Yes, Johnson thought. It certainly was.

~ ~ ~ ~ ~

A week later, Kate sat at a table in Abuela's, one of the island's most popular Mexican restaurants. Gaudy paintings of Catholic icons covered the bright orange, blue, and yellow stucco walls. Tall glass candle holders adorned with saints and scripture sat in the middle of each table. An ornate black and gold cross hung on the wall next to the counter. Behind its wide glass top, a large, elderly woman greeted arriving customers and took their money on their way out. The plaintive whine of Mexican ballads floated over the comforting aroma of lard-infused refried beans, simmering cheese and tangy chili peppers.

Kate self-consciously brushed her fingers over the bandaid on her forehead. The scrape had almost healed and the violet bruise had faded into a sickening yellow. But it was still obvious enough to draw quizzical glances from people who didn't know what had happened. She'd spent most of the last week hiding in her apartment.

The first several days passed in a haze of pain medication and sleeping pills. She hoped the forced rest would help cure the aches in her body, if not her soul. On the third day, Brian brought her a carton of soup and a bouquet of roses. He'd stood awkwardly in her kitchen while she told him she needed some space. She knew he loved her, and she couldn't love him back. It was just too risky. But that didn't make telling him goodbye any easier. That night, an oppressive loneliness settled over her like a blanket of ash from the bonfire of frustration and disappointment suddenly burning through her life.

The next day, she'd gone back to work. No more wallowing in self-pity. The prostitution ring story might be yesterday's news, as far as Mattingly was concerned, but Kate knew there was more to it than what they'd been able to publish so far. Today, she would get a start on finding out how much more.

Kate sipped a Topo Chico while she waited for her lunch date. Benito Muñoz worked in the County Clerk's office and headed the local chapter of the League of United Latin American Citizens. Nothing happened in the island's Hispanic community that he didn't know about.

"Sorry I'm late, mi amiga!" Muñoz cried as he bounded from the door to her table. "I know better than to leave a beautiful woman waiting. I'm just lucky someone didn't snap you up before I got here."

Kate couldn't help but laugh. Muñoz tempered his almost stereotypical machismo with a cartoonish flirtation. No woman could be seriously offended by his overtures.

"It's busy in here today, no? I'm starved. Let's order." Muñoz raised his hand and waved at a passing waitress, who smiled broadly as she hurried over. "Hola, señorita linda! Que es les especiales de la casa?"

Kate listened absently as Muñoz made small talk with the waitress, whose family he obviously knew. He'd probably been present at her baptism, would be an honored guest at her wedding, and would be among the first to kiss her babies after she brought them home from the hospital. Benito Muñoz was almost as important to the island's Hispanic families as Eduardo Reyes, but on a much more personal level. Whereas everyone knew of Reyes, Muñoz knew everyone, probably by name. Kate had seen the two men together at various events and knew they had a cordial relationship. But she didn't think they were close friends. She longed to ask Muñoz what he thought of Reyes' possible connection to the prostitution ring but feared he might clam up if she hit him with such a delicate topic before their lunch even arrived.

Over enchiladas and tamales they talked about a planned community center, fights between rival groups of teens at the local skate park and the likely redistricting of council seats after the next census. When Muñoz pushed his empty plate away with a satisfied sigh and leaned back in his chair, Kate decided she'd taken long enough to ease into what she really wanted to talk about.

"So, what are people saying about last week's prostitution bust?"

A slow smile spread across Muñoz's face. "I was wondering how long it would take you to ask me that. It's the one thing you're really curious about, no?"

"I have a personal stake in that story, after all," Kate said, her fingers flitting again to her forehead. "It shouldn't be a surprise that I want to know what other people think. Right?"

"Si si, amiga. Si," Muñoz said, lacing his fingers together over his stomach and looking at her under knitted brows. He seemed to be figuring out how much to say. "Well, everyone's still talking about it."

"Still?"

"Still." Muñoz sat up and leaned over the table so that his face was just a few feet from Kate's. She could smell his cloying aftershave. "It's not every day the island's patron saint is caught up in a scandal, no?"

"So what's the verdict?" Kate asked, lowering her voice. "Did Reyes know what was going on or not?"

Muñoz gave a big, exaggerated shrug. "No se. Some say yes, others say no. The old women shake their heads disapprovingly. The young men say, 'What's the big deal?'"

"Safe to say it hasn't hurt his image any."

"Amiga," Muñoz said, shaking his head and clicking his tongue as if to say she should know better. "Eduardo Reyes, he is untouchable."

Kate gritted her teeth. How could anyone hold such sway over an entire city?

"What about the hotel manager, Ricardo Peña? What are people saying about him? I mean, even though the DA's not going to press charges, surely no one believes he's innocent."

"No, no. Innocent? No," Muñoz said, shaking his head as he smiled again. "He was always trouble, from the time he was in middle school. Drinking, drugs, skipping school. His papa ran off when he was young, and his mama just couldn't control him. He's lucky Reyes took pity on him and offered him a job. I think Peña knew it too. He would have done anything for Reyes, everybody knows it."

"So what's he going to do now?" Kate asked, her heart starting to beat faster as she thought about the possibilities. "Do you think Reyes will risk putting him to work somewhere else?"

"Ha!" Muñoz said, loud enough to make Kate jump and draw a few surprised looks from nearby tables. "I don't think so. Not for a while anyway. Peña is visiting his mama's family in Mexico...indefinitely."

"He left town?" Kate asked, her voice barely above a whisper. The question seemed too important to risk anyone overhearing, although she quickly realized everyone around her in the restaurant probably knew the answer already.

"His mama didn't want to see him get into any more trouble, although it broke her heart to send him away. Once things quiet down, I'm sure he'll be back."

Kate chewed on her bottom lip as she thought through the implications. Peña was certainly free to leave the country if he wanted to. And it guaranteed he couldn't be hauled in for questioning again, although that seemed unlikely to happen at this point.

"I feel the most for his mama," Muñoz said, tugging his wallet out of his back pocket in a signal the interview was almost over. "He was her only child, and now she's all alone. At least she has someone to talk to who knows what it's like to lose a child."

"What do you mean?" Kate asked absently, snatching up the check before Muñoz could pick it up. The newspaper still paid for lunches with sources, at least for now.

"She and Rafaela Costa have been best friends for years. Their boys were inseparable growing up. Now that both of them are gone, so to speak, their mothers can mourn together."

"Wait," Kate said, looking hard at Muñoz as she tried to process the connections. "Rafaela Costa. Julian Costa's mom?"

"Si, the man who was killed earlier this year. Such a tragedy. And they still don't know who killed him."

Kate suddenly had a hard time taking a deep breath.

"Were the two men still friends?"

"Si, si. Julian refused to drop him, even though he never got into trouble like Ricardo did. They lived different lives, but they were still like brothers."

Kate fumbled with her wallet and a handful of dollar bills fluttered to the floor. Muñoz laughed as he stooped to pick them up.

"You should be more careful, amiga. You don't want to go losing all this money." When he handed the bills back to her, he leaned in and kissed her quickly on both cheeks. "Thank you for lunch. It was a pleasure, always a pleasure."

Kate smiled weakly and waved as he bounded back to the door.

If Ricardo Peña and Julian Costa were like brothers, what were the chances one didn't know what the other was involved in? When Costa died, everyone described him as a clean, family man who had never been caught up in any illegal activity. But Johnson suspected he was doing something he shouldn't have been, even though he never would go on the record about it. Kate remembered his frustration about not being able to get Costa's widow to talk. At the time she'd commiserated with the frustrated detective but hadn't given it much thought after the case went cold. She'd attributed the widow's reticence to her shock, grief, and a general mistrust of the police. Kate was convinced Costa's death had been a surprise to his wife. She'd been at the scene when Muriel found out her husband had been murdered. No one could fake that much grief and despair.

But what if Julian had been mixed up in something with Peña? Or what if he was trying to keep Peña out of trouble? It couldn't have involved the latest prostitution ring because the pimp didn't set up shop at The Clipper until well after Costa died. But based on Miss Kitty's comments, the new girls weren't the first ones to work out of the hotel. And Peña had to have known about it. It seemed likely Costa did too. Was he part of the operation, or was he trying to keep his friend out of trouble? Either possibility offered opportunities for him to get himself killed.

Kate abruptly sat down again as her knees suddenly gave way. The unidentified girl shot in Fish Village had no obvious connection to any of this. But what if she was the first casualty in a clean-up operation designed to keep the group's activities quiet or restore order among unruly participants? What if she wanted out or threatened to go to the police? Kate had to take a deep breath to slow her racing heart and chase away the black spots that had started to float in front of her eyes. A lightheaded fog made it hard to concentrate.

She could think of only one person who might be able to shed light on all the possible connections—Muriel Costa. She hadn't wanted to talk to the police, but maybe she would be willing to talk to a reporter, especially if Kate told her she was working on a story about police incompetence and her husband's unsolved murder. Her conscience kicked her in the gut, making her wince. The first rule of journalism ethics was never misrepresent yourself or your intentions to a source to trick them into giving up information. But surely solving at least two, maybe three, murders justified cutting a few ethical corners. If only the good guys played by the rules, men like the cigarette-smoking pimp and even Eduardo Reyes would never be held accountable.

Kate stood up so quickly she knocked her chair over. Normally the stares of the other customers would have brought a rush of heat to her face, but she didn't even flinch as she scooped it back upright and walked over to the front counter to pay the bill. She could already see the outlines of the fake story in her head, tailored to give Muriel Costa as much incentive as possible to talk. Would it work?

Chapter 24

Kate stood in front of Muriel Costa's front door, her stomach churning. She had been nervous about plenty of interviews during her time as a reporter, but none of those carried this one's potential weight. Ever since she left the restaurant, the images of Miss Kitty lying broken on the rocks, Julian Costa left in a pool of his own blood, and the unnamed girl thrown out like trash in Fish Village scrolled across her memory. She wanted to know what happened to all of them, but more importantly, she wanted someone to pay for their deaths.

Muriel Costa opened the door with a furrowed brow and narrowed eyes, like she didn't immediately recognize her visitor but felt like she should. Guilt rattled the cage of Kate's conscience. Forcing a bright smile, she ignored it.

"Hi, Mrs. Costa," Kate said quickly, hoping to disarm the woman before she could make up her mind not to talk. "My name's Kate Bennett. I'm a reporter with the *Gazette.*"

Muriel's confused look morphed into distaste and she started to shut the door.

"I don't have any interest in talking to a reporter," she said.

"Wait! Please. Can I just tell you what I'm working on? I promise I won't take up too much of your time. And if you don't want to talk to me, that's fine. I'll go away. I promise. Please?"

"I don't care what you're working on. I don't want to see my name, or my family's name, in the newspaper again. It was bad enough when my husband died."

"Look, I understand. I do!" Kate blurted, her words storming the walls of her normal reserve before she could stop them. "My mom died when I was in high school, and I hated seeing her picture and video of our house on the evening news. I hated hearing a reporter casually talk about something so excruciating I could barely even think about it."

Kate never intended to tell Muriel Costa something she didn't even speak about with her closest friends. Her involuntarily honesty caught her off guard and left her temporarily at a loss for what to say next.

"So now you do the same thing to other people?" Muriel sneered.

Kate sucked in a sharp breath. She'd never thought of it that way before.

"It's not like that," she sighed. "It's a long story. Look, I didn't mean to tell you that. But it's true. I understand why you don't want to talk to me."

Kate hesitated. She was about to lie in hopes of getting information. She believed she was justified, but crossing that ethical boundary screeched like nails down the chalkboard of her soul.

"I'm writing a story about the incompetence of the Galveston Police Department. Your husband's death was one of two unsolved murders this summer. And now this prostitution ring. It's like they can't find their asses with both hands over there."

Muriel's face softened slightly and Kate thought she could see the hint of a smile playing at the corners of her mouth.

"And for whatever it's worth, I didn't want to bother you for this story. But my boss insisted I at least try. Normally I might have told him no, but the newspaper's about to announce a round of layoffs. I didn't want to put a target on my back. I need this job."

Kate swallowed back the bile rising in her throat and reminded herself telling half truths and outright lies would be worth it if she could find out something that tied the murders together. Muriel sighed. Her pursed lips suggested she was still trying to figure out a way to tell Kate no. But her resistance seemed to be faltering.

"Five minutes," Kate said. "That's all I need. Please let me just ask you these questions. If you don't want to answer, you don't have to. But at least I can tell my boss I tried."

Kate hoped her pleading eyes would push Muriel over the edge, even though she hated resorting to tricks and manipulation.

"Fine," Muriel finally said after staring at Kate for about 15 seconds. "You can have five minutes, or until the baby wakes up from her nap, whichever comes first."

"Thank you so much!" Kate gushed. Persuading Muriel to let her in was the most difficult part of her plan. Even if the widow didn't answer any questions, her reactions would at least tell Kate whether she was on the right track.

The cramping in her stomach started to ease as she followed Muriel into her living room, stepping around the abandoned toys and discarded shoes that littered the floor. Muriel sat down on a faded couch and pulled her knees up to her chest. On the side table next to the widow, Kate spotted a family photo. It must have been taken shortly after the baby was born, just a few months before Julian's death. His proud smile said he was completely content surrounded by his wife and his three children. He looked like the kind of man who could be driven to join a criminal operation only out of desperation—or by force.

Kate perched on a tattered love seat perpendicular to the couch, balancing her notebook on her knees. "During the investigation into your husband's murder, did the police ever give you any idea they might have a theory about what happened?"

Muriel shifted uncomfortably. "Not really. They couldn't find anything that connected him to anything bad. And I told them my Julian was a good man. Make sure you write that down. The detective kept insisting he was involved in something he shouldn't have been. But they had no evidence! Nothing. I kept telling them they needed to look at some of the homeless people who hang around near the beach. Most of them are crazy. Who knows why one of them would have killed Julian. But maybe they didn't need a reason. Who knows?"

"But the police never questioned any of them, to your knowledge?"

"No, at least they never told me they did. Once they quit questioning me, I never heard from them again. No update on the case, no nothing. It was like they just gave up. And my poor husband's killer is still out there."

Muriel began to rub her hand back and forth along her thigh, as if to keep tears at bay. Kate cringed inwardly at bringing the widow back to something that obviously caused her so much pain.

"What about Julian's friends? Did the police ever talk to them?"

"Yes. Friends, co-workers, family. All of them vouched for Julian. He was a good man," Muriel said quietly, lacing her fingers together around her knees.

Although she spoke with conviction, Kate got the impression Muriel had said those words over and over, until they were almost worn out. Why did the widow feel such a need to defend her husband?

"What about Ricardo Peña? Did they talk to him?"

Muriel looked up sharply with a glare. "Why? What's he got to do with this?"

"Nothing," Kate said quickly, her fingers tingling with excitement as she clutched her pen in a vice grip. "I had just heard they were good friends, and I assume if the police wanted someone who could vouch for Julian going back years, it would be Ricardo."

"I'm sure they did talk to him. And I'm sure he said Julian was a good man, just like everyone else."

Muriel's knuckles had gone white and her biceps stood out as though her arms wrapped around her knees were the only thing keeping her tiny frame from springing off the couch. Kate tried to ignore the fear that suddenly burned in the pit of her stomach. If the widow was hiding whatever her husband had been involved with, what might she do to keep it a secret? She might even be involved herself.

"It must have been quite a shock to see your husband's friend caught up in that prostitution bust," she said slowly. "I mean, I know he wasn't charged with anything, but I hear a lot of people think he might have been involved—"

"What does that have to do with my husband's murder?" Muriel spat, glaring now as she uncoiled and set her feet on the floor. "I thought you wanted to talk about Julian."

"I do. But the prostitution case is another one the police seem to have botched. And it's interesting that your husband's friend was involved."

"A coincidence. That's all."

Muriel stood now, putting her hands on her hips. Kate quickly stood too so the older woman wouldn't have a height advantage.

"Maybe. But that's a pretty big coincidence."

"Your five minutes are up," Muriel hissed. "How dare you come into my house and suggest some kind of connection between my husband and ... prostitutes."

"What about the other murder this summer?" Kate said in a rush. "What about that girl they found in Fish Village? Did the police ever ask you whether it might be connected to your husband's death?"

Kate had hoped to get some kind of reaction from Muriel, but she was unprepared for the look of complete shock that overwhelmed the widow's face. With blanched cheeks and wide eyes, Muriel licked her lips. When she tried to say something, nothing but an unintelligible hissing came out. She crossed her arms over her chest and swallowed hard.

Surprise left Kate breathless. She could barely stammer out her next question.

"Do you think the same people that killed your husband killed that girl? Why? Do you know who she is?"

Muriel shook her head violently from side to side. "No! I have no idea what you're talking about. I don't know about any dead girls. And neither did Julian. He was a good man."

Kate held the widow's panicked gaze. Desperation, sorrow, and raw terror flitted across her face, deepening the shadows under her eyes and the lines that criss-crossed her forehead.

"Please leave now," Muriel whispered. "Please."

Kate briefly considered pushing Muriel, now that she had her off guard. But she doubted she would say much more after the shock of the questions had worn off. Without a word, she turned and walked to the front door, quelling the fear that stabbed her chest when she thought of the other woman standing behind her. She reached for the knob and turned it slowly.

"Someone's going to figure out what happened eventually, you know," Kate said, turning briefly to look at Muriel one more time before opening the door and stepping out into the bright afternoon sun.

The widow didn't say a word but stood on the threshold and watched Kate with wide, frightened eyes as she climbed into her car and drove away.

~ ~ ~ ~ ~

Kate's head was still spinning when she pulled into the newspaper parking lot 15 minutes later. Preoccupied by a replay of her conversation with Muriel, it took her a few minutes to realize something was wrong when she walked into the newsroom. The cavernous space, normally filled with the din of chatting, typing, and laughing, had fallen ominously silent. As she walked past Krista's desk, she spotted a box on the chair. She looked back questioningly at Delilah, but before the senior reporter could say anything, Mattingly came rocketing out of his office.

"About time, Bennett!" he barked. "Meeting. My office. Now."

With a sinking feeling in her stomach, Kate trailed behind Delilah, Ben, Jessica, and Cowel. Hunter Lewis brought up the rear and closed the door behind him. When they were all seated around the conference table, Mattingly let out a long sigh in the heavy silence.

"This morning, Mr. Bells called the department heads into his office and announced we couldn't delay layoffs any longer. We're losing six positions in all, two in the newsroom. Krista will be leaving us, effective immediately. I'll also be letting one of the copy editors go later this afternoon."

Anger flushed Kate's cheeks and tears pricked the backs of her eyes. The fight for truth and justice would limp on, but those cuts hampered the effort.

The reporters glanced at each other around the table. Kate mostly saw relief in her coworkers' eyes. They had survived. Kate suddenly felt a rush of sympathy for Krista. She was an innocent bystander in the mortal combat between profits and purpose. Through the floor-to-ceiling glass windows that separated Mattingly's office from the newsroom, Kate watched as the junior reporter trudged back to her desk, presumably coming from the bathroom. Her eyes were rimmed with red, and between putting things in the box on her chair, she paused to blot her face with a giant wad of toilet paper. Tears began to gather behind Kate's narrowed eyelids, and she quickly turned away.

"For the rest of you, this means we'll be reorganizing our beat structure and asking you to pick up the slack. Hunter and I will figure all that out in the next few days. Any questions?"

"Is this it?" Delilah asked. "At least for now? I mean, are you going to come back and hit us with more cuts or furloughs or something in a few months?"

Mattingly looked hard at Delilah for a few moments before answering.

"I don't think so. I'm pretty sure we won't have any more cuts for a while. But I'm not sure about the furloughs. It mostly depends on our revenue between now and the end of the year. We may have to make more adjustments in January."

No one said anything, until Lewis broke the silence.

"This has been hanging over our heads for a while. Now that it's over, we can get back to work. No one's happy about this, not even the publisher. And I can guarantee you Kenton fought as hard for us as he could. If there had been a way to get the newsroom through this without cuts, he would have found it."

Mattingly just grunted in response and looked down at his hands, clasped in front of him on the table.

"The news business isn't what it used to be," he said. "It's all numbers and profits and margins now. Used to be, all we had to worry about was not getting scooped on the next big story. It's just not that simple anymore."

The managing editor's sagging mouth screamed defeat. Kate's throat tightened so hard it felt like someone was holding a pillow over her face.

"Well, I just hope the publisher knows what he's doing to this newspaper," Delilah said. "Saying it isn't what it used to be doesn't even cover half of it."

When no one said anything in reply, the senior reporter stood up.

"Are we done here?" she snapped. "I have work to do."

Mattingly grunted again but kept his eyes focused on the table as Delilah stalked out, followed closely by Ben and then everyone else. Kate lingered after standing up.

"I know you fought hard for us," she said, tracing circles on the table top with an outstretched finger. "I know it wasn't easy…and I appreciate it."

Mattingly didn't look up, but he nodded in acknowledgement. Pressing her lips together to keep the tears at bay, Kate turned and walked out of the office, leaving the managing editor sitting alone, still staring at his hands.

Kate walked straight to the now jobless reporter's desk and stood there, shifting awkwardly from foot to foot while Krista blew her nose.

"It's not like I didn't see this coming," Krista said between sniffles. "I just kept hoping it wouldn't happen. I have no idea what I'm going to do. I'll probably have to move back in with my parents." The prospect of returning to her childhood home brought on a fresh wave of tears.

Kate cleared her throat while Krista blew her nose again.

"Don't give up! Journalism needs reporters like you. There are lots of other papers out there. I'm sure Lewis will put in a good word for you. And I'll be happy to tell anyone what a great reporter you are."

"Thanks," Krista said, mustering an anemic smile.

"I'm really sorry. If there's anything else I can do, let me know."

Krista nodded but didn't say anything else as she wiped her cheeks again. Twenty minutes later, she walked out of the newsroom. Kate was the only one who waved goodbye.

~ ~ ~ ~ ~

Johnson was shutting down his computer when he heard a knock on the frame of his open office door. He hadn't seen Kate since the mayor's press conference a week ago. She looked as tired and dejected now as she had then, although the bandages were gone. He smiled gently and waved a hand toward her usual seat in front of his desk.

"Take a load off. Looks like you've had a rough day."

"We had layoffs at the paper today," Kate said, perching on the edge of the chair.

"Not you?" Johnson said, his heart skipping at the thought Kate might be stopping by to say goodbye.

"No. Krista, our junior reporter. I think I'm safe, at least for now. The whole thing just sucks. The fewer reporters we have, the harder it is for us to dig up the truth. That's pretty much our whole job, you know?"

Johnson nodded and leaned back in his chair. It wasn't just her job. Kate's search for truth consumed every part of her. A setback for the newspaper was like a blow to her life's purpose.

"It's not all up to you, you know," he said.

"What do you mean?"

"Uncovering truth. Pursuing justice. Even if the newspaper had 100 reporters, it wouldn't be able to right all the wrongs in the world."

Kate frowned. "If you're trying to be encouraging, it's not working."

"I'm just saying, you don't need to feel responsible for fixing everything that's broken. That's not humanly possible."

"If we don't fix it, who will?"

Johnson hesitated. He glanced up at the painting on his wall. He could almost smell the fresh breeze blowing in off the hills. A longing for home stirred deep in his chest.

"Some broken things won't ever be fixed here on earth," he said.

Kate's derisive snort blew away the encroaching fog of the past. She clearly wasn't buying it.

"That's little solace for the people who die violent deaths and the murders that go unpunished," she said. "That's actually what I came to talk to you about."

Johnson sat up straighter in his chair. "The murders? What about them?"

"I had lunch with Benito Muñoz today. He told me Ricardo Peña and Julian Costa were lifelong friends, which made me wonder whether his murder and the prostitution ring were connected. I went to talk to Muriel Costa this afternoon. She didn't tell me anything new, but you should have seen her reaction when I asked about Peña, who is spending an extended vacation with family in Mexico, by the way."

Even as his pulse quickened with excitement, a knot formed in the pit of Johnson's stomach. Every promising lead in the murder cases had turned to dust. He longed to believe his unsolved murders were connected to each other and even the prostitution ring. A common thread would make them so much easier to solve.

"Look, I know you've been told to drop the prostitution case, but I think you should keep digging," Kate continued. "These cases are connected. I just know it. If we keep picking around the edges, something will break loose."

That's what he'd decided to do after talking with the chief. Could this be the thread he was looking for?

"I want to believe there's a connection," he finally said. "I do. But I need evidence I can take to the chief."

"I've just given you evidence!" Kate said, exasperation filling her voice. "Costa and Peña were friends. Almost like brothers. What are the chances Costa didn't know Peña was up to his eyeballs in something shady? There's nothing else in his life that could have gotten him killed, at least not that you've found. Doesn't it seem likely that his death had something to do with what he knew? Maybe he was going to expose whoever Peña was working for. Or maybe he was involved too and wanted out."

Johnson's mind raced. That definitely put Costa's squeaky clean image in a different light.

"That's all possible. Some of it's even probable. But I still need something more to go on."

"You should go talk to Muriel Costa again," Kate said.

Johnson winced at the thought of stirring up the widow's grief. His first conversation with her had been excruciating. But then he suddenly remembered someone else who had been there that day: Father Tomás. If the priest knew the family as well as he seemed to, maybe he could at least point Johnson in the right direction. His face must have betrayed his growing excitement because Kate leaned forward with narrowed eyes.

"What is it?" she asked. "You just thought of something, didn't you?"

Johnson couldn't help smiling. "Maybe. More like someone. I just thought of someone I haven't talked to who might open up based on what you told me."

Kate's exultant grin lit up her whole face. "I knew it! This is not over. We will figure out who's responsible for all of this. And then we'll make them pay."

Johnson's smile faltered. "What if we can't?"

Kate's eyes widened in surprise. She looked as though he'd slapped her.

"What do you mean?"

"I mean, I'll follow this lead, but it might not break the whole case open. You realize that, right?"

"Of course," Kate huffed. "But then we'll just look somewhere else. Keep digging some more. We'll figure it out eventually."

Johnson's heart sank. He was determined to keep looking so he could say with a clean conscience he'd done everything he possibly could. But he knew the whole weight of the case didn't rest on his shoulders. How could he lift that burden Kate felt to make everything right? He resisted the temptation to reach out and take her hand.

"I'll do what I can," he said. "But if we hit another dead end?"

"Then we'll keep digging," she snapped, her eyes narrowing in frustration. "Or at least I will."

"And what if you reach a dead end you can't dig your way out of? Does that mean you've failed?"

Kate broke his gaze and looked down at her feet. A hint of despair tugged at the corners of her eyes and made her suddenly look achingly sad. Johnson stood, walked around the desk, and perched on the edge of the chair next to Kate's. She raised her head in surprise and looked at him searchingly.

"You are not responsible for saving people, or punishing them," he said gently. "You don't have that kind of power, and neither do I."

Kate didn't say anything for what seemed like a long time, but her eyes never stopped searching his face. She seemed torn between wanting to believe him and willing him to change his mind. Johnson waited as she struggled, watching the conflict crease her forehead and crinkle the corners of her eyes.

"But I don't want whoever's responsible for this to get away with it," Kate finally said, her voice barely above a whisper.

Unable to resist any longer, Johnson reached out slowly and took her hand in his.

"They won't," he said softly. "I promise you, they won't."

Chapter 25

Esperanza sat down at her dressing table and pulled a stack of eyeshadow pallets toward her.

El Jefe had told them to get ready for a special night. He was bringing new customers, and he wanted the girls to be on their best, most welcoming, behavior. Esperanza assumed Jim also would be there. He hadn't missed an opportunity to see Gloria since that first night he asked to have her all to himself.

Every time Jim had visited Gloria in the last few weeks, Esperanza marveled at his longing gaze and lovesick smiles. El Jefe had even started to make fun of him to his face, although he did it playfully. Esperanza assumed he didn't really want to offend the man who had become his best customer. But did he worry this man might learn what was really going on and try to do something about it?

Esperanza picked up a stubby black eyeliner pencil worn short with use. As she prepared to sweep it across the edge of her lashes she noticed faint lines feathering out from the corner of her eyes. Fear and constant anxiety had left their mark. But that wasn't all. A growing guilt shadowed her face as well.

Until recently, Esperanza had thought of herself as El Jefe's caged animal, forced to do his bidding no matter what. She thought he had complete control. But she had slowly started to realize he shared some risk too. Once that understanding took root, she began to get a sickening sense of the vicious cycle of fear and desire that really ensnared them. Any one of the customers could expose what was going on in that house by making an anonymous call to the police. But El Jefe counted on their desire to suppress any qualms they might have about taking women against their will. He also counted on fear of exposure to keep them silent. None of the men would want his family to know what he was doing.

Esperanza thought the cycle ended there. But she had come to understand that she and Gloria had a role, too. At any moment they could refuse to play their part in the charade. They could fight, scream, expose the true nature of their plight to the customers. At least that might make it harder for the men to enjoy an experience they likely thought of as a meeting between two, consenting adults. So, why did they keep quiet, smiling when they wanted to scream and opening their arms when every instinct compelled them to fight? Fear of pain, or worse. And the desire for freedom, as elusive as it seemed. She'd come to think of it as their complicity in their own captivity. Fear and desire. That vicious cycle of dependency was the only thing keeping El Jefe in business.

Jim's infatuation with Gloria was a new factor in the equation. Several times, Esperanza had spotted El Jefe watching the man with her sister. Eyes narrowed, lips pursed, he seemed to be calculating the risk of this unexpected complication. Esperanza's heart hammered in her ears and her head started to throb when she thought about the danger this attempt to gain Gloria's freedom posed. What if El Jefe decided to cut Jim off before Gloria could convince him to pay her debt and take her away from this hellhole? What if Jim got tired of paying so much money to see Gloria and decided to satiate his desire elsewhere?

Esperanza took a deep breath and let it out slowly. Having a shred of hope was almost worse than having no hope at all. It gnawed at her stomach and sent her mind spinning in torturous circles. Fear of losing it made her cling to it with a suffocating, isolating desperation. She couldn't let Gloria see how urgently she had come to view this opportunity. Each of Jim's visits only reinforced her belief that he might be her sister's only chance at escape.

A tap on her door made her jump. Gloria slipped inside and came to stand behind her. She wore a sleek black sheath dress that hung almost to her knee. It would have been modest if not for the side slit that went all the way to her hip. She had curled her hair and piled it up on the back of her head in a silky, shimmering cascade.

"What are you doing?" Gloria asked, tapping her sister on the shoulder with disapproving urgency. "It's almost seven. They'll be here soon."

Sweat started to prick Esperanza's brow at the thought of El Jefe's wrath. "I lost track of time. Do my hair while I fix my makeup."

They worked in silence for the next five minutes. After ringing her eyes with heavy black liner, Esperanza dusted several shades of pink powder across her lids. A soft tangerine blush accented her high cheekbones, and fuchsia gloss turned her lips into a beacon of lust. Gloria had twisted her hair into a knot at the nape of her neck and stood holding out an electric blue, slinky shift as soon as Esperanza set down her last brush. She stood and stepped into the dress, turning around so Gloria could help close the back.

"Are you okay, chula?" she asked, looking over her shoulder as Gloria pulled up the long zipper.

The teen nodded but started chewing on her bottom lip. Esperanza turned around and put her hands on her sister's shoulders.

"You're nervous. What is it?"

Gloria smiled hesitantly. Her chest and neck flushed. "I think we're close," she said. "I just have a feeling that tonight could be the night."

Esperanza suddenly had a hard time breathing, like someone had placed a hand over her nose and mouth. "What makes you say that?"

"He's just been more intense with every visit," Gloria whispered. "He almost scared me last time, he was so passionate. He held me so tightly... You said I would know when it was time to ask him to take me away from all this. I think it's time."

Esperanza pulled her sister close and wrapped her arms tightly around her shoulders. Tears blurred her vision. Before dawn they would know whether their plan would work.

"Oh, Gloria!" For a few minutes Esperanza couldn't get anything else past the lump in her throat. "Everything's going to be okay," she finally said, as much for herself as for her baby sister. "You've done so well, been so patient. He's completely obsessed with you. How could he say no?"

She pulled away and looked into her sister's luminous brown eyes. They sparkled with a feverish kind of excitement.

"I can't believe this could all be over soon," Gloria whispered. "It's too good to be true."

"It's not!" Esperanza took her sister's hands and squeezed them tight. "You'll see. He wants you all to himself. All you have to do is tell him that's what you want too. He'll do whatever he can to make that happen."

"What if El Jefe won't let me go?"

Esperanza had asked herself the same question thousands of times, but hearing her sister say it out loud made it palpably terrifying. Fear made her suddenly dizzy.

"Don't say that! Don't even think it," she said, gripping her sister's shoulders for support. "Jim will find a way to set you free. He has to!"

Gloria nodded. Tears glistened in her eyes. They stood like that for several minutes, paralyzed by fear and hope. Esperanza's mind whirled with possibilities. Tonight would be the night.

"I hope you're right," Gloria finally said, as the crunch of tires on gravel signaled the men's arrival. "I hope you're right."

Chapter 26

El Jefe brought four men with him. Esperanza didn't recognize any of their faces, but their hungry eyes and macho swaggers were all too familiar. They looked like little boys at a candy store who'd been told they could have whatever they wanted. When she realized Jim wasn't with them, sinking, sickening dismay made it even harder for her to conjure fake smiles for the others.

She tried to catch Gloria's eye to see how she was taking Jim's absence, but the teen was too busy taking drink orders and trying to avoid the unwanted pinches and caresses of the new customers. Her youth and beauty always drew immediate attention.

About 20 minutes passed before Esperanza heard the front door open again. She glanced up just in time to see Jim slip inside. El Jefe met him halfway across the living room and extended his hand in greeting. But the gesture looked stiff and his usual slap on the back and wide-mouthed smile was missing. He clearly wasn't happy to have an extra guest. A knot of worry began to form in Esperanza's stomach.

After the men exchanged a few words, El Jefe motioned for Jim to follow him back to the kitchen. Across the room, Esperanza could see Gloria trailing them with her eyes. She had to figure out what was going on. Turning to the two men closest to her, Esperanza offered to refresh their drinks. From the bar, she could hear the hushed but tense tones coming from the kitchen.

"I'm not trying to crash your party," Jim said. "I just wanted to see her."

"You see her too much already, mi amigo," El Jefe hissed. "She's not your girlfriend. And you're not the only man she sees. Gloria's very popular, no? You see how the other men look at her."

"Don't," Jim said, the slight whine in his voice revealing how much El Jefe's words pained him. "It's not the same. I really care for her."

"Bah! Care for her. You care for what she gives you, same as the others. Only you've let it become an obsession."

"Just let me stay tonight. I'm not here to cause any trouble."

Esperanza held her breath when El Jefe didn't respond right away.

"Fine," he finally snapped. "But you'll wait until all the others have had a turn. If she's got any energy left after that, you can have her."

As he strode out of the kitchen, he let out one of his barking laughs. Esperanza stood very still as he passed the bar, hoping he wouldn't look her way. After he was out of sight, she let out a sigh of relief and hurried back to the living room to deliver the drinks. He showed no sign of having noticed her absence.

Throughout the night, Jim sat in the corner of one of the overstuffed couches, nursing a scotch. None of the other men paid him any attention, but he hardly ever took his eyes off Gloria. His frown deepened and his color rose every time she smiled at one of the other men. In between delivering drinks and enduring groping caresses, Esperanza watched the two of them. When one of the other men bent down and kissed Gloria's neck, squeezing her bottom at the same time, Jim's whole body stiffened and his lips curled into a vicious snarl. She trembled with dread as she watched his anger boil. She prayed fervently he wouldn't take it out on Gloria. Surely he knew she didn't have a choice.

After a few drinks, the men's attention started getting more insistent. They groped the girls openly, almost challenging them to resist. One in particular wouldn't leave Gloria alone. El Jefe finally sauntered up to the two of them, standing about 10 feet from Jim, and threw his arm around the new customer.

"She's delicioso, isn't she mi amigo?" he crooned. "Hard to resist. Mmmm. No need to deny yourself. Take her back to her room. It's what she's been waiting for all day, isn't that right, putita."

Esperanza's mouth went dry as she watched her sister's eyes widen in alarm. El Jefe saw it too, and it seemed only to fuel his masochistic delight. He reached out and grabbed Gloria's face, shaking her roughly. His fingers sank into her soft cheeks and she let out a whimper of protest. Esperanza felt Gloria's terror as though she audibly cried out for mercy, begging for someone to protect her.

"Ha, ha!" El Jefe barked, his eyes flashing with excitement. "Take her, mi amigo. Take her! Oh, and you should know, she likes it rough."

With one last shake, he released Gloria, leaving only the red silhouette of his fingers and the palpable sense of horror. On the couch, Jim clenched and released his fists, his face flushed a deep red. But he did not make a move to stop the other man from leading Gloria down the hall. Panic clutched Esperanza's throat, making it almost impossible to breathe. She felt so dizzy she might have fallen if one of the other men hadn't sidled up to her and put his arm around her waist. She grabbed his hand and pulled him toward the back of the house. She at least wanted to be near her sister, even if she couldn't do anything to protect her from the man primed to brutalize her.

For the next 30 minutes, Esperanza strained to catch every sound coming from the room next door. Her sister cried out in pain several times. Each yelp felt like a knife sunk deep in Esperanza's gut. The agony of her powerlessness just made the knife twist. When the man with her was done, she quickly slipped back into her dress and walked back into the living room.

"Oh, yeah, she liked it rough," the man who had been with her sister was telling the others. "I'm not sure she'll have much left for either of you."

"That's all right," one of the men said, setting his drink down and heading for the hall. "I'll get my money's worth."

"I guess that leaves you for me," the fourth man said, pulling Esperanza to him. "Let's go, sweetheart."

This time, Esperanza didn't hear anything from the other room. The fear of what that might mean clawed at her mind, shredding the last remnants of her hope for the night. How had everything fallen apart so quickly? When she was free, she got dressed again and went back to the living room. El Jefe sat with the two other men on one couch. Jim still sat in the corner of the other, his mouth set in a hard line, his eyes vacant. Esperanza busied herself behind the bar, where she could avoid notice but still hear and see everything in the living room. A few minutes later, the third man emerged from her sister's room, a smirk on his face. He made a big show of buckling his belt. The others laughed.

"I've got to say, you sure know how to throw a party," he said, raising his hand to his forehead in a mock salute to El Jefe.

"And there's plenty more where that came from, mi amigo," El Jefe said, standing and stretching his arms over his head. "But tonight, it's late. I think we've all had enough fun for one day, no?"

The others stood too, draining the last of their drinks and swapping self-satisfied smiles. El Jefe opened the front door and motioned for the men to head down the stairs. Before following them, he turned to fix Jim with a long, cold stare.

"She's all yours, mi amigo. But make it fast, no? Gloria needs her beauty sleep."

As El Jefe's heavy footfalls echoed down the steps, Esperanza glanced out the side door to the deck. The embers of El Carcelero's cigarette glowed in the dark, a barely perceptible sign of his constant presence. El Jefe had probably warned him to keep a close watch on his unwanted guest. If Gloria could persuade Jim to take her with him tonight, could the three of them overpower their jailer? Esperanza had never seen him with a gun, but she didn't doubt he had one close by.

Esperanza wanted to see her sister before Jim went to her, but she didn't want to delay their meeting any longer. She watched him stand from the couch, draining his drink like the others had done. She tried to read his face. Anger had transformed his gentle features into a rigid mask. She knew he was furious. El Jefe had humiliated him. She hoped that would only make him more likely to heed her sister's plea for help.

He didn't even glance her way as he strode down the hallway and opened her sister's door. She began to tremble, tears stinging the back of her eyes, when he shut it firmly behind him. She hurried back to her own room and pulled her chair up to the wall. For about forty-five minutes she sat with her ear pressed to the sheetrock, straining to pick up any little sound. Her eyelids were starting to get heavy when a long, low moan broke the silence.

"Why, Gloria, why? You know how I feel about you."

Esperanza jumped up from the chair. A spike of adrenaline set her heart hammering. She ran to her door but hesitated as her hand closed around the knob. She couldn't hear anything else. She ran back to the wall and pressed her whole body against it, willing another clue that would tell her what was going on.

Another series of moans slowly turned her anxiety to fear. She had never heard Jim make a noise when he was with her sister. Was he giving voice to his passion or his anger? As he continued to cry out, Esperanza strained to hear her sister. Nothing. But Jim continued to moan, his cries broken by jagged gasps. They finally reached a crescendo and then died away, leaving a heavy silence. For a few minutes, all Esperanza could hear was the thudding of her heart.

Then a long, low howl split the night. It tore through Esperanza's ears, a harbinger of utter destruction.

"Gloria! Gloria! Gloria!"

Esperanza sprinted out her door and burst into her sister's room. El Carcelero was right behind her.

Gloria lay in the middle of the bed, her eyes closed. Jim was on his knees next to her, his hands on her shoulders.

"Gloria! Gloria, wake up." He shook her gently at first then more vigorously. "Oh, God. God! What's happened? I've killed her!"

Esperanza ran to the bed and flung herself on her sister. Frantically, she wiped the hair away from her face and rubbed her cheek.

"Wake up, chula. Wake up! I'm here. It's okay. I'm here."

On the other side of the bed, El Carcelero dragged Jim to the floor and placed two fingers on the side of Gloria's neck.

"No! NO! She's just fainted. It was all too much. Gloria, wake up!" Esperanza's voice rose with every word, until she was finally screaming. "Gloria, WAKE UP!"

But her sister never moved. She looked like she was asleep, but as the reality of what had happened began to sink in, Esperanza let out a long, keening wail. Burying her head in her hands, she screamed and screamed. While the men looked on, seemingly unable to move, Esperanza finally looked up to the ceiling and let out a piercing howl.

"What did you do?" El Carcelero growled, turning on Jim where he stood at the end of the bed, clutching a sheet to his chest. When he responded with just an inarticulate gurgling, El Carcelero shoved him up against the wall. "What happened?"

"I don't know. I don't know! We were making love. I guess I put my hands around her neck. I was so overwhelmed with the other men, all of it. I just wanted her to know how much she meant to me."

"Yeah, you showed her alright," El Carcelero said.

Esperanza was gasping for breath. She felt like Jim's hands were around her throat. Bright spots danced before her eyes. All she could do was wail as she continued to stroke her sister's lifeless cheek. The blow across her jaw caught her by surprise and cut off her cry.

"Shut up! Shut up and let me think!" her jailer shouted. Pointing at Jim, he said, "You, don't move."

El Carcelero's fist had stopped her cry, but it couldn't stem the flow of tears cascading down Esperanza's cheeks. Her sister's sweet face, impossibly serene in death, swam before her eyes. She patted the folds of loose sheet until she found Gloria's hand. Grasping it gently, she brought it to her face and kissed the palm. The last time she had done that, they were sitting at their mother's bare kitchen table, talking about the man who had offered Esperanza the chance to come to America. Gloria had begged to come too. Esperanza refused at first. Her sister was too young to leave school to work in a country where they would have no legal status, no friends or family to help them. Esperanza had read stories of men and women caught by the police and bused back across the border. She was willing to take the risk, but she didn't want her sister to suffer the indignity of being unwelcome in a foreign land.

But Gloria persisted. She wheedled, begged. Their mother even took her side. She would rather her girls be together, she said. You will be a comfort to each other, she insisted, finally persuading Esperanza by telling her Gloria had no prospects of a future at home. When she finally gave in, they were sitting in the kitchen, the warm, spicy punch of chorizo filling the air as their mother cooked dinner. After she told Gloria she would take her to America, she had lifted the teen's hand to her mouth and kissed it. *I'll keep you safe*, she had promised.

The agony of everything they had endured, from the moment the broker handed them over to the men at the dock to the final forced act of intimacy that took Gloria's life bore down on Esperanza, bowing her back and pressing her facedown on the bed. She would do anything to trade places with her sister.

Through the fog of her grief, Esperanza could hear El Carcelero in the hallway, talking on his phone. She didn't even bother to sit up when she heard him walk back into the room.

"You, get dressed," he barked. Esperanza could hear clothes being tossed across the room.

"What are you going to do?" Jim said, his voice trembling.

"I'm going to clean up your mess. And you're going to help me."

"What do you mean?" Jim asked. It sounded like he was putting on his pants.

"We've got to get rid of the body, tonto. We're going to dump it in the Bay. Hurry up."

Esperanza sat up and spun around wildly.

"What? No! No! You're not taking her anywhere!" she said, still clinging to Gloria's hand. She looked frantically from one man to the other. "We have to call the police! He murdered her."

El Carcelero snorted. Esperanza watched, struggling to understand what was happening as he snatched up the sheet piled at Jim's feet and spread it out on the floor. He grabbed Esperanza by the shoulder and yanked her off the bed, sending her tumbling to the floor.

"Grab her feet," he barked at Jim as he hooked both hands under Gloria's armpits.

Dazed, Esperanza watched as they swung her sister from the bed and set her down in the middle of the sheet. Her head made a sickening thud on the wood plank floor. Esperanza screamed, the sound exploding from her mouth in an involuntary rush. She scrambled onto the sheet and threw herself onto her sister's body, wrapping her arms around Gloria's limp shoulders.

"No! Don't touch her," she wailed, rocking back and forth.

From behind, El Carcelero grabbed both her arms, pulling her up and off her sister. Gloria's head fell back again, smacking the floor. Esperanza thrashed and kicked, trying to break free of his vice grip. He grunted when her heel connected with his shin. But that was the only satisfaction she got for all her fighting. He pinned her arms behind her back and wrestled her to the ground.

"Get the tape," he grunted, nodding toward the door to Gloria's room, where Esperanza could now see a roll of silver tape and a pile of rope. When Jim came close enough to hand El Carcelero the tape, Esperanza spit at him.

"Murderer!" she screamed, as El Carcelero wrapped the heavy tape tight around her wrists. He spun her around, so that her back was up against the bed and wrapped more tape around her outstretched legs. He pressed the final piece firmly across her mouth. Over his shoulder, Esperanza could see Jim kneeling over her sister. Tears streamed down his face.

"I never meant to hurt her," he said, looking at Esperanza with pleading eyes. "It was an accident."

"Enough!" El Carcelero barked. "Wrap her up."

"We can't leave her like this," Jim said. "Please, at least let me put her clothes on."

"Fine. Just hurry up."

Powerless, Esperanza watched as the man she had foolishly pinned so many hopes on clumsily redressed her sister in the slinky black sheath she'd put on so many hours ago. He struggled to get it over her head and pull her limp arms through the armholes. When he was finally done, he smoothed the hair back from her face and carefully adjusted the gold heart at her throat. Under the thin chain, Esperanza could see the purple smudges beginning to appear where his hands had clamped down until they snuffed out her sister's life. Tears pooled in her eyes and spilled onto her cheeks.

When Jim finally sat back, El Carcelero flipped one side of the sheet over Gloria and rolled her into the rest of it, until she was completely shrouded in the white linen. Esperanza whimpered uncontrollably as he wrapped tape around her sister's ankles, her waist, and finally around her neck, folding the end of the sheet down to make a tight hood.

"All right," he finally said, straightening up and wiping the sweat from his forehead. "Lets get her to the boat. We don't have long before the sun comes up."

The trickle of Esperanza's tears turned to sobs as the men lifted her sister and carried her into the hallway. She tried to quiet her cries so she could hear what they were doing once they made it under the house. After some scraping and banging, she heard a faint splash followed by the purr of an outboard motor. She held her breath until she was absolutely sure the sound had died away, leaving her enveloped in a heavy, empty silence.

She leaned her head back into the side of the bed, inhaling the fresh scent of her sister's perfume. A wave of nausea sent bile surging into her throat. She gagged against the tape over her mouth, and a fresh wave of sobs shook her body. When the sobs finally melted into whimpers, she slid sideways until she was laying on the floor, her cheek pressed against the cool boards. Her eyelids, swollen with tears, slowly closed and her sister's smiling face faded into the darkness. The image stretched and widened until she could see the whole, bright scene. The memory was so vivid, Esperanza thought for a moment she was really there. Gloria was at home, in the kitchen, twirling around the table to show off the colorful skirt her mother had just finished sewing. She was laughing, her eyes full of life and her face fresh with the promise of future hopes and dreams.

"Lo siento, Gloria," she whispered. "Lo siento."

Chapter 27

A cool wind knifed through Kate's thin hoodie and propelled her toward the knot of police officers clustered at the water's edge. The first cold front of the fall had blown in overnight, rattling the windows in her loft and driving away the last traces of summer's misery. When she woke up, she figured she would spend the day working on a weather story. She was saved from that reporter's hell by a call over the police scanner announcing a body had washed up near Channelview Drive.

The street ran parallel to the island's north shore. Its row of large houses, most of which had private piers jutting out into Galveston Bay, looked across the water to the mainland. Tucked away behind Harborside Drive, past all of the port's docks and warehouses, it had a secluded feel. People paid good money for a house here because they didn't want to deal with the tourists on the West End or the traffic in Offats Bayou.

Kate spotted Johnson among the group of officers standing near the water. Between their dark blue uniformed legs, she caught glimpses of a dingy white sheet.

She hung back until the coroner arrived. When the officers broke their huddle to make way for the gurney, Johnson looked up and Kate caught his eye. The familiar flutters of excitement started to stir. When Johnson held up one finger to let her know he would come give her the details in a minute, the flutters accelerated into a full hurricane.

While she watched from about 50 feet away, the coroner and his assistant lifted the body onto the gurney. It looked like a mummy with duct tape wrapped around its ankles, waist, and neck. Pulling a pair of scissors out of his bag, the coroner carefully cut through the tape around the neck and folded back the cloth until he could lift it away from the body. Kate strained to see but the angle completely blocked her view. Frowning in frustration, she took a few steps forward. Johnson looked up and shook his head at her, almost imperceptibly. But she saw. If she wanted any information, she'd better not take another step.

Johnson pulled a small notebook and pen out of his front pocket and started taking notes as the coroner pointed to the body. His eyebrows rose. He nodded rapidly. His pen made circular motions on the paper, as though he was sketching something. What had him so excited? Kate stomped her foot with impatience. Johnson's head snapped up and he frowned at her. She had to wait through five more minutes of pointing and nodding before Johnson flipped the notebook closed and the coroner wheeled the gurney back to his van. As he drove off,

Johnson walked slowly over to Kate. Butterflies beat a steady rhythm against her ribs.

"Hey," he said, flashing her a lopsided smile.

Heat crept across Kate's cheeks. The memory of their last conversation briefly crowded out all the questions that had been building in her mind.

"Hey yourself. So, what do we have here? Something seemed to have you pretty excited."

"It's another young Hispanic woman."

Kate couldn't hide her excitement as she looked up with wide eyes and parted lips.

"It's hard to tell, but she looks no older than twenty."

"Just like the first murder," Kate said, her hand shaking slightly. "Could you tell what happened to her?"

"Judging by the bruising around her neck, I'd say she was strangled. But we'll have to wait for the coroner's report to say for sure."

"Could you tell how long she's been in the water?"

"Not long. Probably just a few days."

"Well, somebody obviously dumped her after they killed her. I don't suppose she had any ID."

"We won't know for sure until we get her fully unwrapped. But she's wearing a party dress, and I doubt it's got any pockets."

"So, we've got another unidentified dead woman and no way to figure out who she is."

"Maybe. But we may have gotten lucky this time."

"What do you mean?"

Johnson paused and looked at her intently, like he was trying to figure out how much to tell her. "This is off the record. Completely off the record."

"Oh, come on. You're killing me."

"I mean it, Kate. This could be big, and I have to talk to the chief to make sure he agrees with making it public."

Kate signed and rolled her eyes.

"Hey! At least you're the first to know about it. I could make you wait."

"Okay, okay. Spill it."

"She's wearing a necklace, a gold heart pendant. It looks pretty unusual, like it was handmade. Maybe one of a kind. If we can find out where it came from, maybe we can figure out who she is."

"Do you really think it will be that easy? What are the chances it's that unique?"

Johnson shrugged. "It's one more clue than we had last time a young woman was murdered. I'll take anything I can get."

Kate pursed her lips and tapped her pen on her notepad. "When you decide to go public, I'll be the first to know, right?"

"Of course." Johnson grinned. "I can't promise you'll have exclusive access, but I'll call you first."

"Okay. Back on the record? Where do you think she came from?"

"It's hard to say. With the currents around here, it could be the mainland. She might also have been dropped off the causeway, or dumped somewhere in West Bay. If we don't get a hit from missing persons reports or on the necklace, we'll probably have the National Weather Service do some current models to find the most likely point of origin."

Kate looked up and out across the water. A pelican swooped and wheeled just above the white caps, finally plunging beneath the surface. When he rocketed out of the water a few seconds later, a fish tail wriggled wildly from the side of his long beak. Kate shuddered.

"Do you think there's any chance there's a connection between this girl and the one from Fish Village?"

"I have no idea," Johnson said evenly, eyeing her notebook.

Kate closed the cover and tucked it into the back pocket of her jeans. "Not for the story. For me."

"I really don't know, Kate." Johnson sighed. For a minute, the shadows that had haunted his eyes all summer returned. "I would love for them to be related. But who knows? People get killed all the time. We could be dealing with something entirely different here."

Kate nodded. She searched his face for any sign he had more hope than he was letting on. He returned her stare with a look she couldn't decipher. Then he smiled.

"On the other hand, maybe this is the break we've been hoping for."

Kate grinned at him. "Call me when you have something, okay?"

"I will."

She turned to go and then suddenly remembered what she'd been waiting all week to ask him. "Oh! What about that lead you were going to follow up on in the Julian Costa case?"

Frustration furrowed Johnson's brow. "I've left a few messages but haven't heard back. Looks like I'm going to have to follow up in person."

Kate wrinkled her nose in disappointment. But he hadn't given up. That was a good sign.

~ ~ ~ ~ ~

The next morning, Kate's cell phone rang just as she was taking the first sip of her first cup of coffee. The sight of Johnson's number on the screen made her catch her breath. She was still stinging from the berating Mattingly had given her when he found out she knew about a major clue in the case but couldn't use it in yesterday's story. He had already jumped to the conclusion that the body in the sheet was connected to the girl from Fish Village. And he was determined the *Gazette* would be the one to break the news. Kate fervently hoped Johnson had something to tell her on the record as she picked up the phone.

"Your patience has been rewarded," Johnson said, without even saying hello. "And I persuaded the chief to give you an exclusive."

Kate sloshed hot coffee onto her hand as she slammed down her mug and rummaged in her messenger bag for her notebook and a pen.

"That's no small miracle," she said, flipping to a clean page. "I thought he would never forgive us for all the stories about the prostitution ring."

"He's a practical man. He knows we need you guys almost as much as you need us. Plus, Ben might have smoothed things over with his glowing profile of the neighborhood policing plan."

Kate snorted. She had meant to write that story herself before she got so wrapped up in the prostitution ring saga.

"So what do you have for me?"

"We're going public with the necklace today. Press conference at 3 p.m. But I'll give you the details now so you can put up a web story before then. Just make sure you have a photographer there so you can get pictures of this thing. We're hoping someone will recognize it and call the tip line."

"How much of a long shot is this?"

"Hopefully it's not. This thing is pretty unusual. It's definitely handmade, but the craftsmanship is good. I'm sure it wasn't cheap."

"Have you talked to the local jewelers?"

"Yeah, none of them recognizes it. And it's not on any of the pawn shop registries either."

"So, someone brought it onto the island. You just have to figure out whether it was the dead girl or whoever gave it to her. I guess you didn't find any missing persons reports that matched her description?"

"Not yet. We'll be releasing a sketch this afternoon. Hopefully, between the sketch and the necklace, someone will recognize her."

"What about a connection between this dead girl and the other one?"

"It's nothing but speculation at this point. The only similarities are their age and the fact that they're both Hispanic. That's not much of a connection. This girl was well-dressed and groomed. She looked like she'd been to some high-end party."

"Did the coroner find any signs of drugs or alcohol in her system?"

"Not a trace."

"What about signs of sexual assault?"

Johnson sighed. "He said it was hard to tell. There was definitely some bruising and signs of recent trauma. But she had no defensive wounds. In fact she didn't have a mark on her, other than the bruising around her neck. If she was assaulted, she didn't put up much of a fight. It's possible the sex was consensual."

Kate winced. What had this girl been involved with? Whatever it was, she'd bet it wasn't consensual, since it ended with her being wrapped in a sheet and dumped in the bay. But until the police figured out who she was, they'd never know for sure.

"Well, I'd better get going so I can get this story up as soon as possible. Thanks for giving me the exclusive. Mattingly was pretty pissed we couldn't print anything about the necklace yesterday."

Johnson laughed. "Hopefully this will get you out of the doghouse."

"Hopefully." When Johnson didn't say anything in response, an awkward silence hung between them. "Well, thanks again. I guess I'll see you this afternoon."

"Wait. Kate?" Johnson's voice sounded a little strained. "I saw Brian last night. He acted kind of weird when I asked where you were."

Kate's chest tightened and she squeezed her temples with her free hand.

"Yeah ... we're kind of taking a break. It's complicated."

"It usually is," Johnson said.

Kate didn't know what to say. She never expected Johnson to ask about her love life. And she had no intention of trying to explain it to him.

"Yeah. Look, I gotta go."

"Hey, I didn't mean to butt in. It's none of my business. I just wanted to make sure you were okay."

"I'm fine," Kate said tersely. She sighed and willed some of the tension out of her voice. "I mean, I'm fine. Thanks."

After they hung up, Kate picked up her coffee cup and took a long draw of the lukewarm brew. Her pulse had started to pound at the top of her head. She rarely got personal with anyone. Even after dating Brian for six months, she didn't talk much about her family or her feelings. But when Johnson asked, explanations, excuses, and questions almost tumbled out like junk from an overstuffed closet.

He could probably sort out her confusion in half the time it would take her to describe it. The urge to call him back tingled like a deep itch at the back of her neck. The downside to perpetual isolation was that at some point, the human craving for connection shouted down every rational line of self-defense. It bubbled up deep in her soul, a longing to know and be known. She'd been fighting it for years. Was the protracted war winding down? When she finally surrendered, would anyone be left to witness it?

The dead girl's necklace

A heart-shaped pendant could hold the clue to solving the island's latest homicide

By Kate Bennett

The young woman who washed up near Channelview Drive yesterday morning was wearing a heart-shaped pendant police say could hold the key to catching her killer.

During an afternoon press conference, investigators unveiled the necklace and asked anyone who recognized it to call the tip line.

"This is a unique piece of jewelry," Det. Peter Johnson said. "It's not something you could just pick up at any run-of-the-mill jewelers. We're sure someone out there will recognize it."

The 18 karat gold pendant is made of a vine of what look like daisies, twined into a heart shape. At the top, a tiny bird perches, its beak open as if in song.

Before showing the necklace publicly, police took it to all the island jewelers. None of them recognized it.

Investigators believe someone brought the necklace to the island, either the dead girl herself or the person who gave it to her. Although anyone who recognizes the necklace might hesitate to reach out to the police, Johnson insisted investigators would not equate knowledge about the pendant with involvement in the murder.

"Someone knows who this girl is and has probably seen her wearing this necklace," he said. "That doesn't mean they know anything about how she died. Of course, if they do, we definitely want to hear that. But at this point, we'd like to start with her name and try to find out where she came from. Someone's got to be missing her."

Once they know her name, investigators hope to retrace her steps and find out where she was and who she was with in the last few weeks.

Like the summer's first murder, the girl found shot to death in Fish Village, the latest murder victim remains unidentified. She did not have any ID on her body and she does not match the description of anyone reported missing in the area. The necklace offers the best hope of finding out who she is. Twenty-four hours after releasing a sketch of the young woman, investigators have no solid leads on her identity.

Although the two murder victims share some similarities—both were young and Hispanic—investigators say they do not have enough information to know whether they're connected.

"At this point, it's all speculation," Johnson said. "If they are connected, we'll do everything we can to find out how."

Galveston police have one other unsolved murder on the books—longshoreman Julian Costa. But investigators never found any connection between Costa's death and the woman in Fish Village. They have no reason to believe this girl's murder is connected to Costa's either, Johnson said.

Chapter 28

Johnson woke up at five a.m. the next morning and arrived at the station an hour later. After the previous night's newscasts, the tip line rang nonstop for hours. A few of the tips were credible enough to send an officer to follow up, but Johnson didn't believe any of them held the key to solving the murder. At least, not yet. One of the secretaries was taking a call when he walked in, but she shook her head at his raised eyebrow of inquiry.

"Yes, sir, it's entirely possible that the aliens left the necklace when they dropped this young woman off in the Bay," she said, rolling her eyes as she tugged on her headset. "We'll be careful. Thank you for the warning."

Johnson shook his head and walked to the break room to get a cup of coffee. He expected this morning would yield another round of tips as the early newscasts rolled and newspapers hit driveways. When he walked back into the conference room where the bank of phones had been set up to take calls, two more secretaries had arrived. All three of the women were now on the phone. Johnson leaned in a corner, sipping his coffee and listening to them quiz callers to gauge their credibility. After about 15 minutes, he was ready to give up and go back to his office to look over the case file again when one of the secretaries waved at him. Eyes narrowed, pen poised over her notepad, she listened intently to the person on the other end of the line.

Johnson's chest tightened. He rocked forward on the balls of his feet.

"Let me transfer you to the detective who's heading up the case," she said. "He's going to want to talk to you."

Johnson didn't wait for an explanation. Pointing in the direction of his office, he jogged out the door. The phone on his desk was ringing when he burst in and snatched up the handset.

"This is Detective Johnson," he said, perching on his chair and pulling a notepad and pen out of his top drawer.

"Detective, my name is Ephraim Getz. I own a jewelry story in Rice Village, in Houston. I understand you're looking for one of my necklaces."

"What makes you so sure you sold this necklace?" Johnson gripped the edge of his desk as he struggled to keep his voice steady so he didn't betray his rising excitement.

"I didn't just sell it, detective. I made it."

Johnson shot out of his chair, knocking it over. It took every ounce of self-control not to shout. "You made this necklace? How can you be sure."

"I'm looking at a copy of the *Houston Chronicle*, and the photo is very detailed. This is one of a series I made this spring. Each one is unique, but they're all similar. Variation on a theme, if you like. If you bring it to me, I can tell you for sure."

"Would you be able to tell me who bought it?"

"Of course. I keep detailed records for all of my pieces. They are little works of art."

"I'll be there in an hour," Johnson said, jotting down the address before he slammed down the phone.

His heart pounded so hard he could feel it pulsing through the vein in his forehead. This was the only lead he'd had in months. He was one step closer to catching a murderer. He silently prayed this was the break he'd been waiting for.

~ ~ ~ ~ ~

It was too early for shoppers when Johnson pulled into the parking lot of Getz's shop. It sat conspicuously on a corner, where shoppers could catch a glimpse of his glittering merchandise from the street. He had to knock on the glass door to catch the sales woman's attention. While he waited for her to come out from behind the counter to let him in, he glanced at the display on his right. Nestled in a bed of black velvet, surrounded by diamond bracelets, Rolex watches, and engagement rings, sat three heart pendants very similar to the one in his pocket.

"You must be Detective Johnson. Please come in," said a young woman with auburn curls that bounced as she swung the door open wide and ushered him inside. "Mr. Getz will be out in just a moment."

Johnson followed her toward the back of the store, glancing at the expensive trinkets glowing under soft lights behind heavy glass. Everything about the store exuded an understated and effortless opulence. If the dead girl belonged to this world of privilege, surely someone would have missed her by now. If she didn't belong, how did one of Getz's necklaces find its way around her neck?

"Detective Johnson, I'm sorry to keep you waiting," said a short, stocky man with a shock of dark hair and a bushy mustache. He set down a thick, three-ring binder on the counter in front of Johnson, pulled off his horn-rimmed glasses and began rubbing them vigorously with a white handkerchief. "This has been quite an unwelcome surprise."

"I'm sure," Johnson said, taking a small, plastic ziplock bag from his pocket. "I don't suppose any of your jewelry has ever shown up at a crime scene before."

"Hardly," Getz said, unfolding a piece of black velvet and spreading it on the glass between them. Johnson opened the bag and slid the gold pendant onto the cloth. He held his breath while the jeweler picked it up lovingly and squinted at it for several minutes. He took out a magnifying glass and inspected the back.

"Well, I didn't have any doubt this was my necklace, but now that I've seen my stamp, I'm positive." He handed Johnson the magnifying glass and pointed to the tip of the heart. With the help of the curved lens, Johnson could just make out a tiny "EG" etched into the gold.

"If, by chance, someone decided to copy my design, they would hardly bother to include my stamp," Getz said.

"So, can you tell me who bought it?"

"Of course. I've got the records right here, although I don't need to look it up. I just sold this a few weeks ago, to one of my regular customers."

A shiver of excitement danced between Johnson's shoulder blades as Getz opened the binder and flipped to a page toward the back. Under a grid of photos, the jeweler had penned names and dates. He pointed to a photo of the pendant between them.

"James Finney. October 26. I believe he said it was for his daughter."

"How old is she?"

"Ten, I believe."

"She's definitely not our victim then," Johnson said, more to himself than to Getz.

"No, and I doubt seriously Mr. Finney had anything to do with a murder. He and his wife are well-respected members of the community."

Johnson's eyes narrowed. He looked hard at the jeweler. "You haven't called him, have you?"

"No, detective. But I assume he's seen the news reports, just like everyone else. I'm surprised he didn't call you himself. I'm sure there's some very logical explanation for this."

"Mmmmmmm," Johnson said, scooping the pendant back into the bag. "Until we get this cleared up, please don't discuss it with anyone."

"Of course." Getz bristled with offense. "I'm hardly interested in advertising this. It's not exactly good for business."

"Can you tell me where Mr. Finney works?"

"Hemphill and Associates. It's a small oil company. He's the chief financial officer. Their office is in the Galleria."

"Thank you, Mr. Getz. I appreciate your cooperation. If you can just get me a photocopy of that page, I'll let you get back to your morning."

While the jeweler stepped behind the heavy blue curtain that separated the store from his private workspace, Johnson considered his options. If he went to Finney's office and he wasn't there, he would have wasted the trip. But if he called ahead of time, he would lose the element of surprise. He only had one chance at a first interview, his best shot at catching a potential suspect off guard. By the time Getz emerged from behind the curtain, Johnson had made up his mind.

~ ~ ~ ~ ~

Quivers of unease vibrated through Johnson's stomach as he rode the glass elevator from the parking garage to the fifth floor. He did not expect Finney to confess to a murder, but he hoped the man's reactions to his questions, especially if they came as a surprise, would reveal whether he had anything to hide. The offices of Hemphill and Associates sat behind thick wood doors with discreet brass letters proclaiming the company's name. Johnson paused and took a deep breath before swinging open one of the heavy panels and walking inside. Plush green carpet swallowed the sound of his footsteps as he walked past leather sofas and a mahogany coffee table to the receptionist's desk. The young woman sitting behind it glanced over him quickly, taking in his battered boots, serviceable khakis and plain white, buttoned down shirt. She smiled, somewhat dismissively. Johnson belatedly wished he'd thought to put on one of his three ties.

"I'm here to see Mr. James Finney," he said.

"Is he expecting you?"

"No." Johnson pulled his wallet out of his back pocket and flipped it open to his badge, which he held in front of her face. "Please tell him Detective Peter Johnson with the Galveston Police Department needs to speak with him on official business."

The woman's eyes widened at the sight of the badge. She responded to the command as he hoped she would.

"One moment, please. I'll let him know you're here."

Johnson watched as the woman walked to the hallway that ran parallel to the reception area and turned left. He counted to three and followed her. She knocked on a door at the end of the hall and opened it, stopping just inside. When Johnson walked up behind her, she jumped.

"Sorry," he said. "I just thought I would save you the trouble of coming back to get me."

With round eyes and gaping mouth, the woman stood aside and gave Johnson a free path into the room. The man behind the desk looked almost as alarmed as his receptionist. He stood as the detective approached but gripped the edge of the desktop with both hands, as if for support. He had dark circles under his eyes, and although it was only mid-morning, he had already loosened his tie and unbuttoned his collar.

"D-Detective," he stammered as Johnson crossed the space between them. "Please come in."

When Johnson held out his hand, Finney stood a little straighter and offered a weak smile. His handshake was limp, his fingers cold. He motioned for Johnson to take a seat in one of the stiff wingback chairs in front of the deep desk.

"What can I do for you?" Finney asked, gingerly perching on the edge of his chair. He picked up a fat pen and weaved it through his fingers.

"I need to ask you a few questions about a necklace you bought back in October from Getz Jewelers."

Finney fumbled the pen and it hit the top of the desk with a thud. Without the distraction to keep his fingers busy, his hand trembled slightly. Johnson's pulse quickened.

"Ah, yes. Have you found it?"

"Found it?"

"Yes, someone stole it, from this drawer, in fact." Finney pulled open his top right desk drawer and pointed inside. "It was a couple of weeks ago."

Johnson's eyes narrowed as he considered the response. "Did you report the theft?"

"Well, no," Finney said with a slight laugh that sounded apologetic. "I didn't. I felt like I was partly to blame for leaving it here in the first place. I didn't mean to, but I had to get home in a rush the night I bought it. My daughter had a volleyball game I just couldn't miss. I bought the necklace at lunch, you see. And I had intended to give it to my wife that night. But then I left it. When I got to work the next morning, it was gone. I'm sure it was one of the cleaning crew."

"You bought the necklace for your wife?"

"Yes, that's right."

"Mr. Getz thought you were buying it for your daughter."

"Oh? No. No, for my wife, in fact." Finney picked up the pen again. He stared at it as though twirling it through his fingers required all his concentration.

"Well, it turned up around the neck of a dead girl."

Finney winced and dropped the pen but didn't immediately say anything. Johnson's heart beat faster. Most people, when told something like that would have offered exclamations of surprise and horror. Finney swallowed and licked his lips.

"That's terrible, detective. Truly terrible. But I don't see what that has to do with me. As I said, it was stolen. Who knows what happened to it after that."

"Maybe the dead girl is one of your cleaning crew. I'd like to show you a picture, to see if you recognize her."

Finney looked like he was about to protest, but Johnson had the photo in front of him before he could say anything. He took one look at the girl's bloated face and turned swiftly away, his hand over his mouth. Johnson could hear his pulse pounding in his ears now.

"Do you know who she is?"

Finney shook his head violently. "No! I'm sorry. Please excuse me. I've never seen, a … a… " The businessman stood abruptly, walked to a credenza, and poured a glass of water from a crystal pitcher sitting on a silver tray. He drained the whole tumbler before turning back to Johnson.

"I'm very sorry, detective. I'm afraid I can't be of any help to you at all. I have no idea how my necklace turned up on that poor girl."

"Your wife's necklace."

"What?"

"You said you bought the necklace for your wife."

"Yes, of course. My wife's necklace."

"Have you been to Galveston recently, Mr. Finney?"

"Galveston? No. No. I don't think we've been there since last summer. My daughter has a friend whose family rents a beach house every July. We went down there for a few days. That's the last time, I think. I'm afraid I don't have much time for trips to the beach."

Finney smiled weakly. His already pale face had turned downright pasty. He looked like he might throw up in the leather-trimmed trashcan next to his desk.

"What did whoever leads your cleaning crew say when you mentioned the stolen necklace?"

"What? Oh. I didn't mention it, in fact. I doubted it could be recovered, so I didn't pursue it. My wife has plenty of jewelry. It really was just a trinket. I decided pursuing it would be more trouble than it was worth."

"And is the same crew still cleaning your office?"

"Yes, I'm afraid they are," Finney said, a little sheepishly. "Without going into the whole incident of the stolen necklace, I didn't see how I could have our administrator dismiss them. I guess that was probably a mistake."

Johnson looked long and hard at the sandy haired man in front of him. Finney met his gaze, but only briefly, before picking up his pen again.

"I'll need a contact name and number for that crew. Perhaps you could have your receptionist look that up for me before I leave." Johnson slid a business card out of his pocket and snapped it down in the middle of the desk as he stood to go. "If you think of anything else, please give me a call."

Finny rose from his chair, relief flooding his features. "Of course! Of course, detective. Anything I can do to help. I really feel terrible about this. I hope … I hope you catch whoever did this."

As Johnson walked out the office door, he heard Finney pick up the phone and ask the receptionist to look up the contact information he'd requested. Johnson didn't believe for one minute the cleaning crew knew anything about the necklace. But he waited silently while the woman wrote down a name and number on a sticky note and handed it over.

As he stepped into the glass elevator again, he was sure of two things: That necklace had never been stolen and Finney knew the girl who was wearing it when someone dumped her body into Galveston Bay. Now all he had to do was figure out how a middle-aged businessman from Houston was connected to a young Hispanic girl that no one seemed to have missed.

Chapter 29

After he got off the elevator, Johnson sat in his car, key in the ignition, and considered his next move. If he went back to the station and told the chief what he had discovered, he would most likely end up in the DA's office making a case for a warrant. But he didn't have enough evidence to go on yet. Finney's story about the necklace theft would be hard to disprove. Or at the very least, it would be time consuming. He would have to interview all the cleaning crew members, look into their backgrounds, interview their family and friends. And he was convinced it would turn up nothing.

Finney might not be the murderer, but he knew more than he had said. And if he didn't have anything to do with the girl's death, why wouldn't he tell what he knew? He could at least tell them her name. Unless she stole the necklace from him, Finney must have given it to her, which meant he must have known her very well. There were only a few ways a man like Finney got to know a girl like that. Johnson thought about the prostitution ring at The Clipper. This girl could easily have been a high-priced call girl. And the girl shot in Fish Village was just like her, only without the polish. Were they both part of a well-organized prostitution ring operating in Galveston? If so, where did that leave his second murder victim, Julian Costa? Was his death related or just a random outlier?

Johnson tapped his fist against the steering wheel. He had too many pieces and only a hazy picture of how they might fit together.

But if Finney had been spending time with a prostitute in Galveston, he had to have left some clues behind. Credit card charges for food or gas. Maybe a speeding ticket down that long stretch of Interstate 45. Johnson flipped open the laptop attached to the dashboard of his department-issued Crown Victoria. Accessing financial records would take a court order, but he could pull up Finney's driving record right now. He tapped the businessman's name into a search box on the screen, scrunching his eyebrows together in frustration as he waited for the results to pop up.

There it was. A speeding ticket on September 15, issued by the La Marque Police Department at 2 a.m. A man like Finney only had one reason to be speeding home in the wee hours of the morning—a wife. What had he told her he was doing out that late? Surely she didn't think he was working. And if he had a habit of coming home that late, she had to have been suspicious. He'd learned from other cases that wives were rarely as clueless about their husbands' activities as the men thought they were.

But they weren't always willing to sell their husbands out either.

Johnson tapped Finney's address into his computer and pulled up the only other driving record linked to that home. Amanda Finney. Her license photo showed a woman with short blonde hair, sharp green eyes and a strand of pearls around her neck. She looked as shrewd as her husband was soft.

Johnson's pulse quickened as he turned the key in the ignition and pulled the gear lever into reverse. His best bet for getting anything from Amanda Finney would be to surprise her with her husband's connection to a dead girl. Would she tell him what she knew, without calling a lawyer? Or would she circle the wagons and protect her husband, no matter what he might have done?

~ ~ ~ ~ ~

The two-story brick house Johnson pulled up in front of twenty minutes later had black, plantation-style shutters, a red front door, and an immaculately landscaped yard. One of the shrubs had been trimmed into the shape of a corkscrew. As he got out of the car, Johnson looked up and down the street. Three houses down, a lawn crew was mowing the grass. Otherwise, it was quiet and deserted—a world away from the streets of Galveston, which hummed with activity at almost all hours.

The hair on the back of Johnson's neck rose with every step he took toward the front door. The heavy brass knocker slipped through his fingers and crashed back to the wood with an insistent thud. Almost a full minute later, Johnson heard high heels clicking across the foyer. When the door swung open, Amanda Finney stood before him, eyes narrowed and lips scrunched in annoyance.

"Yes?" she asked ungraciously, her eyes flitting from Johnson's face to his boots and back again.

"Mrs. Finney, my name is Detective Peter Johnson, with the Galveston Police Department." He pulled his badge out of his pocket and held it up for her inspection. "I'm here to ask you about a piece of jewelry your husband reported missing."

Amanda Finney frowned. "I'm not missing any jewelry."

"According to your husband, you are. May I come in?"

She glanced over her shoulder, as if looking for an excuse to turn him away.

"I promise I'll be as brief as possible," he said, hoping she wouldn't ask him to wait while she called her husband. "It really is very important."

She looked at him searchingly, as if trying to figure out what she was in for if she invited him in. His heart thudded, but he smiled reassuringly, hoping she couldn't hear it. Reluctantly, she stepped back and swung the door open wide enough for him to cross the threshold.

"Please be brief, detective. I have a lunch date at the country club in an hour, and I simply can't be late."

She led him down a wood-paneled hall into an expansive living room. Flowery curtains banked tall windows that looked out over a glistening pool. Prints of English hunting scenes adorned the cream-colored walls. A vase filled with what must have been at least two dozen white roses sat in the middle of a delicate coffee table. The room had a very masculine feel with a pervasive feminine touch. Amanda perched on the edge of a dark blue leather sofa and clasped her hands loosely in her lap. Johnson sat on the ottoman of the easy chair across from her, where he could easily see her face.

"Now, detective. What is this about? As I've already said, I'm not missing any jewelry."

Johnson pulled the small plastic bag containing the heart pendant out of his pocket and held it out to her. She frowned as she took it from him, turning it over in her hand to examine it.

"Your husband bought this pendant from Getz Jewelry in October. Mr. Getz thought your husband said he was buying it for your daughter. But he told me he bought it for you."

Amanda frowned and handed the bag back to Johnson. Her eyes scanned his face. Although she said nothing, he sensed she was looking for some clue about where the conversation was going, calculating what kind of disruption in her perfect world this unexpected interview was likely to create.

"He told me the necklace was stolen from his office the same day he bought it, before he had a chance to bring it home. Did he mention anything about a theft to you?"

"No. But it hardly seems likely he would, if it was meant to be a surprise gift."

"That's true. Does it seem like something he would buy for you, or your daughter?"

Her eyes narrowed and her white-tipped fingernails dug into the backs of her hands.

"Not especially. But there's no accounting for a man's taste, detective. My husband is easily persuadable. Perhaps Mr. Getz was trying to move some excess merchandise."

Johnson nodded as though carefully considering her answer. He looked down at the pendant and back at her. She had become very still, her face frozen into a brittle mask. Johnson's fingers trembled with excitement. She was hiding something.

"Do you have any reason to believe your husband might have bought this for someone else?" he asked quietly.

Amanda broke his gaze and looked out the window at the pool, where a waterfall trickled over a cascade of rocks into the deep end. Johnson held his breath, exhaling slowly when she turned back to him with hard eyes and a derisive sneer.

"You're asking me whether I think my husband is having an affair, detective. I can hardly see what business that is of the Galveston Police Department."

"Did you know your husband got a speeding ticket on I-45 at two a.m. on September 15?"

"No."

"Do you have any idea what he was doing out that late, or why he was so anxious to get back to Houston?"

Amanda had begun to chew on her bottom lip, her red gloss smearing across her bright white teeth. She shook her head, unclasped her hands, and moved as though to get up. Alarm shot up Johnson's spine, and he scrambled to think of what he could say to persuade her not to throw him out. But after half rising from the couch, she sank down again, sliding up against its tufted back. She crossed her arms tightly over her chest.

"My husband makes frequent trips to Galveston with a group of other businessmen. They fish. And drink, I suppose. Sometimes they're out late. Several times he hasn't come back until the next morning. He swears there are no women involved."

A shot of excitement coursed through Johnson's chest. He tried to keep his face expressionless. Amanda sighed, her features softening slightly to reveal what Johnson guessed was a deeply suppressed vulnerability.

"Obviously, I've had my doubts," she said.

"But you think the group trips are real, not just a ruse to get him out of the house?"

"Oh, no. They're real. I've heard some of the men joking about them at the club, although it's supposed to be a big secret. They call wherever they meet 'The Retreat.' I don't know whether that's the name of a boat or a house. I know they don't spend all the time on the water." Her mouth twisted in disgust.

The muscles in Johnson's shoulders and neck were so tight an ache had taken root at the base of his skull. Excitement surged through his arms and legs, leaving him slightly breathless. He chose his next words carefully, afraid at any moment Amanda would shut down or realize she might not want to be so open with a police officer without a lawyer present.

"You said you thought women might be a part of these trips. Do you think there's a specific woman your husband might have grown attached to?"

Amanda sprang off the couch and stood, trembling. Her mouth compressed into a tight, angry line. Her nostrils flared. Johnson's heart sank as she fixed him with a livid glare.

"Honestly, detective, I have no idea. Why does it even matter? I'm tired of these questions. What do you really want, and why are you so interested in my husband's dalliances?"

Johnson stood slowly fixing his eyes on her face. He held up the bag containing the heart-shaped pendant.

"We found this necklace around the neck of a dead girl who washed up on the island two days ago. We're still trying to figure out who she is. The only clue we have is this necklace, which we know your husband bought four weeks ago. He claims it was stolen. But he also told me he hasn't been to Galveston since last summer."

While he talked, Amanda's eyes grew wider and wider. Her red lips parted in a silent exclamation of shock and horror. When he was done, she clamped her hand over her mouth and sank back to the couch. For what seemed like a long time, the only sound in the room was the loud ticking of a grandfather clock Johnson hadn't noticed before.

The jarring ring of a telephone broke the silence and made them both jump. Amanda looked over her shoulder toward what Johnson guessed was the kitchen. If that was her husband, the last thing Johnson wanted her to do was answer it.

"Mrs. Finney?"

Her head snapped back around, her eyes still wide.

"Do you think my husband killed this girl?"

"I don't know what happened to her. All I know is that she's dead, and she was wearing the necklace your husband bought."

Amanda looked down, picking at the hem of her skirt while she thought. As the alarm faded from her face and she regained some of her composure, Johnson's heart sank.

"But you said he told you it was stolen," she finally said. "That seems entirely possible."

Johnson shrugged. Amanda's features had settled back into the mask of confidence and detachment Johnson first noticed in her driver's license photo.

"When did you talk to him? Does he know you're here, talking to me?" she asked.

"I stopped by his office this morning and then came here. I didn't tell him where I was going."

"Is my husband a suspect?"

"I suppose at this point, I would consider him a person of interest."

Amanda narrowed her eyes and looked hard at him. After a few seconds, she stood abruptly and strode to the other side of the coffee table, putting some distance between them. Johnson stood reluctantly.

"In that case, detective, I'd better not say any more. You need to leave."

Johnson didn't try to stop her when she spun around and marched down the hall toward the front door, her heels clicking with displeasure. He thought for a moment he had seen genuine fear in her face when he told her about the dead girl. She believed, at least briefly, in the possibility her husband might be a murderer.

Had sincere doubt or a deep-seated instinct for self-preservation changed her mind?

At the end of the hall, she held open the door, her foot tapping with impatience. When he reached her, he held out his business card. She stared at it dismissively before finally reaching out and taking it between her thumb and index finger.

"I understand your desire to protect your husband, but if he's involved in this in any way, you need to think of your safety and your own future, not just his."

She opened her mouth to respond but then clamped her lips together firmly without saying a word. Johnson stepped across the threshold and heard the door click softly closed behind him. He hadn't succeeded in convincing her that her husband was guilty of a crime. But he had planted seeds of doubt. He was sure James Finney would have some explaining to do when his wife got ahold of him. If he didn't tell her what she wanted to hear, maybe she would give Johnson a call. If not, she'd already told him more than enough to propel the investigation forward.

He was pretty sure when he left Finney's office that the businessman knew something about the dead girl and how she ended up on Channelview Drive. Now he was convinced. He would get a warrant for Finney's financial records, to see if he could establish a pattern of visits to the island. That should be relatively simple, if not expeditious. Depending on what he found, he might have enough to bring Finney in for a formal interview. The first question he planned to ask him, the question he would have asked Amanda Finney if she hadn't thrown him out: Who were the other men involved and what did they know about the dead girl wearing this necklace?

Chapter 30

Kate's eyes had popped open that morning at six a.m. She'd stayed up well past midnight the night before, trying to weave together the strands of the unsolved murders. By the time she slipped into a deep and dreamless sleep, she'd convinced herself she was just one step away from untangling the knot that tied them all together. She wasn't sure what woke her so suddenly. But as she lay in bed, she felt a lightness she hadn't known for months: hope. She dressed slowly, savoring her coffee with anticipation. The day seemed full of promise.

Kate walked into the newsroom just after eight. It was deserted, as she expected. She drank another cup of coffee in peace and read through her daily batch of two dozen emails. The other reporters trickled in shortly after nine. Everyone was curious about the case. Kate had a hard time convincing them she didn't know anything more than what was in the morning's newspaper.

Shortly after ten, her phone rang. She snatched up the receiver, hoping to hear Johnson's voice on the other end.

"Miss Bennett? This is Father Tomás, at Our Lady of Guadalupe."

"Oh… hi." Kate cringed at the obvious disappointment in her voice.

"I'm calling you on behalf of Muriel Costa."

Kate sucked in a breath and sat up straight.

"Muriel has some information she would like to share with you," the priest continued. "Could you meet us at the church in about half an hour?"

Her heart started to pound hard.

"Of course. Is there anything I should know before I get there?"

"No. But bring your notebook. I'll let Muriel explain the rest."

Kate's head swam as she slowly hung up the phone. She'd left her last meeting with Muriel Costa convinced the widow knew more than she was willing to admit. Had she finally decided to come clean? If so, why was she calling the newspaper and not the police?

~ ~ ~ ~ ~

Twenty minutes later, Kate pulled up outside the church. A bright fall sun shone in a cloudless sky. It was cool but not cold, the kind of day that put everyone in a good mood. Even the salty breeze smelled fresh. Kate walked up well-worn stone steps to the church's tall wooden doors. A colorful stained glass scene of a lion and a lamb sparkled above the arched entrance. She took a deep breath before stepping inside.

It took her eyes a moment to adjust. The church was warm and quiet. Peaceful.

"Miss Bennett, thank you for coming," Father Tomás said, walking down the aisle toward her. His face was serene but serious. He motioned for her to follow him toward the front of the sanctuary.

When they were about half way down the long row of pews, she spotted Muriel Costa, sitting in the middle of the second row. She was looking up at the large cross hanging above the altar. As they got closer, she looked down at her lap. The priest stopped just in front of where Muriel was sitting, motioning for Kate to take a seat in the pew next to her while he walked around to the front row and sat down toward the far end. He was close enough to hear what they were saying but not intrude.

Kate trembled, her nerves overpowering her resolve to stay calm. The weight of this interview pressed down on her chest, making it hard to breathe. This case had consumed her thoughts for months. She was finally about to get some answers.

She sat down gingerly on the pew about six feet from Muriel. The widow's eyes remained fixed on the rosary in her lap, the beads twisted tightly around her fingers. They sat in silence for several moments. Muriel finally sighed deeply and looked up.

"The most important thing you need to know is that my husband was a good man. He loved me and his kids. He only wanted to do right by us. He just made some bad decisions."

She looked at the priest, who nodded encouragingly. Kate slipped her notebook out of her purse, pulled a pen out of the spiral binding, and flipped it open. Muriel looked back and smiled wryly when she saw the blank page.

"Write that down," she said.

Kate's cheeks flushed and she bit back a caustic response. Muriel sighed again and tugged at her rosary beads.

"We were not expecting another baby when I found out I was pregnant again. We were excited, but Julian was worried about how we were going to pay for diapers and everything else. Things were tight, even though he had a good job. He had his mama to look after, too."

Muriel wiped away a tear that had gathered at the corner of her eye. Kate's throat started to tighten.

"You already know his friend Ricardo Peña. He knew how to make money. It didn't matter whether it was legal or not. Julian tried to talk him out of the worst stuff. I think he succeeded about half the time. But Rico still managed to get himself in trouble. For the last year, he'd been pretty clean, at least that's what we thought. One night he came over to have a beer with Julian after dinner. I heard them talking while I was cleaning the kitchen. Julian told him about the baby and how worried he was. Rico said he knew of some extra work Julian could pick up at the dock. He said he could hook him up."

Muriel looked over at Kate briefly and waited for her to stop writing before continuing.

"He told Julian a few longshoremen were working with a group that was smuggling illegal immigrants onto one of the cruise ships and taking them to Houston where they could start new lives in America. All Julian had to do was help transport them from the dock to a warehouse nearby, where they would be put in a van and driven off the island. It seemed simple enough."

Kate's hand flew across the narrow page of her notebook, her marks barely legible, even to her. As she scribbled, frantically trying to keep up with the widow's narrative, her mind whirled around the pieces of the puzzle she already had, trying to figure out where they would fit.

"Julian knew smuggling people into the United States was illegal, and he worried about getting caught. But we don't look at immigrants like you probably do. We understand why people will do anything to come here. And when they get here, they work hard. It's not like they're looking for a handout."

Muriel paused and shot Kate a defiant look. Kate met her eye and nodded. She understood.

"So even though it was wrong, it wasn't like he was selling drugs or anything. He felt like he was helping people. And we needed the money."

The widow swallowed. Tears filled her eyes again. Anxiety hardened into a knot in Kate's stomach.

"It's not like the immigrants came in every week or anything. It was maybe about once a month. A couple of crew members on the ship would sneak them off, hidden in luggage carts. They were drugged, which Julian thought was strange. But one of the other guys told him it was for their own safety, so they didn't risk giving themselves away. The groups were small, two or three, and they were always young women. Julian didn't think anything of it at first. Lots of young people want to come here for a better life than what their parents have back home. But then one day he heard the other guys making crude jokes about them and where they were headed. Julian started to get suspicious."

Tears trickled down Muriel's cheeks. Without saying a word, the priest handed her a box of tissue and took his seat again at the end of the pew. He must have been familiar with the story, but his furrowed brow and sad eyes told Kate it was just as hard to hear again.

"Julian asked Rico about it. He tried to blow it off, but Julian insisted. At first, Rico claimed the smugglers got the girls jobs as nannies and housekeepers. Julian didn't believe him. Rico finally admitted they thought they were coming to work good, honest jobs, but they were headed for the strip clubs in Houston. They were drugged so they wouldn't ask any questions or try to escape before they got there. He said they just had to work for a few months to pay off their debt to the smugglers, then they were free to go. Julian didn't believe him. He told me later he couldn't imagine what those girls had to go through."

Muriel paused as the constant flow of tears turned into quiet sobs. Kate blinked back her own tears. The story grated across her soul with a raw, scarring sorrow.

"Julian told Rico he wouldn't do it any more, that he was through. At first, Rico tried to reason with him. Then he got really angry. He told him the crew wouldn't just let him leave. He said if Julian tried to do anything stupid, me and the kids would be in danger. ... He was stuck."

She looked at Kate, the sorrow in her face underscoring the family's helplessness.

"So, he never said anything. He was too afraid. He told me the other guys had started to stare at him at work, just to let him know they were watching him. He knew then that Rico told them what he'd said about wanting out. Rico sold him out. His best friend. For Julian, I think that was the worst part of all. They were like brothers."

Muriel ran her fingers over the cross on her rosary, as though touching it eased the pain of the betrayal. She took a shuddering breath.

"A few weeks later, the next group of girls came in. Three of them. Everything went just like always. But when they met the men at the ship, they realized one of the girls had escaped."

Tears flowed down Muriel's cheeks. They careened off her jaw and down her neck, wetting the collar of her sweatshirt. She didn't bother to reach for a tissue, as if the pain of the memory paralyzed her.

"They went looking for her and finally spotted her running toward Fish Village. They planned to grab her, put her in the van, and take her back to the warehouse. One of the guys gave Julian a gun and told him to point it at her to scare her, so she wouldn't try to keep running, or scream. He'd never held a gun in his life."

Kate strained to understand the widow. Her tears made her voice thick and the words slurred together.

"Julian told me he wasn't even thinking when they pulled up next to her and shoved him out of the van. He just wanted to grab her as quickly as possible before someone saw her. But she struggled and fought. The gun went off ..."

Muriel buried her face in her hands and sobbed, rocking back and forth. Father Tomás came around and sat on the other side of her, rubbing his hand between her shoulder blades until the sobs became shuddering gasps. She looked at Kate with pleading, bloodshot eyes.

"He was devastated. You have to believe me. He came home that afternoon and just lay in my arms and cried. He took a few days off work. He was sure the police would come for him. I think he almost wanted them to. The guilt, it consumed him. Rico came over two days later and told Julian the police had no idea what they were dealing with. They had no way to tie any of them to the girl's murder. He told him they were just going to lay low for a while and everything would be ok."

Out of the corner of her eye, Kate saw the priest shake his head sorrowfully. Muriel's voice had started to sound hollow, as though telling the story had wrung every last drop of misery from her body.

"But Julian couldn't live with himself. He planned to turn himself in. He came to Father Tomás first. They talked all night. I think Rico must have known, must have followed him. I don't know if he's the one who ambushed Julian the next morning on his way home or if he called one of the other guys. But I never saw him alive again."

Kate's gut twisted when she thought back to that early morning crime scene. Muriel's inconsolable grief was seared into her memory. But something still didn't fit. Why would Muriel let her husband's killer go free if she had the power to help catch him?

"Why didn't you tell the police?" Kate demanded.

Muriel stared at Kate with round eyes and slightly parted lips. She shook her head.

"I was terrified. Don't you see? They killed Julian to make sure their secret stayed safe. You think they would have spared me, or my kids? The only reason we're still alive is because I kept my mouth shut."

Overwhelming sadness enveloped Kate. One bad decision after another. Most were small steps of error. But they had laid a path to desperation and ruin.

"So why come forward now? And why are you telling me and not the police?"

"I am going to tell the police. We're going to the station as soon as we're done here," Muriel looked at Father Tomás, as if for reassurance and strength. "I wanted to tell you the story first because I don't know how much the police will say once it all comes out. And I don't know whether I'll be able to talk then. I don't want people to think Julian was just another bad guy. That he was some cold-blooded killer. It wasn't like that. He was a good man. I want you to make people understand. He was a good man."

Kate nodded. Readers might not sympathize with Julian Costa's decisions, but she would do her best to make sure they felt the desperate situation he found himself in, even if it was a mess of his own making.

"Aren't you still afraid?"

Muriel nodded slowly, as though she was realizing anew what she was about to bring down on her head.

"Yes. But I can't keep looking over my shoulder every day. And I don't want anyone else to die. I thought it was all over after you found out what was happening at The Clipper. I had no idea they had started to bring girls there, but since Rico was involved, I'm sure it was all part of the same operation. And now another girl has turned up dead. How many more?"

"But what about your kids?"

"Father Tomás arranged for one of the deacons to take them to stay with his family in San Antonio. They'll be safe there until this is all over. And hopefully I'll see them again someday soon."

Kate blinked to force back the tears that suddenly filled her eyes. Muriel Costa was willing to sacrifice her own life for the sake of justice. Most people would never know that kind of bravery.

"I keep thinking about that girl who washed up near Channelview Drive," the widow said. "I wonder if she was one of the other two who came in with … the girl Julian…"

She trailed off as if she couldn't bear to say to the words again.

Kate frowned. "Didn't they just get sent to Houston like the others?"

"I don't think so," Muriel said, shaking her head. "When Rico came to talk to Julian … after … he said they were staying here. The boss had something special in mind for them. He said they were very beautiful."

"Something special?" Kate shuddered. "What do you think that was? Not the prostitution ring at The Clipper."

Muriel shook her head again. "Rico said there was some place on the Bay. He called it 'The Retreat.' It sounded like a house to me."

Excitement started to bubble in Kate's chest. "Do you know who the boss was?"

"No," Muriel smiled sadly. "I wish I did. But I only know who the other longshoremen were."

Kate's eyes widened in expectation, her pen poised above her notepad. She leaned forward slightly when Muriel didn't immediately say anything else.

"I'm going to give the police their names. But you'll have to get that information from them."

Kate considered pressing her to reconsider, but Father Tomás spoke up.

"We're trying not to get ahead of the police investigation. Muriel is willing to accept the consequences of her actions. But we are hoping they will show mercy."

Kate nodded. The DA might have less sympathy if he knew the newspaper had all the details of the case before he did.

"We're also asking you to hold off on publishing any of this until the police make some kind of announcement about the case."

Kate pursed her lips in disappointment. She looked down at her notebook and back at the widow. Father Tomás stood, and Kate took the hint. She tucked her notepad back into her purse and tried to think of something that would reassure the widow she had made the right choice in calling her.

"Thank you for trusting me with your story," she finally said softly. "I promise I'll do it justice. I do believe your husband was a good man."

Muriel offered a thin smile and nodded. Kate stood to leave.

"Wait," Muriel said, just as Kate was about to walk back down the aisle. "When you came to talk to me about the murders, you said your mama died when you were young and that it was all over the news. Was that even true?"

Kate's cheeks burned. The familiar nausea started to churn in her stomach. She clenched her teeth together and nodded.

"What happened?" Muriel asked.

Kate looked toward the door, debating whether to be completely honest. Her heart hammered, as it did every time someone asked about her mother. She usually brushed the questions off with a curt reply. But she owed Muriel the truth, after everything the widow had entrusted to her.

"She hung herself," Kate finally said, willing her teeth to unclench enough to get the words out. "She was staying at a mental hospital, where she was supposed to be getting help. Every news report called it a tragedy, but they never bothered to ask the most important question: why? I vowed never to make that mistake."

Muriel held her gaze for a long time before nodding. For a moment, they shared in the camaraderie of suffering.

"Don't ever stop asking why," Muriel whispered. "It's the only question that matters."

When Kate turned to walk away, the tears that had been threatening during the entire interview finally broke through the dam of her self control and flowed freely down her face. She now had the answer to a question that had plagued her for almost six months. But it didn't bring her any peace. Or satisfaction in the assurance of justice. Julian Costa had paid the ultimate price for his crime, but his young wife and children would be the ones to truly bear his debt. And his killer seemed likely to go unpunished. How would Johnson explain the righteousness in that?

Chapter 31

Johnson made it back to the island from Houston in record time. As soon as he got back to his office, he began filling out paperwork and giving the DA the information he needed to pursue a warrant for Finney's cellphone and financial records. The judge didn't hesitate to sign it. Johnson handed off the information about Finney's cleaning crew to another investigator. He didn't believe the janitors had anything to do with the necklace or the dead girl, but he had to follow up on the lead, just in case. After that, he sat down with the police chief to go over what he'd learned.

Johnson was convinced the most recent murder was tied to the first unsolved case and the prostitution ring at The Clipper. He smiled at the thought of what Kate would say when he had a chance to catch her up on all the new information. She'd been the one trying to convince him the day before. Now he was trying to persuade the chief.

"That's a big leap," Lugar said, drumming his fingers on his desk and looking at Johnson through narrowed lids. "You've got a lot of gaps to fill before you can make that case stick. And besides figuring out who did all this killing, you've got one big unanswered question: Who's behind this whole thing?"

"One step at a time," Johnson said, leaning forward eagerly, his hands on his knees. "The first step is to tie Finney to Galveston and then bring him in and see whether he's willing to talk. If not, we've got other leads to pursue. His wife said at least some of the other men on these 'fishing' trips belonged to the same country club. If we can get a warrant for the club's membership records, we might be able to figure out who some of the others are."

"How?" Lugar huffed, loading that one word with more skepticism than Johnson thought possible.

"Do what I did with Finney. Run their driving records. If we get any hits, we can get a warrant for financial records. Or we can interview staff at the club and find out who the Finneys hang out with while they're there. Who does he golf with? Who does he do business with?"

The chief shook his head. "You'll never get a judge to issue a warrant on such circumstantial evidence. This has got to be more than a fishing expedition, no pun intended."

Johnson grimaced and sat silent for a moment. He had one other line of enquiry he wanted to pursue, but the chief wasn't going to like it.

"There is one other possible connection that we haven't talked about," Johnson started, feeling his way through what was bound to be a minefield.

"What's that?"

"The only other Houston businessman whose name has come up in any of these investigations: Eduardo Reyes."

Lugar started shaking his head before Johnson even finished.

"You cannot make that connection without very, and I mean very, good cause," he said, crossing his arms and leaning over his desk, to fix Johnson with a steely glare. "I don't want to even hear you mention that unless you can come in here with watertight evidence that he's involved."

"So, what? We're giving Reyes special treatment now? Why shouldn't we investigate him just like anyone else?"

"That's not what I'm saying," Lugar said, wiping his hand down his face and pinching the bridge of his nose as though just the thought of Galveston's favorite son being involved in something so sleazy—and illegal—made his head hurt. "But you can't go waving that line of questioning around like a rodeo clown with a red handkerchief. Reyes will come down on us so hard we won't know we've been gored until we've bled to death. That's not a fight I'm willing to take unless we've got a very good reason."

The chief's cautiousness sucked away some of Johnson's enthusiasm but not his resolve. He expected opposition.

"Well, I'm not willing to discount the possibility that he might be involved just because he's the mayor's biggest supporter and the island's most vaunted mascot. He owned the hotel where a major prostitution ring set up operations. I know he placed all the blame on the manager, but who's to say he wasn't getting a cut of the take? And now we've got reports of Houston businessmen coming to the island, most likely to meet prostitutes. What are the odds? If he knew about any of this, I'm going to find out. I'll tread carefully, of course."

"You'd better," Lugar growled. "If I get so much as one call from the mayor, I'm shutting you down and you'll just have to wait for someone else to implicate Reyes—and be willing to testify about it."

"Yes, sir," Johnson said, standing to leave. "I'll keep you posted."

"I want an update at the beginning of every day and the end of every day. Oh, and Johnson … be careful."

Johnson nodded and walked down the hall to his own office. He had one last clue he hadn't shared. Amanda Finney said the men called their meeting place "The Retreat." Of course, that might have been a code word. But she suspected it might be the name of a boat, or a house. If he could find it, he would have another major clue and possibly the murder scene.

Sitting down behind his desk, Johnson opened his rolodex and flipped to the card for Galveston Yacht Basin, the island's biggest marina. The manager offered no resistance to pulling up the list of boats moored there. None was named "The Retreat." Inquiries to a few of the smaller marinas produced the same results. Johnson groaned as he hung up the last call. Of course it was possible the boat was kept at a house, but there were only a few places on the island where a vessel large enough to host several men comfortably on a fishing expedition could get that close to land.

Johnson stood up and walked into the conference room, where an aerial photo collage of the entire island stretched along the back wall. He scanned the canal neighborhoods of the West End. That seemed like the most obvious option. But the houses were packed together like sardines. Surely they would have gotten complaints by now about regular parties. A lot of the houses were vacation properties, but the West End's full-time residents liked their peace and quiet.

He continued to scan the back side of the island, finally stopping at Sportsman Road. The isolated finger of development sat well off FM 3005, the only road that ran the length of the island. About forty houses dotted the shore, perched high on pilings, with docks stretching out into West Bay. Large, modern houses sat between older ones, bait camps built in the 1950s and 1960s. They were smaller and surrounded by more property. The island's scrub brush provided a measure of privacy. Johnson squinted as he stood inches from the map, prying as much information as he could from every pixel. It looked like at least some of the houses were almost completely hidden from the road by greenery.

He slapped his palm against the wall in excitement. That was the place to start. He marched with renewed determination back to his office and typed the address for the county tax assessor's website into the browser on his computer. A quick search pulled up a listing of all the property on Sportsman Road. He scanned the list of owners and didn't see any names he recognized. But several of the houses were owned by corporations. It would take longer to figure out who was behind those benign-sounding names. But it could be done.

Springing up from behind his desk one more time, Johnson strode into the main room where officers shared desks. It was nearing a shift change, and uniformed men and women filled the small space, trading good-natured insults and cutting up. Johnson scanned the crowd until he found the rosy-cheeked face he was looking for.

"Conner," he shouted. "Come here a minute."

Officer Dylan Conner looked up, waved in response, and trotted over. If he had a tail, it would have been wagging.

"What's up, boss?"

"I need someone to do a little internet research for me, and I know you're good at that."

"Yes, sir! What am I researching?"

Johnson led Conner back to his office and pointed to the list of properties on his computer screen.

"I want to know who's behind those companies. I'm trying to figure out who owns these houses. Can you do that?"

"Sure can. It might take a little while, depending on how straightforward the incorporations are. But I should be able to figure it out sooner or later."

"Let's say sooner, okay?" Johnson slapped the young officer on the back and grinned. "It's important. Call me when you have something. I'm going to take a drive."

"This is connected to the murder investigation, huh?" Conner asked, his grin pushing his round cheeks so high they squished his eyes into bright slits.

"Yeah, but don't go running your mouth about it. I'm following up on a hunch, that's all. It may be for nothing."

"Got it," Conner said, nodding vigorously. "I'm on it. I'll call you as soon as I have anything."

"Good man," Johnson said as he walked out the door.

~ ~ ~ ~ ~

Kate chewed on everything she'd learned in the last hour as she drove slowly back toward the newspaper offices. *The Retreat.* The name kept ricocheting around in her mind. Without realizing she had turned, she found herself heading down Stewart Road. She loved the West End. It was a little slice of country that felt a world away from the tourists, the souvenir shops, and the downtown boutiques. It felt a little bit like home.

Kate had no plan to drive randomly through neighborhoods looking for a house where young girls might be imprisoned. That would be like searching for one specific crab hole in a sand dune. But she wanted to imagine what it might look like, gaze out over the same placid expanse of wetlands they might see through the windows of their jail. If they were ever allowed to look out the windows.

Kate turned down Sportsman Road. She'd last driven down it in the spring, when she'd come to interview a local environmental activist angry over the new neighborhoods of fancy houses chewing up the wetlands. She rolled her windows down and let the fresh air blow across her face. She laid her head back against the seat and let her mind wander as she rolled by driveways and mailboxes.

She almost missed it.

In fact, by the time she consciously registered the words, she'd driven past it. A small sign nestled in the grass growing a little too high next to a gravel driveway: The Retreat.

~ ~ ~ ~ ~

It was two thirty by the time Johnson got through all the lights on 61st Street and Avenue S and crawled through two school zones. He had his windows rolled down, his left arm perched on the door to soak up the sun's bright rays. It was a perfect day, the clear air and soft breeze whispered promise. He hadn't enjoyed this much optimism in months. For the first time since July, he had hope for some resolution. As he cruised down Stewart Road, he thought back to his last serious conversation with Kate. She had no idea how much the unsolved murders weighed on him, casting a pall over every day and sapping the enjoyment from almost everything. Having faith was not the cop-out Kate thought. He woke up every morning and willed himself to trust God to provide some answers. The months of silence to his repeated prayers crushed his spirit. Each day's supplication became harder and harder to make.

He continually had to remind himself that faith was the hope of things unseen. Today, that was a little easier to believe.

As he drove down 8 Mile Road, Johnson marveled at how much vacant land still remained on the island and how many different environments such a small place could contain. This open expanse of marshy plain stretching into the water felt worlds away from the city's tight, densely populated neighborhoods.

He slowed as he turned onto Sportsman Road. Wetlands spread out to his left. Seagulls wheeled overhead, filling the quiet with their discordant cries. On the right, driveways met the narrow street every thirty yards or so. He peered carefully at each house as he rolled slowly by.

Several houses sat behind tall walls with heavy metal gates. It would be easy to host fairly discreet parties at any of them. He dismissed houses built too close to the road as unlikely sites for regular gatherings.

About half way down the street, the more tightly spaced development gave way to larger lots. The first house sat close to the water, well off the road. But the owners had cleared out all the brush, erasing any privacy they might have had. The house next door was almost completely hidden from view, with only the top of the roof peeking above the trees. Johnson slowed to a stop at the long driveway. It curved before it reached the house, keeping the building obscured. He scanned for something that might show the address, but no mailbox stood at the end of the drive. He was about to move on when a small wooden sign partially hidden in the tall grass caught his eye.

He sucked in a breath. Adrenaline rocketed through his veins, making him lightheaded. Every hair on the back of his neck stood on end. He shuddered with anticipation.

Two words were burned into the wood in small letters: The Retreat.

Johnson forced himself to take two steady breaths to try to slow his thudding pulse. It took every ounce of self control not to gun the engine and speed down that curved driveway. But what was at the end? He looked up and down Sportsman Road, and for the first time, he noticed a familiar car pulled over on the side about 50 yards away. *Kate*.

~ ~ ~ ~ ~

Kate kept to the edge of the driveway as she walked slowly toward the house. It stood up on stilts, a wide deck wrapped around every side. The brown stain on its wood siding had faded slightly, but it didn't look rundown. Just rustic, serene. Kate peeked around a scrubby bush and scanned every window. Blinds covered the glass. The only sign that someone was home was an olive green SUV parked near the staircase that led up to the front door.

When she had pulled over to the side of the road and climbed out of her car, Kate had no idea what she planned to do. Now that she was half way up the driveway she realized how much danger she was walking into. No one knew she was here. And these were people who had already killed once to keep their secret safe. She had just decided to creep back to her car and call Johnson when she heard several loud thumps and a muffled yell coming from inside the house.

Then a woman screamed.

Heart thudding, Kate raced toward the stairs. She pulled her phone out of her pocket and dialed 9-1-1 as she took the steps two at a time. The dispatcher answered just as she was pounding her fist on the door.

"Help! A woman's being assaulted! This is Kate Bennett. I'm a reporter for the *Gazette*. I'm at a house on Sportsman Road..."

Before she could finish, the door burst open and the sharp stench of gasoline rolled over her. A man reached out and grabbed her by the throat. Kate yelped and dropped her phone as her hands flew to the man's arm.

"You!" he snarled. "Figures."

Kate immediately recognized the voice of the man who'd attacked her at The Clipper. Terror racked her whole body and she froze, unable to think or move. The man dragged her inside and Kate saw the source of the scuffle she'd heard. A woman with her hands tied behind her back was kneeling on the floor of the living room.

Blood trickled from a cut on her forehead. Next to her sat a bright red gas can.

The girl gaped at Kate. The sight of her jolted Kate into action. She began to claw frantically at the man's arm. He yelled and slapped her across the face with his free hand. The force of the blow knocked Kate sideways, and threw him off balance. He loosened his grip just enough for Kate to wrench herself free. She shoved him in the chest as hard as she could and he stumbled back into the coffee table. He wobbled a few times before crashing across it and falling on his back between the table and the couch.

Kate seized the girl by the elbow and dragged her to her feet.

"Run!" she screamed as she pushed her toward the door.

~ ~ ~ ~ ~

Johnson swore loudly and pounded the steering wheel. Kate! How had she known to come here? And more importantly, what was she doing there?

Driving up the driveway alone violated every bit of training Johnson had ever received. He would have no idea what he was getting himself into until it was too late. But if Kate was at that house, she was definitely in danger. Fear coiled tightly in his chest. He had to find out what was going on behind those bushes.

He reached for his radio. He wouldn't wait for backup, but he at least wanted to make sure they were on the way.

As he pushed the button on the side of the unit to call dispatch, a loud pop shattered the silence. Crows, startled by the noise, rose screeching from the trees in front of the house. Johnson jumped and fumbled the handset, dropping it between the seat and the center console. He swore and plunged his hand in after it. Just as his fingers closed around it, two more pops rang out.

"Dispatch, this is 58. I have shots fired on Sportsman Road. I repeat, shots fired. Request backup. Over."

Chapter 32

Before dispatch could respond, Johnson heard the rumble of a big engine and the squeal of gravel under spinning tires. A few seconds later, an olive green Ford Expedition careened around the bend in the driveway. It sped toward the police cruiser parked in its path. Johnson yanked the gear lever into reverse and mashed the gas pedal to the floor. The car jumped backward just in time to avoid getting broadsided. The SUV fishtailed as its tires bit the pavement, spraying gravel in its wake. As it sped past Johnson, the driver glanced his way. He had just enough time to take in angry eyes and a snarling mouth. But he didn't recognize the man's face.

Johnson hesitated for only a split second before throwing the car into drive. His heart screamed for Kate, but his tactical training overrode every emotion. Help would be there within minutes. He had to make sure the man did not get away. He threw the car into a sharp U-turn and rocketed forward. But the SUV had a good head start, and by the time he reached 8 Mile Road it had already disappeared.

"Dispatch, this is 58. I've got a man fleeing the scene in a green SUV. I'm in pursuit."

"Ten-four. Do you still need units at your location?"

"Yes! Tell them to proceed with caution but look for possible victims." Johnson's voice caught on the word. "I think there was a reporter from The *Gazette* there."

Johnson gunned the engine as he whipped around a corner. The cruiser's back end swung wide. He clung to the wheel to keep the car from spinning out of control. He looked up just in time to see the SUV turn left. Johnson flipped on his lights and siren.

"Dispatch, this is 58. Suspect is heading east on Stewart Road at high speed. Notify all units in the area to be on the lookout."

It had been a long time since Johnson had been on a high-speed chase. With white knuckles, he gripped the steering wheel. His eyes darted left and right as he watched for other cars. Despite the cool air rushing through the windows, beads of sweat dotted his forehead. The suspect showed no signs of slowing down, let alone stopping. In this sparsely populated area, he didn't have anyone in his way. But in just a few miles, he would hit late afternoon traffic. He prayed everyone would stay out of the SUV's way.

Through Stewart Road's two 90-degree turns, Johnson gained on the suspect. As they neared the airport, other cars on the road slowed their progress. The SUV swerved in and out of traffic. It barreled through the intersection at 77th Street. Horns blared and other cars screeched to a halt to avoid getting hit. Johnson slapped his hand against the dashboard and waved people out of his way as he slowed to weave through the stopped cars. His frustration exploded into a guttural yell. The SUV pulled further ahead.

"Dispatch, this is 58. Suspect is approaching 61st Street."

"Ten-four, 58. I have two units headed your way."

The SUV had reached a school zone. The driver slammed on his breaks to avoid hitting the end of the line of cars waiting for classrooms to disgorge their occupants. Johnson cringed as the suspect pulled into oncoming traffic and gunned his engine. Their frantic pace had slowed and Johnson got close enough to read the SUV's license plate before it rocketed ahead again.

"Dispatch, I have a plate number for you: 50T Y2N."

The SUV rounded the corner in front of another school and had a clear lane to 61st Street. If the driver intended to keep running, he was probably headed for the freeway. Johnson spotted flashing lights ahead. The two units dispatch had called to his aid were parked in the intersection at 61st. The SUV slowed briefly, but just as Johnson thought it might stop, the driver veered to the left and disappeared down a side street.

"Dammit!" Johnson yelled, pounding the steering wheel again. Unless the other officers also had a road block along the minor intersections on 61st, the SUV had an unobstructed patch to the interstate.

Johnson raced down 62nd Street just in time to see the SUV turn right onto Avenue Q 1/2. At 61st Street, it fishtailed again as the driver sped through the sharp turn. He barely kept control of the boxy vehicle as it rocked from left to right. Before Johnson made the turn, the two other units flew past him, lights flashing.

"Dispatch, this is fifty-eight. Suspect is on 61st Street, headed for the interstate. Better notify La Marque, Santa Fe, League City, and highway patrol."

"Ten-four. Units 96 and 31 are also in pursuit."

"I see them."

"The plates came back to a José Vargas. He has a Galveston address, but it's not on Sportsman Road. Priors for drug possession and domestic violence."

"Ten-four. Thanks."

Johnson gritted his teeth. The SUV's brake lights suddenly glowed red before it swerved under the interstate overpass and rocketed up the entrance ramp. With three police units in pursuit, sirens blaring, Johnson thought other drivers would make way. But no one seemed to notice the speeding SUV until it was right up on them. It weaved between cars, picking up speed anytime it found an open stretch of lane. Johnson's speedometer pushed past 85 mph.

Traffic cleared briefly after they crossed the causeway. But as they neared La Marque, cars and trucks started to fill all three lanes. The SUV slowed. Johnson tightened his grip on the steering wheel. They were gaining on him.

Two 18-wheelers blocked their path. There was no way the SUV could squeeze by.

But the driver tried.

The big rig trailer shuddered as the SUV clipped its back left corner. Smoke poured off the tires as the truck driver stood on his breaks. But that didn't stop the rig from swinging sideways. It caught the back of the SUV, pushing it toward the median wall in an out-of-control pirouette. Johnson's tires screeched in protest as he swerved to avoid the disaster unfolding in front of him. The SUV spun once, twice, before its momentum flipped it over. It rolled into the wall, leaving a long black streak along the concrete. It briefly slid along the top of the barrier like a skateboarder riding a rail before crashing back to the asphalt and exploding in a bright orange burst.

Johnson pulled into the emergency lane and jumped out of his car. Hot, angry fire had already engulfed the SUV. He coughed as the acrid black smoke rolled over his head, the stench of melting metal and rubber rushing down his throat. He couldn't even see the driver through the haze of flame. Nausea rolled over him and he turned away, hand over his mouth.

"Oh, man," said one of the other officers as he walked over to Johnson. "That's a helluva way to go. What was he running for?"

"I don't know … yet," Johnson said, coughing again. He ran his fingers through his hair and turned back to the accident scene.

The truck driver was climbing out of his cab. He'd managed to keep the rig upright, nothing short of a miracle. The other two Galveston police cars blocked any traffic that might try to get through. Cars had already started to stack up behind them, with drivers getting out and snapping photos with their cell phones. In the distance, sirens wailed and flashing lights signaled the arrival of state troopers and the La Marque Fire Department.

"I radioed dispatch," the third officer called to Johnson, cupping his hands around his mouth to be heard over the roar of the flames. "They said you should call Lt. Jarrell on his cellphone. He's out at the scene on Sportsman Road."

Johnson's heart thundered in his ears. *Kate*. He sprinted back to his car. Snatched his phone from the center console, he punched in the lieutenant's number.

"You are not going to believe this," Jarrell said as soon as he answered.

"What did you find?"

"Your reporter, for one. How the hell she got tangled up in all this I have no idea. And a young, Hispanic girl who looks a lot like the one who washed up on Channelview."

Johnson could hardly form the words. "Are they dead?"

"No! They're both alive. Frankly, it's a miracle."

Relief buckled Johnson's knees and he sat down hard in the driver's seat. He wrapped his hand around the back of his neck and squeezed, trying to stem the flood of emotion that tightened his chest and made it hard to breathe. Tears filled his eyes too quickly for him to fight back. They trickled down his cheeks.

She was alive.

"Hello? You there?"

"Yeah, I'm here," Johnson said, clearing his throat to mask the huskiness. "Sorry, it's a little crazy out here. Has the girl said anything?"

"Not much that's intelligible. For one, she's hysterical. And then, she doesn't speak much English. Hopefully when she calms down we'll be able to get more out of her."

"Are you taking her back to the station?"

"No, to UTMB. She's pretty beat up. It looks like she's been tied up for a while too."

Johnson cringed. What had this poor girl suffered?

"Is that how you found her?"

"No, she and Bennett were hiding in the brush between the house and the road. The suspect evidently chased them out of the house shooting. Looks like he intended to burn the place down. We found a gas can just inside the door. No telling why he didn't go back to finish the job. Dispatch said his escape attempt didn't end well."

"Not exactly. At least not for him. Did the girl say anything else?"

"Something about 'mi hermana.' That's Spanish for sister, right?"

"Yeah." Johnson blew out a long breath. "I bet the dead girl is her sister."

"I guess we'll find out soon enough. We called Jimenez to sit with her. She should be able to translate too, when the girl is ready. She's going with her to the hospital."

"What about Bennett?"

"She's refusing medical attention."

"That sounds about right. Was she hurt?"

"She said he grabbed her by the neck and slapped her, but that's it. Seems mostly okay. We're taking an unofficial statement now. She promised she'd come down to the station later to answer any more questions. She insists she has to go back to the newspaper office to write her story. I'm sure you'll be hearing from her soon."

Johnson laughed. It bubbled up from deep in his chest. He felt almost delirious from the emotional swings of the last few hours.

"Johnson? You okay?"

"Yeah, sorry. It's been a long day already."

"Well, it's not going to be over any time soon. Pull yourself together."

"Yes, sir. There's not much more I can do here. I'll check in with the chief and head over to UTMB to see if I can talk to the girl."

"I'll let you know if we find anything else interesting at the house."

"Thanks."

After he hung up, Johnson surveyed the scene around him. The firefighters had the flaming SUV reduced to a smoldering, twisted ball of metal. Two state troopers and three La Marque police officers were directing traffic around the scene on the shoulder. The other two Galveston police officers were standing by their cars, looking useless. He strode across the empty lanes to have a word with the trooper in charge. He was only too happy to have the extra officers head back to the island. They would all have to fill out incident reports, but that could wait until tomorrow. Johnson waved his colleagues into their cars and the trio inched into traffic and headed for the next exit.

~ ~ ~ ~ ~

Kate stomped her foot with impatience as the officer assigned to take her statement asked her question after question. When he started asking the same questions, prefaced with "Now let me just see if I have this right," she couldn't contain her frustration.

"If you didn't get it right the first time, why would I bother repeating myself?"

The officer raised an eyebrow at her and glanced at Lt. Jarrell.

"Look, lieutenant, I've told him everything I know," Kate said, throwing her hands up in the air. "The Houston TV stations are going to be all over the island in less than an hour! I need to get back to the newspaper to write my story."

The girl she'd helped rescue had headed off in an ambulance about 10 minutes before. She'd broken down in hysterical sobs as soon as her captor drove away. Kate had used her car keys to tear through the duct tape binding the girl's wrists. She'd been about to go look for her cellphone when the first police car arrived. It had been complete chaos after that. Paramedics arrived a few minutes later, and Kate hadn't had a chance to see the girl again. Would she ever learn the full extent of what she'd suffered?

Kate looked pleadingly at Jarrell, who looked back through narrowed eyes.

"Alright. But expect a follow-up call. I'm sure Detective Johnson's going to want to talk to you."

Johnson. Kate suddenly realized he should have been there.

"Where is he anyway?"

"You just missed him, or he missed you," Jarrell laughed. "He got here not long after you did and saw your car. He was radioing for backup when he heard the gunshots. After the guy took off, Johnson followed him."

Kate's eyes felt like they were going to bug out of her head.

"Did he catch him?"

"Sort of. Guy crashed on his way up 45. He's a pile of ashes now."

Kate's head spun. Relief twirled with horror and disappointment. He would never have to face his accusers or spend years in a tiny jail cell thinking about what he'd done. Still, he'd paid with his life. Maybe that was enough.

"Go write your story," Jarrell said. "And try not to make this a habit, okay?"

Kate just smiled and shook her head.

~ ~ ~ ~ ~

Johnson headed straight for the chief's office when he got back to the station. But one of the secretaries stopped him before he made it halfway down the hall.

"You've got someone waiting for you in the conference room," she said.

"Who is it?" he asked, exasperation giving his voice an unusual edge. "I've got my hands full at the moment, and I need to talk to the chief before I head over to UTMB."

"Well, I think you'll want to make time for this one. She says she has information on one of the summer murders. Her name's Muriel Costa. Wasn't she the one whose husband was killed in June?"

Johnson stopped and stared with wide eyes and a gaping mouth at the secretary, who kept walking.

"Told you it would be worth your time. I'll let the chief know where you are."

Johnson nodded absently. His mind raced over the possibilities. He held out hope for a long time after the Costa murder that the widow would come clean with what she knew. He never believed she was as clueless as she pretended to be about what had happened to her husband. But it had been months. What prompted her to come forward now?

Slightly dazed, Johnson walked toward the conference room. For half a year, he'd foundered in darkness, praying for some sliver of light in his stalled investigations. Now rays of revelation streamed so brightly they nearly blinded him.

When he pushed open the door, Muriel started, as though from a deep reverie. She looked smaller than he'd remembered, more fragile. But at the same time, the deep furrows around her eyes spoke a new determination and strength. He searched her face for some clue about what she was about to say, focusing so hard he didn't notice the priest until he was standing right next to him.

"Detective, it's good to see you," Father Tomás said, holding out his hand. "We've been waiting a long time."

"I'm sorry about that." Johnson smiled apologetically as he shook the priest's hand. "We've got a rapidly changing situation we're dealing with, and I had to go to the mainland unexpectedly."

He looked back down at Muriel. She was fixated on the rosary clutched tightly in her lap. A rush of excitement sent a chill down his back. Was he about to get the answers he'd prayed for daily since the summer?

Father Tomás sat down next to Muriel. Johnson took a seat across the table.

"We come to you today with information you should have had months ago," the priest said. "But I hope, after you've heard the whole story, you'll understand why Muriel stayed quiet for so long."

He looked at his parishioner with a mixture of sadness and pity.

"And I hope you'll have mercy. I know that's not solely your decision, but I expect your word will go a long way with the prosecutor. I've advised Muriel not to ask for anything in return for her information. But we both know that's a leap of faith."

Johnson's gut twisted in anticipation. He looked from the earnest priest to the quiet woman next to him.

"I can't promise anything, of course. But I'll do everything I can to make sure we do the right thing."

The priest nodded. "I know you will. That's why we're here."

An expectant silence hovered over the table for a few minutes. Johnson shifted restlessly in his chair. Three times he stopped himself from urging the widow to speak. As impatient as he was, he sensed she shouldn't be rushed. Whatever she came to say cost her a great deal. Finally, she took a deep breath, let it out slowly, and met his eye.

"The main thing I want you to remember, detective, is that my husband was a good man."

~ ~ ~ ~ ~

An hour and a half later, Johnson leaned against the wall in the hall, his head pressed back against the sheetrock. An overwhelming sadness settled over him like a smothering blanket. When Muriel finished talking, he wanted to wrap his arms around her and reassure her everything would be okay. Every drop of her grief saturated his soul. He promised her he would plead her case with the district attorney, although he doubted the prosecutor would bring charges. Muriel had benefited from her husband's illegal activity and had interfered with the investigation. But surely she'd paid the price, and then some. It was hard to see her as anything other than a victim.

Throughout the summer, he had searched in vain for a connection between the first two murders, finally concluding they must be unrelated. He never dreamed they would be so intimately tied together. He now had the 'how' and 'why' for both murders. But the 'who' was still missing. Who was the girl willing to risk everything for a better life in America? And who had killed Julian Costa over the remorse that drove him to confess?

He was so engrossed turning the details of Muriel's story over in his mind that he didn't notice Dylan Connor walking down the hall toward him.

"Hey boss, you okay?"

Johnson dragged his thoughts back to the present, and tried to focus on the young officer standing in front of him. "Yeah. I'm just processing a lot of information right now."

"Well, I've got something else for you to chew on."

Johnson pushed off the wall and stood up straight, his mind suddenly cleared by the memory of the assignment he'd given Connor a few hours earlier. "You've got a name?"

"Oh yeah, and it's quite a name." Connor grinned wide, obviously proud of himself.

"Let's have it."

"Well, when you left, you asked me to look at all the houses on Sportsman Road owned by companies. But when I heard about what went down with your chase and the girl they found, I figured I should focus on that house. Did you know it was one of the ones you wanted me to look at?"

The hair on the back of Johnson's neck rose. "No. But I guess I should have known whoever owned that house wouldn't want to make it obvious who he was."

"You don't know the half of it. I had to dig through three shell corporations to figure out who that little love nest belonged to."

Johnson cringed. Love had absolutely nothing to do with it. He motioned impatiently for Connor to continue. "So, who owns it?"

"You're really not going to believe it."

"Connor!"

"Okay, okay. It's Eduardo Reyes."

Chapter 33

Almost two hours later, Johnson walked into the hospital. The rapid-fire revelations of the last 12 hours left him punch-drunk. He could hardly lay the case out for the chief, who had waited patiently through his interview with Muriel to get an update on the day's events. Lugar had finally latched onto the case, his previous hesitancy overcome by the indisputable evidence. He showed a true policeman's enthusiasm for every detail, until Johnson revealed Eduardo Reyes' connection to the house. The blood drained from Lugar's face and he put his head in his hands. What could have been a relatively open and shut case would turn into an epic legal battle with Reyes involved. He would hire the best lawyers, put up the biggest fight. He could call half the island as character witnesses. They would all swear he could never be involved in something like this.

And at the moment, they didn't have a smoking gun to put in Reyes' hand. He owned the house, sure, but he could easily claim he lent it to a friend and had no idea what was going on inside. Johnson had another investigator chasing down the details on the man who had crashed his SUV on I-45. They knew who the vehicle was registered to, but they needed to make sure José Vargas was the one behind the wheel when it burst into flames. Johnson fully expected to find a close connection between the dead man and Reyes, but since Vargas could no longer speak for himself, Reyes would be free to put his own spin on things.

The entire case would hinge on witness testimony. And the only person likely to testify willingly was the traumatized girl he was about to interview.

An emergency room nurse pointed him to a room on the third floor. An officer sat outside the door, looking bored. He sat up a little straighter when he spotted Johnson walking down the hall toward him, but he was obviously tired. Johnson patted his shoulder in encouragement. He hoped it was enough to perk up the young policeman until his replacement arrived.

Peering through the small glass window in the hospital room door, Johnson could only see the end of the patient's bed. Officer Lilian Jimenez sat in a chair in the corner, her legs tucked under her and her forehead creased into a deep frown as she watched her charge. When she looked up, Johnson waved. She stood slowly and tip-toed toward the door.

"She's asleep," Jimenez said when the door clicked quietly closed behind her.

Johnson nodded. "How's she doing? Has she said anything?"

"Bits and pieces. Man, detective, I'm telling you .... if just half of what she said is true ..." Jimenez swallowed and then cleared her throat, finally crossing her arms tightly across her chest. "I've never heard anything like this."

A heavy sense of dread settled on Johnson's shoulders, pressing down on his chest and squeezing his heart. This girl's story would probably keep him up at night for months to come, wishing he didn't know so much about man's depravity

"Do you think she's ready to talk?"

"I think she wants to tell her story. I don't think it will be easy, now or ever."

"Jarrell said she didn't speak any English."

"Not much, no. I'll have to translate for most of it."

"Alright. Why don't you let her know I'm here and see if she wants to talk. I would wait until tomorrow, but I need to ask her about a couple of men I'm hoping to get arrest warrants for. I don't want to give them any more time to prepare a defense."

Johnson watched through the window in the door as Jimenez went back into the room and around the corner to the front of the bed. About five minutes later, she peeked around the corner and motioned for him to come in.

He took a deep breath before pushing open the door.

The girl propped up on pillows in the bed looked impossibly young. Dark purple bruises covered her cheeks. One eye was swollen. White tape almost obscured her nose. Johnson guessed it was broken. She watched him with wide, frightened eyes. He'd seen the same look on the faces of cornered animals he'd rescued over the years. She clutched the covers to her chest. Dark red lines encircled her wrists, remnants of the restraints that had recently bound her.

Horror, pity, and an overwhelming sense of injustice rooted Johnson's feet to the floor. All he could do for several moments was stand and stare. By the time he wrestled his emotions into submission enough to step further into the room, the girl's fear had faded into watchfulness. She dropped her hands into her lap and glanced at Jimenez, who nodded encouragement. Johnson pulled a chair from the corner toward the bed, close enough to have a conversation but not too close to make the girl feel uncomfortable.

He smiled gently.

"What's your name?"

"Esperanza." Her voice was hoarse and quiet. But it resonated with the strength and determination that had probably helped keep her alive.

"I'm Detective Peter Johnson. I'm here to find out what happened to you so that we can arrest the men who did this and put them in jail for a very long time."

Esperanza's big brown eyes filled with tears.

"Mi hermana," she whispered. "Ellos mataron a mi hermana."

"They killed my sister," Jimenez translated quietly.

The girl's raw grief stabbed at Johnson's gut.

"Can you tell me what happened? From the beginning? Where are you from and how did you get here?"

Esperanza nodded. She took a few shaky breaths and pushed herself up straighter on her pillows. Johnson kept his eyes on her face, even as he strained to hear Jimenez's translation. Her quiet words fell hesitantly at first but soon tumbled over each other in her desire to be heard.

"I'm from Mexico, from a small town south of Playa del Carmen. There was nothing there for me but poverty and hardship. I wanted a better life. In America."

Johnson nodded his understanding.

"That was the start of all my trouble," she said, her voice cracking under the weight of her regret. "All our trouble. It was a great sin."

Johnson shook his head sadly. "This is not your fault."

"It is. You don't know. But you will." Esperanza swallowed and twisted the covers in her lap. "I heard about some men who could help smuggle people into America on the cruise ships that come every day to Cancun. I told my mama, and she encouraged me to go. The smugglers promised good jobs, as nannies or maids. I knew a few other girls who had gone. Their families hadn't heard from them in a while, but they hadn't come back either, so we knew they hadn't been caught and deported. That seemed like a good sign. I imagined them living good lives in America."

Esperanza looked up at Jimenez and back at Johnson. He nodded encouragingly.

"When my sister heard about my plans, she begged me to take her. She was too young. Just sixteen..." Esperanza's voice cracked and she paused as tears filled her eyes. "I told her no. But she didn't give up. And she was hard to refuse when she wanted something."

"What was her name?" Johnson asked quietly.

"Gloria." Big tears rolled down the girl's long lashes and clung to her cheeks. "She refused to let me leave without her. She finally persuaded Mama, who didn't want to let her go. But she said if we were together, we could look after each other."

Esperanza gave a little, gasping sob and put her hands over her face. Johnson glanced at Jimenez, who was wiping tears from the corners of her eyes. His throat tightened. He thought about the girl in the party dress washed up on the shore near Channelview Drive. Just sixteen years old.

"We met the smugglers at the cruise ship dock late one night. There was another girl there, too, but I didn't know her. They snuck all of us on board the ship and hid us in one of the crew member's cabins. They gave us pills for the seasickness. We slept through the whole trip. When we woke up, we were in a warehouse, tied up and gagged. And the other girl was gone. We were terrified. They kept us there for hours. It must have been a whole day because when we left, it was dark. They put us in the back of a van and drove us to the house."

"Is that where we found you?"

She nodded, pausing for a long time. She seemed lost in the memory.

"There was a man there. He untied us. I thought at first everything was going to be okay. Then he came for Gloria..." Her trembling voice trailed off. Jimenez handed her a box of tissue. "I tried to fight him off. He beat me. Then he... he... he raped her. Then he came for me."

Sobs racked her slender frame. Johnson, who had been leaning forward, his elbows on his knees as he listened, sat back and raked his fingers through his hair. The girl's minimal account of her horror didn't stop his imagination from filling in the details. Bile rose in his throat. He pictured the sisters, alone, violated, terrified. A kernel of anger began to burn in the pit of his stomach.

"He locked us in a room with no food or water. The next day, he came back. He was almost like a different person. He let us out of the room and brought us to the table to eat dinner. We didn't dare run. He told us we worked for him, that we had a debt to pay, for our journey. He told us we would work as... prostitutes. Once we had paid our debt, he would let us go. Gloria believed him. I didn't, but I never told her that. I didn't want to steal her hope. It was all she had left."

Esperanza paused again, overcome by her tears.

"After that, he was almost kind to us. He brought us clothes and things to decorate our bedrooms. A woman came in to cut our hair and show us how to fix our makeup. He never tied us up again, but he left another man to watch over us. We called him El Carcelero. He was always there."

"Did you ever try to escape?"

She shook her head sadly. "We never had a chance. We were never alone. After about two weeks, El Jefe had his first party."

"El Jefe?"

"That's what we called him. We never knew his name."

They might not have known his name, but Johnson bet Esperanza would never forget the man's face. He had a photo of Reyes on his phone. He would show it to her before he left, but he sensed now was not the right time.

"What happened at the parties?"

"It was our job to entertain his friends. Sometimes they would go fishing first. Then they came back to the house for drinks and dinner. And they took turns... with us. A lot of the men came often."

"Do you think they knew you were prisoners?"

Esperanza shrugged. "Maybe. Maybe not. I don't think most of them cared. They never took much interest in us, beyond what they could get from us. But then there was one man..."

Anticipation shivered down Johnson's spine.

"He was like a love-sick boy with Gloria. He acted like he really cared. I thought maybe he would be her way out."

Recounting that hope brought on a fresh round of tears, and Esperanza paused to wipe her face and blow her nose. Johnson waited for her to finish.

"Do you know his name?" he asked.

"Jim."

That single syllable reverberated through Johnson's mind, knocking hard against his already throbbing head. It had to be James Finney. He thought about the businessman's emotional reaction to seeing Gloria's picture. Johnson took his response for guilt, but maybe there was more to it.

"I told Gloria to encourage him," Esperanza continued. "I thought she could persuade him to take her away. We knew she would not really be free. She would still belong to a man. But at least it would only have been one man. And we hoped maybe someday he would give her more freedom, or even just let her go. All she wanted to do was go home to Mama."

Esperanza shook her head sadly and wiped her eyes again. It took her longer to continue, and Johnson's stomach twisted as he realized she was probably getting close to recounting her sister's death.

"That was our plan," she said. "And it seemed to be working. But El Jefe was getting tired of Jim always coming around. One night, he showed up to a party he hadn't been invited to. El Jefe told him he could see Gloria but only after all the other men had a turn. He paraded them in front of Jim and even encouraged them to be rough with her. Jim sat on the couch all night, watching everything but never saying a word. But I could tell he was getting more and more angry."

Johnson pictured mild-mannered Finney's rising rage. Had he taken it out on Gloria?

"When all of the other men left, he went back to her room. I was worried, but I hoped what had happened would give him the push he needed to take Gloria away. Instead he killed her."

Esperanza put her hands over her face. After a minute, tears began to run down her arms. Her whole body shook. Powerless in the face of her suffering, Johnson shifted in his chair to try to ease the vice-grip of anger and sorrow twisting his insides.

"Do you want to take a break?" His husky voice sounded grating in the quiet room.

Esperanza didn't respond at first but eventually shook her head. She managed to get her tears under control when she pulled her hands away from her face, but her mouth was still twisted in an agonized snarl. Jimenez had to lean forward to catch her gravely, garbled words, translating them in a whisper just loud enough for Johnson to understand.

"I don't know for sure what happened. He said he had his hands around her throat while they were in bed and was overcome by his feelings. He squeezed the life out of her! I was in my room, next door, and I never heard her make a sound."

Esperanza gulped a few breaths. Her trembling had become so violent her teeth chattered.

"I ran into her room when I heard him yelling. So did El Carcelero. She was laying in bed, so peaceful. It looked like she'd just gone to sleep. But she never woke up."

Johnson could guess the rest of the story. He thought having all the pieces to this puzzle would provide some relief. But it only brought a numb sense of horror at the depths of evil that lurked in the human heart.

"El Carcelero said they had to get rid of her body, but I kept saying we had to call the police. I wouldn't let her go. So El Carcelero tied me up. They wrapped her in a sheet and carried her away. There was a small boat under the house. I heard them drag it to the water and start up the engine. I don't know how long they were gone. When they came back, Jim left. I never saw him again."

Esperanza looked up, her tortured eyes locking on to Johnson's in desperation.

"Every time I close my eyes I see her at the bottom of the ocean," Esperanza choked out. "She deserved a proper burial."

Pity washed over Johnson and he reached out and grasped her hand before he could stop himself.

"She'll get one! She's not at the bottom of the ocean. We have her body. You'll be able to take her home."

Esperanza gazed at him with wide, wondering eyes. She looked at Jimenez and back at Johnson. Her thin fingers, cold as ice, grasped his hand and squeezed hard. She opened her mouth but nothing came out. Johnson squeezed her hand in return and then sat back, pulling his phone out of his pocket.

"I know you're tired, and you need to rest. But can you just tell me what happened today? And then, would you be willing to look at some photos? I'm hoping you can help me identify these men."

She nodded. "After Gloria died, they kept me tied up. I don't know how many days passed. El Carcelero was on the phone a lot, probably with El Jefe. At first, I just wanted to die too. I hoped he would kill me. But then I realized I was the only one who could ever tell what happened to Gloria. Then I was determined to stay alive. I kept watching for a chance to escape, but none came, until today."

She started talking faster now, anger replacing her tears.

"El Carcelero came to my room and dragged me into the living room. He had a gas can and a gun. I think he was about to shoot me when someone started pounding on the front door. He opened it and there was a girl there. He grabbed her but she fought back. She knocked him backward and he fell over the coffee table. It gave us just enough time to get out the door. He started shooting at us but we made it to the bushes. After we heard him drive off we waited for a few minutes to make sure he wasn't coming back. Then the girl cut the tape off my wrists. I have no idea who she was or how she got there."

Hearing what Kate had done brought a faint smile to Johnson's lips. She really wouldn't let anything stop her from seeking the truth.

"She's a reporter. She's been chasing this story for months. And she had a previous run-in with your El Carcelero."

Johnson asked, holding his phone up for her to inspect Jose Vargas' drivers license photo.

"Is this him?"

Esperanza nodded, her mouth set in a hard line.

"He won't be coming back," Johnson said with a grim satisfaction that surprised him. "Ever. I caught up with him as he tried to escape. We chased him off the island, and he crashed. The car exploded."

"He's dead?"

"Most definitely." Johnson nodded, searching her face for a clue about how she would respond to the other photos he had to show her. "Can you look at two more pictures?"

When she nodded, he pulled up a photo of James Finney and held up his phone.

"Jim," she said, glaring at the placidly smiling face of her sister's killer.

Johnson's heart began to pound as he pulled up the last photo. He took a deep breath and said a quick prayer that this would be the final piece of the puzzle. When he turned the phone to the traumatized girl in front of him, her face contorted into a wordless snarl.

"El Jefe," she spat out, turning away in disgust.

Relief swept over him and he leaned back in his chair. That was it. The last unanswered question. The tension and hopelessness he'd carried for six months slowly melted away, leaving him thoroughly drained. He couldn't remember when he'd been more tired. They sat in silence for a while.

"How did you know?" Esperanza finally asked. "How did you know who they were and where to look for me?"

"Your sister was wearing a necklace. We traced it to the man you knew as Jim. His name is James Finney. The rest was a lot of guesswork. I didn't know to be looking for you, but I was looking for the house."

Esperanza nodded slowly, as though trying to take it all in.

"Did Jim confess to killing Gloria?"

"No, but with your testimony, I'm sure he will."

"Testimony?" Fear filled her voice and creased her forehead. She clutched the sheet to her chest again. "I would have to testify, in court?"

Dread dropped into Johnson's stomach like a stone. He never dreamed she would hesitate to testify against the men who had tortured her and her sister.

"Well," he said, faltering as he tried to figure out how to put it in the least threatening way possible. "We have nothing definite to tie them to what happened to you. You're the only one who can identify them."

Esperanza started to tremble, the anger and determination she'd shown in the last few minutes vanished. She shook her head back and forth, slowly at first and then more quickly.

"I don't know. I don't know! I just want to go home."

"You will go home, soon," Johnson said urgently, hoping to comfort her. "In fact, you can go home anytime you want. We won't keep you here if you want to leave. You're free now. But if you don't testify, I can't guarantee that we'll be able to punish them for what they did."

Esperanza never took her eyes off his face, but she didn't respond. She just stared with wide frightened eyes.

"Rest now," Johnson said, standing up and giving her what he hoped was a reassuring smile. "We can talk more tomorrow."

She nodded and leaned back into the pillows, her eyelids already half closed. She looked so young and fragile. The entire case rested on her thin shoulders. Worry gnawed at the pit of Johnson's stomach as he and Jimenez walked quietly out the door.

What if Esperanza decided she couldn't tell her story to a jury? What if Finney and Reyes walked away, scott free?

He'd once told Kate to take comfort in ultimate justice. Everyone would have to account for their actions some day, he'd promised her. That assurance rang hollow now. He wanted to see these predators in handcuffs, locked behind bars for their crimes. If they didn't pay for what they'd done, justice was a joke. For the first time in years, the sharp dagger of doubt tore a hole in his faith.

What was the point of seeking out the truth if criminals went free?

Summer murders solved

Three deaths are connected to a sex trafficking and prostitution ring operated out of the Port of Galveston

By Kate Bennett

Galveston police announced Thursday they have busted a human trafficking and prostitution ring with tentacles that stretched from Mexico to Texas. They believe the ring is responsible for this summer's two unsolved murders as well as the death of the young Hispanic girl who washed up on Channelview Drive last week.

Seven suspects are in custody, and police expect to issue more arrest warrants soon.

"This is a criminal enterprise the likes of which I have never seen," a visibly moved Police Chief Sam Lugar said during a news conference. "The people who participated in these crimes are guilty of the most heinous exploitation and cruelty. We can all be thankful that their vile house of cards came down around their ears when it did. Otherwise, there's no telling how many women they would have taken advantage of."

While two of the trafficking victims died, at least one survived. Police rescued a young woman they have so far declined to name at a house on Sportsman Road after an officer in the area reported sounds of gunfire. The woman remains at the University of Texas Medical Branch, recovering from unspecified injuries.

A necklace speaks

Also on Thursday, Galveston investigators arrested James Finney, a well-known Houston businessman, and charged him with second-degree murder, solicitation, and statutory rape. They believe he killed Gloria Suarez in a fit of passion sometime within the last two weeks and dumped her in West Bay. Suarez was a Mexican national brought to the island and forced to work as a prostitute. She was just 16 years old.

Investigators identified Finney through the necklace the girl was wearing when she died.

"Although this young woman could no longer speak for herself, she helped identify her killer," said Det. Peter Johnson, who led the investigations into all three murders. "Without that necklace, we might never have found out who she was. Now we'll be able to send her home to her mother, who had no idea what had happened to her little girl."

Finney will be arraigned on Monday. His lawyer, well-known Houston defense attorney Dustin Scruggs, said his client planned to plead not guilty.

"This was a tragic accident," he said. "Mr. Finney is a respected member of the community

who had no idea what he had gotten himself involved in. We are confident that when a jury
hears all the evidence, they will acquit him of
these charges."

The ring unravels

Police also arrested three longshoremen believed to be involved in transporting Suarez
and other girls to locations on the island and
possibly the mainland. Bobby Martin, Javier
Ruiz, and Tony Vernon, all Galveston residents,
have been charged with continuous trafficking
of persons, a felony that could send them to
jail for 25 years to life. Mexican officials
working with Galveston police also arrested
three cruise ship crew members who recruited
the girls and smuggled them aboard the boat to
make the journey from Cancun to Texas. The ship
left Galveston earlier this week, before the
arrest warrants had been issued. The men have
so far not been identified but are expected to
be extradited early next week.

"We are cooperating fully with authorities as
they investigate this terrible crime," the
cruise ship company said in a prepared statement. "We are evaluating our processes to see
how this could have happened and make sure it
can't ever happen again."

Investigators are piecing together the sordid
story of the trafficking ring with help from

Suarez's sister, the unnamed survivor found at the house on Sportsman Road. Although they have not released many details, police said the sisters traveled to the United States willingly, thinking they would be working as maids or nannies. When they arrived, they were taken to the house, held captive, and forced to host parties for groups of men.

Police have not identified the man, or men, in charge of the ring, but they believe Jose Vargas, who died in Tuesday's fiery crash on Interstate 45, acted as the girls' jailor.

"We believe that Mr. Vargas was planning to make a getaway, possibly to Mexico, after he learned our investigators had interviewed Mr. Finney," Lugar said. "Nothing but persistence and good police work kept him from getting away. Our officers had found the house and were about to execute a search when Vargas ran."

Investigators think Vargas was trying to kill Suarez's sister in an attempt to silence a potential witness before he fled. Johnson described her survival as nothing short of miraculous. As she recovers from her ordeal, police hope she will be able to help identify others involved in the ring.

Fish Village murder

Although Suarez and her sister were the trafficking ring's last victims, they were far from the first. Based on statements from another witness, the ring started as a conduit for women eventually taken to strip clubs in Houston.

One of those early victims ended up shot to death in Fish Village in June. Investigators believe she escaped from a warehouse where she was being held after longshoremen took her and two other women off the cruise ship.

"When the traffickers discovered she was missing, they followed her, eventually catching up with her on Barracuda Drive," Johnson said. "We believe they planned to recapture her and take her back to the warehouse. Her death was an accident."

Johnson would not elaborate on the details of how she ended up being shot, but he identified the man who shot her as Julian Costa, the longshoreman who eventually ended up dead himself.

Galveston police are working with Mexican officials to identify the woman and find her family, who likely have no idea what happened to her.

Retribution

After Costa killed the woman, investigators believe he had plans to turn himself in. When other members of the trafficking ring found out, they killed him.

Investigators have not said whether they know who struck the fatal blow, but they are interviewing Martin, Ruiz, and Vernon and hope soon to have a better idea of what happened.

"This investigation is not over," Lugar said. "We are continuing to get new information. We believe this ring goes beyond the people we've arrested so far, and we expect to make more arrests soon."

Chapter 34

Kate dug her fingers into the knots that crowned her shoulder blades. She'd been hunched over her laptop for two hours working on a story about Julian Costa. It was Saturday, but typing and tense chatter filled the newsroom. Each reporter was working on a different story about the trafficking ring, examining it from every angle. The Sunday paper would be filled front-to-back with exclusive coverage of the case.

It had been all hands on deck since Kate came back from the house on Sportsman Road, and the pressure had worn tempers thin.

"I don't know why the rest of us have to work on this. It's been Kate's story all along," Jessica grumbled as she stalked out of Lewis' office. Kate pretended she hadn't heard. Jessica had always made it clear she hated having to work on anything to do with crime or cops. Kate suspected it was because she felt out of her depth, but to the other reporters, she was just being lazy.

"If you spent as much time writing and reporting as you do bitching, your stories might be worth reading,"

Delilah said, catching the exchange between phone calls. "There's no way one person could cover all this. Although we'd probably do just fine without your meager contributions."

"Mind your own business," Jessica snapped as she stalked back to her desk, cheeks flaming.

"I'm about to turn in my first draft," Kate said. "If you need help with something, Jessica, I can pitch in."

The business reporter huffed as she collapsed in her chair and hunkered down behind her computer screen. She didn't bother responding. Kate shrugged and turned back to her computer. Every word of her story resonated with Muriel's sorrow. Going through the details again wrung Kate's heart. Julian Costa did not deserve to die, and his widow didn't deserve to suffer for his crimes for the rest of her life. Kate hoped her story would elicit enough public sympathy that the DA would drop any charges against Muriel. She read through the story one more time and emailed it to Lewis. She was on her way to his office to tell him it was ready for a first edit when Mattingly came rocketing out from behind his desk, bug-eyed and trembling with anger.

"Dammit! Bennett, get in here. Lewis, you too. I've never heard of such spinelessness in my entire life."

Kate's heart sank. Mattingly had been on the phone with the publisher and the newspaper's lawyer most of the morning, trying to convince them to clear a story about the house on Sportsman Road and the man who owned it. After the official news conference announcing the arrests,

Johnson had tipped her off to the person behind the shell corporations. But it was off the record. She had to do the legwork herself to dig through all the layers to get to Reyes' name.

She finally found the last piece of paperwork at about 3 p.m. Friday. She made five calls to Reyes' office, trying to get a comment. Each time, his secretary claimed he was too busy to talk. During the last call, Kate warned the woman they would run the story anyway, telling readers Reyes refused to comment. Fifteen minutes after she hung up, the publisher walked into Mattingly's office and shut the door. Reyes had called and threatened to sue the paper out of business if they published the story. Kate fumed and ranted when the managing editor delivered the news. But Mattingly assured her he could persuade the newspaper's lawyer to give them the green light by the next day. Evidently, he was wrong.

"Here's the deal," Mattingly said, pulling a bottle of Maalox out of his drawer and taking a swig. "Our lawyer says we're in the clear on this. Your story doesn't say anything that can't be backed up by public records. But if Reyes decides to sue, it will cost us several reporters' salaries, even if we prevail. The publisher says we can't afford it. It's not worth it to him to get in a big court fight when it seems likely the police will make some kind of announcement about the house soon."

Kate's white-hot anger from the previous day had fizzled into smoldering resentment. Her pulse thumped a steady rhythm of dismay in her temples.

"What if they don't?" Her pent up frustration exploded a little more forcibly than she intended. "If they don't plan to press charges, they're not going to say a word. And when it comes to Reyes, the DA is as spineless as the publisher."

"They'll have to make some kind of comment about the home's owner. At some point, they're going to have to at least talk to him. And the DA is going to have to explain why he won't press charges, if that's what he decides to do."

Kate threw her hands up in mock surrender. "All this means is that someone's going to scoop us on this."

"Well, if they do, they do," Mattingly barked, banging his fist down on the desk. "It's out of my hands. If you'd worked your sources better, maybe we'd have an on-the-record comment by now that would give us some cover."

The managing editor's unjust criticism knifed through Kate's self-righteous indignation, deflating her satisfaction in seeing a case she'd chased for months finally come to an end. Her simmering anger at this latest setback burst into flame that quickly consumed her better judgment. She opened her mouth to spew a caustic reply, but Hunter Lewis put his hand firmly on her shoulder.

"Kate's done a great job here. Sometimes these things don't pan out like we think they should, so we have to improvise."

Kate crossed her arms tightly over her chest and glared at Mattingly. He took another swig of Maalox.

"What about this girl they have holed up at UTMB?" Lewis continued. "Shouldn't she be able to identify Reyes, if he really was involved?"

"She should," Kate said, only slightly mollified. "And I would think if she had, they would have issued an arrest warrant immediately. I don't know why they haven't. Johnson won't tell me a thing about her. He won't even say how bad her injuries are."

"It's also possible that she's so traumatized that she doesn't want to testify," Mattingly said. "I wrote about a case like that years ago, in Dallas. This girl was attacked and beaten by someone she knew. She was the only one who could identify him. But she just refused. She said she couldn't go through the pain of a trial."

Kate's throat constricted at the thought of Reyes going free.

"If that's what's going on here, Reyes will get away with it. All of it. How is that even possible?" Her voice warbled, but she was too distraught to care. She looked from Mattingly to Lewis, willing them to tell her she was wrong. After a few heartbeats of silence, a sickening dread bloomed in her gut and crept up her chest, burning a trail along the inside of her ribcage.

"He can't get away with it!"

Mattingly shook his head slowly. "It's not right. But it wouldn't be the first time someone got away with something like this, or worse."

"I don't think Reyes is innocent," Lewis said. "But it's possible that he didn't really know what was going on. Vargas could have been the one behind the whole thing."

Kate shook her head. "I'll never believe that. You think Vargas, a petty criminal who dropped out of high school, had the contacts with businessmen in Houston to keep an operation like this going?"

"Well, we only know of one businessman—James Finney. It's possible all the other customers were local."

"How likely is that?"

"Probably not likely. But unless Finney gives them up as part of a plea deal, we'll probably never know."

Kate groaned.

Across the newsroom, her phone started to ring. Relieved for an excuse to escape Mattingly's office, she jumped up and trotted across the open space, snatching up the receiver just before the call rolled to voicemail.

"Kate Bennett."

"Miss Bennett, this is Beverly Pointer, with Eduardo Reyes' office. Mr. Reyes asked me to let you know he will be holding a press conference at his warehouse in Galveston in an hour, if you would like to attend."

Kate's heart raced, thumping like a dozen little hammers beating against her ear drums. What was Reyes playing at?

"I'll be there," she yelped and slammed down the phone.

~ ~ ~ ~ ~

Dark clouds hung low in the sky and an icy drizzle had started to fall when Kate climbed out of her car in front of Reyes' warehouse. The flowers at the gate, which had bloomed so brightly during the building's dedication six months ago, were brown and lifeless. But the same Houston news vans filled the parking lot. Cameramen were setting up their equipment on the loading dock.

Kate climbed the steps, recalling Reyes' exuberance the last time the media gathered there. She nodded to the TV reporters but kept her distance. She was just beginning to wonder how long Reyes would keep them waiting when a familiar black Cadillac rolled into the parking lot. Mayor Matthew Hanes climbed out of the driver's side, and Reyes emerged from the passenger's seat. He waved and flashed one of his trademark grins, only slightly dimmer than usual, at the waiting media. Kate grimaced, disgust mixing with the bile rising in her throat.

As he walked up the steps and across the dock, Reyes shook hands with each reporter, greeting them by name and thanking them for coming. Kate hung back, nodding curtly when he looked her way. For a moment, his sanguine mask slipped and he glared at her with naked hostility. But before she could react, the placid smile returned and he moved on to his next guest. Hanes trailed behind, putting his hands in his pockets and taking them out again in a constant cycle of unease. He looked like he would rather be anywhere but there.

After Reyes had greeted everyone and checked to make sure the cameramen were ready, he took his place at the front of the semi-circle of reporters. He paused, bringing his hands together in front of his torso and tapping his fingers tips, as though considering how to begin. Butterflies beat a nervous dance in Kate's stomach. She didn't expect him to make a public confession, but whatever he said would be nearly as momentous.

"Thank you for coming, on what is, I'm sure, a busy Saturday. All of you have been covering this tragedy that has unfolded on our island. Like my fellow Galvestonians, I have watched all of your reports, read every word of your stories, and wept over this plague of immorality. It has cut all of us to the heart."

Hanes, standing about three feet behind his friend, nodded solemnly. Kate dug her pen impatiently into her notebook, staring at the blank page. Anticipation whipped her butterflies into a hurricane of restless energy. Surely Reyes hadn't called a press conference to talk about how broken-hearted he was over this story.

"I asked you here today because I have a confession to make, one that pains me more than anyone will ever know."

Kate's head snapped up. Her pulse skittered, as a dizzying surge of adrenaline shot through her chest.

"The house on Sportsman Road, where this tragedy unfolded, belongs to me. I bought it several years ago, planning to tear it down and build a waterfront home for my family. But those plans got delayed, as so many of our plans do. In the meantime, I learned a distant cousin of mine, Jose Vargas, needed a place to stay."

Reyes paused to let the information sink in. Kate tightened her grip around her pen until her fingernails dug into her palm. Her left hand trembled, making it hard to read the words she scribbled in her notebook.

"As you all know by now, Jose was a troubled young man. I had hoped that he would be able to put his life back on the right path, with a place to stay and someone he could come to for advice and help. Sadly, that's not the road he chose to take."

Kate's pulse roared in her ears as the full picture of Reyes' plan to make Vargas his scapegoat came into focus. It was the perfect solution.

"This last year has been a busy one for me, expanding my practice in Houston and working to get this warehouse built to help provide some power for Galveston's economic engine. I did not keep as close an eye on Jose as I should have. I will carry regret for that to my grave."

Behind Reyes, Hanes shook his head sorrowfully. He was the quintessential picture of the sympathetic and supportive friend. But he shifted from foot to foot, clasped and unclasped his hands. He couldn't seem to figure out whether to look at Reyes or the audience. What had him so antsy?

"Although I do not know all of the details, it appears as though Jose somehow got involved with this trafficking ring and brought some of the girls back to the house. As for the rest, you all know as much as I do. When it seemed as though the police were closing in on his criminal operation, he ran, with disastrous results."

Kate clenched her teeth together to keep from calling out, branding him the liar every ounce of her intuition told her he was. Nausea swirled in her stomach. Vargas was the ideal fall guy.

"I wanted to be the one to share this information with you because I didn't want anyone to think I had something to hide. I will cooperate fully with the police as they investigate what happened here, not that I'll be able to shed much light. But what I do know, I'm happy to share. I'm deeply ashamed that someone in my family, no matter how distantly related, was involved in something like this. And I'm horrified that I somehow helped enable his criminal activity by giving him a place to operate."

Reyes paused and cast an appraising glance at his audience. Kate met his eye and shook her head just enough for him to catch the movement. She wanted him to know at least one person saw through his pretense. If he noticed, he didn't react.

"I will never forgive myself, but I hope in time the people of Galveston will," Reyes concluded, his hand over his heart.

The other reporters surged forward to bombard him with questions. Kate turned away in disgust, trembling with anger and helplessness. Unless his last victim was willing to testify, Reyes would get away with using and selling women as though they were dirty magazines good only for someone else's gratification. He was a modern day slave trader. Kate took several slow, steady breaths to try to control her shaking. She couldn't even turn back to look at him. Just the sound of his voice set her skin crawling.

While Kate stood with her back to the gaggle of reporters surrounding Reyes, she noticed Hanes drift away from the group and slink down the steps to the parking lot. She watched as he pulled a pack of cigarettes out of his pocket and fumbled with a lighter. She'd never seen him smoke before. Had he known what his friend was up to all along or was he just now figuring it out? Did he share Reyes' deep-seated misogyny?

Kate jogged down the steps and stole up behind him as he was taking his second, long drag.

"That's a nasty habit," she said.

Hanes jumped, almost dropping the cigarette. He scowled at her before catching himself and offering a wan smile.

"It is. Don't tell my wife. She thinks I quit in college." He huffed a mirthless chuckle, smoke curling serpent-like from his nose.

Kate's eyes narrowed. Hanes looked as guilty and nervous as Reyes had every right to be. What was he afraid of?

"Are you confident the police have this investigation under control?" she asked, stalling as her mind raced to figure out what was at the root of his unease.

"Absolutely. As far as I can tell, they have arrested everyone who was involved. Now we just have to wait for the legal process to play out. I have great faith in our courts, as you know."

Kate pursed her lips. He was acting as though the case was closed. What was the rush?

"Chief Lugar said yesterday he anticipated making more arrests, particularly at the port. They're still trying to figure out how many people were involved in this operation. Do you know something the rest of us don't?"

"No, no, no. Not at all." The little bit of color in Hanes' cheeks had drained away. "Really, Miss Bennett, it's like you're trying to put words in my mouth."

Hanes dropped his cigarette and ground it out with his shoe.

"If you don't have any other questions, I have a phone call to make," Hanes said, leaning against his car with one hand and pulling his cell phone from his pocket.

A phone call.

The last time Hanes had tried to dismiss her with the excuse of a phone call was the night she was attacked at The Clipper. She thought he was calling the police chief. What if he was calling Reyes, to warn him his operation had been compromised?

Kate's eyes widened. She opened her mouth to say something when another memory exploded—Hanes stumbling out of the raucous party at Joe Henry Miles' respectable Victorian, followed by a motley crew of dock workers. She thought it was odd at the time. Now it made perfect sense.

"You knew," she whispered, horrified at how far the trafficking ring's tentacles spread. "You knew all along."

"Excuse me?" Hanes turned around slowly and looked at her warily.

"You knew. About the trafficking ring. Probably about the murders. You knew all along."

Hanes scowled, his face bright red. Kate took a step back. All of the final pieces of the puzzle had fallen into place. Excitement swirled with revulsion, leaving her dizzy.

"That's why you told the chief to call off the prostitution task force. You were giving them cover."

"That's outrageous! These are baseless accusations."

Hanes took a step toward her, raising his hand as though he meant to grab her by the shoulder. Kate took two more steps back.

"The night I was attacked at The Clipper, you called Reyes to warn him. They knew I was watching them."

Haynes glared but didn't respond. His angry flush slowly faded.

"And that night the police had to escort you home from Miles' house, you were partying with dock workers. It didn't make sense then, but now... What? Were you celebrating getting away with two murders, your sick little operation undetected?"

Hanes stared. He didn't say anything, but the pallor in his cheeks betrayed him. He pulled his pack of Marlboros out of his pocket and tapped a cigarette into trembling fingers. He lit it slowly and took a long drag. Kate watched in disbelief as a cloud of smoke briefly obscured his face.

"You can't prove anything," he finally said, his voice flat. "And if you try to print any of these accusations, you'll regret it."

They stared at each other for what seemed to Kate like a long time. She wanted to tell him he was wrong. Longed to insist he would pay for his role in making so many women suffer. But as she stood there, she began to realize the scope of the injustice unfolding around her.

Hanes was right. She couldn't prove his involvement. She doubted Johnson could either. And Reyes had the perfect alibi.

Haynes took another drag on his cigarette, looking more confident the longer she stayed silent. Kate turned away. The mission she'd given herself after her mother's death was suddenly too heavy to bear. She'd set herself up as a crusader for justice. But that was a fantasy. Justice was a cruel joke with a punchline that eviscerated her longing for something she could believe in.

Reyes would never be punished. Neither would Hanes. She would have to learn to live with that. But how?

Case closed

Officials say they do not expect to make any more arrests in the sex trafficking ring that left three people dead

By Kate Bennett

Galveston law enforcement officials do not expect to make any more arrests in the sex trafficking ring case, declaring it for all intents and purposes closed.

But that doesn't mean everyone involved will face justice.

"We know there were other people who participated in this operation who are still out there," Galveston Police Chief Sam Lugar said during a news conference Monday. "The Johns, for example. We know at least a dozen men visited the house on Sportsman Road, but we have no way of identifying them."

The one person who likely could identify the men isn't talking. James Finney, who faces murder charges in the death of Gloria Suarez, has so far refused to name other men he saw at the house. Finney has pleaded not guilty and his lawyer has made it clear he intends to take the case to trial.

Last murderer, victim identified

While Finney has been uncooperative, investigators have had more luck with the longshoremen who took the trafficked women off cruise ships and transported them to their next destination. All three men named Ricardo Peña as Julian Costa's killer.

Peña was the manager at The Clipper, the hotel where the trafficking ring operated for a while this summer. After police raided the hotel, Peña disappeared. He is believed to be in Mexico. Local prosecutors have been in touch with Mexican officials, but even if they found Peña, it is unlikely they would send him back to the United States. Peña could face the death penalty, a punishment Mexico staunchly opposes.

Despite their disagreement over sentencing guidelines, Mexican officials cooperated with Galveston investigators to identify the woman Costa shot to death in Fish Village in July. Maria Sandoval was an 18-year-old from Tulum, Mexico, who paid the traffickers $800 to smuggle her to America. Her mother told police she wanted to work in the United States to make money to send home, to help care for her five younger siblings.

Investigators had no leads on Sandoval's death until Muriel Costa came forward last week and named her husband as the murderer. She also provided information that led to the arrest of the other longshoremen involved in the ring.

Although the widow denied for months knowing anything about her husband's death and could have been charged with obstruction of justice, Galveston County District Attorney Nathan Mahoney said yesterday he did not intend to press charges.

"Mrs. Costa has been through enough," he said. "We believe she acted out of fear for her safety, and that of her children. Trying to punish her would only punish them."

Ring leader

During yesterday's news conference, Mahoney thanked Eduardo Reyes for cooperating with investigators trying to piece together how the ring got started. Last week, Reyes revealed he owned the house on Sportsman Road where the ring set up its last base of operation.

Reyes claims he had no idea what was going on there. Reyes also owns The Clipper and said previously he had no idea Peña was allowing the traffickers to use its rooms for illicit encounters.

Based on information provided by Reyes, police believe his cousin, Jose Vargas, was the trafficking ring leader. Reyes said he allowed Vargas to live in the house, hoping a stable living situation would help him turn his life around. Vargas was no stranger to police and had served time for drug-related charges.

Investigators say they have no evidence linking Reyes to the crimes.

Police think Vargas set up the ring with help from contacts in Houston's sex industry. Vargas knew Peña, who used his relationships with the dock workers to make contact with the cruise ship employees. They in turn made contact with smugglers in Mexico. The longshoremen claim none of their bosses at the docks knew anything about the operation.

Tim Hammond, head of the dock workers union, said he was shocked to learn about the ring. He and Port Chairman Joe Henry Miles have pledged to tighten security at the docks and work with cruise ship operators to make sure no smuggling, human or otherwise, happens again at the Port of Galveston.

"The people of this community, and the thousands of people who board cruise ships at the port every week should have confidence in our ability to ensure their safety and run a facility that is above reproach," Miles said.

Final victim

The only eyewitness to the sex trafficking operation was released from the University of Texas Medical Branch on Sunday. Police have not named the woman, citing a desire to protect her privacy.

The woman, who was found at the house on Sportsman Road when police raided it, has returned to her family in Mexico. She provided written testimony that will be used against Finney in his trial for her sister's murder. But police do not expect her to return to the United States to testify in person.

"This young woman has been through a tremendous trauma," Mahoney said. "She has cooperated in the investigation into her sister's death, but she declined to participate in any further prosecutions. While that means some people involved in this operation will escape punishment, we have no choice but to respect her decision."

Chapter 35

The edge of the concrete bench dug into Kate's thighs. But she refused to move. The discomfort provided the perfect accompaniment to her mood. She'd been sitting there, watching the waves rush the shore, for half an hour. The rhythm of the constant ebb and flow did nothing to soothe the anger that still roiled her gut two weeks after the DA declared the sex trafficking ring case closed. She'd watched the final machinations unfold like a slow-motion disaster she was powerless to stop. When the smoke cleared, justice lay broken and bleeding while the guilty walked away unscathed.

For the first few days after that final press conference, she had seethed and railed, pacing her apartment long into the night trying to figure out a way to expose the people really behind all the suffering and death. Hunter Lewis had patiently listened to her pleas and plans—and gently reminded her that she had no evidence to prove Reyes, Hanes, Miles, and Hammond were involved. After her third attempt to get him to let her do a story, he'd ordered her to take some time off. Reluctantly, she'd agreed. She had no choice. Her father had been thrilled to hear she was coming home for a week.

Her car was all packed. She just had to do one more thing before she left.

The late morning sun radiated a welcome warmth through the brisk breeze buffeting her back. A cold front had come through overnight, the wind pushing the waves further from the seawall than Kate had ever seen them. Despite their setback, they continued to reach resolutely for their normal landing spot. When the front blew itself out, the waves would reclaim their territory. Not even Mother Nature could keep them offshore for long.

Kate grimaced at the irony. Only man could twist and alter the natural order to suit his purposes.

She didn't bother turning around when the purr of an engine behind her signaled she was no longer alone. The car door slammed and a mixture of relief and trepidation tingled up her spine as the sharp rap of boots on concrete grew near. Johnson sat down at the other end of the bench, less than two feet from her, without saying a word.

For a while, they watched the waves together in silence. Some of the turmoil that had held her captive for the last week began to recede. Kate pulled her knees up to her chest and wrapped her arms around her legs. Johnson was looking at the granite boulders at the base of the seawall.

"This is the place where that… where…"

"Miss Kitty. Yeah. I still think she was murdered. But I guess we'll never know now." Kate cringed at the bitterness that saturated her words. She longed to let go of her anger, but she didn't know how.

"I wish I could give you a definite answer on that. If she was murdered, Jose Vargas seems like the most probable killer." Johnson met Kate's eyes and held her gaze for several long heartbeats. "If it makes you feel any better, he got what I'm sure you would say he deserved."

Kate huffed. "It doesn't make me feel any better. I would much rather have seen him sentenced to a nice, long stint in jail. Held to account. He got off too easy."

"He was held to account, just not where you could see. And I'm pretty sure he didn't get off easily. I think you can rest assured he's paying the ultimate penalty for what he did."

"I wish I could believe that," Kate said, the words catching in her throat.

Her anger suddenly collapsed into the chasm of hopelessness that had yawned in front of her for years. Her eyes filled with tears.

"How do you get up every day knowing ... knowing that the people really responsible for all of this are walking away scot-free? How do you keep pretending to serve justice, knowing that?"

Before she could dash them away, two tears spilled over her lashes and coursed down her cheeks. Johnson slid next to her and put his arm around her shoulders. He took a deep breath and let it out slowly, fixing his eyes on the waves again.

"It's not easy. But I know there are things at work that I can't see. I just have to trust that there's a reason they're not facing justice now."

"And you're okay with that? You don't have any problem with a God who lets evil go unpunished? Why would he do that?"

Johnson took a long time to answer. Kate watched the shore birds hopping along the wet sand, leaving a trail of three-pronged prints in their wake.

"Honestly? I don't know. When I realized Esperanza wasn't going to testify, that Eduardo Reyes was going to get away with what he'd done to her and her sister and who knows how many other girls ... I struggled to reconcile that with my belief that justice always prevails."

"Esperanza? That was her name?" Goosebumps crawled over Kate's arms. "That means hope."

"I know. At first I thought it was cruelly ironic. But now I think it's appropriate."

"What do you mean?"

"Her survival was nothing short of miraculous. If she hadn't lived, we'd never know what happened. She would have ended up being just another unidentified dead body. Vargas would have escaped to Mexico. But because of her, we were able to put all the pieces together and the whole operation imploded. Think of all the girls who won't suffer the same fate."

"But what good is that when Reyes goes unpunished? How could she let that happen?"

Johnson shook his head sadly. "She'd been through so much. It would have been his word against hers. He probably would have claimed she participated willingly. I just don't think she could face that, even if it meant he would get away with what he did."

"And what about justice?"

"Justice may be delayed in this case, but that doesn't mean it's not waiting in the wings."

Kate took her eyes off the shore and turned toward Johnson, searching his face for any hint that he didn't believe what he was saying. His clear hazel eyes met her gaze unflinchingly.

"I could never believe in a God who let evil have free rein, even for a moment."

Johnson cocked his head to the side. His whole face was so earnest she couldn't look away.

"If you could remove all the evil in the world, would you?"

Kate opened her mouth to spit an incredulous and emphatic response. But before her lips could form the words, the image of Julian Costa laying lifeless in the alley filled her mind. Had he been evil? Had he deserved to die at the hand of his best friend? Did his children deserve to grow up without a father? She thought about Muriel Costa, who refused for months to tell the police what she knew. If she had confessed, maybe Esperanza and her sister could have been rescued. Was that evil? Did Muriel deserve to get away with that?

Kate shut her mouth and looked back out at the water. She thought about the lies she'd told to try to get Muriel to talk. It seemed justifiable at the time. But it was still a lie. Was that evil?

She closed her eyes and shuddered. The last image that filled her mind was all too familiar. Her mother, hanging from a rope. Her eyes were open, staring at nothing. She had suffered from mental illness her entire adult life. Kate always told herself her mother just couldn't struggle against her demons any more. But underneath all the carefully crafted, grown-up excuses huddled a little girl who never figured out why her mommy couldn't fight harder, for her. Had giving in to a longing for death been evil? She'd left so much sorrow and brokenness behind.

Kate brought her hands to her face and let despair wash away her last vestiges of composure. She cried quietly at first, but eventually sobs shook her whole body. She had an odd sensation of free-fall, as though the tower of self-righteousness she'd carefully built, brick by prideful brick, had collapsed under her feet. Johnson's arm tightened around her shoulders.

When her tears started to subside, he handed her a crisp, white handkerchief. She wiped her eyes. Johnson let his arm fall but didn't move away. Kate clutched the damp cloth in her lap.

"There's no way to remove all the evil from the world," Johnson said softly. "It's woven into every molecule. It's just something we have to learn to live with. I wish Reyes were sitting in a jail cell right now. I don't understand why he's not. But there are a lot of things I don't understand. I still get up every day and do what I can to curb the evil in front of me. I seek justice where I can. That's all I can do."

"And that's enough?" Kate whispered, grasping at his words for a scrap of hope she could cling to.

"It has to be. Most days, it's more than enough. And on the days it's not, I remind myself I can never mete out perfect justice because I can't see everything perfectly."

Johnson's humility struck Kate like a slap in the face. She prided herself on being able to see everything clearly and judge people accurately. That hadn't been enough this time. She'd failed. And unlike Johnson, she couldn't fall back on the hope that a higher power would make everything right.

But she wished she could.

"I'm not sure it would ever be enough for me," she finally said.

Johnson took her hand and squeezed it. His eyes shone with hope.

"Maybe someday it will be," he said.

WANT TO READ MORE?

Learn more about Kate Bennett and Peter Johnson in two prequel short stories!

The Jumper tells the story of Kate's first day at the *Galveston Gazette*.

He Must Pay gives you a sneak peek into Johnson's past.

Read them both for free when you sign up for exclusive access to the Galveston Crime Scene!

Join now at GalvestonCrimeScene.com

ABOUT THE AUTHOR

Leigh Jones is a journalist who sharpened her reporting skills at local newspapers in Texas. She's now an editor for the daily podcast of a national news organization.

She fell in love with Galveston while working as a reporter for *The Galveston County Daily News*. She's a Hurricane Ike survivor and co-authored a book about the island's recovery. When not writing mystery novels, she researches and documents historic true crime on the island.

Leigh lives in the Houston area with her husband and daughter. They visit Galveston often.

Printed in Great Britain
by Amazon

64411017R00251